DEPARTURE

ALSO BY A.G. RIDDLE

The Origin Mystery

The Atlantis Gene

The Atlantis Plague

The Atlantis World

DEPARTURE

A.G.RIDDLE

HARPER Voyager

An Imprint of HarperCollins*Publishers*

DEPARTURE. Copyright © 2014 by A.G. Riddle. All rights reserved. Printed in the United States of America. No part of this book may be used or reproduced in any manner whatsoever without written permission except in the case of brief quotations embodied in critical articles and reviews. For information address HarperCollins Publishers, 195 Broadway, New York, NY 10007.

HarperCollins books may be purchased for educational, business, or sales promotional use. For information please e-mail the Special Markets Department at SPsales@harpercollins.com.

FIRST EDITION

Harper Voyager and design is a trademark of HarperCollins Publishers L.L.C.

Designed by Paula Russell Szafranski

Library of Congress Cataloging-in-Publication Data has been applied for.

ISBN 978-0-06-243166-0

ISBN 978-0-06-244956-6 (Barnes & Noble signed edition)

15 16 17 18 19   OV/RRD   10 9 8 7 6 5 4 3 2 1

For those stubborn enough to dream

PART ONE

SURVIVORS

CHAPTER ONE

Harper

IN ONE HOUR, THIS PLANE WILL LAND, AND I'll be forced to make the Decision, a call that I may regret for the rest of my earthly existence. Depending on how it goes, chaos and poverty may follow. Or pure bliss. Fifty-fifty odds, I'd say. Not dreading it all. Barely even thinking about the Decision most seconds.

Like most writers, I don't get out much. Or get paid much. I fly economy, and nine times out of ten I'm sandwiched between a feverish person who coughs when I least expect it and a married man who inevitably asks, "So how's a cute little thing like you still single?" I suspect the airlines have a flag in their system for me: "Not a complainer, reassign to misery row."

Not this flight.

Approximately six hours ago I entered a magical world, a place that only exists for brief periods of time forty thousand feet above Earth's surface: first class on an international flight. This joyous land that pops into and out of existence like an alternative universe has its own strange customs and rituals. I've taken it all in, knowing that this will likely be my last glimpse. The ticket probably cost two months' rent at my microscopic flat in London. I would have rather had the cash, but the ticket was a gift, or, more precisely, an attempt at manipulation by the billionaire who presented the Decision at our meeting in New York.

Which I'm *not* thinking about right now. Yes, at present, I exist in a Decision-free zone.

The flight time from New York to London is just under seven hours. Every fifteen minutes I switch the screen to check where the plane is, willing it to just keep going, to fly until we run out of fuel. Maybe I'll slip the flight attendant a note: "Drop below 40,000 feet and it blows!"

"Hey, who do I have to kill to get a refill here? And what's the deal with the Internet?"

Trouble in paradise. As far as I can tell, there are only two unhappy inhabitants of First Class, Pop. 10. I call this pocket of unrest the Aisle of Brooding and Snide Remarks. Its thirtysomething residents have been waging a drinking and sarcasm contest since takeoff. I know one of them, the individual currently pressing his drink request, and I know what's eating him because I'm involved in it. His name is Grayson Shaw, and I've made every effort to avoid him.

"Hey, I'm talking to you," Grayson yells.

A thin, dark-haired flight attendant whose name tag reads JILLIAN pokes her head out of the galley and smiles weakly. "Sir, the captain has turned on the Fasten Seat Belts sign and suspended drink—"

"For God's sake, just throw me two mini bottles. We're like eight feet apart."

"Ignore him, Jillian," the other brooder says. "Two mini bottles won't fix his problem."

"Thanks, random guy in 2A. Really insightful."

Grayson jumps up as another wave of turbulence rocks the plane. I feel him pulling on the back of my headrest as he wades forward. His long blond hair falls around his face, hiding me from his view, and I'm glad for that. He stops in front of my first-row seat, at the entrance to the galley.

"Okay, it's not that hard. You're a cocktail waitress in the sky. Now hand me the bottles."

Jillian's put-on smile recedes. She reaches for something, but the plane phone rings, and she grabs it instead.

Grayson massages his temple and turns to the side. His eyes meet mine. "You. Jesus, this flight keeps getting worse."

He's about to launch into me, but the other brooder is here now, standing uncomfortably close to Grayson. He's quite handsome, his dark hair short, his face lean, his eyes unflinching.

Grayson stares at him for a second, then cocks his head. "Can I help you?"

"Actually, I came up here to help you."

Normally I don't go in for this sort of macho stuff . . . but I have to say, I like the hero from 2A. There's at once something mysterious and familiar about him.

Grayson opens his mouth to respond, but he never gets a chance. The boom behind us is deafening. The plane drops, stabilizes, then bounces and shakes, like a tiny pebble on the ground during an earthquake. Time seems to stretch out. The two men are on the floor in front of me, rolling around, maybe fighting; the plane is jostling me so hard I can't tell.

Chaos erupts. The flight attendants fight their way down the aisles, bracing themselves on seat backs, stowing articles when they can, shouting at people to get back in their seats and fasten their seat belts. A voice comes over the PA, but I can't make out the words.

Compartments overhead pop open, and an oxygen mask dangles in front of me, a round, yellow plastic bowl with a flat bottom. It bounces up and down on the clear plastic tube like a dangling piñata, just out of reach.

Grayson is gone—to where, I don't know and don't care. The other brooder gets up and steadies himself on the bulkhead. He peers down the length of the plane, squinting slightly, his eyes moving left and right, seeming to calculate something.

Finally he plops down in the seat beside me and pulls the seat belt tight.

"Hi."

"Hi," I mouth, not sure if my voice is audible over the ruckus around us.

"Can you hear me?"

For some reason, his voice is crystal clear. His accent is American, its calmness a sharp contrast to the pandemonium around us. We seem to be in a bubble, he and I, talking casually while the outside world disintegrates.

"Yes," I say, finally hearing my own voice, as if from far away.

"Buckle up and put your head between your knees. Wrap your fingers around the back of your head. Don't look up."

"Why?"

"I think we're about to crash."

CHAPTER TWO

Nick

I'M ALIVE, BUT I'VE BEEN BETTER.

Every inch of my body aches. Gone is the slight buzz of alcohol, replaced by a pounding headache. It hurts worst around my pelvis. I pulled the belt low right before impact, hoping to spare my internal organs. It worked, but not without cost. I start to unbuckle it, but stop.

It's too quiet.

The lights are out, and only faint moonlight seeps in through the windows. I hear a few low moans behind me. This 777 held around 250 people when it took off from JFK. If even a fraction were alive, the cabin would be awash in voices, probably screams. The relative silence is a bad sign.

My mind seems clear, my arms are fine, and I think I can walk. I'm in decent shape, but given how rough the crash was, I bet a lot of the other passengers weren't as lucky as me. I have to help them. For the first time since—well, since I can remember—I feel close to normal, filled with purpose and urgency. I feel alive.

The woman beside me still hasn't moved. She's hunched over, her head between her legs, hands clasped behind it as I instructed her.

"Hey." My voice comes out raspy.

She doesn't move.

I reach out and brush her blond hair back. She turns slightly, a single bloodshot eye peering up at me, and pushes up slowly, revealing her slender face. The other eye is equally bloodshot. A bruise runs from her temple to her jaw.

"You okay?"

She nods and swallows. "Yeah, I think so."

What next? Check her mental status? "What's your name?"

"Harper. Harper Lane."

"What's your date of birth, Harper?"

"Eleventh December." She smiles slightly, not adding the year.

Yeah, she's okay. She looks late twenties or early thirties to me, and she's British; I hadn't realized that before. Probably on her way home to London.

"Stay here—I'll be right back."

Now the test. I unfasten my belt, stand up, and immediately stumble into the wall, hitting my shoulder hard. The plane's settled at about a thirty-degree angle, nose down, tilted slightly to the left. I lean against the bulkhead, waiting for the pain to ebb.

Turning my head, I get my first glimpse back down the aisle . . . and freeze in shock.

The plane's gone. Almost all of it. The first-class and business-class cabins are all that's left. Just beyond the business section, tree branches crisscross the ragged opening. Around the edges, electrical pops flash against the dark forest. The vast majority of the passengers were in economy, and there's no sign of it—only a quiet forest. The rest of the plane could be a hundred miles away, for all I know. Or in a million pieces. I'm surprised we're not.

On the other side of the wall, I can hear a rhythmic pounding. Staggering a little, I feel my way around the divider that separates first class from the galley. It's Jillian, the flight attendant, banging on the cockpit door.

"They won't come out," she says when she sees me.

Before I can respond, she moves back to the wall, grabs the phone, listens for a second, then tosses it aside. "Dead."

I think she's in shock. What's the priority at this point? I glance back at the sparks popping against the twisted metal. "Jillian, is there a danger of fire?"

"Fire?"

"Yes. Is there any fuel in this section?" It seems like a reasonable question, but who knows?

Jillian gazes past me, confused. "Shouldn't be a fire. Captain dumped the fuel. Or I thought . . ."

A middle-aged man in first class lifts his head. "Fire?"

People around him begin repeating the word quietly.

"Where are we?" That seems like the next logical question.

Jillian just stares, but Harper says, "We were over England." When my eyes meet hers, she adds, "I was . . . watching the flight display on the monitor."

That's the first bit of good news, but I don't get to think about it long. The word *fire* has finally reached the wrong person.

"There's a fire! We need to get off!" someone yells. Across the plane, people start scrambling out of their seats. A panicked mass of about twenty people coalesces in the cramped space. Several passengers break away and rush to the jagged opening at the rear but turn back, afraid to jump. "We're trapped!" is added to the cries of "Fire!" and things start to get ugly. A white-haired woman in business class loses her footing and falls. People trample her on their way to the front, where Jillian and I stand speechless. The woman's screams don't slow the crowd.

They rush on, directly toward us.

CHAPTER THREE

Nick

THE SURGING CROWD FORCES JILLIAN TO FOCUS. SHE spreads her arms, but her voice fails her. I can barely hear it over the crowd. Her standing there, defenseless in front of the crowd, jolts me into action.

I move forward, push Jillian behind me, and plant my feet. I shout, my own voice ringing out louder and clearer than I expect. "Stop! People, stop moving, you're hurting that woman! Listen: There. Is. No. Fire." I say each word more slowly and quietly than the last, infusing the crowd with calm. "Okay? No fire. No danger. Relax."

Save for a few shoves, the crowd settles. All eyes focus on me.

"Where are we?" a woman yells.

"England."

The word ripples through the crowd in hushed tones, as if it were a secret.

Jillian moves from behind me and steadies herself on a chair.

All at once, the survivors begin hurling questions at me, like the press corps in the final seconds of a White House briefing.

"Help is on the way," I find myself saying. "Right now, the key is to stay calm. If you panic, people will get hurt, and if you're responsible for harming other passengers, you *will* face criminal charges." I pause and then add for good measure, "The media's going to find out who caused trouble after the crash, so you can also expect to be on the morning news." The threat of public humiliation—most people's greatest fear—seems to do the trick. The uproar subsides, replaced by suspicious sidelong glances, as people wonder if their neighbors will rat them out for bum-rushing the exit.

"If you're in pain, stay where you are. If you have internal injuries, moving is the worst thing you can do. Emergency personnel will check you out when they arrive, and they'll decide when and how to move you." Sounds good, anyway.

"Where's the captain?" an overweight middle-aged man asks.

Luckily (or unluckily), the lies keep coming: "He's coordinating with emergency personnel right now."

Jillian gives me a confused look. She seems to be trying to decide whether this is good news or a lie. I wonder how much help she's going to be.

"Who are you?" another passenger yells.

"He's just a passenger, same as the rest of us." Looks like the drunken jerk in 2D survived, unfortunately. He stares at me with glassy eyes. "Ignore this clown."

I shrug. "Of course I'm a passenger—what else would I be? Now listen up. Anyone who can walk, we're going to leave the aircraft in an orderly fashion. Take the nearest seat, everyone, and wait to be called. This young lady"—I nod to Jillian—"is going to open the emergency exit, and when she calls your row, do what she says. If there's a doctor on board, come see me immediately."

Jillian opens the left exit door at the front of the plane, and I hear the evacuation slide inflating. I stand beside her and look out. The slide snags on the trees around us, but it will get people to the ground, six or seven feet below us. The plane's nose is still a few feet off the ground. This entire section is being held up by trees, but it feels stable enough.

"What now?" Jillian asks, her voice low.

"Start taking people from the back off first." I figure that will minimize the plane's shifting.

Five minutes later a line's forming at the slide, and the picture becomes clearer. It looks as if everyone in first class survived, but a lot of folks in business—perhaps half of the twenty or so—aren't moving.

A woman with shoulder-length black hair, maybe in her early forties, pauses at the threshold next to me. "You asked for a doctor?" She has a slight accent—German, I think.

"Yes."

"I . . . have an M.D., but I'm not a practicing physician."

"Yeah, well, you are today."

"All right," she says, still hesitant.

"Jillian here is going to give you a first-aid kit. I want you to survey the remaining passengers and prioritize treatment. Anyone in immediate danger first, then children, then women, then men."

Without a word, the doctor starts making her way through the cabin, Jillian at her side. I man the exit, making sure that people are spaced out enough to get down the slide without colliding. Finally I watch the last passenger make her way down: the elderly woman who was almost trampled. Her feet touch the ground, and an older man, possibly her husband, catches her hand and helps her up. He nods to me slowly, and I nod back.

From the galley between first and business classes, I hear the clink of glass bottles and an angry voice: 2D berating someone.

I step back there to find Harper standing across from 2D, her face pained. He's got a dozen mini bottles lined up on the slanted table. Half are empty, and 2D's unscrewing the cap on a Tanqueray.

I'd like to get into what he said or did to her, but there are more pressing matters—namely the remainder of the passengers, many of whom might need help and possibly medical treatment.

"Stop drinking those," I snap. "We may need them for medical care." We could run out of antiseptic before help arrives, and liquor would be better than nothing.

"Very true. They're caring for *my* medical needs right now."

"I'm serious. Leave those and get off the plane."

He grabs the corded plane phone theatrically. "Let's have a round of applause for Captain Crash, the mini bottle Nazi." He fakes the roar of a crowd, slugs back the bottle he's holding, and wipes his mouth. "Tell you what," he says, slurring a little. "Let's compromise. You can have these bottles as soon as I'm done with them."

I step toward him. Harper moves between us. A firm hand on my shoulder stops me.

It's the doctor.

"I've finished," she says. "You need to see this."

Something in the doctor's tone rattles me a little. I give 2D a hard look before turning and following the doctor, Harper at my side.

She stops at the seat of a middle-aged black passenger in a business suit. He's propped against the wall, dead still, his face covered with dried blood.

"This man died of blunt force trauma to the head," the doctor says, her voice low. "He was bludgeoned by the seat back in front of him and the bulkhead to the side. He was buckled in tight, but the chairs in the business section aren't as far apart as those in first class. The whipping motion of the descent and crash was deadly for the weaker and taller passengers, anyone whose head could connect with the seat in front. He's one of three fatalities." She motions to the rest of business class, where seven people are still seated. "We've got four who're alive but unconscious. I'm not optimistic about them. One, I wouldn't want to move. Three are pretty banged up, but they might be okay if we could get them to a hospital."

"Okay. Thanks, Doc."

"Sabrina."

"Nick Stone." We shake hands, and Jillian and Harper introduce themselves.

"I wanted to show you this," Sabrina says, "because we've all likely suffered some head trauma. It's imperative that all the survivors keep their blood pressure within a normal range. Any of us might have asymptomatic head trauma, which could result in stroke or cerebral hemorrhaging if we're excited or exert ourselves."

"That's good to know." The truth is, I'm not sure what to do with this new information. I'm not exactly sure what to do about anything at this point. The three women are looking at me expectantly, waiting.

My first thought is of the main section of the plane. If business class fared this poorly, I can't imagine what economy is like, where the seats are closer together and the whiplash as the plane broke up and crashed would have been far more deadly. If there's anyone still alive in the back half of the plane, they're going to need a lot of help.

"We need to find the rest of the plane."

Blank stares.

I focus on Jillian. "Is there any way we could contact the people back there?"

She shakes her head, looking confused. "Phone's dead."

Phone. "What about your cell phone? Do you know the staff at the rear? Their numbers?"

"Yes, I do." Jillian pulls out her phone and turns it on. "No signal."

No luck with my phone either. "Maybe it's because we have American carriers?"

"I live in Heidelberg," Sabrina says. "Maybe . . . no, I've got no service either."

"I'm on EE," Harper says, but she, too, has no service.

"All right," I say. "I'm going to go look for them."

"I'll join you," Harper says.

Jillian volunteers as well, but we decide that she should stay with the remaining passengers until help arrives. While Harper gathers supplies, I notice an Asian man—young, maybe late twenties—seated in business class, hunched over a glowing laptop screen that shines bright in the otherwise dark cabin.

"Hey."

He looks up, scans my face quickly, then resumes typing.

"You need to get off the plane."

"Why?" He doesn't bother to look up.

I lower my voice and squat to look him in the eye. "It's safer on the ground. The plane feels stable, but it's propped up by trees that could give way at any time. We could roll or drop quickly." I motion to the torn metal behind him, where there are still intermittent sparks. "And there may be a risk of fire. We're not sure."

"There's no risk of fire," he says, still typing, his eyes moving quickly side to side. "I need to finish this."

I'm about to ask what could be more important than surviving in the aftermath of a plane crash, but Harper is at my side now, handing me a bottle of water, and I decide to focus on the people who want my help.

"Remember," Sabrina says, "any excess exertion could be fatal. You may not be in pain, but your life could be in danger."

"Got it."

As we leave, Sabrina moves to the young Asian man and begins speaking quietly. By the time we reach the exit, they're practically shouting at each other. Clearly not a doctor-patient relationship. They know each other. Something about the scene doesn't quite sit right with me, but I can't think about that now.

At the bottom of the chute, three people are hunched over on the ground or leaning against trees, holding their heads. But I saw at least two dozen people exit. Where is everyone? I stare into the woods.

Slowly I start to make out glowing lights bobbing in the forest, moving away from the plane—a stream of people spread out in the darkness, a few running. The light must come from flashlight apps on their phones.

"Where're they going?" I ask no one in particular.

"Can't you hear it?" says a woman sitting on the ground right next to the chute, though she doesn't lift her head from her knees.

I stand still, listening. And then, in the distance, I hear them.

Screams.

People crying out for help.

CHAPTER FOUR

Harper

THE DENSE ENGLISH FOREST IS DARK, LIT ONLY by the dim crescent moon hanging above and the smattering of cell phone lights through the trees ahead. The beady white lights thrash back and forth in the hands of runners, their twinkling loosely synchronized with the snap of branches underfoot.

My legs are burning, and my lower abdomen and pelvis send waves of pain through my body every time my feet hit the ground. The words *stroke* and *hemorrhage* run through my mind, along with the doctor's warning: *Any excess exertion could be fatal.*

I have to stop. I'm holding Nick back, I know it. Without a word I let up and put my hands on my knees, trying desperately to catch my breath.

Nick halts abruptly beside me, sliding on the forest floor. "You okay?"

"Fine," I say between pants. "Just winded. Go on. I'll catch up."

"The doctor said—"

"I know. I'm fine."

"Feel light-headed?"

"No. I'm okay." I glance up at him. "If I live through this, I'm going to get a gym membership, go every day. And no drinking until I can run a five-K without stopping."

"That's one option. I was thinking that if we live through this, a stiff drink will be my *first* order of business."

"Excellent point. Post-drink, it's straight to the gym for me."

Nick's staring at the stream of glowing lights, which have begun to converge like a swarm of fireflies on something beyond the trees, something I can't yet see. His face is a mask of concentration. I wonder what he does for a living. Is it something like this? Crisis management? He's good at it, comfortable telling people what to do, for sure. I'm not. I wonder how else we're different, whether we're anything alike at all. And I wonder why I'm curious at all, especially in the middle of all this.

"I'm ready," I say, and we resume our jog, a bit more slowly than before. A few minutes later the forest gives way to open air.

Nothing could have prepared me for what I see.

About twenty people stand close together just beyond the tree line, on the shore of a lake that strikes me as odd. Its shoreline is too round and well-formed, as though it were man-made. But it's the thing that rises from the lake about fifty feet out that terrifies me: a jagged dark hole like the mouth of a massive fish—the open front end of the main section of the plane, broken off roughly where the wings begin. One row of chairs faces us at the front of the passenger compartment, but they're all empty.

The plane's tail must be resting on the bottom of the lake. What's holding up the middle, propping the ripped end up out of the water? The landing gear? The engines? Trees? Whatever it is, it's giving way. The lower edge of the torn fuselage is about fifteen feet above the water, but it's sinking a little lower every few seconds.

It's chilly for mid-November. My breath is a white plume against the night. That water has to be frigid.

Movement inside the plane. A balding man runs up the aisle but stops at the precipice. He grips the seat back as he peers out, his face white with fear, trying to work up the nerve to jump. His decision is made for him. A burly younger man slams into him from behind and they tumble over the edge together, the second man's leg catching briefly on a piece of twisted metal. He spins, hitting the water at an awkward angle but missing the first man. The movement pulls my eyes down to the water, and I realize that two other people are already thrashing there, swimming toward the shore. More who've made it are huddled together on the bank, shivering, drenched. I step closer, trying to discern what happened from brief snatches of shaky speech.

We hit the water going backward . . .

The force—I thought I was going to go through my seat . . .

I crawled across three people. All dead, I think. I don't know. They weren't moving. What was I supposed to do?

I wonder just how cold that water is, how long it will take to die of hypothermia out there.

A man in a navy sport coat appears in the mangled opening. He's crouching at the edge, steeling himself to jump, when Nick's booming voice echoes across the lake.

"Stop! You jump, and you kill everyone left on that plane."

It's bloody dramatic, but it's got the man's attention—not to mention mine and everyone else's on the bank.

Nick steps to the water's edge. "Listen," he calls to the man, "we're going to help you, but you've got to get everyone left alive to the opening."

The man on the plane—around fifty, I would guess, a little paunchy—just stands there, looking confused. "What?"

"Focus. The plane is sinking. When the water starts pouring into the cargo hold below, it will pull the plane down fast. You—and anyone else still conscious—have got to work together. Wake up as many people as you can, then find anyone who's alive but can't move and get them to the opening. You do that, and we'll do the rest. Understand?"

The man nods slowly, but I can tell he's in shock. He can't process it all. Nick seems to realize that, too. He continues, his voice calmer and slower this time.

"What's your name?"

"Bill Murphy."

"Okay, Bill. You're going to get everybody alive to the opening, and then you're going to wait. Everybody to the opening and wait. Understand?" Nick pauses, lets his words sink in. "Bill, is there anybody else conscious in there?"

"I think so . . . yeah."

"How many?"

"I don't know. Five. Ten. I don't know. It's dark."

"That's okay. Go and talk to them now. Tell them to help you get everybody to the opening and wait. Everybody to the opening and wait."

Bill turns and vanishes into the darkness of the cabin. I move to Nick's side. "What's the plan?"

"Still working on it," he says under his breath, glancing over at the crowd. There are about thirty people on the shore by now, bloodied people from the front of the plane and the shivering, wet survivors who've made the swim. He turns toward them, raising his voice. "Do any of you know CPR?"

Two hands go up, one reluctantly.

"Good. I want you to stand over here. Some of the people coming out may not be breathing. You're going to do the best you can with them. If they don't respond after the first attempt, move to the next person." He looks back at the group. "Now, if any of you *cannot* swim, step over here."

Another smart move. He's making volunteering the default—if you want out, you have to step out. Six people shuffle over. I wonder how many of them really can't swim.

A woman shivering on the bank speaks with equal parts fear and force. "I can't go back into that water. I'll die."

"Me neither," says a redheaded man beside her.

"You have to—please, my husband's still on there," an older woman wearing a yellow sweater pleads, her voice cracking.

"This is suicide," says a long-haired teen wearing a Sex Pistols T-shirt.

Nick steps between the group from the front of the plane and the wet survivors, separating them. "You all don't have to go back in the water," he says to the swimmers. "You'll work with the folks that can't swim, drying people on the bank." He goes on quickly, cutting a few protests off. "But first, right now, you need to run back to the front section of the plane and gather all the blankets and the life vests. We need them both to save the people coming out."

It's a good idea. The blanket-to-person ratio in first and business class was unbelievable. There'll be plenty. But I still don't understand what his plan is.

"Besides, the exercise will warm you up and keep your blood pumping." Nick claps his hands. "Let's go. Right now. And bring back a dark-haired woman named Sabrina and the flight attendant, Jillian. Find Sabrina and Jillian, and tell them to bring the first-aid kit. Remember, blankets and life vests—all of them."

Reluctantly the nonswimmers lead the soggy survivors into the woods. The rest of us—twenty-three souls, counting Nick and me—stand and watch them go. To our right, I can hear banging in the plane. Its bottom edge is now only ten feet above the water. I swear it's sinking faster.

On the bank, an overweight man with a nasty gash down his face says, "We'll never make it there and back, dragging someone else. It's too cold. They barely made it across one way, alone."

"That's true," Nick says. "But we're not going to be in the water that long. And none of you are swimming to the plane and back."

A chorus of muttered protests builds, gaining strength by the second as voices join in.

We'll drown . . .

Wait for professionals . . .

I didn't sign up for this . . .

"You have to!" Nick shouts, silencing the crowd. "You have to, okay? We all have to. We don't have a choice. Listen to me. Somebody loves each and every person on that plane. They're somebody's son. Someone's daughter. They're mothers and fathers, just like some of you. That could be your son or daughter on there. Your husband or wife, waiting, unconscious, helpless. Right now someone's mother is checking her phone at home, wondering when she'll hear from her son. In another hour, she'll start to worry, and if we don't go get those people, she'll never see or talk to her son again, and it will be because we were too scared to wade into that water and save him. I can't live with that on my conscience, and I know you can't either. It could just as easily be any one of us on that plane, sitting there, alive but unconscious, waiting to drown. And they *will* drown, without us. If we don't help, *right now,* they die. No one else is coming for them. It's us, here and now, or they die. That's it. We didn't sign up for this, but nobody else is here. No one will save those people if we don't. Every second we waste, another person dies. There are probably two hundred people in that section of the plane, and their lives are in our hands. I have a plan, and I need your help. If you want to sit here on the bank and watch them drown, step out of the group."

No one moves a muscle. Save for the faint commotion in the plane, it's dead quiet. I take a breath, realizing I've been holding it while Nick spoke.

"Good. The first thing we're going to do is make a fire. Who has a lighter?"

"Right here." A middle-aged man wearing a New York Giants sweatshirt steps forward, holding it out.

"Thank you." Nick takes it with a nod. "Okay, everyone run into the woods and bring back as much wood as you can carry. Thirty seconds. Don't bother with anything that isn't already on the ground. Go. Hurry."

He turns to me. "Gather some small branches and twigs and break them up."

We follow the others into the woods, returning with armfuls of kindling. Setting his down, Nick hunches over the pile. A few seconds later, the first tentative flame is flickering. I add my take to it, and as the rest return from the woods with their own twigs and branches, it grows quickly into a small bonfire. God, the heat feels good. And that's not all. Rescue teams have got to be looking for us by now, and the fire can only speed up their search.

"All right. Good work," Nick says, standing up from the fire to focus on the group huddled around the flames. "Here's the plan. We've got enough people to make two lines. We're going to stretch out, spacing ourselves at about arm's length all the way to the plane. When the plane gets to just above water level, we'll wade in quickly, swim to our positions, and start passing the survivors down the lines to the bank. Speed is the key. The people who come off will have life vests on, so those of you in the deeper water should be able to push them to the next person in line. Everybody in the water above their waist gets a life vest, so you don't have to tread water. This is important: don't stay in the water longer than you can stand it. If you get too cold, if you feel your limbs going numb, tap out and come to the fire. Warm up, and if you're able, get back as soon as you can. Once the people coming out get dry and warm, they can go back and join the line. Okay?

"One last thing. If you're a strong swimmer—if you've ever been a lifeguard, or you swim regularly, or even if you're just in really good shape and can hold your breath for a while—come see me right now."

Three people step forward, all younger guys, twenties and early thirties.

Nick turns to me. "How about you?"

"Yeah." I nod, my mouth dry. "I'm good. I'm a good swimmer." Might be a stretch. I was on a team before going to uni, but that was over a decade ago.

He leads the four of us away from the group and speaks quietly. "We'll go out first. Don't put on a life vest, it will slow you down. There are two aisles. We'll split up, two and three." He points to the youngest guy and me. "You're with me. The back of the plane near the tail is probably already filled with water—I doubt it's completely sealed. When we get there, if that's true, the water line becomes our starting point. We can't save anyone below it; they've already drowned. We'll race down the aisle and start checking the people in the first dry row for a pulse."

He puts his hand to his throat. "Press hard and wait. No pulse, move on. Get a pulse, slap them hard with the other hand, try to wake them. No response, unbuckle them, put them over your shoulder, and carry them to the next person in line—we'll try to get the folks still on the plane to help. Check children first—for the obvious reason, and because they'll be lighter, and it's more likely the life vest will keep their heads above water. If you go five rows without seeing a kid, go back and check the adults." He gives each of us our assignments, splitting the seats roughly evenly.

People are coming back with blankets now, dropping their loot near the fire and warming themselves. Nick makes a beeline for Jillian and the doctor, waving the two CPR volunteers over.

"These folks know CPR," he tells Sabrina. "They're going to help you with the people we bring out of the plane." He turns to Jillian. "You know CPR?"

"I've . . . had training but never, you know . . ."

"First time for everything. You'll do fine."

"I don't like this." Sabrina frowns as she looks at the bloodied survivors from our section. "The exertion—any of these people could have severe head trauma."

"No choice. This is what we're doing." Nick's voice is firm, but not condescending or harsh.

I like that about him.

Nick runs to the water's edge again and yells for Bill. He has to call again before the paunchy man finally appears, looking haggard and nervous. The bottom edge of the plane hovers just three feet above the water now, and the sight of how close the water is rattles him further. He peers out at us, frightened.

"There are too many. We can't get them all."

"It's okay. We're going to help you, Bill. We need you to get the life vests from under the seats and put them on the people you've moved to the opening. Understand?"

Bill looks around. "Then what?"

"Then we're going to lower them out of the plane to the rescue teams. It's imperative that you and anyone who can help with that stay there. Do you understand?"

Bill nods.

"We're going to make a line to you. We're coming out soon, okay? Get ready."

Nick turns his attention to the group on the bank. He organizes the lines, placing the very strongest at the front, closest to the plane, the weakest in the middle, and the next strongest closest to shore. I can follow his logic, but I couldn't have come up with it, not here in the cold, under the gun, knowing we're about to watch dozens of people die.

He puts life vests on everyone in the line, in case they have to switch places—a good change to the original plan.

The mood's starting to change. People are pitching in. The fire is having its effect, both physically and psychologically. The non-swimmers are stockpiling firewood, moving in and out of the woods quickly. One of them, a gargantuan guy in his twenties wearing a worn peacoat, reaches for a life vest. "I can join the line if I stay close to the bank."

Two more people step forward, echoing his words as they pull yellow life vests around their necks.

Despite the bustle, I feel my nerves winding tighter. The guys near me, the other strong swimmers, introduce themselves. My hand is clammy as I shake theirs. I can barely take my eyes off the sinking plane as we count down the seconds. *I'm a strong swimmer,* I tell myself. *I have to be, tonight.* But I can't help wondering how quickly the plane will sink when the water breaches the lower opening. And what will happen to the bodies and debris when the plane fills. Will I be strong enough to fight my way out and up to the surface? I bet that water is cold enough to numb my limbs. If the plane fills and I'm still inside, I won't stand a chance. But I can't think about that, for one simple reason: I have to help those people. I can't face the idea of *not* helping them.

Nick's eyes meet mine. "Go time."

CHAPTER FIVE

Harper

FOR WHAT FEELS LIKE AN ETERNITY, EVERYTHING IS silent and still. We're all staring at the dark form of the plane, suspended above the placid lake. It abruptly drops toward the water, breaking the spell, and all eyes turn to Nick and to us, the swimmers who volunteered. I'm no longer aware of the aches in my abdomen and shoulders, or the pulsing pain from the side of my face. I only feel the eyes upon me, the frightened eyes of the almost forty people who face us on the bank, backlit by the crackling fire. Their breath hangs in white clouds in front of them, obscuring their noses and mouths. The beady lights on their yellow life vests glow in the thickening fog like streetlamps on a winter night in London.

And then I'm running, following Nick into the water toward the plane, which is dropping steadily now toward the lake's surface. Three men and a woman stand in the aisles there, staring out, watching, waiting for us.

The cold water is a shock at first, like a wave of electricity flowing across me. I inhale sharply and will myself to press on. I lose a little more feeling with each step, though. Ten feet in, I'm up to my chest. I grit my teeth and plow deeper, pumping my arms, icy water splashing on my face and hair. From here the plane looks miles away, though it can only be another forty feet. Nick and the men are pulling away from me, and I fight to keep up.

One of the younger guys reaches the plane first. Carefully, avoiding the twisted metal tendrils that reach into the water, he climbs into the lower half of the fuselage, where the checked baggage is stored. He turns to help the next swimmer and the next, until all four guys are crouched there in the dark mouth of the plane, almost level with the water now.

I reach the jagged opening last, and Nick's outstretched hand is waiting for me. His fingers clamp onto my forearm. "Grab my arm with your other arm."

Two seconds later I'm crouching beside them in the lower half of the plane, drenched head to toe and colder than I've ever been in my life, my body shaking uncontrollably, every shiver sending waves of pain from my midsection and shoulders. The cold feels like it's eating me from the inside out.

I feel hands around me, running up and down. Mike, the twentysomething guy assigned to my aisle, is rubbing my shoulders and back, trying to dry and warm me. I can't look at him. I just stare at his green Boston Celtics T-shirt. How is he not freezing to death?

I can't help myself, though—I lean in toward his warmth.

Nick's eyes linger on us for a quick moment before he turns and yells for the people on the bank to extend the lines. They surge forward into the water, holding hands. The white points of light from their life vests stretch apart as they go deeper into the lake. As the line of people flows away from the fire, their faces disappear in the dark, the tiny lights the only indication they're there. The two lines of light remind me of a runway at night, pointing this wrecked hull of a plane to the fire, to salvation. *We can do this,* I tell myself.

The men in the passenger compartment above reach their arms down, and I feel hands grasping me, boosting me up. I watch wide-eyed as I pass a little too close to the razor-sharp shreds of metal that protrude from the end of the floor.

The shock and ache of the water is gone now, and I wonder if that's a good thing. But I can still feel my body. I still have control.

I stand for a moment, letting my eyes adjust. It's dark here, even darker than I expected. I don't know if it's all the people, but it feels cramped, airless, like a mine shaft. Faint beams of moonlight filter through the oval windows like lanterns guiding us down to the watery abyss at the end of the aisles. The tail's already filled with water, as Nick speculated.

Those people are already dead. We can't help them, but we can save the others.

Through the lingering pain of the crash and the numbing cold of the lake, I feel my nerves rising. I can do this. I have to. I try to remember Nick's speech, to focus on the key phrases, running through them in my mind, pumping myself up.

If we don't go get those people, they will never see or talk to their loved ones again.

No one else is coming for them. It's us, here and now, or they die.

The floor below us is sinking faster, leveling off, but it still slopes a little, a ramp straight back into the darkness.

At our feet, bodies lie two and three deep in the aisles. Women, children, and a few men, most of them slim. Maybe half have life vests on. Not good. There must be thirty people here. My eyes have adapted to the darkness, and I can make out more of the plane now. There's one row of business, all seats empty, then a dividing wall, and two sections of economy with three blocks of seats—two on each side, five in the middle. I scan the rows that face us. My God. People everywhere. Over a hundred. There's no way. How long do we have? A minute? Two? Once the water starts pouring into the lower half of the fuselage, it will fill fast, reaching a tipping point past which the water will pull it to the bottom. We can't save them all. Maybe—

Nick's voice once again cuts off my panic before it can build. His face is expressionless—no sign of concern, no hint of panic. He sounds like a dad on a holiday camping trip, calm, to the point. He quickly assigns responsibilities to Bill and the seven other people helping inside the plane. Two men will stay at the end of each aisle, passing people with life vests out to the lines in the water. The other four conscious survivors will gather and place life vests on people before they go out.

"Under no circumstances are you to leave this plane. We need your help." Nick points to the unconscious people in the aisles. "They need you. They'll die without you. Got it?"

Nods all around. "Go. Work quickly."

Mike takes off ahead of me, bounding over bodies, stepping on them, crushing them. I take a tentative step and lose my footing, catching myself on the nearest seat.

"Go, Harper! You can't worry about stepping on them," Nick shouts, and with that I'm running, every step a cringing mental effort. Finally my feet hit the carpeted aisle, and I race forward. Mike's got the three seats on the interior, I have the window seats. He's passing me, a body thrown over his shoulder, before I even reach my first aisle.

Water on my feet. I'm splashing forward, and I swear the water's colder here. I had thought the angle would be different, the pool of water would only be at the back, but it's like wading into a zero entry pool; with each step the icy water creeps up my legs another few inches. Where to start? I'm in water up to my waist now. Only the heads of the passengers rise above water here. Can they still be alive? Nick's words echo in my head again: anyone underwater has already drowned. But their heads are above water. I push forward, to the last row where the water is still just below their chins.

I reach first for a teenager, his eyes puffy, black and blue, his face swollen and caked with dark blood. I extend my shaking hand, recoiling when I touch cold, hard flesh. I stand there for a moment, shock overtaking me, my breath flowing out in white streams.

"They're dead, Harper!" Mike yells as he wades up the incline past me, another body over his shoulder. "The water's too cold. Move up three rows."

At the plane's opening, the light seems dazzling now. Nick is yelling and pointing. Bodies go over the edge one by one, splashing. It's working. I have to focus. They're counting on me.

Focus.

Warmth. Warmth equals life. I press my hand to the nearest passenger's throat quickly. Cold.

Then the next aisle. I can't skip them. I won't.

Four rows up, where the water's just below my knees, my fingers wrap around a throat that's warm, far warmer than the others. I press, feeling a faint pulse, and take a second to look at a white-faced boy wearing a Manchester United shirt. I shake his shoulders, yell at him, and finally force myself to slap him. Nothing. I unbuckle him, pull his arm to me, and lift him out. The incline and added weight is murder on my already racked frame, but I press forward, fighting for every step. Finally I reach the queue and lower him to a woman and an older man. They slip a yellow life vest around his neck and pull the cord, inflating it.

I saved that kid's life. He's going to live.

That's one.

The people are going out fast now, one every few seconds. Nick looks back at me and nods. I turn and rush back down the aisle, stopping only to duck into an empty seat as Mike passes.

When I step back into the aisle, I feel something new: running water, pulling at my sneakers and splashing on my ankles. The passenger deck has dropped to the lake's surface. How long do we have?

I race to the next aisle, but they're dead. The cold flesh, the necks, go by in a flash now. I move rhythmically, automatically, reaching, touching, moving on. A few seconds later I pull the handle on the seat belt of an Indian girl wearing a Disney World T-shirt. Next, a blond boy in a black sweater, whose hand I have to peel from the hand of a woman beside him, perhaps his mother. I carry three more kids out, my arms and legs burning with every step. I'm spent. I worry I can't go on much longer.

I push that aside. There's no other option. I *have* to.

Mike grabs my forearm. "That's all the kids. Adults now. You spot them, I'll carry them. Okay?"

One, two, three people go up the aisle over Mike's shoulder.

Every time I glance at the back of the plane, the faces jutting just above the water line are different—a new row of passengers being swallowed by the surging pool. We're sinking, fast.

Mike wades toward me. "It's going under. Unbuckle anybody alive and put a life vest on them. It's their only shot."

I rush from row to row, feeling, reaching, unbuckling. I have to go under to reach the life vests beneath the seats, and the water at the first seat is more of a shock than it was when I waded in the first time. At the fourth seat, I feel the plane under me shudder and roll. The sound of ripping metal vibrates through the cabin, and frigid water rushes over me. The wings. Something's happening. Focus. I stretch, trying to unbuckle someone's seat belt, but I can't reach it. I duck under, and yes, I've got it. When I push up, my head doesn't break the surface.

Panic. I reach up, around, desperately trying to feel for the surface, but it's not there.

Through the dark water, I see a faint light: the opening. I work my arms and kick, trying to swim up to the light, but my foot catches on something. I'm stuck. I reach back, grabbing, but my fingers are lifeless, useless, as though I had slept on them. I try to yank my foot free, but it won't come. I turn back to the opening, waving my numb arms, hoping someone will see me. A body with a yellow life vest drifts past me, blotting me out. I watch it float up toward the dim light of the opening, which grows smaller and fainter by the second.

CHAPTER SIX

Nick

HERE AT THE END, WHEN IT'S ALMOST OVER, I begin to understand what might have happened to this section of the plane. After it broke away from the nose, it spun 180 degrees as it hurtled toward the ground. The treetops around the lake slowed it down before it hit the water. It crashed tail first, and that probably saved a lot of lives: the impact threw people back into their seats instead of forward where the seat backs would have snapped their necks. The bottom of the plane has been propped up by something. Trees would be my guess. Whatever it is has finally broken free, and so has all hell. The water in the fuselage, heavy as concrete, is finally pulling the center down. She'll be on the bottom in seconds.

"Everybody out! Now!" I yell.

The last of the survivors who helped us pass the bodies out climb up the aisle and into the waiting line that stretches to the bank, where bodies lie in uneven rows. All the way to the fire, it's a blur of yellow inflatables around bloodied, swollen faces, some bobbing in the water, others standing waist-deep, all working with their last ounce of strength. The horde hardly looks human, but they've been saints tonight.

The guy in the green Celtics T-shirt—Mike, I think he's called—brushes past me, shivering, his head down. I grab his arm, searching the chaos around us. "Where's Harper?"

Mike coughs and glances behind him. "I thought she already bailed." He nods. "Yeah. I think so."

"All right. I'll make sure. Go." I give him a push, and he walks to the edge of the plane and paddles into the frigid water.

I peer back into the abyss, but all I see are bodies, inflated yellow life vests around their necks, floating up toward me. I turn, walk back up the aisle, and scan the faces all the way to the fire, but I don't see a slender woman with blond hair, no life vest. She's not there. She didn't get out.

Something bursts below me—a life vest, I presume. The spray of water hits my face like a bucket of ice water. I shake my head and focus, staring into the dark aisle. Another body floats past, and then I glimpse a figure, slim arms reaching above a seat. Then they're gone, swallowed by the blackness.

My body reacts before I can even process what I've seen. I dive into the black water and swim through the flooded aisle, my hands gripping the backs of the seats that face me, pushing deeper, past bodies and floating objects I can't make out.

It's her. I can just discern her bruised face. Relief and fear war inside me. I reach for her outstretched hand, but the fingers don't close on mine. She feels lifeless, and that stops me cold. I float there for a moment, panic overtaking me for the first time since Flight 305 crashed.

Then her arms move slightly, as if waving for help. She's alive. Quickly, I move my grip to her forearms and pull, but she doesn't budge. I close the few feet between us, wrap my arms around her in a bear hug, plant my feet on the seat, and push off. Nothing. It's like she's tied down, trapped. My chest is pounding now, either from lack of oxygen or from fear.

I drop lower, grip her just above her waist, and thrust out with my legs, giving it everything I've got, and we're free, floating in the aisle, but she's not moving. My chest feels like it's going to explode, but I keep an arm around her and kick at the seats, propelling us up. She feels unnatural, like a rag doll in my arms. The sensation is sickening, but I keep going, the sparkle of the moonlight through the water brightening slowly as my limbs grow numb and panic consumes me. We break the surface, and I gasp for air. For a moment I lose her. I grab her before she can go under again, then kick with my last ounce of strength, but I can't keep us above water. I'm spent. I try to suck in a breath, but I mostly get ice-cold water.

Voices around me, but I can't make them out. I hold on to Harper, kick toward the shore. My legs don't work. I'm limp in the water, something tugging at me. Water flows into my mouth, and I spit it up, choking. I shut my mouth and eyes and try to hang on.

I open my eyes again and see only yellow rubber, a life vest mashing into my face. I blink. Above me hangs a sliver of moon, stars brighter than I've ever seen them before. And then I'm on the shore, dragged by hands under my armpits. My head falls to the side, and I cough up water until I'm dry-heaving. I feel a blanket enfolding me, hands pushing, turning me toward the fire. The heat assaults me, scorching at first, the contrast to the cold nearly unbearable. Waves of heat wash over me, soaking through my skin to my shivering bones, each blast more bearable than the last. It's as if I'm coated in layers of warm mud; it burns, but I can't bring myself to turn away.

Seconds pass, or it could be hours; I've lost all sense of time. Hands grip me and lay me on my back, and I hear footsteps racing away, returning to the lake for someone else.

I roll over onto my side and search the camp. Harper is beyond the fire, on her back, Sabrina crouched over her, working feverishly on her still body. Sabrina's eyes meet mine. I've seen that look before, when the doctor told us about the dead in first class. My head falls back to the ground. The stars fill my eyes again, and then they fade away.

CHAPTER SEVEN

Nick

IT'S EARLY MORNING WHEN I WAKE. I'M STILL by the fire, which has receded to half the size it was the night before. Bodies wrapped in blankets surround the fire in concentric rings, deflated yellow life vests scattered among them, as if it rained flattened rubber duckies last night.

I feel like I spent the last eight hours bouncing around a giant electric mixing bowl. There's no one point of pain, just radiating waves of ache. I take a breath but stop short, trying not to cough. The crisp air hurts, too. It all hurts.

After I'd warmed up by the fire last night, I moved farther out, leaving the warmest space for those who needed it most. We should have built two fires; it's far too cold out here, even for me.

Footsteps crunch toward me across the gravel bank, purposeful, quick strides, and then Sabrina is looming over me, scanning me with her intense eyes. "How do you feel?" Her accent is thicker this morning, her words more clipped. Or maybe that's just her Doctor Voice.

I let my head fall back to the ground. "Fantastic," I say, and cough.

"That's unlikely. I need you to accurately report your symptoms. You might have internal injuries that I couldn't identify last night."

"Good news, Doc: all my internal injuries are psychological." I sit up, surveying the camp. "Where's Harper?"

"This way."

I can't help holding my breath as Sabrina leads me across the camp to the circle closest to the fire. Harper's lying there on her side, her small body curled toward the fire, wrapped in two fuzzy blue blankets, her matted golden hair spilling over the top. She's not moving.

"She's alive," Sabrina says finally. "But I don't know much more. She wasn't breathing when she was brought ashore. I revived her, but she was delirious. She may have permanent brain damage, or . . . As I said last night, any strenuous exercise was dangerous."

"What do you think we should have done—nothing? Watched? Paddled out and told them we'd love to help but we can't, doctor's orders?"

"No. That is not what I meant to say. I only wanted to point out that her precarious physical state before the excess exertion and oxygen deprivation may have exacerbated any preexisting injuries, making a precise diagnosis more difficult."

"Right. Well, since you put it that way . . ." I take a deep breath and rub my temples, trying to soothe my pounding head. Sabrina probably saved dozens of lives last night, and from the looks of it, she hasn't slept herself. "Look, I feel like hell, and I'm sort of second-guessing the decisions I made last night."

"The fault is likely mine. I'm well outside my comfort zone here."

"Right. You could . . . work on the bedside manner a bit."

"I don't visit bedsides."

"I gathered that. What kind of doctor are you, anyway?"

She turns and steps away from the fire. "I think you should get something to eat and rest."

"Sandwich and a nap. Sounds good to me." Searching the distance along the shore, I listen, but I don't see or hear anything. "So where's the cavalry?"

"Cavalry?"

"You know—helicopters, emergency personnel. They have to be here by now."

"I haven't seen anyone."

"You're kidding."

"I assure you I'm not."

Human interaction just isn't Sabrina's bag, which is probably why she's not a practicing physician, whatever that means. But that's not the biggest mystery at the moment.

Maybe the rescue teams are camped out at the nose section. The plane crashed almost twelve hours ago—they have to be here by now. In the confusion last night, I left my cell phone in my pocket. I verify what I already knew: it's dead and not coming back.

"I'm gonna check the other section, get some food. Want anything?"

"Yes, please. A half-liter bottle of water and a full meal, ideally a thousand calories—fifty percent carbohydrates, thirty percent protein, and the remaining twenty percent fat. Preferably unprocessed with minimal additives."

"Great."

"I can add further parameters if it would be helpful."

"Nope, nope, I've got what I need. Be back."

I trudge through the woods, following the path Harper and I ran last night. She was already winded then. I should have known better—and I should have never asked her to join me and the guys in the plane. I think back to last night and realize I looked directly at her when I called for volunteers, practically without thinking. I shamed the people complaining with that speech I gave, and I can't help but think I did the same with her. I twisted her arm, put her on the spot in front of everyone.

If she dies or is permanently disabled from the rescue, that's all on me.

Guilt presses on my shoulders like the weight of the world, dragging me down.

Ahead, I hear shouts. Two dozen people are crowded around the gray emergency chute that leads up to the door just right of the cockpit.

"It's our food!"

I know that voice—the drunken jerk in 2D. He's standing at the bottom of the chute, shouting and pushing people.

"*We* paid for it." He jabs his finger toward the face of the man in front of him. "*Our* tickets bought the food in first and business classes. Eat the food you paid for in economy. I hear it's back at the lake."

I don't give much thought to what I do next. It's nice to have an easy decision.

I push through the crowd without a word.

"You—" 2D says, snorting . . . before I punch him in the face as hard as I can.

He falls straight back into the chute, bounces up halfway, and lands again awkwardly. Then he's pushing up, lunging at me, throwing a fist at least two feet short. I catch him with another shot to the face, and he flies back, at an angle this time, rolling off the edge of the chute onto the ground.

Every movement hurts, but God, it feels so good. That's the first time I've hit someone since I was ten. I hope it'll be the last punch I ever throw—but it's worth it. Easily.

From the ground, 2D's eyes are daggers. "I'll have you arrested for assault when this is over!"

"Really? How?"

"I've got two dozen witnesses."

"Do you?" I glance back at the crowd, who are all smiles, some shaking their heads.

"And I've got proof," 2D says, pointing to his bloody face.

"Of what? Being in an airplane crash?"

I turn to Jillian, whose eyes are wide. "How much food is left?"

"Some. I'm not sure."

"Start bringing it out. Take two people to help you."

The mob swells forward, but I hold up my hands. "Wait. We need to stay down here. The plane could be unstable. Let Jillian bring the food out, and we'll divide it evenly, okay?"

There's some grumbling but no real pushback. After all, I just punched some random guy in the face, seemingly apropos of nothing.

Behind me, Jillian is struggling up the chute with the help of two guys. It seems a waste to build a stairway when we'll be rescued soon, but someone's likely to get hurt if we don't. I walk over and talk with the three of them about what we might use, everything from luggage to the serving carts. We agree that that will be the next priority, after breakfast is served.

What next? The mob is still here, massed like concertgoers waiting for the show to start. We need real help. Rescue.

"Does anyone here have a working cell phone?" I ask.

Voices around the crowd call out.

No, no service.

Battery's dead.

Been trying all night, nothing.

Nobody has, I've been asking.

That's odd. No, it's unbelievable. Out of two hundred passengers who crash-land in England, no one has a cell signal? Something's wrong.

The crowd seems to be thinking the same thing. A man wearing a tweed blazer over a *Doctor Who* T-shirt and jeans steps out of the crowd. "It's obvious what's happened, isn't it?" He pauses, waiting for the group's attention. "It's started—the Third World War. They've taken out our communications, all electronics. The invasion's begun, that's why they're not bothering with us lot. They've got bigger problems than rescuing us at the moment."

Groans erupt, as well as murmurs of concern. A short, bald man wearing a black sweater and tiny round glasses takes up the dissenting position, speaking with that Down East Maine accent, slowly, deliberately, like a professor dressing down his least-favorite student. "That, sir, is far-fetched to the point of absurdity."

"Is it now?" the *Doctor Who* fan retorts. "What do you know about it?"

"A great deal, actually. I used to work for Northrop Grumman."

"Oh yeah? Big whoop."

"If this *were* World War Three, we'd be hearing explosions. Planes would be flying overhead. We'd probably hear tanks and troop carriers in the distance. Anyway, I doubt World War Three would start in England."

"Maybe they're saving England for last. It's the perfect launching place for an invasion of Continental Europe—history's proved that."

"It is," Northrop Grumman guy counters. "And that's precisely why nobody's conquered it in almost a thousand years."

"Well, maybe it isn't that kind of war. Your lot always assumes the next war will be just like the last, tanks and planes right up to the end, but it's the technology that's the real key. They've taken us back to the Stone Age. They'll wait us out, let us start starving before they invade. They probably got us with a series of EMPs. That explains the crash—the phones, too."

"It does not, sir," Northrop Grumman drawls condescendingly. "An EMP wouldn't have fried our cell phones, but it would have knocked out larger electronics. I just saw a man on the plane with a working laptop."

A middle-aged woman in an NYU sweatshirt speaks up. "The Internet went out during the flight. I was reading e-mail. That was at least an hour before we crashed."

"True," says a tall man beside her.

"Maybe it's just a problem with the satellites."

Northrop Grumman turns to the NYU woman. "A satellite failure could have contributed to the crash, true, but it doesn't explain the cell phones. They connect to land-based towers—well, except for sat phones. The one thing we can conclude is that all land-based towers in the area must be down."

"Or there aren't any," *Doctor Who* says. "Maybe we're not in England at all."

That, I find interesting.

NYU speaks up again. "The little readout showed the plane over England—I saw it."

"It's possible," Northrop Grumman says, considering, "that if the plane had a malfunction, and all external communication was lost, the readouts would have shown us on the original flight path. The plane's position could have been calculated based only on our flight time."

"Then we could be anywhere!" a frightened voice shouts.

"Greenland, for all we know. It's bloody cold enough."

"Or Iceland, or another island off the coast of England. No-man's-land."

"They'll never find us."

An elderly woman steps toward me. "What do you think, sir?"

Every eye turns to me.

"I think . . ." *What do I think?* I take a minute, finally settling on something I'd been chewing on for the last few minutes. "I think that we're going to know a lot more once we get into the cockpit. The computers, or hopefully the pilots, can tell us where we are. And the communications equipment could help us contact help."

It amounts to kicking the can down the road, the proverbial answer we've been waiting for locked just feet away, but it does the trick. The crowd mellows. As food slides down the inflated chute, the group breaks up. People get their half meals and start trooping back to the warmth of the blankets and fire by the lake.

"You won't get into that cockpit."

I turn to find Northrop Grumman standing bizarrely close to me. "Why do you say that?"

"It's reinforced. All airplane doors were, after 9/11, especially on long-haul flights. You'd have a better chance of getting into Fort Knox."

"What about the windows?"

"Same. They can withstand about any impact, even at high speed."

The guy's still staring at me, almost expectantly. He's got more to say. Heck, I'll bite. "What do you suggest?"

He moves even closer, almost whispering. "You can't get in, but if someone is alive inside, they can get out—that's our only hope. It's only been twelve hours. Maybe one of the pilots was just knocked unconscious. If we could wake them up, they could unlock the door."

"Makes sense. So we'll make some noise."

"Exactly. Now, this is important, Mr. . . ."

"Stone. Nick Stone." I extend my hand, and he shakes quickly.

"Bob Ward. Now we need to make sure we—or someone we trust—are the ones who get into that cockpit first."

Someone we trust. My mind flashes to the three guys that followed me onto the plane last night—and to Harper. I can't help wondering how she's doing. Dread fills the pit of my stomach.

"Why?" I ask, trying to focus on the issue at hand.

"Because there's a box inside the cockpit, filled with guns. If the wrong people get to them, this camp will become a very dangerous place." He glances back at the chute, to where I laid out 2D.

"I agree."

"Are we ready to begin, then?" Bob's already shuffling toward the chute. This guy is having the time of his life.

With the help of a few passengers, we make our way into the plane, where Jillian's sorting food in the little galley just behind the cockpit.

"How's the food supply?" I ask.

"This is the last of it."

"Okay, we'll figure out what to do this afternoon. Could you take two meals to the lake—one for the doctor, and one for Harper? And do you remember the three guys who were helping me on the plane last night?" She nods. "Good—can you ask them to join us here?"

"Sure."

"Also, do you know the pilots' names?" Maybe calling them by name will help. "In fact, if you have a complete crew and passenger manifest, that would be helpful."

Jillian tells me the pilots' names and passes me some stapled pages, which I scan. I see my own name, then Harper Lane, and my nemesis in 2D: Grayson Shaw. Sabrina Schröder, passenger in 11G, business class. I scan a bit more and find Yul Tan, the Asian typing on his laptop last night, 10B. I glance down the aisle. He's still there, typing away, the glowing screen lighting his gaunt face. Either that laptop gets great battery life, or he's taken a break—which doesn't look likely. He seems strung out, agitated. There's something off here, but what, I don't have a clue.

"Ready, Mr. Stone?" Bob asks.

"Yeah. And call me Nick."

NOTHING.

We've tried noise. We've tried going through the first-class lavatory. We've been down to the ground, where the nose is dug in now—it settled some last night—and peered through the windshield in the few places where it isn't too heavily cracked. They're in there, three pilots, none moving. We can't tell if they're breathing. The five of us—Bob, the three swimmers from the lake, and me—have been at it for hours, and I'm exhausted.

"I've gotta take a break, fellas," I say. "Heading to the lake. Grab me if you get through."

"You could rest here, Nick," Bob calls, but I'm down the make-shift stairway and hiking away before he can stop me. The truth is, I want to see Harper. It's past midday, and I haven't been able to get her out of my mind. I'm worried, but there's something else, too: a feeling I can't seem to shake off. I ignore a few more calls from Bob as I disappear into the dense forest. He's not one for letting things go.

On the walk back to the lake, I think about why we haven't seen any rescue personnel. Even if we've crashed in some remote part of England, surely the fire would show up on satellites, or helicopters could spot the column of smoke. England is bigger than it appears on a map, but it's also a first-world country with all the kinds of technology that wouldn't ignore a plane crashing in its borders. I make a deal with myself not to worry about it any more until tomorrow morning. Not much I can do right now anyway. Survivors—I'll focus on them. Warmth, food, and medical care could make all the difference between life and death for a few folks.

To my right I hear branches snapping. I turn to see 2D—Grayson Shaw—twelve feet away, holding a stick the size of a bat. He grins at me, revealing blood-covered teeth.

I'm unarmed, too sore to run, and probably too tired to fight. This should be interesting.

CHAPTER EIGHT

Harper

LAST NIGHT I GAVE BIRTH TO A RHINOCEROS. Not just any rhino, mind you: a pregnant rhino, with twins. And three horns. Lots of horns. I birthed a double-pregnant, triple-horned rhino. That's what it feels like, at least.

I'm glad I'm breathing, but I still dislike the pain every breath brings. I'm going to lie here until it doesn't hurt anymore. On the bright side, I'm bound to lose some weight during this period. I have no appetite and can't imagine the pain eating will entail.

I envision myself emerging from this swaddled, fireside solitude. I'll be slimmer and funnier and completely healed; a phoenix rising from the ashes, ready to soar high above the lake and roar in a screeching call of freedom and awesomeness before I retake my pitiful life.

Must rest and wait for those wings to grow in.

DOCTOR'S BEEN BY. SHE'S A good bit sterner than I remember her last night. Dry, to the point, bit of a bore, really. Though her bedside manner needs some work, she seems to know her stuff. And she's filled me in. She fed me some pain pills after I came out of the water last night. I don't remember it, but she says they may have resulted in strange dreams and foggy thinking. (I neglected to mention the rhino and phoenix visions, neither of which seems strictly medically relevant.)

The doctor's most concerned about my leg, which apparently has a nasty gash from where it was caught in the plane. She's bandaged it up and wants to keep an eye on it.

About all I can recall from last night is the euphoria of saving those people, the children especially, the ones I carried myself. Then the cold, and Nick's arms pulling me, and nothing much after that.

AWOKE FEELING EVEN WORSE. PAIN meds must have worn off completely now. Nick sent some food, but I couldn't eat it, so I gave it away. Must sleep.

A FEW MINUTES AGO I spotted a kid walking past the fire, an Indian girl around twelve wearing a Disney World T-shirt.

That made me feel good enough to stand up and take a walk. My right leg is dodgy, sending spikes of pain through my body with every step, but it becomes manageable after a few paces.

Being on my feet hurts a lot more than lying down, but I want to do something to contribute around here.

Most people are huddled together by the fire, but a few are dragging branches in from the forest, adding their take to the dwindling flames. That seems as good an idea as any, so I set out along the branch-swept path into the woods.

About a hundred feet into the forest, I hear a voice, one I know. One I detest.

"Don't worry, it won't be like this," Grayson says in his usual hateful, condescending tone. "I'm going to hurt you when you least expect it."

"I'm not expecting it now." Nick sounds calm.

I walk closer, just far enough to make both of them out. Nick looks exhausted. Black bags hang under his eyes, which are hard, much more so than I remember. Grayson holds a large stick at his side. His back's to me, so I can't see his face.

I inch closer, and a branch pops under my foot. I look up to find both their eyes upon me.

"Jesus, you're like a virus," Grayson says. "You just won't go away." He waits, but I don't speak. "I bet you're loving this. Best thing that could've happened to you, isn't it?"

Nick looks right at me, ignoring him. "You all right?"

"Yeah. You?"

"Yeah."

"Oh, for the love of God. Please excuse me while I go throw up until I die." Grayson marches past me. "Tell your boyfriend to sleep with one eye open, Harper."

A few seconds later I hear him pitch the stick into the fire.

Nick stands before me now, his face serious and tense. I wonder what's happened.

"I put you up to it last night," he says. "Going into that plane."

"You didn't."

"I did. If something had happened to you—"

"Listen, if I had it to do over again, I would do the exact same thing, even if I hadn't woken up this morning, curled up by the fire. I've seen them, a few of the kids I hauled out of that plane. The risk was well worth it. To me, it was all well worth it."

He nods, glances at the ground. His face is still solemn, but I can feel the tension flowing out of him, as if it were a wall of air brushing past me. "Where does it hurt?" he asks.

"Everywhere. My whole bloody body."

He smiles and exhales, laughing for the first time. "Me, too."

He fills me in as we trek back to the fire, gathering loose branches as we go. Nobody's cell phone works, which is strange, but not out of the question in rural England. He's tried to get into the cockpit with no luck. He figures the pilots are dead; he's had a look at the cockpit and it's pretty tight, would have been deadly during the crash. Poor souls.

At the fire, I insist he take one of my blankets, and after a bout of protests, he relents. We sit in silence for a while. I'm dying to ask him what he does for a living, where he's from, anything. I want to know what Nick Stone is like, you know, when he's not rescuing plane crash survivors from an icy lake. I've never met anyone quite like him. He seems to have been delivered to Planet Earth from some other place, some place where normal human weaknesses and shortcomings don't apply.

I'm about to launch into my first lame question, which I've rehearsed in my mind nine times now, when someone runs up to us, almost colliding with Nick.

It's Mike, the guy with the green Celtics T-shirt. He focuses on Nick, speaking between pants. "We're . . . in."

CHAPTER NINE

Harper

IT'S A STRUGGLE TO KEEP UP WITH NICK and Mike through the woods. With each step, I can feel the air temperature dropping and the pain in my lower leg rising.

When we reach the nose section, the two of them bound up an assortment of luggage and plane bits stacked to form a rough stairway. Nick pauses at the top and reaches down for me, as he did when we climbed into the plane in the lake.

I scramble awkwardly up the pile, and he catches my arm and pulls me to the threshold. My body crashes into his, sending waves of pain through me while he holds me close to steady us.

Worth it. So *worth it.*

The other two swimmers—their names escape me—are there already, and someone I don't know, a short, bald man wearing a black sweater. He peers over his small round glasses, fixing me with a skeptical gaze as if he's about to ask who invited a *girl* into his boy's-club airplane tree house.

I'm one second away from asking if this is a boob-free zone when Nick intercedes. "Harper, this is Bob Ward. And you remember Wyatt and Seth from last night?"

Bob's suspicious look vanishes with Nick's words, and after we exchange shakes and nods, everyone turns to the first row of seats. A man in a pilot's jacket lies there, his face crusted with dried blood.

Bob steps forward and kneels by his side, motioning back toward Nick. "Dylan, we've got Nick Stone here." His officious tone would be funny in any other circumstances. "He's managing the situation on the ground. I need you to tell him what you just told us."

The pilot turns his head, trying to pick Nick out of the crowd. His face is so discolored and swollen that I can barely make out the whites of his eyes, but he begins speaking, his voice a whisper.

"We lost all communications about halfway in, somewhere over the Atlantic."

Nick raises a hand. "Stop. I need you to wait one minute."

What's he up to? He marches down the aisle into business, stopping next to a young Asian man who's typing maniacally on a laptop. After a brief exchange, the Asian man gets up and follows Nick back.

"Please continue," Nick says to the pilot, eyeing Laptop Man.

"Like I said, we lost communications over the Atlantic, but we maintained our flight path. The captain has been flying this route for three years. I've been on it six months. Radar still worked, but nothing else. We generally knew where we were, but it was really odd, to go dark like that. The captain swore the problem was outside the plane, but that's impossible. Anyway, we got radio contact—Heathrow air traffic control—a little over two hours before our designated landing time. There was a global situation with communications, they told us, and they would walk us in. We should land normally, but descend to seven thousand feet for safety reasons. That slowed us down, but we did it. Then everything happened at once."

"The blast?" Bob coaxes.

"The first one, yeah."

"Was it above you?"

"No—behind, I think. Or all around. I don't know. We dove, trying to get away from it."

"And there was another blast?" Bob sounds eager, expectant.

"I . . . I don't know. There was something . . . else. But I don't know what. A series of shock waves, tossing us around in the sky. Never seen anything like it. We lowered the landing gear and went down even farther, trying to cut our airspeed, preparing for the worst. We thought it might be some megastorm. We couldn't get away from it, though. Everything after that's a blur. We kept diving, trying to get past it, but it caught up to us."

Nick is still staring at Laptop Man, who hasn't moved a muscle. He's like a statue. *What's going on? You sleep in around here, and mysteries pop up by the minute.* "What do you think of that?" Nick asks him.

Laptop Man avoids eye contact with Nick and speaks in an even, controlled tone. "Like I said, I don't know anything about it. But it sounds sort of like the communications went out during a storm, and we crashed. Can I go now?"

"Nobody's holding you."

The Asian guy walks back to his seat and, after a last glance over his shoulder at Nick, plops down and starts typing away again.

What the hell was that all about?

Nick thanks the pilot and moves back into the galley between first class and the cockpit. Sabrina, who came with us from the lakeside, moves in to examine the pilot.

"You buy the pilot's story?" Bob asks Nick, his tone skeptical.

Nick stares at Bob for a second, as if waiting for him to recant. "Yeah, I do."

Bob nods a bit too theatrically, as if he were a TV detective finally choosing to believe an informant's story. "The other two pilots are dead, so we've got no corroborating witnesses—well, save for ourselves. We tried the radio, but there's no answer."

"All right. I think we bed down tonight, wait for rescue. If nobody's come by daylight, we reassess."

"You're forgetting the most important part." Bob's voice is edging toward panic.

"Right. What am I forgetting?"

"The guns." Bob races into the cockpit and returns with a handgun, holding it by the end, like it's a fish he caught on holiday.

"Put that back," Nick says sharply. "And bring me the key."

Bob mutters but returns with the key, placing it in Nick's palm. "There're four handguns in there. One for each of you." He nods to the swimmers and Nick. I guess I didn't make the handgun club.

"We're not carrying them around," Nick says. "We have to sleep, and someone could take them off us. It's too dangerous." He glances at the key. "And so is this." He hands it to me. "They know the five of us will have been in the cockpit."

I slip the key into my tight jeans pocket, where I swear I can feel it radiating heat. I feel like Frodo Baggins in *The Lord of the Rings,* knowing I may hold the key to the lives of the survivors of Flight 305. Another burden to bear, though not quite as dreadful as the Decision.

The sun is setting as Nick and I make our way through the woods to the fire by the lake. Neither of us says a word, but in my mind, I'm going through the questions I want to ask him. Namely, what he does for a living. Ah, who am I kidding? I want to ask some roundabout question that gets at the real money shot: Is there a woman in Nick Stone's life? A little lady waiting at home. A Mrs. Nick Stone. A soulless, way-too-skinny, fashion-victim, fake-as-Santa girlfriend. That's unfair. My leg hurts. Excuses . . .

At the fire, we settle in and watch the sun set over the lake. As it slips below the horizon, I start my interrogation—nonchalant, of course.

"Where you from, Nick?"

"All over. You?"

"I grew up in a small town in England, but I live in London now."

"This feel like England to you?" He motions to the lake and forest around us.

"Yeah, a bit."

"Yeah, to me, too." He slumps over, pulling the blanket up to his chin. "I'm beat, Harper. See you in the morning."

He's asleep in seconds. I can't help remembering Grayson Shaw's last words to me. *Tell your boyfriend to sleep with one eye open, Harper.*

I settle in between him and the fire and stare up at the stars. Sleep won't come tonight. I've slept too much today already, but that's not really it. Truth be told, it's been a long time since I've slept next to someone I fancied as much as Nick Stone.

CHAPTER TEN

Nick

I EXPECTED TO WAKE UP TO HELICOPTERS, FLASHING lights, and waves of English first responders saying things like "Are you all right there?" and "Let's have a look at you now."

No such luck. The muddy beach by the blue-green lake looks exactly as it did last night: rings of people around a dying fire, wrapped up in navy blankets. Only a few are stirring, mumbling groggily to each other.

I get to my knees and lean over Harper, who's curled toward the fire, sound asleep. I wouldn't wake her for all the tea in China.

As I survey the camp, watching the survivors of Flight 305 wake to another day, two simple facts strike me: It's been over thirty-six hours since we crashed. And someone should have been here by now.

AT THE NOSE SECTION, IT feels like déjà vu. Again there's an angry mob, the second to mass here in as many days. Grayson Shaw is here, too, but at least he's not center stage this time. He's sitting at the back, looking hungover and haggard. He must have finally run out of alcohol. But that could actually make him more dangerous.

The food in the nose section ran out last night, when I was too tired to notice. The crowd's muttering about people hoarding food, calling for searches of the camp and redistribution. "I'd kill a man for a Diet Coke right now," I hear a skinny man in a rumpled suit say. I'll look up Coke stock if I live through this.

Jillian's taking the brunt of the crowd's ire. They're chewing her out like this is simply a disruption to normal in-flight service. The truth is, she's just another survivor now, but the uniform she's wearing pegs her as the person who hands out food. She looks relieved to see me.

"Help," she says, lunging for me and clamping both hands around my arm, pulling me up to stand beside her at the bottom of the makeshift stairway as she faces the crowd.

Bob Ward and Sabrina are here, too. Their faces are solemn, but they nod, encouraging me.

The crowd quiets, people nudging each other and whispering.

That's him.

Yeah, the guy from the lake.

"All right," I say. "We're going to get some food, but it'll take some time."

"We need something now!" a woman in a mud-stained sweater shouts.

"There isn't anything right now, okay? Look, we have to work together here. If we work together, we'll all eat—otherwise, we could all starve."

The word *starve* is a mistake. The crowd picks it up, and it echoes from person to person in panicky counterpoint until it sounds like the Starve Chorus. It takes me a few minutes to unsay it and get their focus again.

"So how we gonna get food?" asks an overweight man with a thick New York accent.

How indeed? I hadn't gotten that far. I can see where this is going. If I let groupthink take over and devil's advocates call the shots, we'll still be standing here at sundown, hungry and undecided. I need a plan, right now.

There are only two logical sources of food: the meals in the other half of the plane and fish from the lake. We might manage to kill something here on land, but with a hundred mouths to feed, it likely won't go far. Unless . . . there's a farm nearby. It's a long shot, but I tuck the idea away for future use.

"Okay, first step," I say as authoritatively as I can. "We're going to take an inventory."

"Inventory?"

"Yes." I point to Jillian—poor Jillian—and Bob Ward, who straightens up and puts on his ultraserious camp counselor face for the crowd. He, at least, is still loving this. "Jillian and Bob are going to come around and ask you what was in your carry-on and checked baggage and what your seat was—or, more importantly, what overhead bin your bag was in. Describe anything that might be of use out here, especially food. Come see me right now if you had any fishing or diving gear in your luggage—a wet suit, even snorkeling gear."

A bloated guy in his forties laughs, turning to the crowd. "Hey, Jack, folks don't do much snorkeling in New York in November." That gets a few laughs, and he grins at me, waiting.

I know this guy's type, and I'd love to stick it to him, but I can't afford to make another enemy. I opt for the high road.

"That's true. I'm thinking about people making a connection, passengers departing from the Caribbean, somebody diving on vacation, making their way home. JFK is a major hub for international destinations. Nassau to JFK to Heathrow isn't out of the question. Or maybe someone on their way to the Mediterranean via Heathrow. I thought maybe we could get lucky."

Jillian starts the survey, but Bob hangs back. "You want to start diving for the food and any supplies in the lake."

"Yeah, it seems like our only move."

"I agree, but there's a problem." Bob pauses dramatically. I get the impression he likes saying "There's a problem" and pausing.

"What's that?"

"All the checked baggage will be in LD3s."

Oh, right. LD3s.

"What's an LD3?"

"It's a unit load device."

A unit load device. Why didn't he just say so?

"I don't know what that is, Bob."

"They're metal cases that hold the luggage. On smaller aircraft, they simply load the bags in. On larger ones, like our fateful Boeing 777, they place the bags in the LD3s, then move them onto the plane. They can get more bags on that way and keep them straight. The 777 can carry up to thirty-two LD3s, and maybe a dozen pallets. I can't remember."

"Pallets?"

"Yeah, with food, supplies, etcetera."

"What does all this mean?" I ask.

"The LD3s will be stacked two wide all the way to the tail. Even if we can dive down to them, they'll be hard to get to. We might be able to get into the first two, but there's no way we can haul them out and get to the rows behind them. Bottom line: we can't count on getting to anything in the checked baggage."

So much for that plan. "That's good to know."

"I'll check with Jillian and the pilot, try to figure out where the pallets might be positioned. If they're near where the plane broke apart, or here in the nose, we could get lucky."

"All right. Thanks, Bob."

Bob Ward. Annoying? Yes. Helpful? Also yes.

The doctor is queued up next, that "Something is seriously wrong, Mr. Stone" look on her face. Then again, Sabrina has had that look on her face since we met, so maybe that's just how she always looks.

"Hi, Sabrina," I say, bracing myself.

"We need to build a shelter."

At least somebody around here gets right to it.

"Why?"

"Most of the passengers suffered mild hypothermia on the first night. Some, such as yourself and Ms. Lane, moderate cases. This morning, I've observed a trend: about half the passengers have a cold. If they remain out in the elements, that could progress. If it rains, they'll fare even worse. We could have cases of bacterial infection or pneumonia soon. At a minimum, I would like to move anyone with a compromised immune system, older passengers, and anyone on an immunosuppressant therapy—which are common for autoimmune diseases—to the nose section and enclose it."

"Okay. Let me have someone check the trees supporting it. It moved some last night. If it collapses under the added weight, we'll be worse off. I'll be back this evening, and we'll reassess then."

"Where are you going?"

"Someone has to scout the area around us, look for food, maybe even help—or a better shelter."

Her eyes grow wide. "Fine. Anyone but you."

"What?"

"You can't leave."

"Why?"

"Because it would be chaos here without you."

I just stare at her, unsure what to say. She's probably right. That worries me, but it also brings a sense of something I haven't felt in a long time: fulfillment. Right now I feel like I'm doing exactly what I need to be doing, that I'm making a difference in people's lives. I haven't felt that way in a very long time.

A BREAK. BOB FOUND A pallet with some food in the nose section. It was tossed around, torn to pieces, but it's yielded enough for two meals. That's brought morale up and quelled most of the complaints for now.

Sabrina has added a request for medications, especially antibiotics, to the luggage survey, but so far the poll hasn't revealed much. There've been reports of fishing gear, and two passengers claimed snorkeling sets—but it's all in checked baggage at the bottom of the lake, locked inside those steel crates. I've felt out a few of the guys who swam out to the rear section with me, and none of them are keen to go diving into the wreckage. I can't say I blame them. Instead, I've sent them out with some of the other passengers who're still in decent shape to scout the surrounding areas. They left a few hours ago in four teams of three, one for each cardinal direction. They'll hike until they find something or someone, or until midday, whichever comes first, then head back, hopefully arriving before sunset. We'll know a lot more then.

I hope.

HARPER'S SICK.

She awoke with a ragged cough, a headache, and a low-grade fever. She swears she's okay, but Sabrina is concerned enough to move her, against her protests, to the nose section.

I've checked the trees supporting the back of this section. They still make me nervous, but I don't see a better option at the moment.

We've hung blue blankets over the open end, but every few minutes an icy draft makes it past them. During the day, it's colder than by the fire at the lake, but I figure it will be much better at night, especially after Sabrina packs it full of patients.

The mysterious Asian, Yul Tan, has come up with a better solution: build a wall. He and Sabrina have stacked the first- and business-class carry-on luggage from floor to ceiling, plugging any holes with deflated life vests. It looks kind of weird, but it works.

Harper takes her old seat in first class, 1D, and stretches out.

"I feel useless," she says, and coughs.

"We all are, right now. Nothing to do but wait. We'll be out of here soon."

"You really believe that?"

"Sure," I say automatically. It's the only response I can make right now. I try my best to keep any doubt out of my voice.

A minute passes, both of us crammed in her pod, watching other passengers file by, coughing as they search for a place to bed down.

"So tell me, what does the mysterious, multitalented Nick Stone do for a living? When he's not rescuing helpless passengers."

"Me?" I hesitate for a moment, debating what to tell her. "Nothing . . . as interesting as rescuing airline passengers. How about you?"

"I'm a writer."

"Really? Anything I might have read?"

She looks down and half laughs, half coughs. "Possibly. I've written six books. None of which had my name on them, though, and none of which I'm legally permitted to discuss."

I wonder what that means. It seems to be a sore spot. But before I can ask, out of the corner of my eye I see someone waving: Mike, standing at the bottom of the stairway. The other two guys who went east with him are at his side. They look tired. They're panting, hunched over, their hands on their knees. Whatever happened to them out there sent them back in a hurry.

I'm up and out four seconds later. "You found something?"

"Yeah," Mike swallows. He's excited, but there's something else: nervousness. "We found . . . something."

CHAPTER ELEVEN

Nick

I BARELY SLEPT LAST NIGHT. I COULDN'T GET the picture Mike took out of my mind: an octagonal structure, all glass and shining metal, glistening in the middle of a field. There's no road or path leading to it, no vehicles, no indication of what could be inside. It's a mystery, a mirage rising out of an expanse of tall green grass.

Mike snapped the picture from a ridge miles away, and then he and his team rushed back as quickly as they could. We don't have any other clues about what might be inside. For the sake of the freezing, starving survivors of Flight 305, I hope the glass structure's filled with food. A satellite phone to get us out of this fix would also be nice. Things are getting desperate.

We'll serve the last of the food this morning, and we have no viable way to get more, at least not enough to feed 104 mouths. I've asked Jillian to organize nut-and-berry-gathering expeditions today, and to assign groups to tend the fire, but that's mostly to keep folks busy and away from each other's throats—to be honest, there's really no one here who knows enough about plants to confirm if anything we find is edible, and Sabrina has warned me that we could be adding to our problems by experimenting.

Again, though: it's something for them to do. I don't remember where I heard it, but lack of purpose often kills more people in situations like this than lack of food.

We have plenty of water thanks to the lake, but that's the extent of the good news. We can last a few days without food, a little longer with some consequences, but this place will start to get ugly after that.

At sunrise the four scouting teams will take the final scraps of food, enough to hike for two days and camp for a night if we need to. That will double our range.

Mike was smart, taking his phone. Today, I'll make sure each team member carries two cell phones—their own, provided it still has battery life, plus another from the other passengers. With four teams of three, that's twenty-four phones total. Phones from a diverse group of manufacturers and on different networks will maximize possible reception. Every hour they'll stop, turn the phones on, and check for a signal. They'll also be taking pictures of anything noteworthy, any potential landmark. The landscape the teams described yesterday—rolling, forested hills and a few meadows—could have been anywhere in Northern Europe, Scandinavia, or the British Isles. But maybe something in a photo will ring a bell with one of the passengers. That might give us an idea of which way to go, or how far we are from help.

Across the lake, the first rays of sunlight break over the tree line. I sit for a moment, watching my breath turn white in the crisp morning air, listening to the crackle and pop of the fire to my right. Finally, I climb to my feet and head back into the forest.

Bob Ward is waiting for me at the makeshift staircase that leads to the nose section. "I'm going with you," he announces.

"You're not, Bob." I pick up my pace, try to step past him, but he shuffles over, blocking my way.

"I've seen the picture Mike took. Could be anything in there. You'll need me, Nick."

Time for tough love. I hate to do it, but 104 souls are on the line, and we're running out of time to help them. "There's plenty to do around here, Bob. We're looking at a grueling hike. We can't stop for anybody who can't keep up."

"I can keep up."

Unfortunately, I doubt it. Bob has to be sixty, and I'm not even sure if *I* can keep up with Mike, who must be ten years younger than I am and in considerably better shape.

I exhale and try for the logical approach. "Look, if you fall behind after noon, you won't be able to make it back to camp before nightfall. You'll be out in the cold for the night. With no food—"

"I understand, Nick. If I can't keep up, I'll make you leave me. I know what's at stake. When do we leave?"

The truth is, I can't stop Bob, and we need to get going. I shake my head, finally relenting. "Now. Grab Mike, and we'll head out."

Inside the plane, I kneel beside Harper's pod. She's asleep, or unconscious. I shake her, but she doesn't come to. Her hair's drenched. So's her shirt. I wipe the sweat off her forehead, brushing her damp hair back. Feeling how hot her skin is scares me. She's dangerously sick.

In that moment, I feel the same way I did that morning by the lake, when Sabrina led me to Harper's limp body lying helpless by the fire. The rest of the passengers were in trouble the second we crashed. Harper was also banged up, but she was fine.

Until I asked her to swim out there and risk her life.

This is my fault. She's going to die because of me.

Finally I force myself to stand up and turn away.

Sabrina is at the back, talking quietly with Yul. "Have you seen Harper?" I ask her.

"Yes." She just stares at me.

"Well, what's the prognosis? What're you doing for her?"

"I'm currently monitoring her."

"That's it?"

"She has an infection. I'm waiting to see if her body can fight it off."

"It can't." I struggle to keep my voice level. "Her forehead's as hot as a firecracker."

"A positive sign. Her body's immune system is mounting a robust response."

"That *robust response* isn't enough. She's getting sicker every day. She didn't even wake when I shook her. She needs antibiotics."

Sabrina steps closer and lowers her voice. "We're almost out of antibiotics. I'm rationing them, saving them for critical cases."

"Harper *is* a critical case."

"Critical as in life-threatening."

I shake my head, trying to compose myself. I'm boiling over. The exhaustion, the crappy, shallow sleep, and the stress of the last forty-eight hours are finally getting the best of me. I'm losing control—I can feel it. I fight to keep my voice level, and I'm not sure I succeed.

"Her life wouldn't be in danger—she wouldn't even be sick—if she hadn't gone into that plane and saved those people. We owe it to her to save her life."

Nothing. No response. My rage simmers.

"Okay, Sabrina, think about what message we're sending all these people if she dies. Huh? You stick your neck out for someone around here, and when we're done with you, we'll leave you for dead. That's what you're talking about, and that's dangerous."

"If I administer antibiotics to her today, when she doesn't absolutely need them, it might be a death sentence for someone else. That's dangerous, too. I'm taking a logical risk to save the most lives. I believe you're familiar with this concept—you demonstrated it at the lake."

"You're a real piece of work, Sabrina. You know that?"

"You're unable to see this situation objectively. You're irrational because you've formed an emotional bond with Ms. Lane—"

"You know anything about that—forming emotional bonds with people? Or did you read about it in a journal?"

"Your bias is easily demonstrated. William Boyd, in seat 4D, has symptoms worse than Ms. Lane's. You have yet to ask about Mr. Boyd."

"William Boyd wasn't in that plane, drowning. Harper was. Hell, she might have been the one who saved William Boyd in the first place! I asked her to risk her life, and she did. And *we*," I almost shout, pointing my finger between Sabrina and myself, "are going to do everything we can to keep her alive."

"Harper did not save Mr. Boyd. He was in the water, in the line that passed the people from the plane to the shore. But this isn't about his role in the rescue operation. You haven't asked about Mr. Boyd because you don't have an emotional connection to him. You're not objective, Nick. I am. In fact, for reasons you've already alluded to, I'm almost uniquely qualified to make unemotional, logical decisions about the care of these people, maximizing the number of lives saved."

Hopeless. I'm arguing with a robot. My jaws are clenched so tight it feels like my rear molars might shatter at any second.

"Give me the antibiotics."

Sabrina stares at me, unflinching.

"You heard me, Sabrina. Hand them over."

"Are you threatening me?"

"You're damn right I am. You're threatening the life of someone I . . . someone we all owe a huge debt to, and I'm not going to let you. You can play your bizarre medical chess game on somebody else."

"I knew this moment would come, but I didn't anticipate it would be from you."

"What moment?" I look at her, suspicion creeping into me. "What did you do?"

"I've hidden the antibiotics, along with all the medicine."

Of course she has. The rage that has been building inside of me settles into a focused, ruthless calm. I'm almost scared of what I'll do next.

I turn and march down the aisle, past Bob Ward, who's got Mike at his side.

"We're ready, Nick," he says, but I don't even look at him.

I pause at Harper's side, slip my hand into the pocket of her sweat-soaked jeans, and fish out the key I gave her yesterday. In the cockpit, I unlock the box and flip the lid back. Four handguns lie there, stacked at haphazard angles.

I learned how to use a handgun as a kid. Kidnapping is a constant risk for every child who grows up the way I did.

I take the top gun out and weigh it in my hand for a moment, telling myself I'm acclimating to the feel of it, telling myself I can do what I'm contemplating. But as I crouch in the cockpit, holding the handgun, I know I can't. It's funny: you can imagine committing a vile act, something completely against your moral code, but only when you physically hold the means to take that action does the decision become real.

Only then do you learn what you're capable of—and I'm not capable of this. I'm not sure if that makes me a bad guy or a good guy.

I hope help is out there. I really do.

Slipping the other three guns into my jacket, I slam the lid shut and stand there for a moment, the key in my hand but no resolve in my heart. My bluff is called. Defeated by my own morals. So be it.

Sabrina stiffens as I approach her, but I just hand her the key. "There's a lockbox in the cockpit," I mutter, turning away from her. "Could be a good place for the meds—it's close by, sheltered from the elements. That's the only key."

She tucks the key in her pocket wordlessly, her intense dark eyes locked on me, not betraying a shred of emotion.

I can only imagine how I must look to Sabrina and the others around us right now. They're thinking *maniac* and *madman,* but they haven't made the calls I have in the last forty-eight hours. I wonder what I would do if I were in my right mind, if I were well rested and well fed, if the lives of a hundred people weren't in my hands at this very moment.

One in particular.

But force won't work on Sabrina. I'm ashamed that I thought it and more so that I almost tried it. However, there is something she's vulnerable to: logic. And she has another weakness: reading people. A solution forms in my mind, as clear as the plan I devised by the lake. It could work.

"In case it affects the calculus on your end, I need to say this. As you pointed out, I have an emotional connection to Harper. I stared into her eyes and asked her to put her life on the line. I feel responsible for what happened to her. If she dies, I'll be depressed. That's a psychological disorder. I assume your training includes psychological conditions."

I wait, forcing her to answer.

"It does."

"In my depressed state, I'll be unable to take on any leadership duties. No more quick life-and-death decisions from me. As you noted previously, this camp would be in chaos without me. That could lead to a loss of life."

Sabrina's eyes move to Harper and back to me, and I can almost see the wheels turning in that biological computer she calls a brain. "Noted," she says.

I search her face for any clue about whether she's bought it, but there's nothing there to read.

I feel every eye in the cabin upon me as I walk past Harper's seat. I did everything I could. I'll see if I can get *myself* to believe that.

Outside, I try to put the encounter behind me and focus on the very important task at hand. I pass guns to the other three team leaders. They'll alter their vectors forty-five degrees today, heading northeast, southeast, and southwest, respectively. Mike, Bob, and I will follow Mike's eastward path back to the glass-and-steel structure, our pace quicker today. Our goal is to reach it before noon.

"Use the guns only if you're threatened by hostile animals—save your ammunition for absolute emergencies. If you don't find help, on your way back tomorrow look out for big game to shoot—deer, moose, cows, whatever you come across. Run back to the camp and get people to help you lug back anything you kill. You all know the situation. I'm not going to give you a speech. The truth is, if we don't come back with help or food tomorrow, we're looking at casualties in the following days. The elderly and weaker passengers are going to starve, and there are people in desperate need of medical supplies. Either we succeed, or people die. That's it. Good luck."

The group breaks up, and Mike, Bob, and I set out through the dense green forest and frosted fields. The tall grass thaws with the rising sun, soaking my pants below the knee as we go. It's cold, but the pace keeps me warm. I try not to think about Harper.

We stop every hour to activate our cell phones and snap photos, but we never get any service or see anything significant. It's like Mike said: hills, fields, and forest as far as we can see, both with the naked eye and with the binoculars Bob found in a carry-on bag yesterday.

Finally we get to the ridge from where Mike took the photograph and spot the octagonal glass structure. It looks about ten miles away, and the hike to it confirms that. We don't even stop for lunch. To Bob's credit, he keeps up, though he's panting a lot harder than Mike or me and looking drained. I could swear he's aging by the hour, but I don't think he'd miss this for anything.

About halfway to the octagonal structure, at one of our hourly stops, I look around through the binoculars and spot something else: a stone farmhouse to the south, maybe another ten miles away. I make a note of its position—if the glass structure is a bust, it will be our next stop. I study the house for a few minutes, searching for signs of life, but there's no movement. It looks abandoned to me.

It's later than I had hoped, midafternoon, when we finally get to the glass structure, which is much bigger than it looked from the ridge. It's at least fifty feet high and maybe three hundred feet across. The glass walls are frosted bluish white, and the frame appears to be made of aluminum.

There's no pathway—dirt, paved, or otherwise—leading to or from it. Very odd.

The three of us walk the perimeter, looking for a door. Halfway around, I hear the sound of a seal breaking. A panel rises from the ground toward the ceiling, a frosted glass curtain revealing a spectacle I can barely believe.

The three of us stand there, our eyes wide.

I know this place. I've been here only once in my life, but that day is easily one of my most vivid childhood memories.

I was eight then, and for the entire week before I visited this place, I counted down the days and hours. It wasn't the destination that excited me. It was the chance to take a trip with my father. He was the U.S. ambassador to the United Kingdom at that time, and we didn't spend a lot of time together. That day, though, I felt very close to him.

I remember the drive, the moment I caught my first glimpse of the site. The morning fog still shrouded it, veiling the ancient treasures towering in the green field. I turned the name over in my mind as we drew closer: Stonehenge. Everything about it seemed otherworldly to me.

I was more mesmerized than my peers. To the other kids on the tour, the prehistoric monument was just a bunch of big old rocks in a field. Not to me. And not to my father. To him, it was not only history but inspiration, the symbol of an ideal. Nearly five thousand years ago, its builders had sweated, bled, and sacrificed to preserve their culture and their vision for future generations. That these mysterious people had erected Stonehenge and some part of it still remained to inspire and inform us, however cryptically, spoke to my father. It was how he saw his own career as a diplomat, I realized that day. He was building his own Stonehenge—America, and specifically its foreign relationships—to help pass down his vision of a better human society, a global one, with freedom and equality at its center. It wasn't that he didn't like me or spending time with me, he just thought his work was more important.

Stonehenge, age eight: that's when I gained a perspective on my relationship with my father that spared me a lot of anguish throughout my childhood. It was a revelation for me, something to hold on to when I found myself wondering why he was never around, why other kids' fathers took so much more interest in them.

But that revelation pales in comparison to the one that confronts me today. Twenty-eight years ago this was a crumbling ruin, chipped away by time and vandals, half the pillars gone, some lying on the ground. But the Stonehenge that towers before me now is no ruin. It looks like it was finished yesterday.

CHAPTER TWELVE

Harper

I AM A BOILING BAG OF MEAT. MEAT soup inside a fragile skin shell.

The fever is consuming me. I've had the flu, and my mum had pneumonia three winters ago. This is neither. This is bad. I'm sick, and scared.

Here inside the first-class cabin, the world around me flickers past in brief glimpses between sleep and foggy awareness.

The doctor's face floats before me.

"Can you hear me, Harper?"

"Yeah." My voice is raspy, barely audible.

"Your infection is getting worse. It's coming from your leg. Do you understand?"

I nod.

"I cleaned the wound when you came out of the lake, but it's gotten infected. I'm going to give you four ibuprofen, then I'll return shortly and we'll discuss next steps."

I swallow the tablets and close my eyes. Next steps. That's funny.

Why? Oh, yeah, 'cause I've got a leg injury. At least the best bit of me is still intact.

EVERYTHING STILL HURTS, BUT THE fever's subsided, and my head is clear. The world is back, and so is the doctor. She turns me to get a better look at my right leg and slides my jeans off. They come off as easily as if they were pajamas.

Dark fluid, black and burgundy, oozes through the white bandage that runs the length of my calf, from just below my knee to my right ankle. The skin around the bandage is puffy and red. I can almost feel myself getting sicker, just looking at it.

My limbs were numb at the end, in the plane, when whatever snagged me dug into my leg, and Nick pulled me free. Now it hurts. I can almost feel the heat rising from it, crawling up my body.

Sabrina stares at the bandage for a long moment, as if she's a human X-ray machine and needs to hold still to capture an accurate image. Then she looks me in the eye.

"You have a severe infection originating at the laceration in your calf. Infection was a risk when you came onto the bank. I cleaned the wound as best I could and bandaged it. Those measures were insufficient. Now we need to make some decisions."

I don't like the sound of this.

"The next step is for me to clean the wound again and monitor it more closely. Normally you would have been getting antibiotics already, but our supply is very limited. Since your infection is one we can access, we have some chance of countering it without oral antibiotics."

"I see."

"If the infection is still advancing by the time the sun sets, we'll have to take a more proactive approach."

I nod, trying to conceal my growing nervousness.

"At that point, I will remove some of the flesh around the wound and sterilize the area a third time."

She speaks at length in the same monotone, listing the risks in detail, using scary words like *sepsis* and *gangrene*. The long and short is, if I don't get better today, she's going to remove some part of my leg. Best case: my summer fashion choices will be limited from here on out. The worst case is . . . a good bit worse. Sabrina ends on the words "permanent loss of mobility." Then she waits. I wonder what she wants me to say.

"Well, writers don't get out much anyway. Haven't played sports in decades." So much for reactivating that gym membership when I get back to civilization.

"I've described your situation in detail because I believe every patient is entitled to know the details of their medical status and to be involved in the decisions for their care, when possible. And your situation is unique at present. Nick has been to see me regarding your care. He's been quite insistent that you receive antibiotics immediately. He has enumerated certain . . . consequences—emotional repercussions for him personally and effects these might have on the well-being of the camp at large—should your health worsen."

Nick Stone cares about me. Now there's something. And something worth getting better for. Not that it's up to me.

Sabrina charges on. It sounds as if she's reading a prepared statement, a speech she's rehearsed a few times. "I've been saving antibiotics for cases of urgent need. My approach is simple: to prolong the lives of as many people as possible, to maximize the number of survivors alive when help arrives."

That's what it's about, then: Sabrina would rather see ten peg-leg survivors flown out of here than only five walk away whole. She's right; their loved ones would agree. I'll bet my mum is one of them.

Sabrina's still barreling on, working up to something, by the sounds of it. "However, given Nick's recent assertions, which I suspect are exaggerated at best and likely false, I face the dilemma of whether to administer antibiotics to you at this juncture. If I'm wrong, and Nick was being sincere, not treating you would endanger the well-being of the camp at large."

"I see." Again I wonder what she wants me to say. She's put no question to me, yet she hovers there by my leg, silently prompting me. She's not good at this part, the talking bit, that's for certain.

"Normally at this point, you would be receiving inpatient care, likely IV antibiotics. All we have are oral antibiotics, and while they might help, I'm not certain they will be one hundred percent effective.

As I said, I'd prefer to save them for patients where there's no access to the infection—and, frankly, where they're needed to prolong a life. For individuals with lower body mass, our limited doses will go further, have a more significant effect."

Lower body mass. "Children."

"Correct."

I get it now. She needs a decision from me—and my help with Nick if it comes to that. So as it turns out, my getting better really is up to me.

Lives and limbs are at stake, no matter who gets the antibiotics. I ask myself what decision I can live with, but it's more complex than that. Down one road, I might not live at all. That's the test, isn't it? I can make a decision I can't live with and save my own life or make one I can live with and risk death.

Sabrina's looking at me, waiting.

I have a plethora of shortcomings. But if you ask any of my friends what single fault most holds me back in life, they'll all tell you the same thing: decisions. Especially about my own well-being. Career decisions. Dating decisions. Where to live. Where to work. When it comes to making calls about my own future, I'm the worst. At least I'm quite capable of picking out an outfit and settling on where to eat (I sometimes find it helpful to state some positives about myself when facing a challenge or major decision). Oh no, should not have thought decision; it's too close to the Decision. Must focus.

My first instinct now is to panic, and panic about my panicking, until I suffer a full-blown decision-dysfunction breakdown. I mean, no pressure: what I say will only determine whether I lose life and/or limb or whether some cute kid down the aisle does. But as the seconds tick by, the panic never comes, only a clear, confident answer that fills me with a reflective calm. No second-guessing, no anguish. Weird. I'll have to sort that out later, when a neurotic yet seemingly competent doctor isn't crouching next to my rotting leg.

"I agree with you, Sabrina. Other people need the antibiotics more. When Nick comes back, I'll tell him that you offered and I refused."

"Thank you." Sabrina exhales and sits back against the galley wall, looking even more exhausted than before. I think this conversation was very hard for her.

I have to say, right now, what I'd really like is to be certain that Dr. Sabrina knows her stuff. I want to know that she sees my kind of injury quite regularly, that she's remedied this sort of thing a hundred times.

I take a deep breath. "What sort of doctor are you, Sabrina?"

She hesitates.

"You see a lot of infections? Trauma? Do a good bit of wound care?" I prod, getting more nervous with each word.

"Not routinely . . ."

"Right. Well, then. What do you do routinely?"

"I work in a lab."

Blimey.

"But I had extensive experience with trauma medicine during my medical school training."

Blimey, blimey, double, triple, quadruple blimey. You know what I remember from university?

Very.

Very.

Little.

I nod as if she's just related today's weather forecast and tell myself that Sabrina Whatever Her Last Name Is just happens to be the number-one trauma surgeon in this makeshift hospital wing, that she is the very best medical care available at the present moment. Must have confidence in her.

She begins peeling away the white tape at the edge of the bandage. "Are you ready to begin?"

Who could say no to that? I mean, she works in a lab.

MEDIEVAL. THAT'S HOW I WOULD describe what just transpired here in seat 1D of the crashed remains of Flight 305. Medieval in the extreme. I've heard people say the treatment was worse than the disease, and now I know full well what they were talking about.

Pain courses through my body, a fire hose I can't shut off.

It's amazing how exhausting pain is. Sabrina says I need to move every so often to keep some blood circulating, but I just can't right now.

In fact, I'm beginning to wonder if I'll walk away from this place at all.

CHAPTER THIRTEEN

Harper

IT'S LATE AFTERNOON WHEN I WAKE UP, DRENCHED and achy. I feel sick all over, but I know I need to move, get some blood circulating. I think I can make a lap around the cabin. Or hospital. Whatever this is now. I push myself up, balance for a moment, testing the leg, and then start out down the dimly lit aisle. Passengers are crammed into almost every seat, most asleep or passed out. A few follow me with their eyes, but on the whole there's very little movement or sound. It's eerie, almost like the moment right after the crash.

I get ten paces before I'm winded and have to lean against a seat in business class, panting, and wipe the sweat from my forehead.

A kid in the seat to my right slowly opens his eyes. I've seen him before, I realize. He was the last kid Mike and I pulled off the sinking plane. I unbuckled his seat belt, and Mike carried him out. He's black, about eleven, I would guess—and he's at death's door. He's sweating, but it's the look in his eyes that makes my heart sink.

"What you in for?" he asks, trying and failing to form a grin.

I shuffle forward and slip into the business-class seat across the aisle. "Bum leg. You?"

"Pneumonia." He coughs into his hand and lets his head fall back.

Neither of us speaks for a moment. Then Sabrina is leaning over him, a single oblong white pill in her outstretched hand, a bottle of water—no doubt from the lake, boiled by the fire—in the other. "Antibiotics," she whispers. "Quickly, please."

He swallows the pill, and Sabrina's eyes meet mine. I give her a single slow nod, wondering how well she'll understand. She nods back.

The last of the antibiotics could buy enough time to save this kid's life. Maybe a few others. I felt pretty sure before, but I'm certain now: I made the right decision.

"You're British?" the kid asks.

"Yeah."

"I like your accent."

"I like yours." He's American, from the North, at a guess. "Where you from?"

"Brooklyn."

"I wouldn't mind living in Brooklyn."

"Kidding, right?"

"Nope. Brooklyn's a good place for writers."

"You a writer?"

"Yep."

"Like a journalist?"

"I was. I write books now."

"What kind?"

"Biographies."

"You like it?"

"I liked it at first."

He's racked by coughs again. Finally the fit passes, and he closes his eyes. Just when I think he's slipping off to sleep, he asks, "You famous?"

"Nah. But I interview famous people. I just write the book, and it gets published under their names."

"Like they wrote it?"

"Yep."

"That sucks."

Leave it to a kid to sum up the state of my career so accurately in two words. And leave it to an adult to rationalize it in three: "It's a living."

"Ever think about doing something else?"

"I have. A lot, lately."

"My mom reads a lot of books. Biographies especially. Says it helps with her work."

"Yeah? What sort of work does your mum do?"

"Lawyer. She's with me on the trip. Can't find her, though. Lot of people are still missing from the crash."

I nod, though I know he can't see me. I can't find the words. I remember the seconds before I first saw this kid, remember touching the cold flesh of the woman's neck beside him before reaching for his neck, feeling the warmth, and ripping his seat belt free. God bless the person with the presence of mind to tell him people are still missing. "Well, she's no doubt very, very proud of you for being so brave."

A silence follows. I'm about to get up when he speaks again. "I'm Nate."

"Harper. You should get your rest, Nate." He's asleep before I finish the sentence. All of a sudden I feel exhausted myself, too tired to even get up.

I AWAKE TO THE CLATTER of rain pelting the plane, so loud it sounds like hail.

The fever's back, stronger than ever.

Nate is sleeping right through the storm, his head hanging awkwardly to one side in a way that scares me.

Struggling to my feet, I reach across the aisle. My hand almost recoils when it meets his burning flesh. He's in trouble.

I look around, searching for Sabrina, with no luck. I shuffle forward to first class, but she's not there either. I collapse into my seat, a wave of pain shooting through my body. Where is she? I'll rest just a minute, then go find her.

Only the faintest light filters through the tiny oval windows. I can't tell if it's after sunset or just dark because of the storm. The dense forest canopy blots out most of the daylight even in good weather.

As I sit, the rain's cadence increases by the second, like a sound track slowly being turned up. A long howl of wind joins the tapping, its hollow sucking sound growing louder, overtaking the rain. It feels like I'm sitting in a wind tunnel with a hailstorm outside.

At the rear of the plane, the gust finally bowls the stacked luggage over, sending sick passengers scrambling.

I close my eyes. The relentless tapping on the metal roof is disorienting, a kind of white noise. Time jumps forward again.

When I open my eyes, Sabrina is hovering over me.

I clear my throat, but my voice comes out scratchy and faint. "Nate. The kid in business—"

"I'm doing what I can for him." She motions to my leg. "I need to have a look."

She's tired. Gone is the poker face she's worn for days. I can read the gravity of the situation on her face, even before the words spill mechanically out of her mouth.

"We need to move to the next phase of treatment. We have two options: be conservative and remove less flesh, or be aggressive, which has a higher chance of stopping the infection. Being conservative now may mean taking more of the leg later if the procedure is unsuccessful. However, taking more flesh than necessary now will have lasting consequences after rescue. There are risks and benefits to both courses of action. You need to decide. You have fifteen minutes to think about it, while I make the rounds and prepare."

She leaves, and I slump back into the chair. Decisions.

My nemesis.

Minutes pass like hours. Vanity or survival? Is there even a chance of survival now?

Through my fever haze, I'm barely able to follow what happens next. The outer door flies open, and people pour in, survivors from the lakeside. The first is hurt, covered in blood. What happened? A lightning strike? A fallen tree?

One by one, more people limp in, some bleeding, some coughing, others hobbling along for no apparent reason. Unharmed survivors guide them, shouting for help.

They're looking for Sabrina frantically, but they can't find her. She has to be here—I just saw her, and the exit's been closed the entire time. Did I pass out again? I don't think so.

There's only one place she can be: the cockpit. I try to tell them, but my voice is so weak that I can't even hear it myself over the storm and the commotion. I reach for a man rushing by, but he brushes past, ignoring me.

Finally I rise and limp toward the cockpit, steadying myself on the galley wall. I'm about to knock on the closed steel door when I hear voices—faint but combative—inside.

"I want to know everything you know." Sabrina.

"I've told you everything." It's a man's voice, but I can't place it.

"You knew."

"That the plane would crash? Sabrina, you think I would board a plane that I knew was going to crash?"

"You knew *something* would happen."

"I didn't!"

"Why were you going to London?"

"I don't know. They said I'd get instructions when I arrived, same as you."

"Where are we?"

"I swear, I don't know!"

"Can you contact them?"

"Maybe . . ."

"Try, Yul. You have to."

"Are you crazy?"

"We're out of food and medications."

"What if *they* caused the crash?"

"Then we're already at their mercy—it makes no difference. Contact them. It's our only option."

The cockpit door opens suddenly, and I'm staring directly at Sabrina and the young Asian guy.

CHAPTER FOURTEEN

Harper

SABRINA MARCHES PAST ME LIKE NOTHING'S AMISS, HEADING down the aisle to the right, where she begins to work feverishly, treating the injured passengers coming in.

I stand there, frozen to the spot. Yul—that must be the trim Asian guy's name—moves out cautiously and faces me, as if he's waiting for me to comment.

My first instinct is to say, "I didn't hear anything," but I bite off the words in time, thank God. Nothing says "I heard every word" more loudly and clearly—I might as well say, "Hey, so I hear you might be connected to whatever caused the crash, and part of an ongoing conspiracy. Care to comment?"

I settle for looking guilty and a barely audible "Hiya."

Yul walks down the left-hand aisle without a word. When he gets to his row in business, he glances back at me for just a little too long before sliding into his seat.

I slump against the cockpit wall, taking the weight off my right leg, and press my burning forehead against the cool surface. It feels good. So does the cold wind blowing in through the door. Since they moved me to the plane I've swung between chills and fever, but now it's only fever, burning relentlessly inside me. I know what my decision has to be, if I want to live. And I do want to live.

When I glance up, the shock of what I see consumes me. Am I hallucinating? Sabrina's gotten the first few incoming patients cleaned off. They're . . . old. I recognize some of these people, from the lakeside, but they seem to have aged decades in a single day. Their faces are wrinkled and hollow, but it's more than that. These people are really old, all over, not just starved and exhausted.

I'm not the only one unnerved by this. Sabrina's losing control. Her eyes are wild, her motions quick and sloppy. Something very, very strange is happening here. Does she know what it is? Or is she finally losing it? Either way, it's not good news for any of us.

Pushing away from the wall, I step forward into the first-class galley, ready to lunge into my seat in the first row. There's a brief flash in my peripheral vision to the right—a man running through the door, carrying a woman. They collide with me before I can turn, the woman landing on my right leg.

AWARENESS. PAIN. I'M IN MY seat again, my legs outstretched. It's pitch-black outside now, night for sure. Still raining.

A woman I don't know sits on the floor in front of me, her back flat against the wall. She rises and holds out her open hand, on which rests a large white pill. "Sabrina said to take this."

I take the pill and toss it back. My throat's so dry it takes half a bottle of water to get it down.

I let my drenched head fall back to the headrest and watch as passengers drag three limp bodies past me toward the exit. All dead.

I focus on the faces. Nate isn't among them. Neither is the Indian girl in the Disney World shirt. It's the new arrivals, the people that just came in from the lake. Two more go by. How many have died? Another body passes. The faces are even older than when they arrived. What's happening here?

Behind me I hear Sabrina's voice. Her droning monotone has

turned to a sharp bark, harsh and urgent. She's interrogating passengers, barely waiting for their responses: "Where do you reside? Have you visited any of these clinics: King Street Medical in New York City, Bayside Primary Care in San Francisco, or Victoria Station Clinic in London? Did you get a flu shot at any of these locations? Do you take a multivitamin? What brand? Do you use an air freshener at home? Do you have any chronic medical conditions?"

Then she's at my side, no preamble, hammering me with the same list of questions, barely waiting for answers. The only doctor I've seen in years is my gynecologist, I tell her. I didn't get a flu shot this year, and I take a women's multivitamin. When I fumble for the brand name, she leans in and grills me like a murder suspect at Scotland Yard. I finally come up with the brand, and she scribbles it down, nodding, like it's the clue that will nab Jack the Ripper. Then she's gone.

I sit up, glance out of the pod. They're hauling two more people out.

The pain moves down a notch, mellows. I know this feeling, know what she gave me: a pain pill.

Sleep comes in seconds.

I AWAKE TO DARKNESS AND silence. The pain is back. I turn, looking back down the aisle, but I can't make anything out. There's almost no moonlight filtering through the small windows. It's still raining, but not as hard, just a steady pitter-patter now.

I lie there, letting my eyes adjust.

On my right, a slim figure slips by. Yul.

Faint footsteps behind me. A woman, black hair, about my height. Mechanical walk. Sabrina.

Three seconds later I hear the click of a thick metal door closing.

I stretch my good leg out into the aisle, test the other. Not good. I limp, hop, and drag myself through the galley, keeping as quiet as I can.

They're being more careful this time, and I have to stand close to the door to hear anything.

"We did this," Sabrina insists.

"You don't know that."

"I do."

"Correlation is not causation, Sabrina. You ask every passenger the right questions, and eventually you'll discover that they all know somebody who knows Kevin Bacon."

"Who's Kevin Bacon?" Sabrina asks urgently. "Another agent? A passenger?"

"No—"

"How does Bacon figure into this?"

"Christ, Sabrina. Forget Kevin Bacon."

"I want to know everything they had you do, every move you made before we boarded the flight."

"All right." Yul sounds exasperated. "What are they dying of?"

"Old age."

"What?"

"They're dying from different diseases, conditions that I assume would have developed in time as they aged," Sabrina says. "But it's happening to them all at once."

"Why aren't we affected?"

"I don't know. Only half the passengers seem to have the condition."

The voices begin to fade, and I lean closer, trying to hear them. A sound, a low rumble, is blotting them out. It's not coming from the cockpit. It's outside.

As I step back from the door, a bright spotlight breaks through the small oval windows, running quickly along the length of the plane. Through the rain, the roar grows louder. Then the light blinks off, and the sound recedes.

The cockpit door flies open, and Yul and Sabrina rush out. They don't stop to interrogate me with their eyes this time. Yul jerks the exit door open and peers into the dark, dense forest, where rain drips unevenly down through the trees.

He glances back at me.

I nod. "I saw it, too: a beam of light ran over the plane."

Yul looks at Sabrina, opening his mouth to say something, but a crunching sound outside the plane stops him. Boots, grinding the fallen underbrush into the forest floor. Someone is running straight toward us, though I can't make out who.

Someone from the lake? A rescue team? Or . . .

Yul jerks a phone from his pocket, activates the flashlight app, and holds it out. The light is weak, but it's just enough to reveal shapes moving out there. At first it looks like rain catching on invisible, maybe human forms—three of them, barreling toward the plane.

Before we can react, the first form charges up the rickety stairs and stops on the landing. It stands over six feet, glittering in the cold glow of Yul's phone, like a glass figurine.

It raises its right arm toward Yul, then Sabrina, then me, firing three rapid shots, almost silent pops of air with no flash of light. My chest explodes in pain.

CHAPTER FIFTEEN

Nick

FOR SEVERAL SECONDS MIKE, BOB, AND I STAND there, staring at the tall stone columns of Stonehenge, perfectly formed and aligned. How? No, *how* isn't the right word. When? There are only two possibilities: we're in the past (a past we don't understand at all), or we're in the future—a future in which this huge monolithic monument has been rebuilt.

I scan the octagonal glass and metal structure for clues but find none—no writing, no symbols, no hints of what the year might be.

The glass panel reseals behind us with a soft click, breaking the silence. Bob opens his mouth to speak, but a neutral, computerized voice drowns him out.

"Welcome to the interactive Stonehenge exhibit. To begin your tour, follow the path to your right. For your safety and the preservation of this historic monument, please do not leave the path."

Tour. I look down, realizing for the first time that there's a glass-tile pathway around the perimeter. It lights up, flashing green arrows that end at a pulsing red target, a bull's-eye where it wants us to stop. Without a word, the three of us follow the path, stopping at the red circle.

"What you see now is how scientists believe Stonehenge would have appeared approximately four to five thousand years ago, when it was completed. Follow the path to continue your journey into the past, exploring the stages of Stonehenge's construction."

The glass tiles once again glow green, guiding us to another red bull's-eye twenty feet away.

"Structure's probably solar-powered," Bob whispers as we shuffle toward the red beacon waiting in the path. I glance over at him, noticing that he looks even older now. The hike must have really taken a lot out of him.

The computer's voice changes slightly. "Would you like to hear about Stonehenge's connection to the solar calendar?"

We glance around at each other, confused, for a moment. "Maybe it can help us figure out what's happened here," Bob says. "What year we're in."

So he's made the leap, too.

"Let's try it."

For the next fifteen minutes we pepper the computerized voice with questions. But it doesn't know anything, save for every possible thing there is to know about Stonehenge. Off-topic questions like "What year is it, by the way?" receive a curt, stock response: "Unfortunately, I cannot answer questions unrelated to Stonehenge. We need to keep your tour moving so that other visitors will have ample time to enjoy the exhibit."

Clearly its programming doesn't include checking the line outside.

Mike, Bob, and I pace to the next red bull's-eye, lost in thought, wondering what to do next. Before us, the tall stone columns dissolve, leaving a vast green field that seems to extend beyond the far glass walls. Oxen pull giant stones through the field. Looking closer, I notice wooden tracks shaped like a trough below the stones. The tracks hold carved wooden roller balls that move the giant pillars along. Ingenious. For the time, anyway. Groups of people wearing animal furs direct the oxen through the field to the monument area, moving the tracks and balls to stay ahead.

"What you see now is the early construction of Stonehenge. Scientists believe Stonehenge was built over the course of a thousand years . . ."

It's a simulation. The whole structure is a hologram. Projectors of some kind must be recessed into the frame.

"End tour," I say.

"Would you like to switch to the self-guided tour?"

"Yes."

"Enjoy your tour of Stonehenge, brought to you through the generous support of the Titan Foundation."

The field, oxen, and prehistoric workers dissolve, leaving only the crumbling stone ruin I saw twenty-eight years ago—or however long ago it was now. The glass enclosure must have been built to protect Stonehenge from the elements and vandals, to preserve this little piece of history for future generations.

Above us rain begins to pelt the glass ceiling, providing a sound track for this bizarre moment.

Mike points to the center of the green field. "Nick, look."

Bodies. There must be a dozen of them, long dead, their bones protruding from tattered clothes.

Mike steps off the path toward them, but I catch his arm. "Be careful."

The computer booms warnings about staying on the path, but we ignore it, which isn't hard—the rain's so loud now it almost drowns it out.

Mike creeps the last few feet to the bodies, kneels, and begins sifting through them.

"No IDs," he calls.

"Doubt they'd have them in the future," Bob says.

He's probably right. A printed, laminated ID would look archaic to the people who created this structure. They've probably moved to embedded chips, fingerprints, or even retinal scans.

Mike shakes his head. "No watches, phones, nothing. Just bones and clothes."

Bob and I walk across the grass to join him. "They could have been picked clean by vandals." Bob coughs. He's looking rough. Haggard.

I nod. Mentally, I try to organize my questions. How does this help us? What do this ruin and these bones tell us?

"Gentlemen," Bob says, his voice weak but formal, "I believe we've just obtained a crucial piece of information." He pauses, apparently awaiting guesses from his two favorite pupils.

I raise my eyebrows, prompting him.

He points to the bones. "This tells us that organized, effective government no longer exists in England. And hasn't for many years. Stonehenge is a World Heritage Site, but it's especially important to the British. If the government were still functioning, if civilization existed here, they wouldn't leave bones at Stonehenge. Not for a day, not for a week. These bones have been here for many years—decades, I would guess."

Mike and I nod. That makes sense.

"What's next, Nick?" Bob asks.

"The farmhouse we saw on the way in. It's our only shot." I glance up at the glass roof. The rain is really coming down now. I'm famished; we didn't stop to eat on the way in, and I'm sure Bob and Mike are hungry, too, though neither has said a word.

"Let's get a bite to eat, see if the rain lets up some."

The three of us move away from the bones into a grassy area, sit Indian style, and have our late-afternoon picnic at Stonehenge. Surreal only begins to describe it. We consider sitting on an overturned pillar nearby, but it seems wrong somehow, whether there are any people left in this world or not. As I eat, I'm still preoccupied by the mysteries, even the small ones. The grass is better kept than on any golf course I've ever seen, for one thing. The structure must maintain the climate and grounds, too, somehow.

If we're in the future and a massive catastrophe has occurred, that would explain the lack of roads—or any sign of civilization, for that matter.

Mike shoves the last bit of his sandwich in his mouth and, still chewing, gets at the real mystery. "Can't get my head around the idea that we're in the future," he says to no one in particular.

Bob clears his throat. Poor guy is struggling even to keep up with our eating pace. I set my sandwich down. The rain is pouring down;

we have some time. "Time travel is scientifically possible—actually, it happens every day," he says. "Einstein theorized it with relativity, and we've been measuring it for decades. In fact, every person who has ever flown on a plane has traveled in time."

Mike squints at me with a "Here we go" look, but I glance over at Bob, interested.

"The rate at which time passes changes throughout the universe, depending on gravity and velocity. Let me give you an example. Let's say twins were born today. One is placed on a spaceship and launched into space. The ship simply orbits our solar system, but it does it at an incredible speed—say ninety-nine point nine percent of the speed of light. That's what Einstein correctly identified as the speed limit for mass in our universe, though we're pretty sure some particles are capable of faster-than-light travel—which, by the way, opens all sorts of possibilities: quantum entanglement that enables data to travel faster than light, for one. But Einstein's limit, at least for particles with mass, may still hold." Bob stops and scans our blank expressions. I'm really starting to like this guy, but he does get carried away sometimes.

"Anyway," he continues, "back to the twins: one on Earth, one in a ship in space, going really, really fast. In fifty years the ship returns. The twin who stayed on Earth is fifty—a middle-aged man. The one on the spaceship? Still a baby, though he's aged a little, since the ship couldn't reach the speed of light without transforming into energy, and it takes some time to get up to speed. Bottom line: moving fast slows down time. So does gravity."

"It's interesting, Bob." I pause. "But you're talking about spaceships—pretty far removed from what we're dealing with here."

"Okay, here's a real-life example: GPS. GPS was developed by the Department of Defense in the seventies to help get military assets exactly where they needed to be. It currently consists of twenty-four satellites in high orbit, around twenty thousand kilometers from Earth's surface. That's so far up there that Earth's gravity doesn't exert the same influence on the curvature of space-time. As I said, gravity slows time down. The stronger the gravity, the slower time passes. So the closer to Earth you are, the slower time goes. If you get close enough to very, very strong gravity, say a black hole, time almost stands still. If you crossed the event horizon of a black hole in a spaceship, you would watch the entire fate of the universe unfold in the seconds before you were sucked into the center.

"But away from gravity, time goes faster—you experience more time, like a video on fast-forward. That's what happens to GPS satellites. General relativity predicts that the clocks in each GPS satellite should get ahead of ground-based clocks by forty-five microseconds each day. So for every day that passes here on Earth, up there, twenty thousand kilometers away from the gravity we experience, the GPS satellites experience one day and forty-five microseconds. Doesn't sound like much, but it's time travel. The satellites are moving into our future. But that's only half of what's going on up there."

Mike rubs his eyelids. "You're making my brain hurt, Bob."

"Stay with me here, Mike. There's another part of the GPS time travel puzzle: velocity. Remember our example with the twins?"

Bob waits, but neither Mike nor I volunteer an answer. It doesn't deter him at all.

"Right. So like our spaceship, these GPS satellites are flying really fast. They're not in geosynchronous orbit, like many people think. They circle the globe roughly every twelve hours, and they have to move at about fourteen thousand kilometers per hour to do that. That's fast. The speed of light is around a billion kilometers per hour, so it's only a fraction of that, but still fast enough to dilate time. But in this instance, instead of speeding up time, the velocity actually slows it down. Remember our twin on the spaceship? Time flowed slower for him. Gravity and velocity both slow time down. Special relativity predicts that, based on their velocity of fourteen thousand kilometers per hour, we should see these GPS clocks ticking more slowly by about seven microseconds per day—and they do. So the satellites' velocity slows time down for them by seven microseconds, while the lower gravity up there speeds it up by forty-five. When you put the effects predicted by special and general relativity together, each satellite should travel forward in time by about thirty-eight microseconds per day. And that's exactly what they do: clocks on the GPS satellites record thirty-eight microseconds each day that we don't observe here on Earth."

"Yeah, but I mean, what does this have to do with our flight?" Mike asks.

"Everything. In fact, if we had landed at Heathrow, we would have traveled slightly back in time. JFK to Heathrow is a seven-hour flight, most of it at about thirty to forty thousand feet, flying at around six hundred miles per hour. We would have landed slightly younger than everyone who stayed on the ground. The time difference would have been insubstantial—a fraction of a second, maybe a hundred nanoseconds—but nevertheless, less time would have passed for us than them. And it gets even stranger: if we'd flown westward, against Earth's rotation—say, from JFK to Honolulu—we would have had a lower velocity than clocks on the ground, and landed slightly older.

"Bottom line: the closer you are to strong gravity, and the faster you move, the slower time goes. If you go fast enough, you can almost stop the flow of time, though you experience it as normal—from your point of view, the world outside you progresses at a faster rate."

"Interesting," I murmur, still taking it in. "But you're talking about fractions of a second." I motion to the structure around us. "It seems like a lot more time has passed than that."

"True. My working theory, Nick, is that our plane passed through a patch of space-time where gravity was distorted. It's the only reasonable explanation, given current scientific understanding. A gravimetric distortion would dilate space-time, making time flow slower or, in our case, faster. Say this distortion created a bubble in space-time, and our plane was in this bubble, where time passed at an incredible rate. If the bubble popped, it would dump us out at whatever time the clock stopped. There are only two possibilities: the gravimetric distortion was a natural occurrence—"

"Natural?" I ask.

"It's conceivable. We're pretty sure black holes exist—in fact, there may be one at the center of our galaxy. As I mentioned, they distort time, making it flow slower as objects approach. There could be other sorts of gravity depressions throughout the universe, some working in reverse, making time flow faster. We could have just gotten caught in a gravity storm—some natural phenomenon we don't yet understand. To be honest, we're still in the dark ages of aerospace science."

I'm with Mike now: this stuff is making my brain hurt. "You said there were two possibilities?"

"The other, which I actually find more likely, is that this *wasn't* a natural occurrence. Someone brought us here, with a technology beyond our comprehension—possibly with the help of someone on the plane."

"Very interesting." I don't know why, but my mind flashes to Yul Tan, the quiet man in business class, obsessed with his laptop. There's something there, I think. I'll have a long talk with him when we get back.

We sit in silence for a while, Bob coughing, the rain coming harder and faster, the clouds overhead a dark slate gray, far-off thunder rumbling. Mike stretches out on the grass like a college kid on a lazy day.

"What sort of work do you do, Nick?" Bob asks me between coughs.

I tell him, and he seems impressed, asking a lot of questions. He asks Mike the same thing. Mike races sailboats and isn't all that interested in talking about it. He was on his way to his sister's wedding outside London, at the family home of his future brother-in-law, who's "in banking or something." He expresses no remorse at having missed the wedding.

After a few moments, Bob's tone turns grandfatherly. "You should never retire," he advises us. "Retiring ruined me. Worst decision I ever made. Should have kept something to do."

His second wife recently left him, he says, and he was on his way to London for a job interview, though he quickly adds that he's under an airtight NDA and can't talk about it at all. Neither Mike nor I press for details, which seems to mildly disappoint him.

I feel a little sorry for Bob Ward. I understand him now, somewhat, in the way I began to understand my father during our visit to Stonehenge so long ago. Bob still has a lot of fight in him, a lot of life left to live, and he never knew it until he retired. The crash of Flight 305 might be the best thing that's happened to him for a while. It's given him a purpose, a way to apply himself. And if I'm to be completely honest with myself, it's done the same for me. I was in my own rut when Flight 305 took off from JFK, and though I would rather our flight had landed at Heathrow, every single one of those passengers alive, the crash has revealed a side of me that I never knew existed. It's shown me what I'm made of in a way the world never did until now.

Bob coughs again, violently, and stops, staring at his fist. He quickly wipes it on the inside of his shirt, but I glimpse the blood. Our eyes meet. He looks so much older, and for the first time I realize something: he *is* older. His face is lined, his eyes are slightly jaundiced, and even his movements are less coordinated. What's happening to him?

For a moment the only sound is the relentless tapping of rain on the glass dome above us, the din like static on an untuned TV, filling the cavernous space. It's dark out now, either from the storm or nightfall.

Through the frosted glass wall, I think I see lightning, but the flash doesn't subside. It grows, getting wider, raking over the ground. A searchlight, from above, moving toward us.

CHAPTER SIXTEEN

Nick

THE SEARCHLIGHT SWEEPS OVER THE TALL GRASS AROUND us, barely missing the structure that surrounds Stonehenge. I jump up, Mike at my heels.

Bob tries to push up, but collapses back to the manicured grass.

"Stay here, Bob!" I yell.

Mike and I rush to the glass wall, to the partition that opened, allowing us in. We stand impatiently as the glass slowly rises from the bottom, the computer voice barely audible above the rain and the engine in the distance. "Thank you for visiting the Stonehenge interactive exhibit . . ."

Outside I spot the searchlight's source: an airship, or that's what I would call it. It's shaped roughly like a helicopter but much larger, and it has no rotors on top or on the tail. Yet it hovers somehow, moving slowly forward. I'm not even sure how it hangs in the air.

I step forward, shouting and waving my arms, but it's already moving past us, back toward the crash site.

I start through the field, still waving. "Stay here," I call over my shoulder to Mike. "They could circle back."

Behind me, he begins shouting and waving his arms, too.

I run flat-out through the damp green grass, wind-driven rain pelting me. At the top of the ridge, I stop. The airship is almost out of sight, and it's making good speed. I scan in every direction with the binoculars, but I can't see another searchlight. The sun has set, and it's getting darker by the minute.

I jog back to the structure, where Mike's standing, his short hair and Celtics T-shirt drenched.

We walk back into the glass octagon in silence. Inside, Bob is hunched over, coughing. He looks up at us eagerly, but I shake my head as I try to squeeze some of the water out of my clothes.

"Looked like it was headed for the crash site," he says.

"Yeah, I think so."

"You have to leave me," Bob says. "You promised you would, Nick."

He's probably right. If the wind and rain have extinguished the fire by the lake, those airships could miss the crash site. On the other hand, if another ship is close behind that one, we won't make it to camp to restart the fire in time. Staying here is our best shot at being seen and maybe Bob's only chance of survival.

"You promised, Nick," Bob says, his voice growing weaker by the second.

"Another ship could be searching the area. This landmark and field are our best chance of getting spotted. What if they miss the crash site? Besides, marching back in this storm would be foolish—it would slow us down and we might be covered by the tree canopy when the next ship passes. We'll wait here for a break in the storm or another ship, whichever comes first."

"You need to get back, Nick. If it's scenario two—if somebody brought us here—that may not be the rescue we're hoping for. They may be hostile." Bob coughs again, wiping the blood away quickly.

"We don't know that."

"We have to assume it. Those people will be taken by surprise. You and Mike have the upper hand. You have to move now."

"We wait. That's the decision."

BOB IS DEAD. MIKE AND I were napping in short shifts, trying to conserve energy for the hike ahead. I awoke to coughs, and looked over at Bob in the dim light. His breathing was shallow, his face even more wrinkled, eyes sunken and yellow. His hands trembled slightly as he drew one last breath, shuddered, and went still.

It's the strangest thing I've ever seen, the way he deteriorated over only a few hours. He'd been fit enough for a twenty-mile hike twelve hours before. Something is very wrong here. What could have killed him that quickly? A contagion? A bug he caught here at Stonehenge when the glass parted? Could the structure have sealed a virus or bacteria inside for all these years? I glance at the bones in the short, manicured grass. Is that what killed these people? Whatever it is, it doesn't seem to have affected either Mike or me—at least, not yet.

Looking down at Bob's still body, I can't help but think he would have liked passing away here, in a place devoted to science, technology, and history, a monument that has represented those things for thousands of years.

We feel we should do something with Bob's body, give him some kind of ceremony, but the reality is, we don't have the time or the tools for a proper burial. In the end we lay him close to the other bodies and fold his arms over his chest.

At the edge of the structure, I pause. "We'll have to move fast, for our sake and the camp's. We only stop to rest when absolutely necessary." Mike nods, and we step under the glass door into the field.

WE'VE MARCHED ALL NIGHT THROUGH the wind, rain, and cold, but we have to stop, try to warm up and rest, to prepare ourselves for whatever awaits at camp. We're exhausted, hungry, and freezing, but we're almost there.

We've seen no sign of the airship, but we'll know soon whether it found the crash site. And whether it's a friend or foe.

AS THE FIRST FAINT RAYS of sunrise paint the treetops, I climb a ridge a mile from the crash site, draw the binoculars from my jacket, and scan the distance until I find the camp by the lake. The fire's long extinguished; I can't see the faintest trace of smoke. Blue blankets dot the muddy bank, all empty, not a soul in sight. That's either very good or very bad.

I pan left, searching for the nose section of the plane through the dense forest, but something else swims into view through the lenses first: three long tents, plastic stretched over arched metal supports, like round greenhouses. What is it? Shelter for the survivors? A field hospital? Beside the tents, white body bags are stacked in neat pyramids like firewood. There must be fifty of them. My mouth goes dry, and I scan more quickly, searching for a clue about what's going on.

The door to the nose section is open, and there's no movement inside.

I pan out farther, searching. The airship I saw at Stonehenge—no, two of them—sit in a clearing. They're huge, three times the size of the plane's nose section. The ships' outer doors are closed, and there's no sign of movement around either vessel.

I run the binoculars over every inch of the forest, but I can't see any movement. Whatever's happening is hidden by the trees or the long plastic tents. We'll have to get closer.

CHAPTER SEVENTEEN

Nick

ABOUT A HUNDRED YARDS OUT FROM THE THREE clear plastic tents, I draw the binoculars again and focus them, trying to make out the blurry objects inside. They're narrow beds, evenly spaced, some empty, some occupied by bodies. Beyond the tents the forest suddenly erupts in a burst of heavy footsteps and cracking branches.

I scan with the binoculars, quickly spotting the source: figures in what look like bulky space suits, barreling through the dense brush. The suits' large helmets indicate that they're built for total containment. Strange. From here the suits' inhabitants appear taller than normal humans. Or are they human at all? They could be machines, or . . . who knows. It's obvious why I didn't spot the figures before: as they move through the woods, their suits briefly take on the browns and greens of the trees and fallen leaves. Adaptive camouflage. They flicker as they move, the suits struggling to keep up with the colors and patterns around them. No rescue team needs suits like that. It's equipment for the military, or for those who need to operate in secret. If they're here to help us, why would they need to hide from us?

What happens next confirms my worst fear. The figure leading the charge raises an arm, there's a popping sound, and I hear a crash, something large falling to the ground somewhere in the forest. I scan feverishly through the binoculars, trying to identify who or what they're shooting at. Finally I see a man, middle-aged, slightly overweight, writhing on the ground as if he's being shocked with a Taser. The last time I saw his face was yesterday morning—when I sent his team northwest to search for help. That team must have been returning this morning as well. One by one the suited figures hunt down the three of them, shooting each with some weapon I can't make out. The invaders hoist the limp bodies on their shoulders and turn, making their way to the domed plastic tents—and directly toward us.

In unison, Mike and I sink to the ground behind a rocky outcrop. A few minutes later, I risk a glance.

The figures carry the three search-team members into the nearest tent and emerge a minute later, carrying a stretcher with an unconscious passenger: Sabrina. They take her to the middle tent, then bring out another passenger: Yul Tan. And a third: Harper. A white cylinder encloses Harper's right leg from her knee to her ankle, and a bag hangs above the stretcher. She's the last one.

I take the handgun from my jacket, prepared for anything.

Mike's eyes lock on the gun, then drift up to me. "What's the plan?" he whispers.

I'm about to tell him that I don't know when I hear a rapid pop behind us, like an air gun.

Mike's eyes go wide as he seizes, and I dive for him. The rock where I was just crouched echoes as the shot meant for me slams into it.

I hold the gun out and fire blind, in the direction I think the shot came from. Then I scurry around to the other side of the rock, scanning the woods all the way to the plastic tents. Yes, the figure's on the other side of the rocks. I peek above the rock and spot it, staggering through the woods toward me. It's hit.

I raise my gun to fire again, but I never get a chance. The ground behind the figure explodes, and the blast sends it flying through the air and knocks me to the ground. I roll through the woods, finally slamming into a large oak tree. My ears ring and nausea sweeps over me. Pain starts in my ribs and surges through my body, causing me to convulse. For a moment, I think I'll throw up, but it passes as pieces of dirt and splinters shower me.

When my head finally clears, I hear more blasts in the distance, a relentless barrage. Through the canopy I see an airship hovering over the crash site, firing into the woods surrounding it, in the direction of the clearing and the two other ships.

I spot their targets a second later: four suited figures running toward their ships, zigzagging wildly as they try to dodge the fire from the airship above.

I make my way back to the other side of the rocks and roll Mike's limp body over. He's alive, his breathing shallow but steady. A spidery metallic burr is dug into his back. I try to pry it off, but I can't get a grip on it.

In the distance the cadence of the firefight changes. Earlier the firing was targeted, like laser blasts, but now it rolls over the treetops like thunder. The explosions shake my chest and deafen me. The sensory overload is disorienting, and I fight to focus.

The fire from the incoming airship is now being returned. Two ships hover in the air for a long moment, neither budging, drilling each other with shot after shot. A column of smoke rises from the field, almost hiding the far ship. I bet one of the ships on the ground was destroyed.

Focus.

I attempt to rise, but collapse again. The ground shakes. Around me the forest rains limbs, twigs, and shattered trunks.

I finally stand, staggering on wobbling limbs, my equilibrium gone.

The camp. The tents. They're open. The arched metal frame has retracted into a series of small boxes on the ground. The plastic sheets that were stretched over the frame blow through the disintegrating forest, bunching, turning cartwheels like milky plastic tumbleweeds. They collect bits of falling wood and leaves as they go, taking on the colors of the forest, slowly camouflaging themselves, making their escape.

Escape.

Rows of hospital beds lie open to the elements and falling debris. The passengers are waking up.

The retreating invaders . . . they set the passengers free. Why? I bet it's so that we wouldn't fall into enemy hands. It has to be. We're the prize here. Bob was right. The . . . *things* in the bulky suits brought us here, and they seem to be at war with someone.

In the air the tide is turning. The incoming aircraft is beating the defender back, out of the black cloud of smoke, but it keeps firing. How long do we have?

How long does Harper have?

Through the trees and slowly falling debris, I see her sit up in her bed and look around, confused. I race to the tent, falling three times as I go, but I feel no pain. Adrenaline carries me on.

When I reach Harper, her eyes go wide. I can't imagine what I must look like. I grab her by the shoulders. "We have to go!" I shout, but I can't hear my own voice. I can't even hear the exchange of fire above anymore, only feel the rumble. My hearing might be permanently damaged.

Harper shakes her head and mouths, "My leg," but then suddenly looks down at it, shocked. She whispers a phrase I can't make out, then swings her legs over the side, planting her feet on the ground, smiling.

I start toward the woods, but she catches my arm, her grip strong. It's a good sign.

She points to Sabrina and Yul, who are just getting up. Slowly, so I can read her lips, she forms words: "They. Know. Something."

We rush toward them, waving at them to come with us. When I turn around, about half the survivors are converging on us, shouting, staring.

"Run!" I yell, flinging my arms out. "Spread out. Go, you hear me? Go!" I grab Harper's hand and sprint through the woods. She's right behind me. In fact, I think I'm slowing her down. Incredible. They healed her. Or maybe Sabrina did—but that's not possible; she's in better shape than when we crashed. Even her skin glows.

I glance back. Yul's gone.

I stop and grab Sabrina's arm. "Where's Yul?"

Thankfully my hearing's returning some, but I still have to strain to hear Sabrina say, "He had to go back for his computer."

"Why?" I ask.

"He needs it," Sabrina says.

"*He* needs it, or *they* need it?" Harper's voice is hard, surprising both Sabrina and me.

Sabrina looks down. "I don't know. . . . I think . . . I think they both need it."

I take the gun out, slip my watch off, and hand it to Harper. A smile curls at the corners of her mouth, and I can tell she's trying with everything she has to suppress it. She turns the watch over, reading the inscription: *For a lifetime of service. —United States Department of State.*

Her eyebrows lift. "You . . . worked for the State Department?"

"My dad did. Listen to me, Harper. If I'm not back in ten minutes, keep going. Promise me."

Harper keeps staring at the watch.

"Promise me, Harper."

"Yeah. Okay."

I take off, pushing my still shaky legs as hard as I can toward the nose section. The rows of beds that the tents rested on lie empty now, and so does the camp. The trees are still shedding debris. It drifts down like falling snow, covering the stacks of white body bags with a fine coat of green and brown. It's quiet, creepy. I can only hear the airships in the distance, their firing now intermittent.

I don't see Yul as I approach the camp, but I don't stop. I bound up the staircase of luggage and plane parts into the nose section and barge through the first-class cabin. He's pulling bags out of the overhead, ransacking them, searching—

Behind me I hear footsteps. I turn to see a suited figure, camouflaged even here, bearing down on the two of us. I raise my gun, but I'm too late. His arm is outstretched. I expect to hear the soft pop of air next, but a gunshot rings out, a piercing noise in the small space. The figure topples forward, colliding with a first-class seat and landing hard, his suit shimmering and flashing, crackling with electrical sounds.

Grayson stands in the first-class galley, a handgun held out.

I turn to Yul. "You have it?"

"Yes."

"Let's go," I say, my eyes locking on both of them.

They follow me out of the plane, and we take off into the woods.

The suited figures will hunt us down now. They brought us here for a reason, and we have what they need.

PART TWO

TITANS

CHAPTER EIGHTEEN

Harper

I'M A NEW WOMAN. LITERALLY. MY HEAD IS clear, my skin is smooth, and my muscles feel supple and strong. There's no hint that I was on my deathbed twelve hours ago. (I guess it was technically my death lie-flat seat—in first class, no less—but never mind that.) The bottom line is, those suited *things* that invaded the crash site healed me. And did a bang-up job. It's quite a mystery, given how the meet-and-greet started.

I don't remember anything after the shimmering monster stormed into the cabin and shot Sabrina, Yul, and me with what must have been a sedating device. I awoke the next morning on a narrow bed. My eyes focused just in time to watch the steel hoops above me retract, letting the plastic roof take flight, drifting into the woods. I thought it was snowing at first, but I soon realized that tiny bits of leaves and limbs were falling, as if a grinder were shredding the treetops. The sound of explosions in the air assaulted me next. Two ships hung unmoving in the sky, firing relentlessly, the booms of their guns like thunder in my chest.

And then Nick was there, rescuing me once again, though this time I was in far better shape than he was. He looked a fright, his face covered in dirt, grime, and caked blood, his eyes sunken, his cheeks gaunt. Scared me worse than the bombs bursting in the air.

He and Yul returned from the nose section a few hours ago with Yul's carry-on and, in my opinion, a far less valuable piece of baggage: Grayson Shaw.

"He's coming with us," Nick said when the three of them rejoined Sabrina and me, and no one's said a word since. The five of us have simply marched through one forest after another, avoiding the fields, our pace steady but not quite brisk, for Nick's sake. He's in the worst shape of all of us. He's been holding his right side—his ribs, I'd guess—and breathing hard almost the entire way.

When we finally stop for water, I beg him to rest for a bit, but he insists we go on. Sabrina tries to have a look at his injuries, but Nick won't hear of it.

"They're hunting us." He motions to Yul's bag. "And whatever's in there."

Yul stiffens.

"We'll talk about it when we get to the farmhouse we saw on our way to the glass structure."

"The structure?" Sabrina asks.

"It was . . . nothing," Nick says, still trying to catch his breath between sips of water. "We'll talk about everything at the farmhouse, when we're not out in the open."

A FEW HOURS LATER THE five of us stand at the edge of a forest, eyeing an old stone farmhouse in the middle of a rolling green field. It looks deserted. There are no cars, no road or drive of any kind, for that matter, just three small stone buildings.

Nick instructs us to stay under the cover of the trees as he and Grayson set out to search the house. I want to ask whether Grayson Shaw, who's apparently come away from the crash site with a handgun he found in one of the plastic tents, is the ideal partner with whom to storm our only potential place of refuge, but they're halfway across the field before I can object.

I wait anxiously as they slip through the wooden door, guns drawn, crouched like the Metropolitan Police raiding a terror suspect's apartment block.

Beside me Sabrina and Yul stand in tense, awkward silence.

No one says a word about what I heard back at the plane. The two of them know what's going on here. They're part of it—they've known since the beginning. I wonder if they're dangerous. What a fix to be in: Grayson on one side, Sabrina and Yul on the other, and some mysterious army hunting us.

Nick and Grayson trudge back through the green field, handguns stowed.

"It's empty," Nick calls. "Come on, quick." The second the wood door closes behind us, he says, "Stay inside and away from the windows."

He lays the last bits of his food on a simple wooden table. "We split it five ways."

Nick doesn't eat his share, though. He just staggers away, exhaustion finally overtaking him. I follow him into the bedroom, where he climbs into the narrow bed and lies facedown, not bothering to remove any of his soiled clothes.

I close the door, walk around the bed, and squat down, facing him. "Where are we?"

"Future," he murmurs, eyes closed.

The future. How? It's a shock, but it explains the suited figures, why rescue didn't come.

"What year?"

"Don't know."

"What was in the glass structure?"

"Stonehenge."

"Stonehenge?" I whisper, half to myself. So we *are* in England.

Nick's drifting off. I touch his shoulder. "Sabrina and Yul—I think they may be involved in whatever happened to the plane."

"Yeah. Gotta rest, Harper. Rough night. Don't let them leave. Get me up at sunset."

"Okay."

His breathing slows, and just when I think he's gone to sleep, he whispers, "Harper?"

"Yeah?"

"Glad you're okay."

Before I can answer, he's gone, out cold.

I settle onto the floor, looking at him, thinking. Then I rise, roll him onto his back on the bed, and take his shoes off. His socks are soaked through. I peel them off, freeing his waterlogged, swollen, blistered feet. I almost gasp as I unbutton his shirt, revealing more of his injuries. Dark bruises cover his arms, chest, and ribs, as if he rolled down a mountain. What happened to him?

We need real help. Rescue. But for now, I'll do what I can for him.

CHAPTER NINETEEN

Harper

I PULLED THE CURTAINS CLOSED RIGHT AFTER I got Nick settled, and now through the thin white fabric I watch the sun setting over the green fields, the serenity a sharp contrast to the turmoil inside me.

Nick hasn't moved a muscle for hours. The blankets covering him are yellowed with age—who knows how old they are—and his wet clothes hang over the edge of the white tub in the bathroom. I sit in the corner, on a wooden rocking chair that creaks loudly if I make the slightest movement. It's been a kind of concentration test—move and the alarm goes off, and Nick wakes up. I've passed so far.

These silent hours in the small farmhouse bedroom have given me time to think, to wrap my head around everything that's happened since Flight 305 crashed in the English countryside. Since then it's been nonstop, with people's lives—including my own, or at the very least a limb—on the line. Now, as Nick sleeps, I can't stop thinking about the passengers who perished in the crash, as well as the people who died in the days after, seemingly of old age, and those who fled the crash site earlier today, who I imagine aren't as warm and comfortable as I am right now. I wonder what happened to Nate, the kid from Brooklyn who will never see his mother again; about Jillian, the flight attendant who became so much more in the chaotic aftermath of the crash; about the girl in the Disney World shirt. I wonder where they are right now, if they're safe and happy.

I am. Despite my fears about what might come next, I'm sublimely happy. I'm happy that Sabrina didn't have to take part of my leg off to beat the infection. I'm happy that I can walk on my own two legs. And more: I'm happy that I survived the crash, and that Nick did, too, and that he's here, alive and relatively healthy. I feel . . . extraordinarily lucky just to be alive and well. I've taken that for granted, just being alive and healthy. It wasn't until I was at risk of losing my life or my leg that I fully appreciated how lucky I've been.

Why is it that we only appreciate things we're at risk of losing?

Here and now, I feel a strange mix of near euphoria and profound guilt—for surviving, for not having done more for the other passengers. At any turn, things could have gone differently, and they did for a whole lot of folks. My actions determined the fate of some, and for the past few hours I've replayed every event and decision, until I can't take it anymore. I'm caught in a circular mental loop with no answer, no resolution.

I have to get out of here, do something.

Maybe it's the turbulence in my mind, but I'm not that hungry. Or maybe those camouflaged figures fed me somehow, or gave me an appetite suppressant. Another mystery.

I slowly rise from the wooden rocking chair, cringing as it cries out, but Nick doesn't stir. In the kitchen, roughly two-fifths of the food waits on the table. Strange: for all the secrecy and mistrust between the five of us, there's honor in the dining department. I take the remaining food back, place it on the bedside table, and leave the room again, closing the door behind me with care.

I set about searching the small stone farmhouse. We definitely need more food, and that's my goal, but I can't help taking in each room, looking for clues to when or exactly where we might be. There's dust everywhere, bugs here and there, but no animal tracks. The former owners locked it up tight.

The bookshelves in the living room are almost bare, save for a few photo albums and a Bible. Not exactly bullish news for printed book sales. There's no sign of a TV, although a large, slightly frosted clear plastic film on the wall, like a giant piece of tape, indicates that people still watch something.

The kitchen cupboards contain no food, only mugs, utensils, and the like.

I descend the steep, narrow wooden staircase to the cellar, the light from above growing weaker with each step. I start to go back up for a candle, but stop. Yellow light glows at the bottom of the stairs—a candle on a sconce. Someone's down here. I hear banging in the distance, at the end of the cramped stone corridor.

I step toward the noise. Cabinets slamming. Yes, maybe there is a pantry in the cellar—and one of the others had the same idea. I see a candle burning atop a shabby bar-height table in the room ahead, a black object lying beside it. I clear the threshold to the pantry and pause. Grayson straightens up. It's hard to read his face in the flickering candlelight, but I see him glance quickly at the table, at what I can now see is a handgun.

I open my mouth, hesitate for a moment. "I was just looking for food."

He turns back to the shelves, pushing jars around, peering behind them. "Haven't seen any. Anything edible, at least, but I'm not looking for food."

I walk to the nearest shelf, which is filled with jars of fruit and jam that look as if they spoiled a long time ago. "What *are* you looking for?"

"Something drinkable."

"They may have given up drinking in the future."

"Doubtful. Drinking's the only solution to some problems."

"You think it's the answer to your problems?"

"It's the only thing that's ever worked."

"Is it the only thing you've ever tried?"

Grayson finally faces me. "What do you know about my problems, Harper?"

"Enough."

"You know what *he* told you. His side."

"True. But I've seen your situation countless times. I've been writing about families like yours my entire career."

"So I'm told. Did he tell you what I intend to do?"

"He did."

He returns his focus to the shelves, rummages around, and finally finds a bottle. Scotch. "Wonder how old this is. A hundred years? Two hundred? A thousand? Can't wait." He uncorks it and inhales deeply, a smile spreading across his face. "The irony is that my book'll be a boon for your career. My tell-all will probably send sales of your 'officially authorized' biography through the roof, make you a millionaire. You'll never have to work again, thanks to me."

I hear footsteps on the stone floor behind me, and Nick appears in the narrow doorway, looking a good bit better. He's still gaunt, but his color is back, and so is the calm intensity in his eyes.

"You okay?"

Grayson answers him before I can, the sneer returning to his voice. "Yes, Prince Charming, she's okay. Her head won't explode if she talks to me."

"We need your help," Nick says flatly.

"With what?" Grayson asks, his eyes returning to the bottle.

"Yul and Sabrina. They know something about the crash. You and I have the only guns."

"No, we don't. Yul found a hunting rifle upstairs," Grayson says absently, still inhaling the aroma from the uncorked bottle.

Nick's eyes meet mine, then he focuses on Grayson again, his tone calm, matter-of-fact. "We need your help. We need you at your best."

Grayson's eyes flash as he glances up. "You telling me not to drink, Dad?"

"No. I'm just telling you that we need your help. And that's all I'm going to say."

Nick walks out of the doorway, and I follow him down the hall. I'm about to ask him the plan when he pauses and nods to another narrow stairwell that lies at the end of the corridor, past the stairs I descended. Voices, faint, drift up. Yul and Sabrina.

"Wait," Grayson says as he closes the distance to us. "They've been down there the whole time, working on something."

I whisper quickly, telling both of them what I overheard back at the nose section—Sabrina and Yul's hushed conversation behind the closed cockpit door, her accusations that Yul knew the plane would crash, that he had a hand in it, her theory that their actions before the flight had led to the plague that aged the survivors in the days after the crash.

Both men listen in silence, nodding in the cramped, candlelit passageway.

"How did the conversation end?" Nick asks.

"It didn't," I whisper. "The camouflaged invaders showed up."

"Okay," Nick says. "We don't leave this house until we know what's going on." He turns and leads us down the stairwell, even deeper underground, into a large room with concrete walls. What I see shocks me.

Yes, Yul and Sabrina know what's going on here.

CHAPTER TWENTY

Harper

THIS UNDERGROUND CHAMBER MUST HAVE BEEN BUILT LONG after the original farmhouse. It's adjacent to the basement and deeper. Instead of rough stone walls, the room is lined with smooth concrete, painted white. There's no need for candles here: a bright computer panel glows on the far wall just next to a large, arched alcove that holds what looks like a black tram car. But there are no wheels under it, only a steel platform. Does it sink into the ground and connect with a rail system?

I bet it does. It's like a single-car tube station, buried below this farmhouse.

The black car's long sliding door is open, revealing brown leather couches on three sides and a large wooden table in the center.

Sabrina and Yul turn away from the panel to face Nick, Grayson, and me. The rifle leans against the wall, within Yul's reach.

Nick breaks the silence. "What is this?"

"We're not sure," Sabrina says, her voice flat. Yep, she's back to normal as well—her normal, anyway.

"I doubt that," Nick says, stepping closer, scrutinizing the car and the glowing panel.

"Our theory is that it's a mass transit apparatus."

"Connected to?"

"Everywhere, it would seem."

Nick looks up. "You were going to leave us."

Yul just cuts his eyes away, but Sabrina says, "Yes."

"At least you're honest."

"I've never been dishonest with you, Nick."

"That may be, but you also haven't told us the full truth, have you? The two of you know what's going on here, maybe what happened to the plane. I think we're entitled to answers."

Sabrina opens her mouth, but Yul speaks for the first time. "We don't have them."

"I don't believe you. What year is it?"

"I don't know," Yul insists.

"What year do you *think* it is?"

Yul hesitates. "We believe we're in the year 2147."

"Why?"

Yul shakes his head and glances at Sabrina. "This is what I mean: we don't have time for this. If we start answering questions, we'll be here for three hours, and we still won't know any more than we did before. And neither will you—you'll just be more confused."

"So confuse me," says Nick. "Start talking. I want answers."

"Our *answers* are mostly conjecture, based on incomplete information. That's why we're going to London."

"And leaving us here."

"For your own safety." Yul gestures to his bag. "I believe they're after Sabrina and me, and possibly what's in my bag."

"Which is?"

"Explaining that will take more time than we have."

Nick pauses, thinking. "What's in London?"

"We don't know."

"Then why go?"

"Because seeing London will give us some idea of what we're dealing with. Look," Yul says, "stay here. You're safer. They may have placed a tracking device on the two of us, and it's possible they can monitor activity on the Podway."

So that's what they call this underground network.

Nick shakes his head. "We're not splitting up. And you're wrong: we can't stay here. We're out of food. We'd have to venture out just to feed ourselves. It's only a matter of time before they find us. Finding help is our only hope. You know that as well as we do. You're looking for answers in London, but that's not all, is it? You think you'll find help there."

"Yes," Sabrina says. "We have reason to believe we'll find help in London. Our plan is predicated upon that assumption."

"If there's help in London, then we are *all* going to London." Nick steps closer to the panel. "Now how does this work?"

"We're not sure," says Yul. "We've been trying to learn the system before we connect to the network, just in case they can track us."

"That's the other advantage to London," Sabrina says. "It's a short trip. Hopefully we'll be far away from this network by the time they're aware we used it."

"Makes sense."

Yul taps the panel. "It keeps asking for a GP, which we assume is a universal identification device, possibly implanted. Its backup is fingerprint ID." The panel switches to a screen that reads, STEP CLOSER TO THE TERMINAL TO SIGN IN. There's a small box in the lower right-hand corner with text inside it: DON'T HAVE A GP? PRESS YOUR THUMB TO THE SCREEN HERE.

Nick motions for me to step forward, and I press my thumb to the cold surface of the lighted panel. Red letters flash on the screen: NOT RECOGNIZED.

"Try it again," he says.

Three tries later, the screen still blinks a rejection notice.

Grayson tries his thumb next, with the same result. Not recognized.

Nick glances at Yul and Sabrina suspiciously, then presses his own thumb to the panel.

NICHOLAS STONE. ENTER YOUR DESTINATION.

"So the three of us"—Nick motions to Yul, Sabrina, and himself—"can use the Podway, but neither of them?"

"It seems so," Yul says.

"Why?"

"I don't know."

"Speculate."

Yul shakes his head. "Where do you want me to start? It could be any of a number of reasons."

"Give me a few, just for kicks."

"Okay, then: when this transit network was created, Harper and Grayson could have been living outside London and not been registered."

"Or we could have died long before this was even invented." Grayson sounds mildly amused. "We'd all be dead by 2147."

"True," says Yul. "The most likely scenario is that Harper and Grayson used alternative forms of transportation in the future. An automobile, an airship, or a teleportation booth. Who knows? Satisfied? Can we go?"

"Not satisfied at all, but we should definitely go," Nick says. "Will another empty car arrive after this one departs?"

"Yes. Within a few minutes if the panel is correct."

"Good." Nick nods at Yul and Sabrina. "Since only three of us can activate this thing, we'll split up: Grayson and Sabrina in the first car, Yul in the second, and Harper and me in the third."

Yul smiles. "You're splitting us up to keep an eye on us."

"That's right. Because we don't trust you. Because you've been keeping secrets from us. Because you were going to leave us. How's that for full disclosure? Get used to it, because you're going to do a lot of it when we get to London, no matter what we find."

Grayson moves closer to Nick, standing shoulder to shoulder with him. He stares at Yul, silently communicating our numbers and firepower advantage.

Yul mutters to himself, but grabs his bag. He glances at the rifle but decides to leave it, which is a relief.

Sabrina works the computer panel, entering the destination, then she and Grayson climb into the first car and pull the door shut. The floor below it parts with a barely audible hum, the car descends, and two minutes later an identical car rises into the alcove. Yul loads up and leaves without another glance at us, and Nick and I slip into the next car.

Inside, the car feels almost like a train compartment. We sit across from each other on the brown leather couches, the glossy wood table between us. The imitation windows on each side simulate an idyllic English countryside flowing by peacefully. In fact, this is the first moment since the crash that Nick and I have had together without the immediate threat of death, starvation, or mutilation—either to ourselves or others.

Nick speaks before I get a chance. "I heard you and Grayson talking in the cellar. What's up with you two?"

"He hates me."

"And you hate him?"

"Not really. I don't know him. His father is Oliver Norton Shaw."

"The billionaire."

"Yeah. You know him?"

"I've met him."

"Me, too. Only once, a few days ago in New York. He flew me out—that's actually the only reason I was in first class. It was a perk, a gift to try to convince me to write his officially authorized biography."

"And Grayson's upset about that?"

"Not per se. His father is planning something big. Shaw wants to give his fortune away in grand style, establishing a new kind of charity. He's calling it the Titan Foundation. He wants the book to detail his life and his journey to a series of revelations about the human race, lay out his vision for the role his fortune and foundation will play in the future of humanity."

"Certainly thinks a lot of himself."

"He does. And not much of his son. Grayson will get nothing when the foundation is established. Shaw sees it as a way to force Grayson to finally forge his own path in the world. When I was waiting to meet with Shaw, Grayson was in with him. He was furious, shouting that he was being cheated out of his inheritance. Called his father a glory whore reaching for the spotlight one last time after his business career was over, among other even worse things. He stormed out, and that's the first time I saw him. Shaw told me Grayson was threatening to sell his own tell-all book to a publisher in London. If he didn't get the inheritance promised to him, he'd air the dirty laundry, as they say."

"Interesting."

"It's funny, I've barely thought about my dilemma since the crash, but it was all I could think about on the flight."

"Dilemma?"

"Whether to write Shaw's biography."

"What's the problem?"

"The problem, more or less, is that I don't know what I want to be when I grow up." ·

"Who does, these days?" Nick laughs quietly.

"I was a journalist for a few years, then a ghostwriter, but Shaw's biography would be my first chance to have something published with my name on it."

"Sounds great."

"It does. It's what I thought I wanted. But I've also been working on a novel, what I hope will be the first in a series. That's my real love, and I'm afraid that if I write Shaw's biography, I'll never finish it. My whole life will change. I just want to know if I could make it writing fiction. If I knew that, the decision would be so much easier."

Nick nods, and we sit in silence for a while.

"What about you? Any career angst?"

He laughs. "Yeah, I'm . . . at a bit of a crossroads, too."

"With work?"

"With everything."

He leaves it at that, suddenly looking a lot more tired. He's not very talkative—about his personal life, at least. It's funny, I've heard his voice so much the last few days: His speech by the fire in the cold dark night that saved all those people. The way he organized the camp, keeping everyone fed and away from each other's throats. His instincts and quick decisions. But in the face of a simple question about his own life, it's like every word is an anvil in his bowels, yours truly trying to reel it up from the depths with a flimsy fishing line.

"I meant it last night," he says.

"About what?"

"That I was really glad when I got there this morning and saw that you were alive."

I take a deep breath, calming myself. "Yeah. Me, too. Wasn't sure if I would make it another day. And seeing you when I opened my eyes . . . that was nice, but God, you looked a fright. Scared me half to death."

"Rough couple of days."

I move around the table to sit next to him and touch his forehead at the hairline, inspecting the wounds where I wiped the dried blood away. I smile. "But, hey, you cleaned up okay."

He reaches for my arm, closes his fingers around my wrist, and puts his thumb in my palm, half filling it.

I feel myself holding my breath.

Neither of us says a word, but our faces edge closer, slowly. I'm not even sure if he's moving or if I am. Or both of us.

The booming computer voice shatters the silence. "You have reached your destination."

But I don't look away. And neither does he.

Behind me the door slides open, and I feel the rush of cool air on my back. Nick's eyes go wide, and I turn, getting my first glimpse of what's become of London.

CHAPTER TWENTY-ONE

Harper

THIS IS LONDON LIKE I'VE NEVER SEEN IT.

In the subbasement of the farmhouse, there was some debate before we left about where to get off the Podway in London. We considered Parliament, 10 Downing, and Scotland Yard, among others, reasoning that if any form of civilized government or law enforcement still existed, it would be found at one of these locations. The rub, however, is that the powers that be and the cloaked beings hunting us may be one and the same.

In the end, we settled on a compromise: a stop in a residential section, Hampstead—at least, it was mostly residential in 2015. We also reasoned that a stop outside the center of power would give us a peek at the state of things in the city and would likely be unguarded, increasing our chances of escape if things went awry.

We were right on one count: the Podway station is unguarded. In fact, it's utterly deserted.

Nick and I stare out of our pod for a moment, taking in what seems to be a converted tube station. Sabrina, Yul, and Grayson are waiting outside. At the sight of us sitting so close in the pod, Grayson rolls his eyes and wanders off through the cavernous stone and concrete space, which is almost unrecognizable now. Where tracks used to be and trains moved through, a series of large booths now stand, each providing access to a single pod. The sight of the dark, empty rows and columns of pod booths rattles my nerves a bit.

It's surreal, seeing what was once a busy tube station devoid of its shuffling crowd: people talking and staring at cell phones, coursing through every nook and cranny. At peak times, people once covered every square inch. You could barely breathe then.

You could hear a pin drop now.

Outside, on the street, there's still no sign of life—human life, anyway. Some buildings are boarded up, some battered, their windows smashed in, glass scattered across the empty sidewalks and streets. Grass and weeds shoot up from cracks, and vines twine up buildings, the lush green in bizarre contrast to the crumbling ruins of civilization. This city, which I love so much, which was built by the Romans more than two thousand years ago, which has survived endless conquerors and countless plagues, including the Black Plague and Nazi bombing raids, has finally fallen. But to what?

The sun has set now, and dim moonlight casts a strange glow over the empty streets. I walk out into the empty lane and stand there, awestruck by the total silence, something I've never experienced in London. It's almost transcendental, hypnotic. I feel like I'm in an overbudgeted television program, though it's terrifyingly real.

"What now?" Nick asks sharply, looking at Sabrina and Yul.

"We . . . hadn't gotten that far," Sabrina says.

"Wonderful." Nick glances back at the station. "I don't think we should stay here. We should get out of sight—and talk."

"My flat's three blocks away," I say, almost without thinking, the mystery irresistible to me.

"Okay. We'll check it out and stay just long enough to work out a plan."

CLUES. THE THREE-BLOCK WALK TO my flat has provided a cryptic set of leads as to what went on here, passed along in the form of modern cave paintings, if you will: graffiti. Many of the messages are incomplete, washed away by the wind and rain, some obscured by weeds, trees, and vines. But fragments remain, and they reveal a city on the brink.

PANDORA WAS INEVITABLE.

MAKE US ALL TITANS OR NONE.

TITANS BETRAYED US.

WE DESERVED THIS.

THE TITANS WILL SAVE US.

GOD BLESS THE TITANS.

HUMANITY DIED YEARS AGO. THIS IS JUST THE CLEANUP.

WE WILL WIN THE TITAN WAR.

On the street, the outer door to what was once a town house, long ago converted to eight flats, stands open. We climb the narrow stairwell to the third floor, where my cramped flat used to be.

As we ascend, I suddenly become self-conscious, nervous about showing my place to visitors . . . one in particular. But that's silly. It isn't actually my place, not now. I mean, if we are in 2147, then I certainly don't live here, haven't for maybe a hundred years. Yet it's still a bit nerve-racking for Nick to see where I live.

On the landing, the door to my unit stands slightly ajar. I push it open. Incredible.

It's bigger.

The future owner joined it with the adjacent flat. My furniture's gone, but the style, the feel . . . it's mine. I must have decorated this place. Or . . . my daughter did. Someone with my taste. I'm frozen in the doorway.

Nick peeks his head around my shoulder. "Everything okay?"

"Yeah, fine."

I wander in, the voices and movements behind me fading away. My first stop is the bookcase. On the top row, a dozen hardcovers with dust jackets line the shelf, all authored by Harper Lane. All have the same look and feel, block letters over mostly black-and-white photos on the covers. Biographies. The first is *Oliver Norton Shaw: Rise of a Titan.* The next biography is of David Jackson, a name I'm not familiar with. I briefly scan the row below, looking for a different kind of book, in another style, a book about someone named Alice Carter. She's the one I care about. But she's not here. Just thick biographies, all in the same style. The lettering runs together as I scan again. There must be twenty or thirty Harper Lane–penned biographies in all. Not a single work of fiction.

There are also no photo albums. Picture frames cover the tables and small shelves on the wall, but they're blank. They must be digital, their memories lost to whatever catastrophe occurred here in the absence of power. I ransack the bookshelf, hoping to find something printed, a yellowed photo of me and a smiling gentleman or a child playing in the ocean at sunset. But as I move down the shelves, I find only reference books, two dictionaries, a thesaurus, and an assortment of worn novels, favorites from my youth.

I hear Nick's voice—my name, the word *Titans*—but I move to the bedroom in a trance.

Again, it's my style.

It's brighter in here. The moonlight glows through the two windows, almost reflecting off the blue walls with yellow accents. I collapse onto the bed, sending a cloud of dust into the air. The floating motes sparkle in the shafts of light, as if my bedroom were a life-size snow globe with me inside.

My arm drifts down, out of the moonlit haze, to the side of the bed, to the place where I hide them, where visitors, even my closest friends stopping by after a shoddy day, could never find them. I would be mortified.

This will clinch it.

I slip my fingers into the crack between the mattress . . .

Yes, I live here.

CHAPTER TWENTY-TWO

Harper

LYING IN THE BED THAT WAS ONCE MINE, in the flat that was once mine, I bring the two notebooks out from under the mattress. A second ticks by while I struggle to choose which to open first. In my left hand, I hold the notes for the novel I've been working on since university. Yellowed, tattered pages hang out of three sides. In my right hand lies my journal, a black-leather-bound volume, one of many I've filled in my life.

Answers first.

I flip the journal open, and stare at the first entry. Third of August 2015. Incredible. This is the same journal I was writing in before I boarded Flight 305. How? I usually fill one every year. My journaling rate must have slowed considerably. Or . . . the entries stop soon after 2015. I hadn't thought of that. This could reveal what happened here.

For a moment I consider taking the journal back out to everyone in the living room, but I need to read it first. I almost dread discovering what it will reveal about me.

I page to the place where my next entry would have been—the day after the plane should have landed.

———————————————————————————————— 15 Nov. 2015

Certainty. Certainty is certainly the word of the day. See what I did there? Yes, of course you do, because I would, and I do. That was certain. And so is my fate, because I've selected certainty.

Okay. I'm giddy. It's the relief, the lifting of the burden, the crushing, paralyzing decision made: I will write Oliver Norton Shaw's biography, the sure-to-be-self-aggrandizing, overhyped tome that will change nothing, except for perhaps my fate. I will be well paid. That is certain. I can then use that money to pursue my true passion: *Alice Carter and the Secrets of Eternity* (note: I have renamed it since yesterday, when it was *Alice Carter and the Knights of Eternity*; let's face it, everybody likes a good secret, and with knights we rather know what we're getting, don't we?).

The biography will take a year to write, nine months if I can swing it, and it will be out in another year. The printers will kill half a forest to get the door stopper into stores. Critics will pick it apart. Some readers will love it. Some will hate it. And most will forget about it (the worst possible outcome). But the bottom line is that within two years, I will have cash in hand (my advance is to be paid a quarter upon signing, a quarter upon approval of the finished manuscript, a quarter when the hardcover is published, and the final portion upon paperback publication). Every six months, royalties will be paid, via check, minus my agent's 15 percent (well worth it, I still think). Two years to financial freedom. That is certain.

Certainty. I've decided to write Oliver Norton Shaw's biography. I am certain that in two years I will be a full-time fiction writer, my life dedicated to a young British girl, Alice Carter, who discovers that she's capable of far more than she ever imagined, that her choices and her unique abilities could change the course of history and save her world. I like that very much. That's something to look forward to. Twenty-four months to go.

So I took the job. And how did it turn out? Luckily I hold my own autobiography in my hand. I flip through the pages, reading the dates scrawled in my handwriting, searching for a day around two years on . . .

---

21 Oct. 2017

Success. I am A Success. Foregoing capitals grammatically uncalled for but necessitated by the following facts:

- The *Sunday Times* #1 Nonfiction Author? Harper Lane
- The *New York Times* #1 Hardcover Nonfiction Author? Harper Lane
- *USA Today*? You guessed it.
- Reviews. Not all bad. Few punches to the face here and there, but my editor has assured me, "The owner of the *Post* hates Shaw, has for years. Ignore it." On another hatchet job: "Gibbs thought he'd be selected to write the book. No mystery why he's got a bee in his bonnet. Don't let him chop you up with the ax he's grinding, Harp." And on and on. But the consensus is clear: it's a hit.

It's not just the critics and the charts. The readers—and there *are* readers—people are actually reading this thing and loving it and writing to me, saying so, saying that it gave them some perspective, some courage to go out and change their lives. That's powerful. Every day, when I open my e-mail, there's another dose of it.

That's one difference. With ghostwriting, I wrote to please my editors. They approved the checks, and the praise and pay came sporadically. Now the encouragement is delivered fresh every day, digitally, one click away. I'm writing for *them* now. I'm writing for happiness. For pride—in my work, and in the decision I made.

Interesting. I flip through the pages, searching for the thing I really want to know. Several months later, I spot the key phrase.

---

7 Feb. 2018

I've met someone. He's smart (very, very smart), charming, well traveled, and knowledgeable beyond belief. In a word, captivating.

But it's not like that. He's old enough to be my dad. He's one of Shaw's closest friends, another Titan founder, and his story demands to be told. The world would be a better place if it were. He says I'm the only person who can write it, that he will approve and support no one else. It's me or no one. If I say no, the world will never hear his story, never know the trials, triumphs, and reversals of David Jackson. I've agreed to do it.

I turn the page, surprised at the date. She's pouring every ounce of energy into Jackson's biography and not much into keeping the journal. Another page turn, and I'm at the book release.

_____ 16 Sep. 2020

In this business, they tell you anyone can get lucky once (I don't believe it). You do it twice, and they start to believe you're the genuine article.

I'm gathering believers.

They say the biography of Jackson is better than Shaw's, his life painted in richer tones, transporting readers to the place where he grew up, where he became the man who conquered the financial world and traded the fate of nations like pieces on a Monopoly board. Most of all, they come to understand his conversion at sixty, why he decided to join Oliver Norton Shaw, dedicating his life and his fortune to the Titan Foundation and the betterment of humanity. They see, in vivid brushstrokes, what being a Titan means to him, how it has made Jackson's life, all his sacrifices, worth it. In short, people understand him. Not just people on the street, but even his most intimate acquaintances. Men like David Jackson aren't overly personable, don't form close mates, aren't apt to emote by the fire with a drink in their hand. He's told me that even his closest friends have rung him up, saying that they finally get him. People he's known for forty years have come up to him at parties and confessed that they finally understand something he did decades before, and what he's trying to do now. Best of all, he's had calls from enemies, people he's feuded with in public and private, people who now want to bury the hatchet and join him and Oliver, to become Titans.

He rang me yesterday, related it all, insisting that I did this, that my biography did this.

I swore it wasn't true, and I believe that. It's his life, his story, his fortune, that will make whatever happens possible. I'm just a storyteller, and his is a story people want to hear. I was just in the right place at the right time.

I had lunch in Manhattan with Jackson and Shaw last Tuesday. They billed it as a celebration, but they're connivers to the end. There was a woman there, another Titan candidate, remarkable in her own right. Not as captivating as Shaw or Jackson, but her story speaks to me. And I know it will to others, to every woman, especially those who grew up in rural corners of the world, where opportunities come rarely and only the lucky escape. I like her, and I like her story. I agreed to write it then and there.

In my mind, I held them up, weighed them: my new subject and Alice Carter.

One is real. The other is a figment of my imagination, a bedtime tale at best.

One may inspire girls for generations. The other might be a hit for a few weeks or even a top-ten-grossing film in any given year, quickly buried by the sands of time and the hype of the next potential blockbuster. People won't remember Alice Carter. But they'll remember Sabrina Schröder because she's real. Every second of her struggle is true. Her triumph is an inspiration. Her story needs to be told.

It's an easy choice.

Whoa. Didn't see that coming. The bio must be on the bookshelf outside, one of the ones I skimmed past, looking for Alice Carter. I'll check after I finish with the journal.

After 2020, the journal entries change. The inner dialogue stops. There are no more thoughts or feelings. It's a bloody almanac now, a history of stats—mostly sales numbers—years, and the biographies I penned. No wonder the journal was never filled.

Then, suddenly, fifty years later, the terse, just-the-facts entries give way to something else.

Alone. Another year. And so is he. Nothing to do but write, my only friend. We've confessed our feelings to each other. He has a plan. He's so brave. It would change everything. For the first time since my mum lay on her deathbed, I've been praying. I want it so much. It's the only way. Without it, he's unreachable. No, *I am.* Forbidden.

The Titans—our last enemy. It's ironic. The controversial cabal I sold to the world is now the only barrier to my immortal happiness.

And that's it. No more entries. You've got to be kidding me. Maybe there's another journal. I'm about to ransack the flat when the bedroom door swings open and Nick leans in. "Hey—" He narrows his eyes, taking in the sight of me lying in bed with the journals, the sadness on my face. "Everything all right?"

Oh, sure, nothing amiss, just found out I abandoned my dream and passed away a spinster who wasted her final years pining for an unavailable man.

"Just resting," I lie, trying too hard to sound casual.

Nick sees right through it. He already seems to know me so well. Or is reading people part of his job, whatever that is?

He comes in and sits down beside me, letting the door close behind him. My heart rate climbs. Butterflies multiply and rise like flames from a newly kindled fire. God, I've turned into a twelve-year-old. I should be in a mental institution.

"What's the matter?" he asks.

I hold the notebook up. "Been reviewing some of my life choices."

"And?"

"Looked good initially, but things . . . didn't exactly work out."

"For her."

"Her past is my future."

"It doesn't have to be." He seems so sure. God, how does he do that? It's effortless for him.

I set the notebook aside, and he motions to the living room.

"I think we've made a breakthrough. There's a museum that may tell us what happened here. And Yul and Sabrina have agreed to talk there."

"Museum?"

"It's called Titan Hall."

THE MARCH TO TITAN HALL feels endless. In reality, it's only four blocks from my flat.

Sabrina and Yul lead the way, with Grayson alone in the middle, and Nick and me bringing up the rear.

We're silent for our own safety, but I have the sense that everyone is deep in thought, contemplating this strange, deserted London of the future—waiting for answers, for the final shoe to drop.

With each passing block, with each empty street, hope that we'll find help slips away. This is my city and my neighborhood, and I feel their emptiness keenly, but I don't think I'm the only one affected. The vacant alleys, looted stores, crumbling office buildings, and abandoned residential towers all confirm the truth that every one of us is fearing but no one has yet stated:

London is empty—there's no help for us to find here.

Finally, we turn a corner and Titan Hall comes into view. It occupies an entire city block, most of it green space. What must have once been a splendid park is now overgrown; it feels like a nexus for nature's reclamation of London, the point of origin for weeds, vines, and trees that are slowly burying the last evidence of man's existence.

In the middle of the park sits a simple stone and timber building, barely visible through the lush overgrowth in the dim moonlight. The hall's modest size and simplicity, in sharp contrast to the crowded, overbuilt London around it, actually makes it far more striking. The effect likely didn't come cheap. I know this block; it used to be occupied by office buildings and large homes, any one of which would have cost a fortune.

And now they're all gone, replaced by this small, single structure.

We trek through the overgrown park, climbing over fallen trees and scrambling through tangled vegetation. At the hall, Nick pushes the wooden double doors open, revealing a small reception area with a raised desk. We wander past the reception desk into a wide room with twelve doors. It reminds me of the loading zone for an amusement park ride. This must be where visitors queued up.

To my surprise, lighted green arrows flash on the floor, pointing us to the first door.

"Must be solar-powered, like Stonehenge," says Nick.

Right, like Stonehenge. I'd love to hear that story at some point.

The five of us follow the arrows into a room that's far bigger than I expected, its floor dark stone. It's empty, as far as I can see, but from the room's shadowy perimeter we hear footsteps, faint at first, then louder, heels clapping on the stone floor.

Nick and Grayson draw their guns and form up in front of Sabrina, Yul, and me, positioning themselves to greet whoever's approaching. We've become a paranoid bunch, for good reason.

The figure that emerges from the darkness seems unconcerned by the guns. She's dressed in timeless formality: a simple black dress, a single strand of pearls. Her hair's shoulder length, about the same as mine, and silvery gray. Her face is lean, lightly lined; I would guess she's in her sixties.

She stares at the five of us, unflinching. "Hello. I'm Harper Lane."

CHAPTER TWENTY-THREE

Nick

BESIDE ME STANDS THE THIRTY-YEAR-OLD HARPER, LOOKING AGHAST at a version of herself that's perhaps double her age, though it's hard to tell—she's aged quite well, I think. Future Harper has no reaction to us, which, given the two guns drawn and pointed at her, is the first sign that something is very wrong.

Before anyone can get a word out, she continues, "I'm the curator of Titan Hall and official biographer for the Titan Foundation. I want to welcome you to the first part of this tour, which will take you on a journey through the history of the Titan Foundation, from its creation to the release of the first four Titan Marvels, and how they changed civilization forever. After this brief introduction, you'll have a chance to explore Titan history in depth, selecting the topics that interest you the most. So prepare yourself to go into the origins of the Titan Foundation, the organization that has given us all so much."

I step forward, extend my hand, and run it through Future Harper: she's a projection. This revelation seems to do nothing for Harper, who's frozen in shock. It's not just the projection. The journals from her flat disturbed her deeply. Seeing her city like this, learning what became of her life, and now, seeing her future self, standing here in faux living color, talking—it would be a lot for anyone to process. But it's not just that. I think it's the contrast between her and her future self that's rattled her. The first thing I noticed about the Harper Lane I met was the playful vibrancy in her eyes. It's captivating—but in the future Harper Lane, it's gone. The eyes of this formally dressed tour guide are devoid of life and passion, and I don't think it's just because this is the umpteenth take. She's changed, fundamentally. I don't blame Harper for being shaken. I'd love to let her take ten, process this, but we don't have the luxury. We need answers. If we don't start unraveling what's going on here and where we can get help, we won't last much longer.

Around us, the empty stone room morphs into a wood-paneled study, its tall windows looking out on New York's Central Park. Harper seems to recognize it, and so does Grayson, who steps forward, his eyes wide.

An older man sits at a table by the window, speaking to a woman in her thirties who looks like a bad knock-off of Harper—not as pretty, and without the aforementioned sparkle in her eyes.

Future Harper drifts closer to the man and woman sitting by the window.

"In 2015 I had a fateful meeting with a billionaire named Oliver Norton Shaw, who asked me to write his biography. Shaw wanted to tell his story to the world, but that wasn't his true motive. He wanted to issue a call to arms to the world's elite, a challenge to the bright, the powerful, and the wealthy—the individuals who, he believed, could change the course of history if they worked together.

"In our first meeting Shaw outlined his vision for a new force for good, a group he called the Titans. Shaw believed the Titans could work to effect change on a global scale, change that would eventually end hunger and poverty, achieve world peace, and bring education and opportunity to every corner of the globe. There was one problem, though: Shaw wasn't exactly sure *how* to accomplish these ambitious goals. That was about to change, though. Only days after I first met

Shaw, he sat down with Nicholas Stone, the man who would become Shaw's cofounder of the Titan Foundation. Here's Titan Stone in his own words."

Future Harper walks away from the table, and the couple slips out of view. Seated in a high-backed leather chair on the other side of the study is . . . me. I'm in my sixties, I would guess. My short hair is about the same length, though the black has mostly turned gray.

Okay, Harper, I get it now. This is bizarre. Surreal with a side of nausea. I dread what this guy will say, what he might reveal. But . . . I wonder if it might also reveal the key to our survival here.

"When Oliver Norton Shaw approached me about the Titan Foundation, I was at a crossroads, personally and professionally. I was lost and . . . very, very unhappy with my life, and I couldn't figure out why. I made a lot of money in my late twenties, very quickly. Back then, I always felt it was a stroke of luck, that I'd just been in the right place at the right time. I had this insatiable hunger to prove to myself that I was worthy of the success I had experienced, that *I'd* accomplished it, not just fate, or the fickle hand of the universe, intervening on my behalf. I was pressing myself harder and harder, taking more risks, setting bigger goals, and accomplishing more and more. I was also growing unhappier with each passing year. It was like I was sinking into a well, drowning and dying of thirst at the same time. I was miserable, lost."

Humiliating. Worse than peeing yourself on the first day of school. I have to stand here while this jerk pours out the feelings I haven't told a soul—not my mother, sister, or closest friends—rattling my secrets off with a smug smile on his face, like he's proud of it.

I glance over at Harper. She's staring directly at me, not the Future Me droning on. Against my will, I shrug slightly and let a sad smirk cross my face. She walks closer, and I think she's going to reach for my hand, but she simply stands there, shoulder to shoulder with me, almost touching.

Now Future Me's voice shifts, from reflective, sentimental sap to inspiring visionary. This should be good.

"The Titan Foundation gave me what I sorely needed: a cause greater than myself. It saved me. It was a true opportunity to build something that will do good long after I'm gone. That's what the Titan Foundation is to me: a beacon that will guide humanity into eternity. We knew we were building something special when it began, but at the time Oliver and I thought we were just putting together a small group of really important people who could target big, global objectives, tasks larger than national governments or major nonprofits could tackle. Luckily we were wrong about the scale of our impact."

The study, along with Future Me, fades away, returning us to the stone-floored room, which seems to have no beginning or end.

"The rest, as they say, is history," Future Harper says. "In late 2015 Mr. Stone pooled his personal fortune with Mr. Shaw's, and they made several fateful investments. The first was in a completely unknown start-up called Q-net, which would go on to revolutionize the Internet. The second, Podway, was a mass-transit start-up that had purchased the patents of a failed mining company. The third, Orbital Dynamics, had a big dream: to launch humanity's first permanent settlement in space, a city in the shape of a ring orbiting Earth. In the years that followed the launch of the Titan Foundation, Shaw and Stone focused all their energy on these three companies, working in private. Publicly, the Titan Foundation was judged an overhyped failure. Behind closed doors, however, they were making progress on the first three Titan Marvels—and attracting powerful devotees, wealthy and powerful individuals who would become Titans and join with Stone and Shaw to make their visions a reality.

"The world stood in awe when Q-net launched, providing instantaneous data connectivity around the world. The Titans provided access to quantum network patents to anyone willing to build chips, and in the years that followed, superfast free Internet around the globe became ubiquitous.

"The Titans weren't through knitting the world together. They next set their sight on moving people, not data. The Podway first united Europe, then Asia, and finally the rest of the world, enabling safe, convenient, cost-effective mass transit. The Titans were shrinking our world, and their next marvel would bring us closer together in a way no one imagined."

Small white dots fade into the room's black background, and a view of Earth from space rises from the floor, giving us the sensation we're walking through the sky high above. A ring-shaped space station hangs in the distance.

"For years the world watched the night sky as Orbital Dynamics' first twinkling ring formed. To the world, Titan Alpha was something we hadn't had in a very long time: a shared dream, an audacious goal that tested humanity's collective ability and intellect. We stared up at the stars, for the first time seeing them as not a mystery but a destination within grasp. We had a new land to conquer, to colonize, and the people of the world, from every nation and race, united, rising to the challenge."

The space station fades, and we're once again on Earth, standing on a sandy beach. A massive dam, larger than any I've ever seen, stretches out before us. It must be a thousand feet high, and miles long. At the far end of the dam a green mountain range rises. To our right, on this end, a gray-white cliff juts above, throwing its long shadow across the breathtaking structure. In the center of the dam, five towers rise. I focus, not believing my eyes. The towers are shaped . . . like the fingers of a hand. They curl slightly toward the dam, a giant's hand of glass and steel, reaching up out of the concrete monstrosity. About halfway down the concrete dam a waterfall spills forth, looking puny in proportion to the dam. The foamy water falls hundreds of feet to the basin below, which is perhaps a few miles wide. A river snakes out of the left-hand side, winding through the rocky green and brown basin. The sound of the waterfall is hypnotic, and for a moment I almost forget where I am. The projection is that good.

"The final Titan investment wasn't in a company at all. The Gibraltar Project was the Titans' most ambitious initiative to date, and the largest construction project in history. At the time their plan seemed laughable: to build a dam across the Strait of Gibraltar and drain the Mediterranean Sea, leaving only a river through a vast, fertile new land that joined Europe, Africa, and the Middle East. The technical hurdles were unimaginable, but as Titan Stone says, the greatest hurdle wasn't technical at all: it was political."

Future Me and Future Harper walk into the scene, making tracks on the beach. My future self stands next to her, a mirror of the Harper and me standing here in this time. The dam looms behind them, and the wind tugs at the loose strands of her hair.

I feel a little nervous as Future Me begins to speak.

"In the early years of the foundation, the Gibraltar Project was really a stretch goal. It was the marvel Oliver and I talked about the least, something we saw, frankly, as almost too grandiose. And to some extent it was outside our wheelhouse at the time. My background was in technology, Internet start-ups in particular, so the first Titan Marvel, Q-net, was really familiar to me. Podway showed us that we could build something in the physical world on a grand scale, but I think the launch of the first orbital colony really gave us the confidence to get serious about Gibraltar. By that time we were hungry to do something really big, on a scale that would top our first three acts. Gibraltar was about the only thing left.

"No public works project of this magnitude had ever been attempted. We studied the Panama Canal and the Three Gorges Dam, both the technology and the politics involved. And year after year, Oliver and I kept hammering away at the project, twisting arms. We made a decision halfway through that we were going to start talking about the project as though it was already happening. We called the nation we'd create Atlantis; its capital, which we put right in the middle, just outside Malta, would be Olympus. Our idea was to tie in to mythology, the stories people have been hearing for centuries, to make it seem more real. Life imitates art, I suppose.

"We had these artists' renderings of the dam, and we had them do some of the new capital city. We brought them to every meeting, and slowly the pieces started falling in place. We got lucky—a lot. It felt like fate. The nations along the Mediterranean shouted us out of the room at our first meeting. I mean, they saw their entire way of life—everything from fishing to tourism—disappearing. But over the years, as the economies of Spain, Italy, and Greece weakened, they actually became the project's biggest supporters. They saw in Atlantis what we saw: the opportunity to gain a new, prosperous neighbor on their southern border, and jobs, almost limitless jobs, in the construction process. For Germany and northern Europe, where the standard of living and birth rates had stagnated, here was something they had sought for a long time: new land, close by, with a great climate. My father was a career diplomat, and I had always stayed out of politics, but in the Gibraltar Project I found the chance to join my business experience with all the diplomatic knowledge I had absorbed as a child.

"With the political buy-in, things turned to technical challenges, questions like rising sea levels, alteration of ocean currents and weather patterns, and a desalinization process that was actually effective. With each solution, we were actually tackling much larger global problems that humanity would have had to solve sooner or later anyway. For us, the creation of Atlantis really demonstrated what the foundation was capable of, but also what the human race, working together, could accomplish. Atlantis was proof positive that we could change the face of the Earth—literally."

The future version of me fades away along with the sandy beach and dam, and Future Harper once again stands in the empty stone-floored room with us.

"At the opening of Atlantis, the Titans had one more surprise, one final marvel that had been kept from the world. It was a revelation no one saw coming, an unparalleled achievement. Follow the green arrows into the interactive portion of the tour to learn about the opening of Atlantis and the final Titan Marvel, as well as hundreds of other topics."

The green arrows light the floor, directing us through an archway ahead.

Future Harper slowly fades away, and the room shrinks until we're standing in a square space about fifteen by fifteen feet. Frosted glass panels line the sides, ceiling, and floor, the only break in them dead ahead, where a panel stands open, revealing another room with similar panels.

Grayson and Harper are the first into the next room, which is roughly the same size as the first. The panels here appear to be giant touch screens. They display a list of topics, some highlighted with pictures. Only a few panels are operational, however. Most are cracked, covered in spidery white lines and spray-painted black block letters: TITANS KILLED US ALL.

We spread out in the room, scanning the panels.

Harper taps a link labeled MUSEUM STAFF, then HARPER LANE.

The panel changes to a page with a photo of Harper at a glass-topped desk and a lengthy write-up below. My eyes don't get past the title and subtitle:

HARPER LANE

1982–2071

She was eighty-nine.

Beside me, Grayson is working the panel to the left, headed THE GRAYSON SHAW AFFAIR. I can't help but scan it. The article details his self-destructive life and how he came to be the public voice of opposition to the Titan initiatives, arguing that his father and the Titans were desperate for fame and attention. The irony.

At the bottom, a little note says that Grayson Shaw hasn't appeared publicly in several years. There have been rumors that he's undergoing late-stage treatment for irreversible cirrhosis of the liver.

The only person not working the panels is Yul. He stands in the center of the room, deep in thought.

"You know what all this means, don't you?" I ask him.

He glances up at me slowly. Reluctantly, he nods. I can't tell if it's guilt or fear in his eyes.

CHAPTER TWENTY-FOUR

Nick

GRAYSON, HARPER, AND SABRINA TURN AWAY FROM THE frosted glass panels to focus on Yul and me in the center of the room.

I step closer to Yul. "You said you'd give us answers after Titan Hall. What happened here, Yul?"

"I only know about some parts."

"Which parts?"

"Q-net."

"What about it?" I ask.

"I created it."

Interesting. "I thought the Titans did."

"I've been working on it for years. I think the Titans only invested in it, provided the money, to make it accessible to everyone."

"What is it?"

"A quantum network, a new Internet. It's a way to move data around the globe instantaneously, using quantum entanglement. It will revolutionize computing. Or rather, it did revolutionize computing.

"It was all experimental until a week ago—a week ago our time— when the first Q-net nodes went active. For months I've had this problem with data corruption. Every time I sent a burst of data, it came out wrong on the other end. There was a pattern to the corruption, so I wrote an algorithm to filter it out. When I looked at the data the filter had extracted, I realized it was organized."

"Meaning?"

"It was a message."

"From?"

"The future. *Now.*"

Yul's words hang in the glass room for a second.

"The sender claimed to be from the year 2147," he presses on. "I thought the stress had finally gotten to me. I took a day off, went to the doctor, got a full workup. I was fine. The next messages proved beyond a doubt that they were from the future."

"How?"

"They predicted events that would happen the next day. The exact vote tallies for parliamentary elections in Poland, for example—right down to the votes cast for every candidate for every office. The arrival times, down to the minute, of every flight that landed that day all around the globe, including every delayed and canceled flight. A few days went by, me demanding proof again and again, them answering correctly every time."

"How's that possible—messages from the future?"

"They were altering entangled particles that existed in their time, organizing them to make a readable message in our time."

Oh, now that makes sense.

Yul reads the expressions around the room and spreads his hands like a high school science teacher giving the complex lecture that's over his students' heads, the one he dreads every year.

"Imagine we're back on the beach we just saw, but we're in the year 2147. Imagine we can put on a special glove, and when we reach down to touch the grains of sand on our beach in 2147, it makes a copy of that beach, in every instant in which it's ever existed. There's a string that reaches across space-time, connecting the grains of sand on our beach to those same grains on that beach in every other moment. We can adjust its length, choosing which beach our string connects to. So now the grains of sand on our beach in 2147 are connected to the same grains on the same beach in 2015. We bend down and draw a message in the sand, and it appears in 2015. I saw that message—on my beach in the past. That shared beach is Q-net, and the data on my hard drive, the digital bits, they're the grains of sand. Because this was the first moment that Q-net existed in our time, it was their first opportunity to send a message back—this was the first instant when the quantum particles that form the network became entangled. Those particles are the grains of sand in the analogy."

The four of us just stare at Yul, no one quite sure what to say. Grains of sand on a quantum beach? I'm so far out of my league here. I ask the question that seems most relevant: "What did the sender want?"

"To help us. They told me that a global catastrophe was imminent, an event that would cause the near extinction of the human race, an event they had barely lived through and were trying to prevent. They asked me to contact Sabrina, whom I didn't know. I was asked to pass a series of instructions to her. They didn't make any sense to me."

"Nor to me, at first," Sabrina says. "Then I realized what it was: a breakthrough in my research—a new treatment."

"For?"

"Progeria syndrome."

Now that surprises me. Since we reached London, I've nursed a theory about how humanity might have vanished from the face of the earth: a pandemic. To me, it's the most viable theory as to how the human race could have fallen so far, so fast. My suspicion was that Sabrina, more than Yul, was connected to it. But this doesn't add up.

"I assumed you worked in infectious diseases," I say to Sabrina, unable to hide my suspicion.

"I don't. Never have." Sabrina pauses, searching for the right words. "That was, however, a logical assumption, given what we've seen."

"Progeria syndrome . . ." I whisper, trying to reconcile the information with my working theory.

"It's an extremely rare genetic condition that causes premature aging. Affected individuals die of old age in their teens. The messages asked me to take several actions, what I believed were preventive measures against some biological event: an outbreak or mass mutation, perhaps. I believed I was distributing a vaccine that might propagate, saving the human population in 2015. It seems, however, that I was only inoculating some of the passengers on the plane."

It takes me a few seconds to process that. Everyone's studying the dark floor, trying to wrap their heads around it. Finally Yul breaks the silence.

"I also received instructions. Schematics. I used them to build a device they said would allow enhanced communications. Both of us"—he motions to Sabrina—"were told to come to London, and that we'd receive another message when we landed."

"That's why you wanted to come to London, even after the crash?"

"Yes," Yul says. "Those were our last instructions. They were all we had to go on."

"The device you built—you think it crashed the plane, or played a role in bringing us here?"

"I've . . . entertained the idea. The plane broke apart roughly where my carry-on was. The device, however, survived the crash unharmed."

"You've been working on that device since the crash?" I ask.

"No. I've been trying to connect to Q-net, to make contact with them."

"And?"

"Q-net is different now. The protocols have changed. It's like dial-up in the nineties: every time I connect, I get booted off instantly. My hardware is okay. It's like I don't have the right software. The data packets I'm sending aren't formatted correctly, and I have no guide to how they should be formatted."

I consider that for a moment. "Or they are formatted correctly, but someone's trying to keep you off. Maybe connecting would reveal your location, endanger you."

"True," Yul says.

"How long have you known we were in the future?" I ask. It's not strictly relevant, but it's a hot button for me. I feel we could have saved some time, and maybe even lives, if Yul had at least told some of us, enlisted help earlier.

"The first night," Yul says. "The stars. At first I thought the crash event could have caused a widespread blackout, eliminating all the light pollution. The first clue was that the international space station was gone. Where it should have been I saw a large, lighted ring in orbit. That's how I knew we were in a different time completely."

"And you told no one?"

Yul shrugged. "Who would have believed me? You?"

I can see where this is going. There's no time for replay or the blame game. We need to focus. I wonder if we should move. We've been here too long . . . but the panels might reveal details we still need. I motion to the cracked, spray-painted panels.

"You think the Titans sent the messages?"

"I don't know," Yul says. "They were involved in Q-net, and seemingly in the catastrophe that occurred. In 2015 the senders identified themselves only as the Friends of Humanity. For all I know, it could have been the Titans' enemies; they seem to be at war."

"The question, to me," Sabrina says, "is why it took the . . . rescue teams four days to reach the crash site."

"Yes. Very curious. When I returned from Stonehenge, two factions were at war. What were the tents? Some kind of medical experiment?"

"Perhaps. I'm only certain of one thing: they were treating the passengers for wounds." Sabrina glances at Harper. "And doing an excellent job."

Through the doorway, I hear footsteps. The intro restarting?

I open my mouth to ask another question, but stop. Figures. In the doorway. Suited. The beings from the crash site. They stop ten feet from us. No one moves. I glance behind me, desperately hoping someone activated another simulation from the menu.

The closest figure raises his arm, pointing it toward us.

No, it's not a simulation.

CHAPTER TWENTY-FIVE

Nick

TIME STANDS STILL IN THIS GLASS-PANELED ROOM, DEEP inside Titan Hall. No one moves. Yul and I stand closest to the two suited creatures. Harper, Grayson, and Sabrina are behind us, still near the panels where they explored Titan history.

Up close, the suits appear to be made of small, overlapping tiles, like a reptile's scales. They shine slightly, like milky glass, but I imagine they're made of a polymer we haven't invented yet. Every inch of the helmets is covered in these milky scales—no opening for eyes, mouth, or nose. The lack of any semblance of a face make these beings look even more alien.

There's only one play here. I begin to reach for my handgun. I'll get one shot—

"Don't."

The voice emanating from the suit is a computerized imitation of a human voice, neither male nor female, devoid of any intonation or hint of emotion. It makes my skin crawl. It continues before anyone can act. "We're not here to harm you."

"What *are* you here for?" I ask.

"To help you," the voice answers.

"Is that why you brought our plane here?"

"Yes."

And there it is: they did this. For the past five days, we've been like rats in their postapocalyptic maze, struggling, scurrying, scratching to survive. Rage burns inside me. "Cut the shit. You brought us here to help yourselves."

"You're here to help both of us. We can't talk here. You have to come with us right now."

Too risky. Way too risky. "Take the suits off first."

"We can't."

"Why not?" Why would they need suits, when we don't? I'm not liking this.

"You have to trust us, Nick. We don't have time to debate."

It knows my name. And the voice . . . despite its computer camouflage, I know that voice. How? Who?

A low drone rumbles above us, growing louder. I glance up, trying to place it. My mouth goes dry. I know that sound. It's an airship, the same type that raided the crash site.

The figures disappear without moving, their camouflage activated. I hear only their echoing footsteps pounding the frosted glass floor. The neutral computerized voice, disembodied in the dark cavern, calls back to us. "Stay here."

Grayson and I draw our guns. I glance around the group. Going by the look on their faces, not a single person favors staying here.

We charge out of the small room, through the first chamber where the Titan history lesson played, and out into the reception area. Through the cracked wooden double doors, I see flashes in the night, what look like targeted laser blasts from two airships battling each other. Some of the vegetation is already burning, sending thick black smoke into the air. That's the cover we need.

I turn to the group, my eyes on Harper, who is clutching the two notebooks to her chest, and flash back to that day on the lake bank, when my eyes met hers as the plane was sinking, when we stood on the precipice together, ready to wade into the breach. A strange, almost intoxicating combination of fear and excitement, a feeling that I never knew existed until five nights ago, washes over me.

Through the crack in the wooden doors, I watch the symphony of light and destruction playing out in the overgrown park, like a laser light show in Central Park. Shots rain from the sky. Fire reaches up like a crowd responding. The darkness flows toward us as thick black tendrils of smoke curl around the building. Time slows down, and my senses intensify. I feel a preternatural focus come over me.

In slow motion, I watch Yul secure his bag. Sabrina stands still as a statue, gazing at the destruction outside. Fear clouds Grayson's face as he glances between the gun in his hand and the battle outside. Harper pulls her shirt up and tucks the two skinny books against her abs, securing them at the bottom with her waistband. She nods at me once, silently saying, *I'm ready.*

I turn to the group, speaking quickly. "Follow my lead. Grayson, bring up the rear, and shoot anything that shimmers. If we're separated, run away from the ships and make your way to . . ." I pause. I don't like it, but there's only one place I'm sure everyone knows. "To Harper's flat. Wait twenty minutes for any others, then move on in case they find it."

I push the door open. The focused firing from the two ships above slows as shots rise from cloaked figures below, the one-sided assault transforming into a back-and-forth. The quiet, overgrown park is now a full-on jungle war zone. Several large fires burn hot and bright, converging on one another, their black smoke rising, blotting out the airships as smaller clouds cover Titan Hall. Through the smoke screen, I hear quick, pulsing blasts. Every few seconds an explosion blows a wall of force and smoke toward us.

I wade into the black cloud of smoke and break right. Behind us a bomb hits the structure, spraying us with fragments of stone and wood. I glance back, making sure no one is hit. I see only grimaces and determined looks.

The dense vegetation was a nuisance on the way in. Now it's a current fighting our every move, trying to pull us in. A fallen tree lies at an angle, and I try to slip below it, but the brush is too thick, tangled into an organic mesh fence. I back out, climb, and tumble over, waiting for the others, helping them down. I bound forward over the next wall of green, limbs and thorny brush scratching my face and hands. Four ships are above us now, pounding each other at close range, none giving an inch.

Sabrina makes it over the web of fallen trees and vines, then Yul.

Behind us, I hear a scream through the smoke. Harper.

I jump and spin back over the vine-covered tree, rushing toward her.

She braces herself on a trunk, reaching for her abdomen. Her eyes meet mine for a second, then she spins around as another shot hits her. She disappears into the undergrowth, swallowed by the green ocean. Grayson is twenty feet behind her, and he turns, firing wildly into the woods. The smoke is clearing now as the battle shifts to the air.

One of Grayson's shots connects. A shimmering figure, not ten feet from him, reels back into a tree. It flickers as it slides to the ground, falls forward, and lies there, a glittering hump of dull glass against the foliage.

"Harper!" I yell.

Grayson turns to me, and I'm about to call to him when a rapid barrage of fire fills the air, pressing down on us. It's deafening, disorienting. I slip my gun in my jacket as trees bend and shatter all around me. A ship barrels down through the black cloud, nose first, right for me.

I turn, stagger to my left, fall, and push myself up, leaping across branches, climbing over everything in my path. The trees and brush cut my hands, arms, and face, but I push on, clawing for every inch. The ground below me booms and disappears. I'm thrown ten feet forward into a vine-covered tree. The ship is bulldozing the overgrown park, throwing dirt, plants, and bits of trees into the air.

There's no use running anymore. I'm just one of the pieces of debris riding a wave of scorched earth. Just when I think it might stop, the ship explodes, launching me again into the air, much farther this time.

I land in a sharp, prickly bed of green, my head spinning. My hearing is gone. My limbs are numb. I sit up, but my head's spinning. Have to get up. The fallen airship burns. Smoke fills the space from me to it. Harper. She's right beside it. Fire will burn her. They will get her.

I blink. Can't keep my eyes open. Have to.

Focus.

In the air above, the chorus of death and destruction still plays, silent now, flashes through the clouds of smoke, ships moving, semi-synchronized, lighting each other up.

I roll onto my stomach and push up, standing for a second, but I can't control my body. It plummets back down to the ground as if a magnet's pulling my midsection. I close my eyes, but the spinning gets worse.

A faint sensation. For a few seconds, I can't place it. Then I realize what it is.

Hands, gripping me, dragging me through the park.

CHAPTER TWENTY-SIX

Nick

I AWAKE IN DARKNESS, TO THE SOUND OF bottles clinking in the distance.

My body is battered and sore, but hey, what's new? The headache is ruthless, but my biggest concern is my left arm, which I must have landed on during the mayhem at Titan Hall. I was too pulverized to notice at the time. A single finger touching my elbow sends a radiating wave of pain.

I reach for my jacket pocket, hoping . . . but the handgun is gone. The binoculars are in my other pocket. Still there. Yes, my captor removed the gun. Not an entirely positive sign.

I have one good arm to fight with and no information to go on. Wounded and uninformed: the theme of my life since Flight 305 crashed.

I wait for my eyes to adjust, to get a glimpse of where I am, but it never comes. The darkness is absolute. I'm indoors, I know that. The floor is hard and there's no wind; it's cold, but not unbearable.

Muffled footsteps. A large door swings open, revealing faint light.

I hold my hand up, squinting, but I can't make out who it is. The person closes the door quickly, without a word, then stands there a moment, unmoving.

A match strike. The light from the flame lights my captor's face from beneath. Not captor, rescuer . . . I think.

Grayson Shaw.

His face is bruised and caked with dried blood. Dirt and debris from the forest litters his long blond hair. There's no hint of a smile. He touches the match to a candle in his other hand and sets it on the floor beside me.

We're in a supply closet—in a store, I would guess. Shampoo and dish detergent line the shelves. Guess those weren't in demand when humanity fell.

"How do you feel?" Grayson asks. It's a question I never thought I'd hear come out of his lips.

I pause. Could this be a charade? A ploy to get me to talk? Could we both have been captured by the suited figures, who have enlisted him to facilitate their interrogation? It's possible. There's a fine line between paranoia and brilliance. I'm not sure which side I'm on right now.

I'm sure of only two things. One: I'm extremely lucky to be alive and in reasonably good shape. Very lucky indeed. Two: I need to find Harper. There were over a hundred survivors when I left for Stonehenge, and some are probably still out there somewhere, but she's the one I'm after, the one I have . . . what were Sabrina's words? *An emotional connection to.* Sabrina certainly has a way with words, a very clinical, unsentimental way, but if I'm being honest, she's okay. She and Yul hid things from me, but I see why now. Messages from the future? Nah, wouldn't have believed that five days ago.

Grayson fidgets as he waits for my response, and I realize his question must have felt awkward to him, too, given our history: snarky comments escalating to casual threats culminating in a punch to the face—his face, two punches, in fact—and subsequent, more serious threats.

"I'm all right." I sit up. "Just a little banged up."

He sets a bottle of water on the floor and holds out his hand, waiting to hand me something. I extend a cupped hand, half expecting him to yell "Psych!" and punch me in the face. I suppose it would make us even—or closer to even, at least.

To my surprise, two small pills drop into my hand. "Aspirin," he says.

I wash them down with the water. Figure it's a fifty-fifty chance they're cyanide. Given the full-body pain right now, I'll roll the dice. "The others?"

"They have Harper for sure—saw them carrying her off after the first ship came down. Not sure about Yul or Sabrina."

Harper's alive . . . but captured. Elation and nausea.

"Where are we?"

"The back room of a small pharmacy across the street from Titan Hall."

He reads the shock on my face. "Only option. I couldn't carry you far. Between the smoke, the battle, and the darkness, I don't think they saw us slip away. They probably think we're under the rubble somewhere."

"How long have I been out?"

"Four hours. Figured they would have found us by now, but there've been no signs of them. A few ships flying over—that's it."

What to do now? To me, there's only one play.

"Listen, Nick," Grayson says, his voice quieter. "On the plane . . . I was in a state. My dad had just told me he was giving away his fortune and cutting me out of his will, leaving me with nothing. He was putting me out on the street so I could finally, in his words, 'learn to fend for myself.'"

Harper told me as much, but I stay silent. It feels like this is something Grayson needs to say.

"Imagine every assumption you lived your life under instantly changing, your whole life upside down, uncertain, for the first time. It felt like a total betrayal, the rug pulled out from under me just like that. I was scared. I felt double-crossed by the person I had depended on my entire life. It seemed like just a whim, a little game he wanted to play: see if his coddled son could cut it in the real world, starting from scratch at age thirty-one. I thought it was cruel not to tell me when

I was in school, or just after, when I could have changed my life and taken a different path, before I developed all my . . . habits."

He waits, but I'm not quite sure what to say. The awkwardness builds. Finally I say, "It's never too late to change your life."

"That shit might sell T-shirts, but it doesn't help me." His voice is bitter, a brief flashback to the Grayson I met on the plane. He pauses. "Sorry. It's just that . . . changing is a hell of a lot harder when you're older, especially after you've come to expect and . . . depend on certain things."

"That's true."

"I should have snapped out of it after the crash, but I was still so . . . upside down."

Incredible. He really has changed this quickly. I have to admit, when he first started up with his story and explanation—apology?—I half expected it to end with a joke on me, accompanied by that classic Grayson Shaw sneer and nasty laugh. But I don't see either now, just humility and a longing for understanding and forgiveness.

I don't think it's the battle outside Titan Hall that changed Grayson, but what he saw inside: that panel that detailed the Grayson Shaw affair. I think seeing what his decision in 2015 led to, what he became, has given him some perspective. I wonder what the world would be like if we could all glimpse our future before every major decision. Maybe that's what stories are for: so we can learn from people living similar lives, with similar troubles.

"Don't worry about it. Look, we've all done things we're not proud of at some point. Just part of being human. What counts is what we do right now."

The air slowly flows out of Grayson, and he glances around at the candlelit storage room. "What *are* we going to do right now?"

"Now we're going to go on the offensive."

TO HIS CREDIT, GRAYSON JUST nods after hearing my plan. Skepticism and worry are clear on his face, but his only question is, "How do we get there?"

We agree that the Podway would be unsafe. I have an idea, but I wonder if this particular transportation technology is still in use, over three hundred years after it was invented. It requires no fuel, has no electronics, and can do about thirty miles an hour, depending on the operator and terrain. It can operate in urban, rural, or off-road environments with no preexisting infrastructure, which Planet Earth happens to be fresh out of at the moment. It's perfect . . . if we can find it.

It's still dark when we make our way out of the narrow pharmacy. We hurry down the street, away from the charred, smoldering remains of Titan Hall.

We don't spot what we seek on the next street, nor the one after that. Finally I see a shop that might suffice. Grayson and I climb in through a shattered plate-glass window. The technology has changed a bit, but it's still basically the same. And there's no learning curve.

Once you learn to ride a bike, you never forget.

WE RODE UNTIL THE FIRST rays of sunrise, stopping only to duck out of cover when we heard an airship in the distance and to gather food. We spotted an apple orchard a short ways outside London, and now we sit in an interior office of a large, dilapidated warehouse, eating apples and trying to stay warm.

Our plan is to rest the entire day and strike under cover of night. It's about our only chance.

The cramped room is dark save for a narrow sliver of light that seeps in between the bottom of the closed door and the floor. Grayson and I lean against opposite walls, an old oak desk between us. I can just make out half of his bruised, haggard face, one of his exhausted eyes staring at the floor.

"In the video, you said your dad was a diplomat."

"Mmm-hmm," I say between bites of apple, wishing we had something more.

"You didn't follow in his footsteps?"

"Nah."

"You're what, an investor?"

"Venture capitalist. Early-stage companies, technology, mostly IT."

"I've had ideas for companies. Tons of them. Figured, what's the use, though? It's not like I needed the money. And any company I started would be measured against my father's empire. I'd always come up short. No-win situation. Plus, once you've been to a few parties and heard the way the gossip machine feeds on the failures of the rich and famous, once you've . . . joined in on the feeding, it becomes nearly impossible to put yourself through the grinder. Who wants to try and fail, when you can drink and laugh with no consequences?" He takes a bite of apple. "I bet that's the stupidest thing you've ever heard."

"It's not. Not even close. I grew up with people just like you, Grayson, in boarding schools all over the world. It sounds crazy from the outside, but everybody's scared of failure and being seen as a disappointment. The longer the shadow is, the farther you have to walk."

"You made it out, though. You did all right for yourself."

"I guess."

"How'd you do it?"

"Changed the scorecard. I opted for a career different from my father's. No comparisons that way. After college, I got on a plane to San Francisco, got lucky, won the IPO lottery, and have been placing calculated bets ever since. Still getting lucky."

"Being in a plane crash wasn't lucky. And it wasn't luck that got the people out of the lake or kept the camp out of chaos. That was skill: strategy, leadership, real-life action-hero stuff."

"Yeah? You want to hear the crazy part?"

Grayson waits.

"Until six days ago, I had no idea I had it in me."

JUST AFTER SUNSET, WE SET out again, pedaling harder this time. If we can't make it there tonight, we'll lose a lot of the element of surprise.

People who've never been to this place don't realize how far outside of London it is. It's our only play, the only place I have reason to believe there may be people—verified humans—who actually want to help the passengers of Flight 305.

The second day at camp, after Bob and Mike got the cockpit door open, the pilot said something I didn't realize was so important until now. After the first bout of turbulence, the plane lost all outside connectivity: satellites, Internet, communications. The pilots were flying blind on their preprogrammed course. When they got closer to Heathrow, however, they received radio contact again. The controllers at Heathrow said a global event had affected communications. They told the pilots to maintain their course, and that the controllers would guide them in.

My working theory is that the device Yul created in 2015 allowed the plane to travel into the future—that the turbulence and radio blackout happened when the plane jumped forward in time. Whoever brought us here must have intended for us to land as planned at Heathrow. But something went wrong. Maybe the suited figures intervened. Or maybe there was a technical problem with the device Yul built, or an issue on their end.

Either way, *someone was at Heathrow,* a human voice at least, and it was trying to get us there six days ago. That's really the only clue I have. In fact, it's the only place on the planet where I have reason to believe there are still any people left.

But as Grayson and I pedal past the road signs for London Heathrow, I feel my nerves winding up. We've expended the better part of twenty-four hours on this little adventure. What if I'm wrong?

I draw the binoculars and scan the sprawling airport, looking for a sign, a literal light in the darkness that proves someone's there, waiting for us. The view isn't promising. The side closest to us is dark. But on the other side of the sprawling airport, a dim glow lightens the night sky.

Someone or something is here.

CHAPTER TWENTY-SEVEN

Nick

HALF AN HOUR LATER I DO A CLOSER scan of Heathrow—or what's left of it—and then hand Grayson the binoculars.

The airport buildings lie in ruins, caved-in heaps of concrete, steel, and glass. Here and there shards of the color-coded signs that once directed passengers around Europe's busiest airport stick out, fragments of red, blue, and green dotting the gray mounds. A different shade of green predominates, though. Vegetation is slowly retaking the land. Grass, weeds, and moss creep across the lumpy ruins, but trees have yet to take hold. Perhaps they'll rise in the coming years, when the wind, rain, and snow have pulverized Heathrow's remains into something more like soil.

Beyond the buildings we spot the source of the light—three long white tents, apparitions glowing in a sea of tall grass. It's hard to tell from here, but I'd guess that, put together, they'd be about the size of a football field. A halo of light rises softly above them, giving them a hazy look in the night.

They've cut the grass on one long runway—I'm guessing because they expected Flight 305 to land here. I count that as a positive sign at first, but then the optimism that has been rising steadily since I saw the light and the tents fades. Beside the tents, at the end of the mowed runway, loom three airships, their silver skin hatched with long, dark marks—the scars of the two previous battles I've witnessed, and who knows how many others. Each is about a hundred feet long, I would guess, and maybe twenty feet tall. I still wonder how they fly. More important, I wonder if the things inside are friend or foe. Here in the darkness, across the sea of grass and the crumbling ruins of Heathrow, there's not a single clue.

For a long moment Grayson and I just stand here, the rusted remnants of a barbed-wire-topped fence collapsed on the ground at our feet. Finally we step carefully across it toward the tents, committing to our course.

"What do you want to do?" Grayson's voice is low.

Though there's little chance they can hear us from here, I answer quietly and quickly. "Find cover and wait. Watch for signs about what's going on."

Ten minutes later we've taken up position on the other side of a broken-down wide-body aircraft of a make unfamiliar to me. Time is slowly dragging it—like the airport, and London itself—into the ground. Grayson and I take turns peering over the mangled hulk at the camp, our bodies huddled close together, trying to trap any warmth between us.

I'd love to catch some sleep, but it won't come. I'm too nervous, too cold, too sore.

Sitting with my back against the metal of the aircraft, I look up as it starts to rain. It's just a drizzle, not near as bad as the frigid, pounding downpour we endured on the ride here. But still, I could do without it.

AN HOUR LATER WE'VE SEEN nothing, not a single indication about how to infiltrate this place. Two hours to sunrise. We'll have to decide soon: go back or make a move. Neither option appeals.

We've made a little shelter under an overhang in the wrecked plane to keep out the cold and the rain. During this time, I've made a decision:

If I live through this ordeal, I'm moving to Arizona and never going out after sunset again.

MOVEMENT. A FIGURE IN A glass-tiled suit just came out of an airship. It walks quickly to the closest tent, slipping through flaps I hadn't been able to make out before. I watch intently, waiting for it to emerge again. I wave Grayson off when he reaches for the binoculars, ready for his shift. I need to see this.

Thirty minutes later my arms are cramped, my eyes are tired, and there hasn't been another movement. Time to roll the dice.

THE JOG TO THE GLOWING white tents seems endless. Through the haze and drizzle, the three round-topped structures loom above the grass horizon like rising suns.

This is a crazy move. Desperate. But it comes down to this: try to find help elsewhere or see what's behind the curtain—or tent flaps, literally. I'm freezing, waterlogged, and hungry, and the flaps are a hundred feet away now. Turning back, going for help elsewhere doesn't seem like an option. I'm not even sure anybody is out there. I *know* someone is here. And the odds are good that the passengers are, too, one in particular, if the battered airship extracted her from the Titan Hall battlefield. As Grayson and I reach the flaps, guns drawn, I tell myself this is our only play.

Neither of us hesitates at the threshold. He pulls the flap back and stands aside, allowing me to enter.

The room is small and empty, its walls made of white sheet-plastic.

Warm, misty air engulfs us from above and the sides.

Must be a decontamination chamber of some sort.

A glass door dead ahead clicks. I pull the metal handle.

Another room. White walls again, hard plastic this time. Glass-tiled suits hang on the right side, white suits made of a rubbery material on the left. Helmets with only a horizontal slit for the eyes sit on a shelf above.

Without a word, Grayson and I begin pulling the rubber suits on over our wet clothes. Leaving those here would quickly give us away.

The suit has a small tank on the back, on the interior, and when I seal the helmet, it pressurizes. For a second I panic, wondering if . . . but I can breathe.

The transparent eye slit is the only thing that might give us away. Speed is the key now.

With my eyes, I try to communicate that to Grayson.

We leave the suit room via a sliding glass door. Unlike the hinged door behind us, it makes a tight seal. Another chamber, another spray of mist from all sides, and a metal door ahead slides open, revealing a long corridor with ten doors on each side. Wide windows are set into the wall between the doors, stretching from waist height to the ceiling, about twelve feet above us, giving us a glimpse into each room. They're . . . labs. Ten labs on each side, each containing a long metal table, open shelving on one wall, and some kind of platform at the back, which I can't make out from here.

From our vantage point in the chamber I can see movement in the closest few labs, figures wearing containment suits like ours. No one has looked up at us yet. They're hunched over their work, which I can't quite make out.

Grayson turns awkwardly in the suit. Through the slit in the helmet, I see fear in his eyes. We're like two turkeys in a shooting gallery: ten firing stalls, shooters on each side, any one of whom could recognize us. The labs are each about twenty feet wide. Two hundred feet to the sliding glass doors at the end. Might as well be two hundred miles. We'll never make it without someone realizing we don't belong, but we can't turn back—that could draw even more attention.

I set out, my pace brisk but hopefully not rushed enough to raise suspicion. I don't dare risk turning my head toward the labs, and I'm relieved to see Grayson following my lead.

The first lab passes. Then the second. Through my peripheral vision, I see flashes of what's going on here. Autopsies. Human bodies laid out on metal tables, split open. Organs in pans around the room.

The third lab passes.

Fourth.

Fifth. Halfway to the doors.

At the seventh lab, the pattern changes. The body on the table isn't human. It's an ape. I can't help but cut my eyes over. I can't be sure, but I think the suited figure hunched over its body stops working and looks up. The eyes inside are human—I think. I pick up my pace, hoping he won't take notice of us.

We pass the eighth lab. Empty.

Behind us I hear the sweeping sound of a hinged glass door opening. Footsteps in the hall. I can't tell if they're moving toward us or away.

Ninth row of labs. Also empty.

I can see through the sliding glass doors ahead now. Rows of rolling tables hold domed plastic tents.

Just past the last two labs, Grayson reaches out and punches the round, unlabeled button beside the sliding doors. Neither of us look back as they open and we step out of the corridor, into an open space.

The sliding doors seal off the sound of footsteps behind us, leaving us in total silence.

The tables are steel, each about eight feet long and three feet wide. There are three rows of seven, lined up neatly.

I move to the closest and peer inside the rounded, clear plastic chamber. A human body. I don't recognize the person. I move to the next row. A woman, middle-aged. I've seen her before. She was in the main section of the plane that sank in the lake. She was one of the first to jump and swim ashore. The last time I saw this woman, she was shivering on the bank in the dim moonlight, pleading with us to save her husband, who was still on the plane. The next chamber holds a black kid, around ten. He looks familiar, but I'm not sure.

I scan the final row. Mike. Jillian. All still, eyes closed. What is this? Are they dead, or sedated?

To the left, a short passageway connects this tent to the next. More of the rolling tables with plastic domes over bodies crowd the connecting section. I bet the other tent's filled with rolling tables.

On the far wall to my right a mechanical droning breaks the silence. A conveyor belt. It runs the length of the wall, from a dark tunnel along the backside of the labs to a small, windowless room in the corner. The belt jolts into motion, surging forward unevenly. Grayson and I wait, watching it. Slowly, a plastic-wrapped package emerges from the tunnel. A body. One they're finished with. And suddenly I know what this complex is:

A massive assembly line for some kind of experiment.

An experiment—that's why they brought us here. I'm sure of it now. And I know what we should do: get out. But I'm not leaving before I find out whether Harper's here—and if she is, I'm not going anywhere without her.

The sliding doors behind us open, and Grayson and I freeze. I hope the suited figure will take the next body, wheel it back into the lab section . . .

It walks past the first row, still approaching us.

"I think we should have a talk."

The voice from the suit's speaker is human, and it booms inside the space.

I sidestep away from the table, into the aisle from the labs to the small room on the far side of the tent. Grayson mimics my movement awkwardly in his white suit, but neither of us turns. We march, probably a little too quickly, along the wide path parallel to the conveyor belt, overtaking the plastic-wrapped body.

"Hey!" the voice yells.

The sliding metal doors open as we approach, revealing a room that's empty except for a large machine that runs the length of the right-hand wall: an incinerator is my guess. I bet there's another at the opposite corner of the tent, serving the labs on that side.

One look at Grayson tells him what I want to do: set a trap.

He nods, draws his gun from the loose kangaroo pouch in the front of his suit, and steps diagonally back into the room's blind spot, beside the door, where the machine meets the wall.

I draw my own gun, clasp it behind my back with my other hand, and stand my ground, trying to appear calm, as if I'm waiting patiently.

The doors slide open. The face is human. A middle-aged man. He doesn't seem alarmed at the sight of me.

He takes one step inside. "Nicholas—"

Grayson brings the butt of his gun down on the man's helmet, sending him to the floor. It doesn't knock him out, however, and he pulls Grayson down with him. I bring my own gun out, waiting for an opening as they roll around on the floor, wondering . . .

Before the double doors can close, another figure rushes in, hands raised. I freeze, unable to look away from the eyes.

His gloved hands slowly reach for his helmet. He pauses, staring at me, waiting for the double doors to seal.

On the floor, Grayson and the man stop struggling, both looking up in shock. The man standing before us lifts the helmet off, and I'm staring at . . . me.

Down to the very last detail, he's an exact replica of me.

CHAPTER TWENTY-EIGHT

Harper

IF I HAD A QUID FOR EVERY TIME I've woken up sore, alone, and in the dark in the last six days . . . I close my eyes, hoping for a little more rest. Sleep comes quickly.

THE SECOND AWAKENING'S MUCH BETTER. At least I can discern the pain's focal point this go-round: my left shoulder.

In the dim light I run my fingers across my shoulder, feeling for the source of the hurt. I stop on a round metal device, cool to the touch. Its tiny tendrils dig into my flesh. I instinctively scratch at the edges, trying to pry it free. It's no use; the little metal insect is dug in too tight.

My eyes have adjusted a bit, and I take in my confines, which seem like a coffin at first. There's a ceiling a few feet above and dark walls on three sides. I can just make out a dim light to my right. I'm in a cubby, just big enough for my body, on an incredibly comfortable mattress.

I push up, but pain explodes in my abdomen, races up my chest, and slams me back into the bed.

My fingers reach for the pain, gently, afraid to ignite it again. My journal—it's pressed against my stomach, against the hurt. No, it's on the outside. The Alice Carter notebook is closest to my bruised abdomen and ribs. Running my hand down the journal's hard cover, I find the silver spider dug into it. The sharp legs reach deep inside, almost to the back cover, like a staple through a stacked sheaf of papers, but not quite deep enough to get through and wrap around. The journal stopped the first shot at the park outside Titan Hall, and that's probably a very good thing.

I hold the small book up and flip it open. The last, unpierced pages are blank. I set it aside and move to Alice Carter. She's survived unharmed, and I realize that I'm happy about that. I'd choose her over the journal any day—I'm not sure I want to know any more about myself. The first walk down Future Memory Lane was jarring enough.

The bed vibrates slightly, then shakes a little more violently. It reminds me . . . of turbulence, and at first all I can think of is Flight 305. Then it's gone, and I can breathe again.

I swing my feet out of the bunk, onto the floor. Faint light rises from below, illuminating the space. Three double bunks are arranged in a U-shape. Both of the others on the bottom level are occupied, but the row above is empty. They look almost like sleeping quarters on a military ship (I once ghostwrote the autobiography of a British admiral; many ship tours were involved). Maybe I'm aboard the airship I last saw at Titan Hall. The more I think about my situation, I realize it has to be. I lean forward to look at the other bunks. Yul lies to the right. He's alive and asleep. But the bag he has vigilantly guarded since the crash is missing. Sabrina occupies the other bunk, and I'm relieved to feel a faint pulse in her neck as well.

The double doors directly ahead slide open, flooding the room with blinding light. I hold my right arm up, squinting, barely able to make out a suited figure. It taps a panel, and darkness overtakes me.

THE PAIN'S GONE WHEN I wake up, and so is everything else: the cramped bunk, the metal burr in my shoulder, my journal and notebook—and my tattered clothes. I feel a little self-conscious as I sit up in a massive bed, inspecting the tight, layered white garments someone has dressed me in.

The room I'm in is spacious, spotlessly clean. Across from the bed, there's a desk against a long wall. To my right, a wide window looks out on the sea. A glass door opens to a glittering bathroom. Beyond the bathroom, another door, solid wood, presumably leads out of the room. It feels like a posh hotel.

I stare out the window for a moment, searching for clues about where I might be. All I can see is a featureless expanse of blue ocean all the way to the horizon, punctuated only by whitecaps on the surface and birds in the air. My first thought is that I'm on a huge ship, but I don't sense any motion.

The outer door hisses open when I approach, revealing a long corridor and similar wooden doors. I step to the first, but can't open it. Panicked, I move back to my own. To my relief, it opens. Must be keyed to me somehow.

What to do? Stay and wait, or make a go for it? The stay-and-wait option is unappealing, but hey, the make-a-go approach hasn't exactly worked lately either.

I march to the metallic door at the end of the corridor and pause anxiously. It parts, revealing a wider hall that runs perpendicular with a different character: that of an office building. No. A hospital. Still not right—something in between.

In contrast to the first wing's carpeted floors and wood-paneled walls and doors, this space is all tile, glass, and concrete, clean and clinical. A series of glass doors lines the walls, and to my surprise, a door on my side of the hall to the far right swings open.

I inhale, unable to move.

Two people in white coats stride out quickly, purposefully, fully engaged in their conversation. They turn right, away from me, toward the end of the hall, but their words still carry in the high-ceilinged space.

"Is there a backup plan if they can't make it work?"

"Not really, besides weathering the attack."

"So that's a no."

They exit through sliding doors at the end of the hall, letting in a warm gust of wind with a salty tang.

I venture closer to the nearest glass door and peer in. The room is empty—a lab, similar to what you might find at a university. High tables with black tops and sinks cover the space. Glass cabinets line the windowless walls.

Two silver tables on casters lie just inside the door, each with a zipped body bag on top.

I push through the swinging glass door into the lab, closing the distance quickly to the body bags. A device that looks like an air pump sits at the foot. I pull the zipper of the first one back. A plume of frigid, foggy air rises. When it clears, I'm staring down at Yul. I stagger back, panting.

God.

I zip the bag shut. I'm pretty sure of what I'll find in the next, but unable to stop myself, I rush to it and pull the zipper down just enough . . . Sabrina. Also motionless. Dead.

Outside the lab, I hear the double doors at the end of the corridor open.

Without taking the time to zip up Sabrina's bag, I run to the other side of the lab and duck, crouching behind the farthest table.

Footsteps echo, drawing close.

In my mind, I can see the fog rising from Sabrina's body bag like smoke from a signal fire, screaming, "Hey, she's in here." Instead, I hear real voices in the corridor.

"The access log says she just exited her room."

"Should have posted someone by the door."

I don't dare look. When I hear them enter the residential wing, I bound up, out of the lab, and down the corridor, pausing only for the doors, which seem to take forever to open.

The area outside is a vast concrete promenade that looks straight down into an endless canyon, a wide river flowing through the center. Why is this so familiar?

I can't tear my eyes away from the drop-off. We must be a thousand feet up. . . .

I *have* seen this place. From another angle, from a sandy beach—in

Titan Hall. This is the Gibraltar Dam, and that means we must be in the mini-city at the center of the dam. One side looks out on the sea, as my room did. This side towers over the valley the Titans created between Europe and Africa.

The doors open behind me.

"Harper! Stop!"

I know that voice. But . . . it's impossible. I turn anyway, not believing my eyes.

It can't be.

CHAPTER TWENTY-NINE

Nick

FOR A MOMENT, THE ONLY SOUND IN THE small room is the low hum of the incinerator to my left. Then the droning cranks louder as the plastic-wrapped body on the conveyor belt reaches the device. The buzzing is a subtle yet vivid reminder that these people are dissecting the passengers of Flight 305 as if they were lab rats and discarding their bodies unceremoniously. My mind rifles through possibilities, plans of action, how Grayson and I can escape this sprawling tent complex at Heathrow.

My clone stands there, his hands up. On the floor, Grayson and the stranger who chased us from the lab wing release each other, both staring from one Nick Stone to the other.

"It's over, Nick," my doppelgänger says.

"What are you?"

"I'm you."

"How?"

"We'll get to that—"

"Let's get to it now." I raise the handgun slightly so he can see it.

He smiles, his expression reflective. "Sorry, I'd almost forgotten what I was like at thirty-six. That was over a hundred and thirty years ago for me."

He's almost 170 years old? He doesn't look a day older than I do.

"You want answers, here and now, right, Nick?" my clone says.

"I'd say we deserve some answers."

"You certainly do." He gestures toward the rows of body bags behind him, through the steel double doors. "But this is a biological hazard zone. We can't talk here."

"What kind of biological hazard?"

"A plague, the likes of which you can't imagine—an extinction-level force we've been fighting for seventy-six years. Unsuccessfully, until six days ago."

"That's why you brought us here? To fight your plague?"

"That's only half the reason we brought you here. You're here to help us cure the plague in our world and ensure it never occurs in yours. We can save both our worlds, Nick, but I need your help. We still have a very powerful enemy standing in our way, and the clock is ticking. I can't tell you how happy I was when I found out that you had come here. That was very smart."

He bends over and picks up his helmet. "I'm going to leave the way you came in. If you want to help us, I'll be in the closest ship outside. You don't need that gun—no one here is going to harm you—but you're more than welcome to keep it if it makes you feel safer." He turns to Grayson. "And there's someone who's very eager to see you: your father."

THERE ISN'T MUCH DEBATE ABOUT what to do. If these . . . people wanted Grayson and me dead, we wouldn't still be alive. We need answers, and medical care, and food. This seems like the only place to start.

Inside the ship, after I've gotten the suit off and some dry clothes on, the future version of myself and I sit down at a small wooden table in a narrow conference room. There are no windows to the outside, but a wide interior window looks out on a sitting area where Oliver Norton Shaw and Grayson sit in navy club chairs, leaning forward, talking, smiling, both crying. The older Shaw looks the same age as he did in the simulations at Titan Hall, mid-sixties.

"Oliver hasn't seen his son in seventy-six years. I can't tell you how happy this makes him. It's been a long time since any of us around here were happy. We've been . . . hanging on."

"For us to arrive?"

"For any hope."

"Let's back up. I want to take it from the top—but first, what should I call you?"

"Nicholas," my future self says. "I haven't gone by Nick for some time. So, from the top. Give me a minute to collect my thoughts. No one talks about the past around here." He grins somberly. "We all lived through it. It's not a pleasant subject."

"I imagine. I saw London."

"London got the best of it. Most places were much worse. But . . . the beginning. The Titan Foundation. In some sense, you're the only person on this planet who truly understands the origins of the foundation, how I felt back then. Lost. Confused. All the things I thought I wanted in life no longer made me happy. In fact, I didn't feel anything, and that scared me the most. More money. Better parties. A growing contact list. Yet every day, life felt a little less interesting, like I was watching it happen to someone else. Every passing day felt emptier than the last. Medication didn't help. My only hope was to make a change. A drastic one. Joining with Oliver, starting the Titan Foundation, was that change. A big, scary goal. I was willing to try anything, just to see if it revealed a clue about what might make me feel alive again."

This is even more jarring than the monologue in Titan Hall. These are my darkest thoughts, the secrets I've kept, the fears about what my life would become if I didn't turn things around. Truths this deep are impossible to fake. This guy knows me. He *is* me. He pauses, letting me process his words, and when I give a slight nod, he continues.

"How far did you get in Titan Hall?"

"To the second chamber. The Gibraltar Dam."

"Okay. So you know about Q-net, Podway, and Orbital Dynamics. The opening of the Gibraltar Dam is when things got . . . more complicated. The press and history books called it our great mistake, the Titan Blunder.

"The dam opened in 2054, on the thirty-ninth anniversary of the Titan Foundation's birth. It was the marvel of the world, a political and technical triumph that would carve out a new nation—Atlantis. We believed it would usher in a new era. Here was a new country, stretching from Israel to the Strait of Gibraltar, from Athens to Alexandria, from Rome to the ruins of ancient Carthage, a nation at the crossroads of Europe, the Middle East, and Africa. A nation that could unite the world. It was our crowning achievement: a microcosm that could demonstrate the potential of human civilization. We wanted it to be the ultimate example of what a peaceful, prosperous society could be, and we wanted to export that way of life north, south, east, and west, across the globe.

"The world rejoiced. The jobs from the building and opening of Atlantis pulled Europe out of a prolonged recession. Atlantis was a new world, a sort of New America at the heart of the Old World, and from around the globe it attracted hardworking, determined immigrants hoping to make a better life for themselves and their families.

"The first orbital ring, Titan Alpha, had been completed five years before, and settlers were arriving there every month, populating the first permanent human colony in space. The Podway was spreading around the world, linking us physically. Q-net was ubiquitous by this point, making free high-speed Internet a reality everywhere. These four initiatives—the Titan Marvels, as they were called—were little more than ideas when I brought them to Oliver at our first meeting.

"There were one hundred Titans when Atlantis opened in 2054. In thirty-nine years, that small group had radically transformed the world. And there was one last marvel, a secret project we thought would have more impact than any other.

"The last marvel is one Oliver was already working on when we met. Did Sabrina tell you about her research?"

"Only that it was related to progeria syndrome."

"Exactly. Sabrina had one sibling, a younger brother. He died of progeria when she was in her teens. She dedicated her life to finding a cure. Oliver had been funding her research for several years when we first met in 2015, though he had little interest in progeria. His deal with Sabrina was simple: he agreed to fund her research until she found a cure, provided she would then turn her attention to a project he was keenly interested in."

I think I see where this is going, but can't quite believe it yet.

"People who've had a lifetime of success think differently from other people. They assume they'll succeed. They plan for their success. This was certainly the case with Oliver Norton Shaw."

I can't help but glance out the conference room window at Shaw, who would have been in his sixties in 2015, and is almost two hundred years old today.

My suspicion grows.

"At our second meeting Shaw posed a simple question: What if we're successful? What if Q-net, Podway, the orbital colonies, and Atlantis become a reality? What then? How can we ensure that the march of innovation continues? The inevitable answer was: establish the right culture and recruit the right people at the Titan Foundation. But that's risky. Cultures can change. You can't count on great minds in every generation. One lost generation might destroy everything we were building.

"But what if the world's best and brightest never died? What if the one hundred Titans lived forever? Imagine a world in which Aristotle, Newton, Einstein, Shakespeare, Jefferson, and Washington had never died—imagine what their innovation and continued leadership could have done for humanity. Shaw envisioned such a world, a new Renaissance with no end.

"Sabrina found the cure for progeria in 2021. She completed her anti-aging therapy in 2044. Shaw, who was in his early nineties then, eagerly volunteered to be the test patient for her therapy. It worked, and we administered it to all the Titans in the following years. Shortly before the opening of Atlantis each of us underwent surgery, returning to our physical state at the moment we became Titans. We did so more for the shock value at the unveiling than for our own vanity, though there was some of that.

"At the opening of the Gibraltar Dam and Atlantis we all walked onstage, revealing our fifth and final marvel: Titanship itself. It was our vision for redefining the core of human existence. Our proposition was simple: Dedicate your life to making the world a better place, and if you reach high enough, if you work hard enough, if you inspire one of the one hundred Titans to give up their place, you will become a Titan yourself, immortal, frozen in time from the day you earn that status. We envisioned it as a meritocracy of the world's best and brightest. *Dream big, work hard, live forever*—that's the promise we held out to the world that day. Never again would humanity's greatest works be left unfinished. Never again would our mortal limits claim a mind before its time.

"In the years after 2054, if you asked any child, anywhere in the world, what she wanted to be when she grew up, she wouldn't say an astronaut or president. She'd say, 'A Titan.'"

If I weren't staring at the proof, I probably wouldn't believe it. Incredible. They actually did it—immortality. They transcended *death*. I shake my head. "I don't understand. You said this was your blunder?"

"Our blunder wasn't the innovation, the immortality therapy itself.

"Our blunder was not accounting for human nature."

"Human nature?"

"We didn't know it at the time, but we had set ourselves on a collision course, started the countdown to a war that would destroy our world.

"The first few Titans inducted in the years after 2054 were mostly scientists and researchers, replacements of a sort. Most of the original hundred Titans had been innovators in their fields, people like Sabrina and Yul. They chose younger versions of themselves, people who could make further advances in their field, carry the torch with new energy."

"The original Titans allowed themselves to be replaced? Gave up immortality?"

"Not at first. But as the years passed and they watched their friends and family die one by one, they changed, became withdrawn. They focused on their work, but they found that there, too, their energy and passion had run its natural course. The ideas they thought might await them in eternity weren't there, just a new kind of loneliness they never knew existed. Many began to see immortality as only a tool—a way to prolong a life unfinished. It turns out change—fresh blood—will always be required for progress, and they sought out the best and brightest to carry on.

"Conferring Titanship required a majority vote of the Titans, with the nominating Titan abstaining—fifty votes out of ninety-nine. For almost two decades the elections were uneventful, the politicking and negotiations done in private.

"In 2071, however, we faced a crisis, and Oliver was at the center of it. By this time Grayson Shaw was eighty-eight, and in extremely poor health. He'd already had two liver transplants, and the doctors said his days were numbered. Grayson was Oliver's one true regret, and Oliver had begun to talk about him more and more, to lament not what he had done in life, but what he'd left undone. Giving Grayson one more shot at life became Oliver's obsession. He nominated him for Titanship, but behind closed doors, it became clear early on that the vote was doomed. Oliver called in favors, demanded this one last act as payment for all he had done. He and I cajoled, threatened, and bribed, but the Titans wouldn't budge. They saw making Grayson Shaw a Titan as the ultimate mistake, an error that would forever poison the well. They had been sold on the idea of a meritocracy. They believed that choosing only the worthy was the sole way the world would accept Titan immortality. The Titans were probably right, yet Oliver persisted, as he always did. Persistence had been the secret to our success, and we weren't about to give up without a fight. We had remade the world, after all, so getting fifty people to agree to something seemed easy." He shakes his head and looks away. "We were very wrong."

"About?"

"Human nature, once again. People will fight to the death to save their own lives, but they'll wage war to preserve their way of life for future generations. To our fellow Titans, it wasn't a single Titanship at stake, it was the Titan way of life, their vision for the future. Grayson's election endangered their entire belief system."

"And it didn't yours?"

"Very much so—but I also saw it as an opportunity, and was willing to lend my weight. I'd met someone, you see, someone very near death. Like Oliver, I was terrified, utterly unwilling to face life without her. I had made my own proposal to save her, but it was defeated as well. Oliver and I were desperate to save our loved ones, and we made a fateful decision: to steal the immortality therapy. It was the most heavily guarded technology in the world, but we had access—in fact, we were probably the only people in the world who could pull it off. We succeeded, but again we failed to account for one thing."

"Human nature."

"Exactly. The downside of employing thieves is—"

"They steal."

"Precisely. The loot in this case was the most valuable object in the history of the world. The thieves we'd hired never showed up at the meeting point, and a week later, nations around the world announced that they had developed their own immortality therapy. Chaos ensued. Nations had long seen the Titan Foundation as the greatest threat to their continued existence. When Atlantis opened, they thought it would eventually become the first global nation-state, reducing all other governments to local authorities. They were probably right. They saw all the Titan Marvels, including Q-Net, Podway, and especially immortality, as eroding their ability to maintain power over their populations. And now they held out immortality to their citizenry, with different nations defining varying criteria for eligibility. Where they expected a new wave of nationalism and loyalty, anarchy erupted. Some populations begged for immortality to be made widely available; others demanded that it be permanently banned. Everyone blamed the Titans for the upheaval. Millions died in the unrest, including the great love of my life. Grayson Shaw died of complications of liver failure three weeks after the chaos began. The Titans convened, and we searched for an answer. We announced to the world that we would provide a solution, asked them to believe and have faith, promised that help was on the way. To some extent, we did feel responsible. But we couldn't have predicted what happened next: a pandemic."

"Pandemic? How?"

"A mutation. The immortality therapy Sabrina created changed somehow. The therapy uses a retrovirus to alter the genes that control aging. That retrovirus mutated in the wild, or maybe someone altered it, by accident or on purpose. We figure private labs and government facilities were doing a lot of work on the virus in the weeks after it was stolen. This mutated retrovirus was deadly. Instead of turning off the genes that control aging, it sent them into overdrive, causing a cascade of rapid aging. It was almost like the victims had a severe case of progeria, with adult onset. Those infected died quickly, some within hours, some in days, in a few weeks in rare cases.

"The casualty reports started coming in the day after our big announcement of a solution. It was a trickle at first, nothing that even made major news outlets. A couple of people died in Europe, four in America, half a dozen in Japan. Then it exploded around the world. People were dying in droves, all after aging rapidly.

"Sabrina was terrified. We all were. She worked day and night, pushing herself to the brink. Ten days after the first cases, half the entire human population was dead."

"How could it spread so quickly?"

"That was the question. What we discovered far too late was that the retrovirus could exist benignly in virtually any animal host. Every animal on earth is a host for countless viruses. Viruses exist to replicate, to spread their DNA, so they actually don't want to harm their host; they want to exist undetected, replicating. And that's exactly what this virus did. It was everywhere. Birds, fish, land animals, they were all carriers, and none of them were harmed . . . except for humans. We were the only host in which the virus caused death, but it didn't harm humans at first. It lay dormant for days, then struck at once, quickly, killing without warning. I remember the horror on the day we learned that the entire human population was already infected, that there was no chance of containment or stopping the outbreak."

My mind flashes back to the bodies I saw in the tents outside. The faces. Now I understand why I didn't recognize them. I'd seen those people before, at the crash site, but they looked much younger then. It's like they had aged decades during my trip to Stonehenge and back.

"The passengers from my flight, they're infected, too."

"Yes. The virus is airborne. You were all exposed the second you crash-landed."

"The virus still exists? Seventy-six years after the outbreak?"

"Eradicating it is impossible. It's everywhere. We'd have to treat every animal on Earth. That's impossible."

I turn the revelation over in my head, trying to understand the implications. And I wonder, what will happen to me? Will I suffer the same fate as the bodies out there? My doppelgänger continues on before I get a chance to ask.

"The virus, however, was about to become the least of our problems. Everyone thought the outbreak was the Titans' solution: killing the population. Governments launched their dying armies against us, hoping we would capitulate and turn over a cure. We were immune to the condition, presumably because we had been given the pure form of the therapy, and that sealed the case against us. They killed sixty-two of us in the Titan War. We went into hiding, but we didn't have to hide long. Forty days after the first cases, every person on the face of the planet—except for the remaining thirty-eight Titans—was dead."

The graffiti in London, at Titan Hall—it all makes sense now. Every person on the planet dead? The magnitude of the revelation is overwhelming. In the cramped conference room, I sit stunned.

My words come out a whisper. "What do you want from us?"

"Your help. For the last seventy-six years, I and the remaining Titans have dedicated every waking hour to bringing your plane here. You and the rest of the passengers of Flight 305 are humanity's only chance for survival."

CHAPTER THIRTY

Nick

NO PRESSURE. JUST THE HUMAN RACE'S ONLY CHANCE at survival. For the last six days, I've had my hands full just trying to keep a hundred people alive, and it looks like I've failed at that. I ask Nicholas the obvious question: "What does that mean?"

"As I said, the retrovirus that triggers rapid aging is ubiquitous on the planet. We have no hope of eradicating it, but there is a solution: a vaccine."

"You have a vaccine?"

"Sabrina, for all her faults, is sublimely intelligent. Within a year of the outbreak she had created a vaccine she thought was viable, though all she had to go on were computer models."

It doesn't make sense. The Titans are immune to the virus, and everyone is dead. What good is a vaccine? The answer seems just out of reach, but Nicholas speaks before I can, as if he's reading my mind.

"A vaccine is our only chance of survival. We can't eliminate the virus from the environment—we can only vaccinate the remaining humans who haven't been exposed."

"Wait—I thought you said everyone on the planet except for the Titans died."

"Everyone *on the planet* did die."

The genius of the plan hits me like a gust of cold air. "The orbital colony."

"Exactly. For the last seventy-six years the five thousand inhabitants of Titan Alpha have been waiting for the day when they can return home and reclaim Earth. The children up there right now are the second generation who've been born looking not up at the stars but down at the ground, at a land they've never set foot on, a new frontier they've been told will someday be their home, as it was their ancestors'."

"Incredible."

"Those five thousand colonists are humanity's last chance to repopulate the planet."

I shake my head, trying to put it together. "Then I don't understand why we're here. You have them. You have a vaccine."

"A vaccine we weren't one hundred percent sure would work. Imagine the colonists' position. They have three life rafts—three vessels on which to send people down. But who do you choose? We felt the vaccine would be effective, but we weren't certain. They asked us what our backup plan was, if the vaccine didn't work for the people sent down on the first two rafts. What if we had only one raft left? What then?"

"You couldn't risk it at that point."

"That's right. We'd have to get more trial subjects somehow."

"Interesting." *Trial subjects.* I turn the words over in my mind, afraid of what he'll say next.

"The question became, if the worst happened, how could we get human test subjects who hadn't been exposed to the Titan Virus? As I said, Sabrina survived the Titan War, and so did Yul. Their two minds were the keys to our plan, in our time and yours. Yul devised a solution that we all thought was crazy. To us the exercise was academic, an effort to show the colonists we'd exhausted all alternatives, rational and irrational."

"Q-net."

"He told you?"

"Only that he had received messages claiming to be from the future."

"It took our Yul three years to create a modified version of the Q-net that could communicate with the past. When it worked, we were all shocked. The first moment he could possibly contact was 2015, just before your flight, when the first Q-net prototype became operational. In the course of our Yul's research, he had determined that altering the quantum states of the particles in the past would actually create a copy of our universe. He theorized that after the moment of contact, there would be two timelines: yours, in which the future after 2015 is uncertain, and ours, where everything's already happened up to 2147, where we are right now. That created a moral dilemma for us, which I'll get to in a minute. The next part of Yul's plan was a quantum experiment on a much larger scale. Yul thought that with enough power, he could dilate the existing link between our universes, making it big enough for something to pass through."

"Big enough for, say, a 777."

"Exactly that size. In fact, that was about all we could manage with the electricity generated from the Gibraltar Dam. But it's all we needed. Yul believed he could build the endpoints for this quantum bridge within a few years, but it proved to be far more complicated than the Q-net alterations. It took him sixty-seven years. When we were ready, Yul sent the schematic for the device back to himself in 2015. He also sent directions for *your* Yul to pass to Sabrina."

I see it now, the last piece, the answer to why some of the passengers died of old age, and others didn't. "The vaccine."

"Correct. We knew who would be on Flight 305, and we told the Sabrina in 2015 that she needed to carry out a series of experiments outside the lab, making sure that the vaccine reached the passengers well before they boarded the flight. We assured her it was related to her progeria research, and it probably looked that way to her. There were two groups: control and experimental."

This seems like as good a time as any to ask whether I'm doomed to die of a plague in which I age rapidly and perish in days. "Am I . . . which group—"

"Relax. You were in the experimental group. You received the vaccine before takeoff," my clone says casually, as if I'm worrying about a nagging cold.

"How exactly—"

"Did we administer it? You really want to know?"

"Actually, no." That would probably just freak me out.

"After the experimental group was vaccinated, the last piece was for Yul and Sabrina to board the plane with Yul's device. That brings you up to the point right before things went very wrong during the flight."

"Very wrong, as in a plane crash."

"That was unintended, and extremely unfortunate. It was however, only a consequence of a larger problem. As I mentioned, the Titans had a moral dilemma. In creating your separate timeline, we had created a world destined to repeat our mistake, in which every person on Earth, save for our thirty-eight, would perish.

"Oliver and I still felt responsible for the fall of our world, and we couldn't bear to see your world suffer the consequences of another of our well-intentioned experiments. We arrived at a very simple solution. Your plane would land at Heathrow, where we'd evaluate the passengers. If the vaccine worked, roughly half, a hundred and twenty or so in the experimental group, would live. That would tell us if we had a viable vaccine. We confirmed that our vaccine works from survivor autopsies yesterday. For Oliver and me, the next step was clear: do nothing."

"Nothing?"

"Our plan was simple: let your plane and the survivors remain here in 2147. In your world, in 2015, Flight 305 would simply vanish over the Atlantic, never to be found. And that disappearance would save the lives of over nine billion people roughly fifty-six years later."

It never occurred to me. "Because of who was on the plane. Sabrina, Yul, and me."

"And Grayson. We had an incredible opportunity: a flight where the key people involved in the Titan Foundation and in our great mistake could be taken out of your timeline, ensuring the catastrophe never happened. To us, the loss of two hundred and thirty-four lives from your world for the safety of billions was a simple choice. There was only one problem: Yul and Sabrina."

"I don't follow."

"They wouldn't hear of allowing the passengers of Flight 305 to stay. They argued that removing those two hundred and thirty-four passengers from your timeline could have unintended consequences, create a far worse catastrophe that might strike the next year, or in ten years. Philosophically, they believe that changing another universe is a dangerous game. If the quantum bridge between our worlds remained open, someone from your universe might eventually find it and make their way here when they needed something from us, which could be perilous. They advocated noninterference, reasoning that if interfering with another universe was a viable survival tactic, we would have already been visited many, many times."

"Fascinating. You compromised, then?"

"You've had some experience with Yul and Sabrina by now?"

"A bit."

"Then you know that compromise isn't their style. Oliver and I had no choice. Yul and Sabrina controlled the science, which was the key to the plan. Our only option was to sit and wait. Yul designed the quantum bridge so that it could be reset, removing all traces of Flight 305 from our timeline and restoring it to yours. In 2015 it would be as though our experiment never happened, as if your plane had stayed on course and landed at Heathrow as planned. He intended to reset the bridge right after we had verified the vaccine's efficacy here in 2147.

"Oliver and I couldn't allow that to happen. Shortly after Flight 305 crossed the bridge into our time, we struck. We made our move here at Heathrow, attempting to take control of the quantum device on our end. The Titans were split. About twenty were loyal to us, and believed in trying to save both worlds. Yul and Sabrina's group made up the other eighteen. Yul tried to reset the quantum bridge when he found out we were trying to take control."

"That caused the turbulence, the crash."

"Yes. After that, we had no idea where your plane was, or if it had even survived at all. We thought maybe it had broken up in midair or crashed in the Atlantic or possibly on land. But that wasn't our biggest challenge at that point. We were fighting for our lives."

"That's what this has been about: the airships, the battles. It's a Titan civil war."

"Yes. In the battle here at Heathrow, half of the remaining Titans perished, including our Yul and Sabrina. The surviving members of their faction began frantically searching for your plane. It's their only play."

"I don't follow."

"Both factions have been doing their best to find and recover the passengers—to determine whether the vaccine is viable so we can bring the colonists home. But their faction has been looking for two passengers in particular: Yul and Sabrina."

"Why?" I ask.

"Yul truly is brilliant. And somewhat untrusting, as perhaps you've seen."

"I have."

"He designed the quantum bridge so that only he could operate it, hoping to ensure his survival. The other faction escaped with the device, which was very unfortunate. They've taken it back to Titan City, at the center of the Gibraltar Dam. Their plan was to capture the Yul from your timeline, so he can operate the device, resetting the quantum bridge. And they need Sabrina for a futile experiment."

"Yul and Sabrina were with us, outside Titan Hall, at the battle."

"Yes. The others took them. Along with a woman."

My mind flashes to the scene in the burning green park, to Harper falling after the shot. "Harper Lane."

"Yes. The biographer. So this is it, Nick. Right now Yul is in Titan City, working on the quantum bridge, trying to figure out his future self's notes—seventy years of research, crammed into a few days. If he's successful, and the bridge is reset, you and everyone from Flight 305 will disappear from this world and return to your timeline with no memory of the crash, as if none of this ever happened. In the coming days you'll establish the Titan Foundation with Oliver Norton Shaw, and in fifty-six years you'll watch the entire rest of the planet die. That's what the other faction wants. That's what the Yul and

Sabrina of my time wanted to do. And I believe their younger selves will agree to finish their work."

Nicholas stands and moves away from me, giving me space. This is what he's been working up to.

"Here's the decision you have to make, Nick. If we capture the device and stop Yul from resetting the quantum bridge, you'll be trapped here in 2147. You and the other passengers of Flight 305 will never go home. But the people you left, everyone in 2015, they'll have a chance of surviving." He holds my eyes. "What's your call, Nick? Are you in?"

"If I say no?"

Nicholas shakes his head. "Then you walk out of here unharmed."

What a call to make. My decision will determine the fate of my world and his. Nicholas needs me. He can't take Titan City alone, and perhaps a few of the other passengers will follow me. The whole thing turns on what I say next.

Faces flash through my mind, the people I might never see again in 2015: my sixty-one-year-old mother, smiling up at me in her light-filled sewing room; my sister, holding her firstborn child, a daughter named Naomi; my three college roommates, drinking and laughing in the ski lodge we rent every year in Park City. I'll never see any of them again. They'll attend my funeral and move on with their lives. But their children will have a chance to grow up, and so will their children's children. Then I see other faces: the passengers of Flight 305 I've come to know in the past week. But there's really only one face for me in this group, one person I can't get out of my mind.

I wonder, if we're successful—if we can stop Yul from sending us back to 2015—what my life will be like here in 2147, in this desolate world, alone. Or maybe not alone. Either way, I'll be starting over. In some sense, that's what I wanted to do before Flight 305 took off six days ago, to try something new. Maybe this is fate, a blessing some-how. Maybe, through this bizarre set of circumstances, I've wound up in exactly the right place at exactly the right time. Even if the right time is 2147.

Nicholas waits by the long window, glancing from me to Oli-ver and Grayson Shaw, no doubt having a similar conversation on the other side of the window. Despite the enormity of the stakes, he seems completely calm.

"I think you already know what I'm going to say, don't you?"

"I do," he says. "I know what I would say. That's why I was so glad when you showed up. There are only twelve of us left, Nick, and we could really use your help. We're about to make an assault on the most advanced, secure structure on Earth. The Titans built the Gibraltar Dam to last an eternity and the city at its center to endure just as long. Bringing it down is our last chance to save both our worlds."

CHAPTER THIRTY-ONE

Harper

IT'S IMPOSSIBLE. SHE'S DEAD. I SAW HER LIFELESS body in the lab not two minutes ago—unmoving, frozen in a body bag. Yet here Sabrina stands, living and breathing.

She inches toward me, and I instinctively take another step back, toward the edge of the platform at the top of the Gibraltar Dam. I glance over, down the thousand-foot drop-off to the rocky basin where the Mediterranean Sea used to be. For a moment the only sound is the waterfall crashing into a pool far below. The five towers—fingers—rise above me; Africa, what was Morocco, spreads out to my left, and Europe, what was once Spain and the territory of Gibraltar, lies to my right. Two battered, burned airships sit on the platform at the base of the buildings. I briefly consider running, but both sides are miles away. I'm trapped.

More people pour out of the building, but I focus only on the two I know, or at least recognize: Sabrina and Yul.

I squint, searching their faces, but I can't find a single difference between them and the bodies I saw in the lab. How?

"It's me, Harper," Sabrina says, taking a step closer.

I edge back. "I saw your body."

"That wasn't me. I'm the person you met on the plane, after the crash."

I shake my head. A cool gust of wind blows my hair across part of my face. I'm six feet from the precipice.

Sabrina steps forward. "You injured your leg during the rescue at the lake, when you and Nick and the others saved all those people. Your leg got infected. It was bad. Nick insisted I give you antibiotics. He was very angry with me when I didn't. You helped me, agreed with me that we should conserve the antibiotics, use them to save more lives. It's me, Harper."

I don't know if it's the fact that I saw the other body with my own two eyes or simply all the surreal stuff I've been through in the last few days, but I just can't believe her. Paranoia is getting the best of me. Maybe they interrogated Sabrina before killing her and cloning her. I'll issue a test. "After the crash, I became suspicious of you and Yul. Why?"

Sabrina answers without hesitation. "You heard us talking in the cockpit, arguing about what might have caused the crash and whether we were involved in it. We didn't explain that conversation until Titan Hall, right before the battle began"—Sabrina motions to the people around her—"right before these Titans rescued us."

Rescued.

"Step away from the ledge, Harper. We'll explain everything."

MY HEAD IS GOING TO explode. For the past hour Sabrina has conducted a one-on-one history lesson and Q&A session with me about what in the world has been going on.

Quite a lot, it turns out. And to top it off, there are two worlds—the one we left in 2015 and this one, where we crashed six days ago. It seems I'm involved in a conspiracy that spans space and time and a conflict whose outcome will determine humanity's fate in two separate universes.

I'm never flying again.

And I'm not exactly thrilled about being used as a lab rat for a vaccine either.

"That's where the issue arose," Sabrina says, sitting on a stool before a raised lab table.

"Issue?" I ask.

"The plane crash."

A plane breaking in half and crashing in the English countryside might constitute more than an *issue* in my book, but I let that one go.

Sabrina continues her history lesson as I perch on the stool across from her in the empty lab like a bad pupil at detention.

"But the plane crash wasn't due to a technical fault," she says. "Yul's devices—the one built in the past and the one here in the future—performed as they should have. It was the Titans—some of them, that is—who caused our plane to crash."

Now that surprises me.

"Shortly after our plane crossed into this universe, a civil war between the Titans broke out at Heathrow, and they've been fighting ever since. The battle at the crash site and Titan Hall are just the two we've seen."

"War over what?"

"Over *whom*. To put it simply, they've been fighting over us, the passengers of Flight 305, two in particular. After Yul proved he could connect to Q-net in the past, the Titans debated what to do with the passengers once Flight 305 arrived. Oliver and Nicholas—"

"Nick?"

"I'm told that the Titan in 2147 goes by Nicholas."

"Oh."

"Oliver and Nicholas wanted to keep the passengers of Flight 305 here. They thought that extracting Nick, Yul, and me from our world would prevent the Titan Foundation from achieving its goals, in particular derailing the immortality cure and thus preventing the subsequent plague.

"The other faction, led by Yul and Sabrina in 2147, wanted to reset the quantum bridge between the universes after the passengers were evaluated and the vaccine was verified. They believed that the Titans had no right to take two hundred lives from the other universe, half of whom wouldn't survive exposure to the virus. This universe's Yul and Sabrina favored nonintervention, but the Titans felt they had a moral obligation to prevent the pandemic in our universe. They wouldn't approve any plan that didn't include saving our world. Yul arrived at another, even more incredible solution: a reset for the quantum bridge."

"Reset?"

"When activated, the reset would close the quantum bridge, sending Flight 305 and all its passengers back to 2015 with no knowledge of what transpired here.

"But it didn't matter, because the other faction never really cared about any of this. Not the vaccine, not the passengers, not the disruption of time. It was all a cover for their true goal: ensuring that the passengers of Flight 305 remained in this universe forever."

"What? Why?"

"Love. Oliver and Nicholas chose Flight 305 because it carried two people they loved very much, at crucial points in their lives."

"Grayson."

"Yes. Oliver wanted to fulfill his last desire: to give Grayson a second chance at life. Flight 305 was perfect—it took off at a turning point for Grayson, right before he would throw his life away."

"And for Nicholas?"

"Love of a different sort. Flight 305 was his only chance to see the love of his life again, a woman who died in the aftermath of the outbreak. For seventy-six years he'd dreamed of the day he could bring her here, start over with her, the woman he could never be with in his time, not as long as he was an immortal Titan and she wasn't. For Nicholas, the object of bringing Flight 305 here was you."

CHAPTER THIRTY-TWO

Harper

FOR A MOMENT, SABRINA'S VOICE ECHOES IN THE empty lab, her words hanging in the air, waiting for me to respond. But my mind is blank. I can't wrap my head around it. Nicholas, the future version of the Nick Stone I've come to know, crashed Flight 305 to bring *me* here.

"*Me?*"

Sabrina gives a curt nod. "In the years after the creation of the Titan Foundation, you and Nicholas worked very closely together. You became close friends, then much more. In 2071 he stole the immortality therapy to save your life."

The passages from my journal . . . My forbidden love. It was him. Nick. No. Nicholas. God, it's so confusing. I turn the facts over in my mind, trying to make sense of them. He stole the therapy for *me*, my future self, to make me a Titan so that we could spend eternity together. It's bizarre and dramatic, but at the same time . . . it's so very romantic. I'm not used to that.

"Nicholas's plan was simple. After you received the therapy, you and he would undergo surgery to alter your appearance, then depart as settlers on a new orbital colony sponsored by the Titans. Oliver and Grayson would join you."

I can only sit, in a daze. My mind is completely blown at this point.

Sabrina drones on, oblivious to my catatonic state. "When you and Grayson died after they stole the therapy in 2071, Nicholas and Oliver were devastated. Since that day, they've devoted their lives to recovering the two of you, to starting over. They manipulated the Titans, steered Yul and Sabrina here in the future, and us in the past. They tricked and connived, all to get you and Grayson here. Nicholas will go to any length to be with you. He's killed for you, and he's planning to kill again."

It's hard to imagine the Nick I know taking a life, but I have to remind myself that this is another person, separated by over 130 years' time, someone who has changed a great deal, no matter what he may look like.

Sabrina pauses, reading my expression. "After our plane crossed into this time, Nicholas and Oliver launched their attack at Heathrow. Their first targets were Yul and Sabrina, the keys to resetting the quantum bridge and returning the passengers of Flight 305 to 2015. During the fighting Yul tried to reset the bridge, but he was unsuccessful—he only sent a series of disturbances along the link."

"Which crashed our plane."

"Yes. Nicholas killed Yul and Sabrina before the bridge could be reset."

"Those are the bodies I saw in the lab next door?"

"Correct. About half of all the Titans were killed at Heathrow. Ten remain loyal to Oliver and Nicholas. There are twelve here. Since the crash, they've all been looking for the three of us, but it was . . . my future self's faction that found us."

"Why?"

"They want Yul and me to complete our counterparts' work, to reset the bridge and return Flight 305 and its passengers to 2015."

"Is that possible?"

"We're not sure. We've been working on it. And another project, the original plan to save the world we came from."

Sabrina's usually stoic mask fades a bit. That makes me nervous.

"We believe, however, that we may be almost out of time. A few hours ago one of our surveillance drones spotted Nick—the Nick you and I know—and Grayson entering the Titan camp at Heathrow. We believe they were searching for the three of us. Motivations aside, Nick and Grayson are with Oliver and Nicholas right now, who are no doubt feeding them misinformation, enlisting their help in a final assault."

Don't like the sounds of that. "Final assault?"

"They're coming here, to Titan City. Their goal, as I said, is to destroy the quantum device, ensuring that the bridge can never be reset. Only one thing has kept them from destroying the city and the quantum device with it."

I raise my eyebrows.

"You, Harper. You're Nicholas's one true desire; he would never risk killing you. So long as you're here, Nicholas and Oliver can't make a direct strike on the city. They'll have to come in to extract you."

"So, I'm . . . bait?"

"Leverage."

Now we're playing word games with my life.

"You're the only thing that's prevented everyone here from being killed already. I've told you all of this because I believe you might determine all of our fates. When the time comes, when Nicholas, Oliver, Nick, Grayson, and their Titans invade the city, you'll have a decision to make."

Oh, God, anything else. I put my face in my hands. I'd like a stiff drink about now.

"Harper, are you listening to me?"

"Do I have a choice?"

"No, you don't. In a few short hours, you'll have to decide whether the passengers of Flight 305 return to our time or stay here in 2147."

Blimey.

CHAPTER THIRTY-THREE

Harper

I THINK SABRINA IS AS PAINED BY OUR hour-long discussion as I am. We keep going back over the same things, debating, running through scenarios and what-ifs, but in the end it's all quite simple:

Once Nicholas has me, this whole place will go up. Game over. And the passengers of Flight 305 will never have any chance of returning home. Those hundred and twenty-one souls who didn't get the vaccine, who either died in the crash or the outbreak after, will be dead forever, and the rest of us will be trapped here. It will be as if Flight 305 disappeared over the Atlantic. The world will assume it crashed, all passengers and crew lost.

We'll never see our families again. They'll bury us. Mourn. Move on (hopefully). But they might also avoid the pandemic that claimed every life on Earth in this time, save for the Titans who now wage a civil war over the fate of Flight 305.

And then there's the other side, the possibility that Yul and Sabrina will succeed and we'll all return to Flight 305, unaware that anything ever happened. I will have never met the Nick Stone I came to . . . know (I want to use another word, but I won't let myself; it will only make my dilemma worse). Must keep emotion out. Must make a rational decision. So easy to say . . . but the Nicholas from this world and my future self, they . . . Okay, last time I'm thinking about that.

"What's your decision, Harper?" Sabrina presses.

They're anxious to know what I'll do when Nicholas and friends arrive. I wonder if they'll jail me if I say the wrong thing.

"I don't know."

"Unacceptable."

I let my face fall into my hands and mumble while I massage my eyelids. "I don't know, Sabrina, okay? It's a lot to take in. I just need . . . some time, all right?"

"We don't have time."

I just stare at her.

"Very well. Perhaps some rest will give you the perspective you need."

She walks to a cabinet and retrieves two notebooks I recognize well. "I believe these are yours."

The tranquilizing burr is still stuck through my journal, and the Alice Carter notebook is as I remember it.

"Thanks," I mumble. I glance around the lab, unsure where to go. "Can I . . ."

"You're free to go anywhere you wish, Harper. This isn't a prison."

Sabrina runs down the layout of Titan City, which contains five towers, each dedicated to one of the original five Titan Marvels and shaped like human fingers, together forming a hand reaching out of the massive dam toward the sky, the ocean to its backside, its palm facing the new land the Titans created, waving.

I'll give it to them for originality.

Our current tower (finger?), which houses the labs, lies in the middle, rising slightly above the two on each side, to symbolize the central role of science and research. Facing the Atlantic, the tower to its right is a hotel; the ring finger represents the Titan union with humanity and visitors. The shorter, narrower tower closest to Gibraltar holds the Titan apartments. On the left side of the lab tower, the pointer finger holds an office complex, and the thumb, which points toward Africa, is dedicated to support staff and storage.

I leave the lab tower through the double doors and walk awhile along the promenade that overlooks the waterfall, down the dam into the shadow of the five fingers, which I had been too close to make out before. There I stand for a long time, staring at the ribbons of sunlight that slip through the fingers. From here I can see the Atlantic all the way to the horizon to my left and the deep, jagged canyon the dam created to my right. The charred airships sit placidly at the base of the hand of Titan City, awaiting their final battle. My hair blows around again, strands lashing my mouth and eyes.

In the sky just left of the last finger, I notice a streak like a red-hot poker, driving down through the clouds. It wasn't there before. What could it be? A meteor? A comet?

BACK INSIDE, I EXPECT TO find Sabrina in the lab where she and I spoke at length, but it's empty. She and Yul must be inside the lab tower somewhere.

On the second floor I hear a voice—Sabrina's—talking at length, with no give and take. Not surprising. I approach the door, but something makes me wait. The tone . . . it's different somehow. It's Sabrina, yet not as robotic.

"Okay, I'm telling you this . . . well, just in case."

Sabrina pauses.

"I want to walk you through my notes on the therapy, but first, there's some personal things I want to say, that could . . . help you if you manage to make it back with these memories."

It's Sabrina—future Sabrina—talking with herself.

"The first is to stop seeing your social limitations as an excuse not to socialize. For most of my life I saw my social inability as a reason not to build personal relationships. I felt I was incapable and that it was therefore useless to try. I was wrong. Every mind has limits. Some have a relative disadvantage in language production, short-term memory, math, or spatial ordering. Your mind has a significant limitation in social awareness and interaction. You have some capacity, and it will only erode with lack of use. You must see your mind differently. If math is a weakness, you must do math to get better. In the same way, you must socialize and try to form bonds with people to get better at it. It will be awkward. You will believe it's a waste of time, but it isn't. Your range is limited, but it exists—I know for a fact. I've had a hundred and sixty-seven years to prove it. When you get back, you must commit yourself to making an effort, and when you fail, ask yourself what you can learn. I kept a journal and reviewed my findings regularly, drawing correlations from my experiences. Your social shortcomings are like anything else: you must practice to get better. You must try, fail, learn, and try again to ever improve.

"There's one other thing. Steven, in your lab, has a huge crush on you, but he's far too intimidated by you to ask you out. In three years he'll marry another tech in your lab. They will never be happy, and she will leave him in another five years. He'll never be the same after that. Ask him if he wants to have coffee after work, and tell him there's only one rule: you can't talk about work. See where things go from there.

"Now. On to my notes. For years I made very little progress. The breakthrough was realizing that a person dies with the same neurons they are born with. Neurons don't age like other cells. They don't divide or die off and are rarely replaced by new ones. You are born with and die with the same roughly one hundred billion neurons. However, over the course of your life, the electrical impulses those neurons store changes. The electrical changes are your memories. Like the nodes in Q-net, the neurons in your brain are made of the same particles in both worlds. The only difference between here and there is the placement of electrons. . . ."

I inch around the glass door to the lab, just far enough to peer in. Sabrina sits on a stool with her back to me, hunched over a lab table, her black hair unmoving. There's another Sabrina staring out at me, her eyes not quite as lifeless as the ones I've come to know. She's still talking. It's a recording, playing back on a giant screen on the far wall of the lab. The future Sabrina made a video, a just-in-case encapsulation of her notes. These people think of everything.

Instinctively I back away. The technical talk is beyond me, but I'm sure of one thing: whatever future Sabrina is telling her past self, it can't possibly have to do with the vaccine—that's already been solved.

So it's a new experiment—something Sabrina didn't tell me about. I'm lost in thought as I turn the corner. The next corridor is the same as the last: glass doors set in marble walls. In the echoing space, I hear another voice. Yul. As before, I draw close enough to the door to hear him. It's another recording, but it may as well be in Chinese; I can barely understand a word. It's all mathematical theories and variables and stuff I can't even wager a guess about.

Then it loops, starting from the top. Yul must be working while listening to the recording in the background.

"Okay. Sabrina wants me to make this video as a backup, a guide to my work in case . . . the worst happens. And I agree there's a chance of that, but the truth is this: there's little chance you're ever going to complete my work—"

Someone shouts offstage—Sabrina, I think—and the video cuts out. It resumes a second later.

"I guess this is take two. I'm supposed to provide personal guidance to you, anything that could help you live a better life, assuming you make it back to 2015 with your memories, which, again, is doubtful—"

Another shout, and the camera cuts out again. The voice resumes after a few seconds.

"Anyway, on to the task at hand. The first thing you should know is that your understanding of quantum physics is incomplete. Woefully. In a few years—your time—an experiment at CERN will change the way you see the quantum world. Space-time isn't what you think it is. It's far stranger. Your current understanding is simplistic and limits your thinking. The discovery at CERN will be the breakthrough that makes everything in the next hundred and thirty years possible. So I'm faced with the impossible task of condensing over a century of breakthroughs in particle physics down into a two-hour video course. Even though I'm teaching a younger version of myself, I still believe it's impossible, that it will take you years to even grasp the concepts my work is based upon, much less achieve the level of understanding necessary to complete it in weeks or days. Nevertheless, here we go. You've been warned.

"And before you get any wild ideas, let me stop you: time travel to the past is impossible. Even under the new paradigm, matter can only travel into the future, as your plane did. We can, however, change the state of linked particles that exist in both times. The problem is power. The more massive the particle, the more power you need. The dam only generates enough power to change the state of very small particles, those with a minute amount of mass. Electrons are the most useful, for our purposes. That's how I sent the messages via Q-net. Here's where it gets tricky. . . ."

What follows is the balance of the lecture I caught the end of, again in a language wholly foreign to me, spoken in English but in the vernacular of mathematics and physics.

After a few minutes of listening, I come to a conclusion: we're screwed. I mean, why didn't the Yul of the future just program an off switch on the thing? I guess to ensure his safety. Or maybe it's more complicated than that. It certainly sounds like it. Or maybe the task at hand isn't related to the quantum bridge at all. Maybe it's another experiment completely—possibly related to Sabrina's work. I feel like a revelation is just out of reach, a piece I haven't connected. There's something they aren't telling me.

I peer around the doorframe. Inside the lab, Yul's head rests on his crossed arms on the raised table in the center. He's not working. Or is he . . .

I push the door open, and he looks up at me with bloodshot, watery eyes.

"What's wrong?" I ask quietly.

"I can't figure it out. He's right."

He shakes his head.

"And I've got a migraine. It's killing me."

"Sabrina can't help?" I ask.

"We're not . . . speaking right now."

"You have to, Yul."

He sets his head back on his arms. "I'll die first. We're all probably going to anyway."

I back out of the lab, pace out of the wing, returning to Sabrina's lab. I pause outside, waiting for the deeply personal part where she talks about the tech in her lab to pass, then push her door open.

She turns, surprised to see me. Her hand moves quickly to the table, and the screen blinks out.

"Harper . . ."

"Yul needs you."

CHAPTER THIRTY-FOUR

Harper

AFTER THE YUL-SABRINA INTERVENTION, I WANDER AROUND THE lab tower a bit more, then the Titan apartments, which are lavish in the extreme. The guardians of humanity weren't exactly slumming it. Then I make my way back to the hotel tower, to the room where I awoke. I guess this is home. Maybe forever.

I've turned the decision over in my mind until I'm ready to scream. Stay here, doom the other passengers, possibly save our world. Go back, and all the passengers will live. We'll disembark. Maybe Nick and I will pass by each other, strangers. Maybe he'll help me get my bag down, just another anonymous person he shared a flight from JFK to Heathrow with. Then . . . history repeats itself. Possibly. Or maybe not. Is the future already written? I suppose it comes down to that question.

I have realized one thing, why the antibiotics decision was so easy, back at the nose section of the plane: it was only *my* life I had to decide about. I was willing to sacrifice myself to save those others. I still am.

When I was at the lake, that was another easy decision, made without a second of hesitation. *Yeah, I'm a good swimmer.* And that's how it's been my whole life—when others are involved, when my actions help somebody else, it's easy. I never realized that before. But when it's just me, my career, my love life, I fall apart. I know what I want: to stay in this ruined world with my memories and everything I've learned about myself, to stay here with Nick. But if I do, I'll be sacrificing the lives of every passenger who died in the crash or from the plague in the days after. They will stay dead. Perhaps that's the only certainty in this whole thing.

I'm caught in a mental loop. I need to get away from it for a bit.

I sit down at the wood table under the picture window that looks out on the seemingly endless Atlantic. In the air, the burning streak is gone, just a line of white smoke now. Next to it, a new, slender line of crimson is forming. What is it? I was so lost in the videos at the labs that I forgot to ask Sabrina. I consider returning, but something else calls to me more powerfully: the Alice Carter notebook.

I flip it open, and a loose piece of paper falls out. It's my handwriting, a note, apparently to myself.

It's never too late to start, never too late to finish. And I will. I've worked far too long on others' dreams, put off my own love, this one and the one I can't speak of. After all this time, I realize that it's like Tennyson once said, "Tis better to have loved and lost / Than never to have loved at all.' I know that now. I know that I would have rather tried and failed than never to have tried at all.

I gently place the note on the table and flip the pages, reading my old scribblings for a story about a girl who receives a letter on her eighteenth birthday . . . from her future self. In the letter, Alice tells her younger self that she alone holds the keys to the Eternal Secrets, three ancient artifacts that allow their owner to control time. Hunted by a shadowy cabal with technology almost indistinguishable from magic, Alice descends into a strange world where her decisions will determine the course of history and the fate of everyone she loves.

Huh.

At university, I had envisioned Alice Carter as a time-travel fantasy series, an escapist tale, a mix of *Harry Potter* and *Back to the Future*. But right now the setup strangely hits home.

I turn the page, and the faded ink ends. New strokes, darker, from a different pen. I resist reading them. It feels almost like cheating, peeking at the answers.

I flip the pages quickly, barely feeling the Braille-like indentations on the backside. On a new page, I repeat the mental ritual I developed in college: I write the first line that pops into my head, then the next, until I have ten or half a page. It's like mental jumping jacks, a warm-up to get the words flowing. It's not about quality; it's about starting, which is the hardest part. I usually throw out this initial bit, but occasionally there are nuggets of solid gold, the kind that only turn up when you're panning with reckless abandon, when you're writing without editing or judging what's coming out. To my surprise, I hit the strike of all time. The ideas pour out of me. The outline for book 1 comes quickly, and then the next: *Alice Carter and the Dragons of Tomorrow*. A setup for book 3 arises naturally—*Alice Carter and the Fleet of Destiny*—and more after that. *Alice Carter and the Endless Winter. Alice Carter and the Ruins of Yesteryear. Alice Carter and the Tombs of Forever. Alice Carter and the River of Time*. Story arcs for seven books, the entire series. My hand aches.

It's like the ideas were always there, hidden just under the surface, ready, waiting for me to break through that top layer that covered them.

And from the plots, the ideas, the scenes I can't wait to write, comes a theme: decisions and time. Time, our fate, the future—it isn't written. It can be changed. Time and again, Alice chooses a new future with her decisions. She chooses to fight the future, to bet on humanity, to have faith in our ability to learn from our mistakes and make better decisions. Today's decisions are tomorrow's reality. I like that.

To me, this is what great books are about, revealing our own lives in a way only stories can; we see ourselves in the characters, our own struggles and shortcomings, in a way that's nonthreatening and nonjudgmental. We learn from the characters; we take those lessons and inspiration back to the real world. I believe that a good book leaves its readers better than they were before. And I think these stories will. That's why they're important.

I've also realized what I want to do: stay here, remember, and make a life with Nick, if that's possible. But what I want to do and what I need to do aren't always the same thing. I think the passengers of Flight 305 deserve a chance at their own future. Like Alice Carter, I reject the idea that the future is written, that our world is doomed to repeat the same mistakes as this one.

So I decide:

I'll let Sabrina and Yul and the Titans here use me, like the cheese in their trap, to catch Nicholas, to buy time. Whatever they need to get everyone home.

I glance once again at the sea through the window. There are three lines of white smoke now, the third glowing ember recently extinguished. The sun will set in a few hours.

I gently close the notebook and move it aside. I will likely never see it again, or remember the work I've done. Outside the hotel room my footsteps echo loudly on the marble floors of the lab tower.

In the hall that holds Sabrina's lab, an alarm rings out overhead, a shocking, pulsing sound synchronized with red flashing lights. There's no announcement, no indication of what's wrong. It's like the whole place just turned into a disco, the DJ gone, his last beat on repeat.

I race to the glass door to her lab. It's empty.

I turn, run to Yul's lab. Empty.

I pound up the stairway, onto the next level of the lab tower. All empty.

The alarm assaults me now, boring into my head. Focus.

Back in the stairway, through the floor-to-ceiling glass windows that look out at the sea, I spot the two airships at the base of the towers rising, moving away. Heading off to battle?

On the next level, through the fourth glass door, I spot Sabrina, standing, her back toward me. A large machine almost fills the room. It has only a single opening, a round portal just big enough for a body. A metal-topped table extends from the opening, a body upon it.

I throw the door open. A screen on the wall to my left displays the two hemispheres of a brain, lit in a blooming kaleidoscope of color. A brain scan.

"Harper," Sabrina says, turning.

"What is this?"

"A contingency."

"For what?"

"In case we succeed."

Sabrina never fails to offer up a cryptic answer. I struggle to put it together: her future self, lecturing her on neurons, how they don't change over time, how memories are simply stored electrical charges. Yul's video, talk of power from the dam being just enough to change the state of linked electrons in the past.

There's another revelation. It should have been obvious: Why did this faction need Sabrina? They already have the vaccine. If Yul held the key to resetting the quantum bridge and sending our plane back, what's Sabrina's role?

This is it: the experiment they've kept from me.

"You're trying to send your memories back, aren't you?"

Sabrina raises her eyebrows. Impressed?

"Yes."

"Why didn't you tell me?"

"For your sake," she says flatly.

The table finishes sliding out of the machine, and Yul sits up, shaking his head.

"My sake?" I look around at the lab. "This was the plan all along, wasn't it? For Flight 305 to return to our time and for the two of you to have your memories, to remember everything that happened here and prevent the Titan catastrophe."

"Yes."

Incredible. "Why didn't you tell me?"

"It's too dangerous, Harper." Sabrina glances over at Yul, who looks haggard, almost like he's hungover. "We aren't sure it will work. We could awaken in 2015 with brain damage, or not wake up at all. If I told you, I knew what your decision would be. It could be a death sentence."

There's the whole picture. Either Sabrina and Yul wake up in 2015 with their memories, or they turn up vegetables. Either way, they figure the immortality therapy will never be completed. Our world will be saved. There's something oddly heroic about Sabrina not telling me. She wanted to save lives back in 2015, including mine, and she and Yul are willing to risk theirs to do it. I like that.

The mysterious machine looms before me; a way for me to remember everything that's happened here, what I've become, what I've learned about myself . . . who I've met. I wouldn't be risking others' lives; just my own. That has been my breakdown point, I'm unable to make decisions where only my fate is at stake. When someone else's life is on the line, I'll risk everything. But when it's just me, I descend into decision paralysis. Here and now, though, my thinking is so very clear. I've seen what my life becomes down the road I chose, a road I might choose again. I want to change my life, make a different choice, take a risk. I want to pursue my dream. That path is uncertain, but hey, certainty is overrated. I believe it's better to have tried and failed than never to have tried at all.

"Put me in the machine."

"No, Harper. It's too risky."

"I'll take that risk. I want to remember."

"It's not worth it."

"It is to me. This is the deal, Sabrina. You and Yul have kept me and Nick in the dark since that plane crashed. We're all grown-ups, old enough to make our own decisions. You have to start trusting us. You want me to help you contain and capture Nicholas? You make me part of the plan. If I don't wake up in 2015, so be it. And you'll give Nick the same choice—the same chance—when he gets here."

Sabrina shakes her head. "We couldn't be sure we had the right Nick."

"I'll know. Now what is that incessant alarm?"

"They're here."

CHAPTER THIRTY-FIVE

Nick

OH, YOU KNOW, JUST A TYPICAL TUESDAY AFTERNOON here in 2147, waiting for my buddy Mike to wake up. Apparently it takes a few hours for the bodies to thaw out.

I'm losing it. Really cracking up. The weight of what I've done and am about to do hits me all at once. This is crazy. The whole thing.

Sitting in the small airship conference room where my future self debriefed me a few hours ago, I rub my temples, trying to focus. I'm clean-shaven and showered, and this is the first moment that I've really had alone since Flight 305 crashed nearly a week ago. Against my will, my mind replays the events of that week. But mostly I think about my decisions, calls that at every turn meant the difference between life and death for my fellow passengers. The bodies in the large tent outside this ship, lined up on the rolling metal tables—they're alive or dead because of me. At the crash site, by the lake, I could have focused more. Could have made a better plan. What if we had thrown out the luggage in the overhead bins first? Would the plane have sunk slower? Probably. Those precious seconds, minutes maybe, would have saved lives. How many? Two, three, half a dozen? Maybe we should have barricaded the belly section, keeping the water out. That would have added minutes. The whole thing went under fast after the water breached the bottom lip. I should have seen that—

The door swishes open, and Nicholas strides in. Now that my wounds are cleaned and my six days of scruff gone, we're mirror images, in appearance if not in thought: his cheeriness strikes a sharp contrast to my anguish.

He sets a single white pill on the wood table and hands me a bottle of water. I glance from the pill to him, unable to hide my hesitation. He's me, I'm sure of that—but I've also only known him for a few hours, and it's been a weird, weird week.

"Stim tab," he says. "It'll clear your mind. Right now you're replaying every moment since the crash, your decisions, pondering whether any of those metal tables could hold a living body instead of a dead one, if you'd just done something differently."

I pick up the pill, scrutinize it one last time, and swallow it down. This feels like it could turn into a therapy session, and I'm not even remotely up for it. I attempt to change the subject. "I take it coffee's out of style?"

"No, we love coffee around here; just can't afford the beans."

It's a dumb joke, but I laugh anyway.

"Don't worry," Nicholas says, "I hold the all-time record for mental replay and what-if syndrome. I sat in a room slightly bigger than this one and stared at the Atlantic all day, every day, for over sixty years, regretting, plotting to set things right, seeing the faces of the people my actions killed, one in particular. We don't have time for survivor's guilt, Nick. You did the best you could. You're innocent. At least you have that. I'm not. I got past it, and Oliver and I killed everyone we ever loved. Everybody else, for that matter."

He waits for my response, but I just take another swig of water. What do you say to that? And what would that much guilt do to a person's mind? How would it change him? Maybe in ways I can't imagine.

"We get it from Dad, you know. The replay obsession. When he was in the moment, in the thick of negotiating an agreement or managing a diplomatic situation, he was as focused as a laser beam. Total blinders. After that he bounced around his study, pacing, talking on the phone with everyone who had been involved, going over every second."

He's right. I never thought about it before.

"How did you get over it?"

"I didn't. I got *past* it. I made this deal with myself that I would focus only on making it right, and that in return, I would allow myself only a single reward for the rest of my life. I stopped allowing myself to think about what had happened. Told myself that every moment wallowing in my guilt was one moment stolen from making it right, from redeeming myself. Since that decision, I've focused only on the next step in bringing humanity back to Earth, on starting over. That was the key to my survival, pouring it all into that one goal. We're close to that goal, Nick. When we destroy that quantum device in a few hours, we'll be home free." He walks to the door. "You ready? Mike and the others are almost awake."

WE AGREED THAT I SHOULD be there when the passengers awoke. They were captured after Nicholas and Oliver drove the other faction from the crash site, so this would be a bit jarring for them. Given my role at the camp, Nicholas thinks they will respond to me, that seeing me first will put them at ease.

After our first talk, we strolled through the three-tent complex, leaning over the tables, surveying the faces, slightly obscured by the plastic sheets, selecting the passengers who would join us on the raid of Titan City as if we were at a farmers' market picking out steaks for tonight's barbecue. *How about him, Nick? Sure, add him to the list. He looks strong, what do you think?* So weird.

I originally came up with eight people, passengers who had received the vaccine and who I had seen perform under pressure at the crash site. Nicholas prodded me, insisting we needed more. We settled on eleven. Mike is among them, and so is one of the other strong swimmers from the lake, a half dozen people from the line that passed the bodies along, and three of the guys I sent on the scouting missions before the camp was invaded. I couldn't bring myself to include Jillian; she's been through so much, and this will be intense (weapons and diving training is next up on the agenda).

The first of the bodies are starting to awaken, and Nicholas and I stand in one of the twenty labs Grayson and I saw earlier, waiting. Mike sits up on the metal table, rubs his sleepy eyes, and shakes his head. He's still wearing his green Celtics T-shirt.

"Nick . . ." His voice comes out scratchy, sounding like it hurts to speak.

"Take it easy, Mike. We've got some catching up to do."

Not to mention the weapons training.

IT'S LIKE A SCI-FI SUMMER camp. The eleven passengers and I sit in a makeshift training room inside the third tent, the eleven Titans and Nicholas by our sides, helping us learn the suits and orienting us to their technology.

The glass-tile-covered suits that make their wearers invisible are even stranger inside. Holographic images inside the helmet display everything from biometric data to infrared scans and video feeds from the other team members. Panels on the forearms of the suits control it all. The Titans can use their eyes, but according to them, that takes more practice time than we have.

After the suit orientation, the talk turns to the assault plan.

Nicholas stands before the group, a large screen behind him flashing images and schematics in sync with his words. I wonder if he controls the screen with some neural link, or if one of the other Titans is assisting. Just one more mystery.

It's actually a pretty simple plan, but simple plans aren't necessarily easy to execute.

We'll suit up and drop into the Atlantic, a few miles from the dam. The suits were designed for total containment, to avoid another mutation in the event the Titans ventured from their stronghold in Gibraltar. The oxygen will last far longer than we need.

We'll use backpack diver propulsion vehicles to reach the dam, entering Titan City through the massive water intakes in the power plant. Things get dangerous at that point, but the plan accounts for the contingencies, so assuming we survive, we'll split up and fight our way up the dam, then into the five finger-shaped towers, searching for the quantum device.

Nicholas is fairly certain it will be in the middle, tallest tower, the one that houses the labs.

The screen changes to photos of Sabrina and Yul.

"Most of you have seen these two individuals, Sabrina Schröder and Yul Tan. They have been deceived by members of the other Titan faction and are working against us. They will likely be close to the device and may be able to activate it on short notice. We can't allow that to happen. If you encounter Schröder or Tan, shoot them on sight. After we've neutralized the device, our priority will be preserving as many lives as possible."

The words hang in the air for a moment as Sabrina and Yul's enlarged faces stare out at us. From across the room Grayson's eyes meet mine, a mix of concern and sympathy on his face. I feel the same. Yul and Sabrina lied to us, kept things from us, but I hope they don't lose their lives in what's to come. Grayson agrees. His father sits beside him, his Titan mentor. The time they spent training with the suit was the happiest I've ever seen him, though, to be fair, he's been either drunk, hungover, ticked off, or somber for all six days I've known him. Maybe this really is a new chance for all of us.

Nicholas is wrapping up the briefing now, detailing the backup plan, which is even simpler: placing explosives in the power plant. If we think the other faction is on the verge of resetting the quantum bridge, Nicholas will detonate the charges, bringing down the dam and Titan City, destroying the device—ideally after we get out.

He calls for last questions and comments, and I stand facing the two dozen people in our assault force, half passengers, half Titans.

"There's another person we need to look out for: Harper Lane. Many of you know her. She's another passenger. Late twenties, early thirties. Slender. British. Blond hair. She was recovered along with Yul and Sabrina at Titan Hall, and we assume she's in Titan City with them as well. She's an innocent bystander here, a hostage, and we should do everything we can to save her. She may also have information that could help us find or disable the device. If anyone spots her, notify both Nicholas and me."

The group breaks up, the eleven passengers and Grayson returning to their Titan mentors for more suit training. We've got another hour and a half before sunset, our launch time.

Before, at the crash site, everything happened so fast that I never had time to be nervous. That's not the case here. With the briefing over, I wish the whole thing were happening right now.

Nicholas drifts over to me. "You good on the suit?"

"Yeah, think so."

"The woman . . ."

"Harper."

"Right, Harper. You seem very interested in recovering her."

"She was with me from the start. Helped at the lake. She's very brave. She's done all she could to help the passengers."

He grins. "So it's all about her altruism."

I just shrug.

"Remember who you're talking to."

"All right, you got me," I mumble.

"We've got some time before we launch. I want to hear all about her, everything that's happened since the crash. It will take your mind away from this."

IT'S AMAZING HOW TALKING TO Nicholas has helped me sort through my own thoughts and . . . feelings about the crash. For the past hour, we've sat in the small conference room, running through the events. He's a mirror, a wiser version of myself with insights that have completely changed my perspective on so many things in the short amount of time we've spent together. I wonder what life in 2147 will be like with him here to guide me. He's the type of person I've never had in my life before: someone who cares, who can teach me what life holds and where the land mines are. It's exciting.

I open my mouth to speak, but I don't get a chance. The ship's overhead speakers erupt in a high-pitched wail, and a screen on the wall activates: the five finger-shaped towers of Titan City, glittering in the last orange and pink rays of the setting sun. Two airships at the base rise and move off. The camera angle changes, following them out to sea.

"We launched drones to keep an eye on them," Nicholas says, focusing on the screen.

The first ship passes, and a flash consumes the feed. They shot the drone down.

The black screen fills again, this view much farther away.

The airships fly in a straight line, then halt, hovering over the water. The feed zooms. Boats in the water. They're round, unlike any I've ever seen.

"The colonists," Nicholas says. "They've evacuated the orbital ring."

"They've already vaccinated their population?"

"They did that days ago. They've had the vaccine queued up for years, just waiting for confirmation that it works. The other faction verified it at the crash site before we drove them out."

"What do the colonists want?"

"Peace." Nicholas shakes his head. "They just don't want to see Mom and Dad fight. My guess is that they're going to take up residence in Titan City, act as human shields to try to stop us."

What a twist. If that happens, it certainly rules out taking the city down. Humanity in this time would be finished.

"What now?" I ask.

"Now we launch. We have to beat them to the city." He points at the airships. "This is a huge opening for us. If we can catch those airships outside Titan City and keep them away, it'll leave the entire place wide open."

CHAPTER THIRTY-SIX

Nick

IN THE CARGO AREA OF THE TITAN AIRSHIP, Nicholas and I stand next to Grayson and Oliver, two rows of people behind us—Titans, then survivors from Flight 305. We all wear the glass-tiled suits, only our heads revealed, our helmets tucked under our right arms. A second ship flies beside us, but it carries no passengers or cargo, only weapons. Using the panel on his arm, Nicholas pilots both ships. I watch as he programs the final autopilot instructions set to start when we depart. The long and short is that both of our ships will fight to the death, then pick up any survivors from our side—if we happen to make it out.

On the wide screen in the cargo hold, Titan City rises, sparkling in the moonlight. The placid Atlantic swells on one side, and on the other a dark, jagged valley waits, a sort of allegory for the precipice upon which we stand. Or fly, rather.

We rush toward the dam, the seconds to arrival counting down on the screen.

At the base of the hand, an airship rises into the sky. Our two ships are barreling between it and another airship that hovers several miles out, above the three landing craft bobbing in the Atlantic. One of the landing craft is already empty.

Nicholas steps out to address the group. "We can assume a third of the colonists were on that raft that was just evacuated to the city. Nothing changes. That leaves thirty-three hundred colonists out in the Atlantic—easily a large enough genetic pool for repopulation. If they arm the colonists in the city, we treat them as combatants. If they stand in your way, do what you have to do. We still deploy the explosives in the penstock at the base of the dam."

The words stop me cold. Nicholas's eyes lock on mine. A flash of realization crosses his face. He speaks quickly, more gently.

"Ladies and gentlemen, I want to remind you one last time of the stakes. If we fail, if they reset that quantum bridge, we doom the world we Titans created, the world you passengers came from. We have to be willing to trade a few lives for the fate of billions."

I remind myself: Isn't he doing what I did by the lake? Sacrificing some lives to save others? But just like before, I can't help feeling something's wrong here, something I can't put my finger on.

A blast rocks the ship, almost throwing Nicholas off his feet.

The screen reveals the battle outside. Our two airships are pounding the lone ship coming from Titan City. We circle it, hitting it with bolt after bolt of focused fire. It wobbles, returning fire as well as it can, trying to fight past us.

Nicholas and Oliver are taking their time destroying it. They're trying to lure the other ship out, the one that hovers over the colonists' landing vessels, but it doesn't budge. It's in the only safe place. We can't fire on it as long as it hovers above the colonists, can't risk debris falling on them—this world's last hope for a new human population.

On the screen, the enemy airship is finally succumbing to the assault. It hangs in midair, burning, circling, before crashing into the Atlantic.

A new wave of blasts rocks our ship—fire from the city. In the briefing, Nicholas told us that they fortified the dam and Titan City during the war, that the aerial defenses were way too sophisticated for us to try to land, making an underwater attack our only option. He was right. We won't last long up here.

"Suit up!" Nicholas yells, marching to the rows of packs that hang on both walls.

I slip my arms through my pack, put my helmet on, and grab a rifle. The hologram inside the helmet materializes, Nicholas's face appearing before me. I'll never get used to this; it's as if I'm talking to myself.

"The propulsion vehicle in the pack is preprogrammed. Relax and hang on tight to your rifle. I'll see you on the other side."

The floor below us sinks, revealing the moonlit sea. More blasts. I grab the wall, hanging on to the cargo net. The helmet shows the scene outside. Our other airship is covering us, standing firm between our ship and the city, taking the barrage full-on. It's on fire, a floating torch in the night. Just before the crack in the floor gets wide enough to exit, the ship covering for us crumbles and falls. Our own ship shudders as it takes fire, throwing half our people to the metal floor.

Nicholas races forward, dives through the small opening, and I follow.

Serenity. Nothingness.

Falling.

Fire above me. Moonlight on the glass sea below me. A faint thundering in my chest, my heart beating or the battle in the sky, I'm not sure which.

As the water rushes up, my fall slows. How?

The rotors in the pack must work in the air and underwater. They slow me, and I hit the water gently, the suit taking only the slightest impact. Below the surface, they reverse, propelling me forward, pulling me under. I follow my last instruction: Hang on to your rifle.

Darkness. Only the deep. The seconds seem to stretch out like hours. What will it be like, the fight in the towers?

I'm comfortable telling people what to do, making decisions in the moment. I've learned that about myself. The question is, can I take a life? How would I even know? No amount of training prepares you for this—and it's not like I've had a ton of training.

I feel my course adjusting.

The glass inside my helmet flickers, a night-vision filter rendering the dark depths in a grainy, green image.

We're forming up. Nicholas is ahead, the point of our underwater dart, two dozen zooming suits racing to the bottom of the dam.

Ahead, a giant gate looms, the lattice tight enough to keep fish (and humans) out. The intake. The gate opens for us—Nicholas's access codes still work. We swim down the descending slope of the penstock, a dark underwater ramp with no end sight. A minute later, the glowing green image reveals the turbine, a boat motor half the size of a football field. The sight of the blades sends a chill through me.

But they're still. I feel myself exhale, and I push harder, swimming deeper into the tunnel.

This was the test. Nicholas's plan was to turn the turbines off with his remote access, and if they didn't respond, to disable them with explosives. The advance probes were right: they're off. We're safe.

Nicholas's face appears in my helmet . . . but his words are sucked away.

No, I am.

The pull—the turbine is spinning to life, its lights flooding the shaft. The water around me is a vacuum, dragging me deeper down the ramp, into the churning blades.

It's a trap.

CHAPTER THIRTY-SEVEN

Harper

INSIDE THE THIRD-FLOOR LAB, THE SCREEN THAT DISPLAYED the brain scan splits. I watch the two charred airships take off from the base of Titan City and race over the Atlantic. They stop at the three life rafts and hover.

"The colonists," I whisper, studying the screen. "Why?"

"To protect us. If we can get them to the city, we can prevent Nicholas and Oliver from destroying it and the quantum device."

She doesn't add *and us*, but we're all thinking it.

The drama unfolds on the screen as Yul, Sabrina, and I watch.

One of our airships recovers the colonists from the first raft and deposits them here at the base of the towers. It heads back to the landing site, but before it can make it there, two more airships arrive. They fire on our returning ship, destroying it before taking fire from the city. Glittering specks spill out of the second ship into the sea. What are they? Then I realize: suited Titans. Nick. Hopefully. But as Sabrina said, I don't know that. He could already be dead, left at Heathrow . . . replaced.

Yul gets up from the white table. He's recovered some, the focused look back in his eyes.

Sabrina pulls her left sleeve back, preps her arm, and injects herself with a syringe lying on the raised metal table. Without a word, she hops on the platform, and it starts sliding into the machine.

Yul punches a control panel as the massive machine swallows Sabrina up. The frozen image of Yul's brain on the split screen gives way to a new set of lobes. Waves of color wash over it.

"The mapping procedure takes about an hour," says Yul.

The floor rattles below us, and the other half of the screen blinks red.

Overhead, a new alarm blares out.

I'm not sure we *have* an hour.

As if thinking the same thing, Yul grabs my arm, pulling me to the swinging glass door, but I throw off his grip.

"Where are we going?"

"To hide, Harper."

I glance back at the machine that encloses Sabrina.

"We can't leave her—"

"We have to, Harper. He's after you."

"I haven't been scanned."

"It'll have to wait. They're in the power plant now. We have to hurry."

THIS HAS BEEN THEIR PLAN all along: cat and mouse. Once Nicholas has me, he won't hesitate to bring this place down. He has no intention of preserving the lives here. Once he's captured me, he'll destroy the dam, the quantum device, and anyone else in the city along with it.

Alarms shriek all around us as Yul leads me to the residential wing—the little finger of the five towers, to the far right of the complex. I explored some of it earlier, but only looked into a few apartments.

"Any preference?" Yul asks.

"Where will we be the safest?"

"At a random place. He'll probably search my apartment, and Sabrina's, and his."

I nod.

As we move through the posh, carpeted, wood-paneled halls, Yul places small silver cylinders on the floor.

"What are those?" I ask.

"Mines."

"For what?"

"Nicholas will send nano drones to make an infrared scan. These will destroy them. Buy us some time."

He isn't through buying time. At each apartment we pass, he walks inside and turns the shower on, setting the temperature to max. Steam fills the bathrooms and drifts out into the bedrooms and corridors. Clever. I don't know if the steam and heat will fool the Titan sensors, but condensation will coat the suits, making them visible. My mind flashes back to the crash site, to that dark night when the rain poured down, revealing the Titans racing to the plane like glass figurines.

Halfway up the tower, Yul pauses at a bathroom. "This is as good a spot as any."

"All right."

"One last thing, Harper. Only Sabrina and I know where the quantum device is." He pauses. "And there's a chance neither of us, none of the Titans here, will survive the night. But you will. Nicholas wants you alive. I think you should know where the device is and how to activate it. Try to get to it if the worst happens."

He tells me where the device is and how to reset the quantum bridge. I listen, nodding like I'm being inducted into a secret order, which is sort of true—Yul finally letting me in on his and Sabrina's circle of secrets.

He moves to the door.

"Wait! Are you—"

"I'm going to finish, then see if I can help with the defense."

As if on cue, explosions erupt in the adjacent tower, sending vibrations through the floor.

"What's the best-case scenario here, Yul?"

He glances away. "Best case? We contain the threat tonight, then spend the time we really need figuring out the science to get the memory transmission right. Maybe a few years, a decade, however long it takes. Then we go back to 2015 with a real shot at remembering."

"How likely is that—winning tonight?"

"Pretty good."

He's lying, but I don't object. The steam in the well-lit marble-floored bathroom engulfs us now, a blanket that hides our faces, allowing us both to lie with less effort.

"Overall, we have the numbers," he says, now a disembodied voice in the fog. "But the colonists won't take up arms. Which means Nicholas and Oliver's team has us two to one in armed manpower, assuming their people survived the trap in the power station."

"What are their orders? For Nick, if they see him?"

"Nicholas, Nick, there's no way to know, Harper. It's shoot on sight for any of the Titans entering the city."

So that's containment.

"It's not so bad, Harper. If this works, you'll see Nick again in 2015."

And he'll be a stranger. It will be as if we had never met, as if none of this ever happened.

"Stay put. I'll be back," Yul says, his voice fading as he leaves the room.

I take a seat on the floor, stretching my legs out on the cool marble. The warm steam feels good, a contrast to the chill on the bottoms of my legs. I run my hands down my calves, over where the infected gash used to be. Closing my eyes, I let my head fall back against the wall, willing myself to relax. Some time later, the first tremors from the blasts run through the floor.

CHAPTER THIRTY-EIGHT

Nick

FOR A MOMENT, THE LIGHT FROM ABOVE THE turbine is blinding. It cuts through the murky darkness like a giant searchlight. The turbine gains speed, and the beam transforms into a strobe light, outlining our twenty-four-person force like an underwater rave. We're spread out, dark, floating spots of ink in the water, flowing with the current, helpless.

I spread my arms, trying to swim back up the penstock, but it's futile. The walls are concrete here, smooth. There are no ladders or grates to grab onto, just a featureless shaft leading to the flashing turbine. I gain speed, rushing downward. My heart pounds. Sweat breaks out across my face, and I give up, stop pumping my arms and legs. I reach for the control panel on my forearm, desperately trying to activate the underwater propulsion system. The autopilot route that brought me here is disengaged, and I have no idea how to work it manually—our crash course in Titan technology didn't cover it.

Above me, I see the first inkblot disappear into the flashing light.

The turbine didn't stop, didn't even slow down. The flashing grows faster. Who was the figure? Mike? Nicholas? Oliver? Grayson? Another. Then another member of our team disappears into flashing lights, the giant blades shredding them with no remorse, no hesitation.

I try to focus on my arm, try to ignore the pull. The propulsion pack sputters to life, pulling against the turbine's vortex. My descent slows but doesn't stop. I accelerate to maximum. An energy warning flashes, and I dismiss it. I glance up in time to see another figure disappear into the light.

I've slowed, but not enough; I'm still sinking, my fate only delayed.

Around me, I see other figures floating, their descent velocity matching mine. We'll be the last to die.

A figure drifts down to the turbine, slower than the first people taken, the propulsion system clearly engaged. Two objects are pulled away from their hands. It's not a rifle—

The explosion propels me back. My helmet display goes offline. I slam into the wall, roll, the air knocked out of me. I try to suck a breath, but it's no use. It's quiet now. I feel debris brushing past me.

A hand grabs my arm, and I feel someone turning me around. My helmet display is offline, but through the clear glass, I'm staring at myself—at Nicholas. His suit must be offline as well. He mouths the words *stay here,* then releases me and kicks into the now dark water.

A second later, I see a small light flick on from his wrist. It rakes across the darkness and I get my first glimpse of the carnage. Pieces of the turbine drift past, motionless, suited figures mixed in with the scraps of black metal.

One by one, members of our team swim toward me, and we link arms, pressing ourselves against the smooth concrete wall.

Nicholas returns and hands me a rifle (I dropped mine in my rush to activate the propulsion system). He moves down the row, passing out rifles and tapping at each person's forearm. He's looking for someone with a working suit. Why? What's his plan? With the turbine off, we can swim into the power plant above it—we don't need the packs to swim the rest of the way.

I peer down the row. We are sixteen strong now. Eight people—a full third of our force—perished here. And we haven't even reached our enemy yet. Our long odds have just become impossible odds. I try not to think about that. I'm glad we're in a line, glad we can't see each other's faces.

Nicholas is before me again, signaling, but I can't make out anything. I think he wants me to stay back. He points to my rifle, then pulls his own rifle close to his body, holding it tight. I get it: *hold on to your rifle*. My stomach turns, and I feel my mouth go dry. I swallow hard but it doesn't help.

Nicholas faces the group now. He points to the light on his wrist, turns it off then on, then draws a line across his throat. *Keep your light off.*

Nicholas motions to two others, and they kick away, descending fast, leaving us in the darkness.

A minute later, through the faint light, I see someone break from the line. A wrist light illuminates the face: Oliver. He motions for us to follow and kills his light. We huddle close, holding our rifles, kicking with our legs, a school of fish diving in the darkness.

We reach the turbine, what's left of it, and have to pass single file through the web of jagged metal. On the other side, I can just make out Nicholas and the two others waiting above us. When the last of our group clears the turbine, the two Titans with Nicholas activate their propulsion units, apparently at maximum velocity, because they surge toward the surface, clearing the water.

Weapons fire crisscrosses the chamber above, but I only hear faint echoes, then a cascade of thunder—two explosions. The force sweeps gently through the water. The divers deployed the explosives above the water. They were clearing the opening.

Oliver motions for us, and we're kicking again, rushing to the surface, rifles at the ready. Just before we reach the surface, gunfire rakes across the room, into the water. The two divers activate their packs again, rushing to the sources of the shots. Two more explosions, smaller than the first, and the room is quiet again.

When I clear the water, I feel an arm grip my forearm, pulling me out. Mike. I scramble out of the way, and he pulls the next person up. There are two entrances to the domed chamber, and I raise my rifle, ready to fire, scanning the room. Bodies are strewn across the metal floor, a dozen at least. A few moving, trying to push up. A shot from the darkness catches the Titan beside me full in the chest. I raise my rifle and fire without hesitation. My first shot ricochets off the wall, but my second brings the man down. I watch, but he doesn't move. And neither do I. I stare at the man, my breath filling the helmet, fog blotting him out, as if trying to erase what just happened.

I tear the helmet off in time to see one of our Titans rushing to one of the openings. He tosses something, a ball that bounces off the walls, the sound of metal on metal. The dark mouth of the corridor breathes fire when it explodes. A second later the other corridor explodes, and I hear someone yell "Clear!" behind me. Then they race around the room, inspecting the fallen enemy combatants, kicking weapons into the water.

Titans cover the two entrances, their rifles at the ready, while Nick addresses us. "There are two ways up: the power plant and the maintenance tunnels. The tunnels will be harder to pass: they're more narrow and easier to defend—or booby-trap. The power plant offers more open areas to fight, fewer choke points, and more opportunities to bypass resistance if you meet it. Oliver, you'll take the bulk of the group. I'll take two Titans." He motions to the two divers who set off the explosions that allowed us to surface. "We'll try the maintenance tunnels."

Oliver shakes his head. "Nicholas—"

"There's a chance they've ignored the tunnels."

"It's suicide," Oliver says.

"We have to take the chance. This is what we're doing." Nicholas's voice is final, but not condescending. I see myself, hear myself by the lake a few days ago.

The group breaks, and Oliver begins giving us a quick rundown of the power plant, planning angles of attack and contingencies.

Nicholas takes the diver propulsion pack from one of the operational suits, replacing his damaged unit, then heads toward me, ushering me away from the group. "You have a much better shot at reaching the quantum device than I do."

He waits, then glances at the unmoving soldier in the opening. "If the time comes, you can't hesitate."

"I won't."

CHAPTER THIRTY-NINE

Harper

THE SWISHING SOUND OF THE DOUBLE DOORS OUTSIDE, in the corridor, brings me back to the moment, to this posh bathroom in the Titan apartment. I can barely see through the thick steam. The cool marble sticks to the backs of my legs; a thin layer of warm condensation coats me. I wasn't asleep. Or awake. Rather in a daze, somewhere in between, an unfocused state where I hoped time would pass and everything would be okay.

Through the pitter-patter of the shower, I can just make out boot-steps in the bedroom, padding quietly on the carpet.

I sit still, hoping . . .

The footsteps come to a halt. I can't see the figure through the cloud of steam. Maybe they can't see me.

More footsteps. Walking away.

I exhale.

A sliding sound.

Steam flows past me, out of the room, past the balcony. The figure opened the sliding glass door, and now the rectangular opening is sucking my cloud of safety away, revealing me. The figure marches through the mist, each step unveiling more of its body.

I expected a glassy, semitransparent suit, but the outer shell on this suit is gone. Half the glass tiles are missing, revealing black, rubbery lining beneath, gashed in half a dozen places to expose cut, burned flesh.

But I focus only on the face. Nick's face.

Or is it Nicholas?

Is this the Nick I know, who saved so many after the crash of Flight 305? Or is it Nicholas, the man who caused the death of so many, who came here to take even more lives—just to be with me?

"Harper." His voice is a whisper.

I want to start my interrogation, get right down to which Nick Stone he is, but I can't help pushing up off the cold marble floor and racing to him, scanning the gashes and bruises all over his body. He's in bad shape. A gentle touch on his blackened, exposed side draws a wince.

"I'm okay." He makes a pained smile. "Harper, this might sound crazy, but there are two of me. The version of myself from this timeline is still alive."

I have limitations. Decisions have always been one. And lying is another. I can't even play poker.

Here in the steam-filled bedroom, I just try to look confused. At least I've had a lot of practice with that this week. I don't know if he buys it, but he goes on.

"Nicholas, the other . . . me, told me what's going on here. Yul created a device, a quantum bridge that connects our two worlds. He and Sabrina are going to use it to send us back to 2015. It will be like none of this ever happened . . . except our world will end up exactly like this one. We have to destroy that device so it can never be reset. But we'll never go home."

I nod. My mind races, trying to formulate—

"Do you know where it is?"

Wind blows in through the open balcony, a cool gust that drives the steam back even more. The moon is bright tonight, but my eyes lock on the twinkling lights of the airship hovering out over the Atlantic, waiting to bring the last colonists home.

"Harper."

I search every micron of his blood-caked face. The hair is the same. The features—

"Harper, come on, we don't have a lot of time here."

"Yeah. Yul told me where it is."

"Thank God." He starts toward the door, leading me. But I stop.

"After the crash, you found a glass structure. What was inside?" I ask, trying to mask my nervousness.

He turns, confused. "What?"

I speak softly. "Please answer."

"Stonehenge."

"Before you went there, you and Sabrina had a row. What about?"

"She wouldn't give you antibiotics. You were at death's door. What the hell is going on here?"

"We can't destroy the device."

"What? Are you crazy?"

"If we do, those passengers who died in the crash and in the outbreak after will be dead forever. They'll never have a chance at growing up or living the rest of their lives."

"That's the price of saving our world, Harper."

"It doesn't have to be. Yul and Sabrina have another solution. They're going to use Yul's quantum device to send our memories back. Flight 305 will return to our time, and the four of us will remember everything that happened here."

"Why didn't they tell Nicholas?"

"They did. Nicholas and Oliver betrayed them. Bringing Flight 305 here wasn't about testing that vaccine. Not for them. That was secondary, a cover."

"Cover for what?"

"Bringing Grayson and me here. I'm what Nicholas is after."

Nick turns away from me. Hurt? Confused?

His voice comes out hard, determined. "He's here for you *and* the device, right?"

"Yes. What do you want to do?"

"I want to finish this."

STEAM SEEMS TO HAVE PERMEATED every square inch of the residential tower, but Nick and I march through it, descending as quickly as we can. On the first floor, on the landing of the stairwell, a pool of blood surrounds a clump of stacked bodies. I recognize the face at the bottom of the pile. Yul.

Nick steps over him and jerks the stairway door open.

I bend down to check Yul's pulse, letting my fingers linger even after I feel the cold flesh.

"Harper, come on!"

I glance up, still unable to move.

"I'm . . . sorry, but there was nothing I could do. He was dead when I got here." He stares at me a moment, and says quietly, "Sometimes we have to skip the back rows—save the lives we can."

The airplane on the lake. I swallow hard.

"Harper, we need to go right now."

I rise unsteadily, and he grabs my hand and pulls me through the dark passageway toward the cacophony of gunfire and other blasts ahead.

The five towers, fingers of Titan City, meet in an elaborate promenade aptly named the Palm—it's shaped like a palm, but it's also dotted with palm trees, both inside and outside.

The Palm I saw before was pristine. Now it's battered and bloody. Shredded leaves and bark cover the previously spotless white marble floors. Scorch marks pock the walls. Half the glass panes in the wall of windows that looked out on the promenade are gone, letting the breeze in from the valley side of the dam. The rush of the waterfall is punctuated by firing, screaming, and occasional grenade blasts. The sound is sickening.

Nick and I pause in the dark corridor, waiting, watching for a break in the carnage. We're at the base of the little finger. The device is in the ring finger, the hotel tower adjacent to the Titan apartments, so we don't have far to go. That's a break. But still four people stand in our way, crowding the entrance to the hotel tower: two colonists, dressed in simple gray garb, and two Titans loyal to Sabrina and Yul. The Titans hold rifles, watching the battle unfold, their faces pained, as if they're resisting the urge to join the Titans on their side below, who are steadily losing ground to Nicholas's assault force moving up the Palm.

We edge closer to the corridor's threshold, the shadows giving way to moonlight through the seven-story wall of glass.

The Palm is actually seven levels of restaurants, shops, and sundry stores, all long since abandoned. Two lavish marble, glass, and steel staircases shaped like DNA helixes flank the open space that looks out on the valley and waterfall.

Suited Titans are fighting their way up the twisting stairwells, shooting and taking fire from combatants hidden in the shops and restaurants on each level. It's like mall warfare, an elaborate game of laser tag, but these shafts of light draw blood. Occasionally a Titan is shot off the stairwell, plummeting down to the massive fountain on the bottom floor.

"Stay behind me," Nick says.

I want to ask what his plan is, but if there's one thing I know, it's that Nick Stone is good at thinking on his feet. There's no one I would rather follow. We just need to reach—

He steps out into the promenade, raises his rifle, and fires point-blank at the Titans guarding the entrance to the hotel tower, catching the Titan on the right with a deadly shot to the head.

The two colonists shield the remaining Titan with their bodies, standing shoulder-to-shoulder in front of her, but Nick doesn't hesitate. Two blasts from his rifle. They drop. Two more, and the Titan falls, her rifle still by her side.

Shock and fear consume me. I'm only vaguely aware of him pulling my arm, dragging me to the entrance of the hotel tower.

Down the dim corridor the moonlight fades with each step, replaced by the soft glow of emergency lights. We're on the first floor, near my room, where I awoke in the white layered garments I still wear, where I finished the outline for Alice Carter, the girl whose decisions determined the fate of her world.

He's still dragging me, almost forcibly now.

"Harper, focus."

His face is inches from mine.

"What room?"

I close my eyes. Swallow.

"It was just two colonists, Harper. They have five thousand more—plenty to repopulate the planet. Now where is it?"

I say the word fast, hoping . . . "Two three oh five."

He lets out a laugh. "Clever."

We bound up the stairway, my legs burning, but I push, trying to keep pace, knowing what's at stake. The stairway is straight up, but the tower actually curves, the finger curling slightly toward the Mediterranean. I don't know how many floors it is to the top, but I know the rooms on the first twenty floors all face the Atlantic—as mine did that first morning. Higher up, they look out on the valley where the Mediterranean once was.

At the landing to the twenty-third floor, he stops and pants, smiling at me.

"Room five?"

I gasp for air. "Yeah."

He throws the door to the corridor open and leans out quickly, rifle first, peeking.

"Clear," he announces before storming down the hall. I follow slowly, watching him charge into the room the same way. I need to catch my breath. Need every ounce of energy for this.

He's searched the room by the time I reach the threshold. He stands in the center, just between the bed and desk.

"Where is it?"

"Balcony." I almost choke on the word.

He glances behind him, to the glass door, the dark, rocky valley beyond it, and then squints, scrutinizing me. "Balcony?"

"So they could pick it up with the airship, evacuate it if needed."

He turns his head slightly, as if hearing a noise.

Then he takes a step toward the sliding glass door. I follow, my pace matching his. This is far enough. I plant my feet, bend my knees a bit. One chance.

If I'm right, the passengers of Flight 305 will live. If I'm wrong . . . we're all doomed. I have only one thing to go on: the Nick Stone I know would never have killed those four people in cold blood, not that quickly, not that easily.

He slides the door open, and I take off, running full-on across the room.

He turns just in time to see me charging for him. There's horror on his face.

He opens his arms a second before I reach him, bear-hugging me as I bowl us both over the rail of the balcony.

Time stops.

The air grows colder as we fall, flying toward the jagged valley floor. The hotel tower is just left of the middle tower and the wide waterfall below, but we'll miss it. We'll hit the hard, rocky bottom.

He pushes back so he can see me. The shock is gone. There's no horror on his face anymore. A sad smile spreads across it. Then he hugs me tight. Behind my back, I feel him fidgeting with his hands, tapping his forearm, still bear-hugging me.

We move in the air. The pack on his back sputters, slowing us.

A spray of cold water assaults me, pelting my body—the waterfall. He almost loses his grip, but he holds tight as the deafening spray envelopes us. Through the rush, I hear the pack choking on the stream, but then the coughs turn to a rumble and a new jet of water erupts from the bottom of the device—a vortex of white foam. It can't stop our descent, but it could slow us—and it might be just enough. I reach back, fighting his hands, but he simply tightens his grip.

His somber grin turns triumphant.

CHAPTER FORTY

Nick

THEY CALL IT THE PALM. I CALL IT hell.

A seven-story mall with a wide-open space in the center, a round granite fountain on the ground floor. The statue in the center of the fountain features a smiling Oliver and Nicholas, their arms raised, hands intertwined on the day Titan City opened, the day they revealed their immortality. It lies in pieces where bodies have pummeled it, some falling from a single story up, others from the second, third, fourth, and fifth stories—each level we've taken. We've paid for every inch with lives, our blood spilled here, some deposited in the now-red water of the fountain.

Mike, Oliver, Grayson, and I reach the sixth floor and retreat into an abandoned shop. Glass trinkets—molds of the Gibraltar Dam, the faces of the first hundred Titans—line the glass shelves. It's weird, seeing glass replicas of my face in all sizes staring back at me. I took a shot to the arm on the third floor, but I've tied my arm to my body, and I think I'm okay otherwise.

For the last hour, it's been a deadly game of hide-and-seek. We make a move up the grand, helix-shaped stairway, take a floor, then recede into the shadows of the dark shops, hoping they'll come after us. We harass them with fire until they do, or until we think they've retreated enough to take another level.

We're a distraction force. An attempt to buy time.

Everything changed in the power plant. We met heavy resistance. We lost four of our twelve-person force down there, two to booby traps, two to enemy fire. We finally broke through, but it was clear we weren't going to reach the towers.

Nicholas, however, caught a lucky break. He's cleared the tunnels and should be close to finding the device by now.

In case he can't find it, he and Oliver devised a backup plan. We placed bombs at key locations in the power plant. If we can't make it to the device, we'll set them off, bringing the entire dam down, destroying the quantum bridge with it. It's a high price to pay, but it's worth it to ensure the other faction can't reset the bridge and send Flight 305 back to 2015, dooming our world to repeat the mistakes made here. Those are the stakes.

I hope Nicholas finds the device soon, and we can get out of this place. We can't leave the way we came in, via the power plant, not without functioning suits and oxygen. When we make it to the top, to the promenade on the Atlantic side, we'll jump and swim to safety. It's a bit of a drop, but we're assured we'll make it. Besides, it's our only shot. Once Nicholas has what we came for, we'll make a run for it. We just have to hold out, distract them a little longer, wait for the signal from Nicholas.

Oliver has a handheld device, a backup link that shows Nicholas's location. Oliver checks it every few minutes, letting us all follow along. Nicholas finished the search of the apartments a half hour ago; now he's moving up the hotel tower, hopefully closing in on the device.

I slump behind a counter, let my back fall against it, and lay my rifle across my legs.

Grayson collapses next to me. "How you doing?"

"Peachy. You?"

"Been better." He lets the hand he's been holding against his stomach fall forward, revealing a deep gash. Blood fills his palm in the few seconds it lies open.

Crap.

Pings. Metal on marble, like a ball bouncing.

"Stun grenade!" Mike yells.

Unfortunately we've all become quite familiar with stun grenades and a few other choice combat weapons in the last few hours. Oliver, Grayson, and I duck our heads and cover our ears. I squeeze my eyes shut, but the blast is still overwhelming, a wave that slams into me, pulverizing my hearing and sight.

I'm vaguely aware of Mike reaching up, plopping his rifle on the glass-topped counter, and pulling the trigger, his head held below, firing indiscriminately, hoping to repel any forces rushing in after the blast.

Twinkling sounds, faint, like someone playing a tiny piano at the bottom of a well. It's the glass from the shelves and the tall window panels shattering, falling on the marble floor, a sea of shards from us to the open area and stairwell. My hearing normalizing, I can just make out shots raining down on us. Mike keeps firing, and I push up, ignoring the pain from my wounded arm. I lay my rifle next to his and fire wildly as well. We keep shooting until their fire subsides, no one connecting. These rifles seem to have an endless supply of electric charges—they don't use projectiles as far as I can tell, and there's no magazine.

We settle back against the counter, once again in darkness and quiet, everyone saving up energy for the mad dash to freedom, to the promenade, which has to come soon, for our sake.

A soft, pulsing alarm rings out from Oliver's oblong tablet. He draws it out, holds it up. Nicholas's location beacon is sailing out of the hotel tower, down the Mediterranean side, toward the basin. Why? He should be on the other side.

His pack activates, steering him into the waterfall, but it's too late. His velocity. There's no way he'll survive the fall. Fear fills Oliver's face.

"Did he send the signal?" I ask. "Does he have it?"

"No. He sent no signal," Oliver says, punching his thick fingers on the tablet.

The view switches to a video feed of the outside of the dam. A drone. That was smart.

There's no sign of Nicholas.

Oliver works the tablet, backing the video feed up. A speck—a body—flies up from the dark pool at the bottom of the dam to high in the hotel and back inside. He pauses the feed, zooms in, moves forward. It's still too dark, and he adjusts the settings, making it lighter. It's grainy, but I can just make out the figure of Nicholas inside a hotel room on a high floor. The moonlight casts just enough light through the sliding glass door for me to see him searching the room. Maybe he found the quantum device and decided that jumping was the only way to destroy it.

An errant shot hits the shop's floor, sending a spray of glass shards into the back of the counter.

Mike throws his rifle up on the counter and squeezes three rounds off.

Silence.

We all lean in, focusing on the video.

It creeps forward.

Nicholas pauses. He seems to be talking to someone. He pulls the sliding glass door open and scans the empty balcony. Confusion.

He turns his back to the passing drone and focuses on something in the room. His arms spread. Another figure, rushing out of the shadow.

Blond hair. A face I thought I might never see again.

The video inches forward.

Harper slams into him, driving him the few feet to the rail, then over. Oliver works the feed, panning, zooming, following them down. They're freefalling, then suddenly they veer into the waterfall and thread in and out of the white stream. Nicholas holds Harper tight while working the control panel on the forearm of his suit behind her back. Their descent is slowing. A small shred of hope emerges inside me. Maybe . . . But Harper twists, reaches for his arms. She's fighting him. Stopping him. Why? My mind burns, trying to unravel it.

Whatever she was trying to do, she did it. The slow descent becomes an unstoppable plummet.

They hit the surface of the water at a deadly speed, disappearing into the black abyss.

My mouth goes dry. My heart pounds in my chest.

Oliver lets the panel fall to the floor. A shadow passes over his face, and then his features grow hard. He taps the panel angrily, calling up the remote detonator for the array of explosives we planted in the power station at the base of the dam. He activates them, putting the main array on a timer, set to five minutes, with a few peripheral charges set to sixty seconds.

The numbers fill the screen, ticking down.

My God.

"What the hell are you doing?" I yell at him.

"It's over, Nick." He slips the narrow panel back inside the sleeve of his suit and begins to pull on his glove, but I reach for him, grabbing for it.

He shoves me back, pushing me to the ground. Pain from my arm racks my body.

Oliver pulls Grayson up and drags him toward the door, speaking quickly, his voice low. "When the charges go off, we'll run up to the next level, shoot out the far windows—they overlook the Atlantic. Jump and don't look back."

Grayson looks back to me, lying there at the base of the counter.

Through the pain, I try to piece the puzzle together.

Oliver couldn't care less about the thousands of colonists—or any of the lives in Titan City—at this point. He's focused only on Grayson. That's what this was about for him. And his loyalty to Nicholas. Harper killed Nicholas. Why? *It's over, Nick.* I go through what I know, what Nicholas said to me. His guilt. *Oliver and I killed everyone we ever loved. Everybody else, for that matter.* I've missed something—something crucial. *Think.* Oliver stole the immortality therapy for Grayson, the prodigal son he wanted to give one more chance, the confused boy in a thirty-one-year-old body who peers back at me now, his father's arm around him, the father who never loved him in his time.

But why did *Nicholas* help Oliver steal the therapy? His words: *I'd met someone, someone very near death. Like Oliver, I was terrified, unsure what life would be like after she passed. I had made my own proposal to save her, but it had been defeated as well. Oliver and I were desperate to save our loved ones . . .*

My mind runs through every moment with Nicholas. He knew me, coached me. Worked me. He needed the passengers for this assault, but what did he come here for? To destroy the quantum bridge? They would do it at any cost—to keep the passengers here. So why risk an assault? Why not just bomb the place as planned?

What had he become?

The power of seeing the world he created, the arrogance. And the sorrow of seeing it ruined by his hubris, killing the only thing he loved. The only person he loved.

Focus.

The question I need to ask is: Why Flight 305?

Nicholas's words run through my mind again. *We had an incredible opportunity: a flight where the key people involved in the Titan Foundation and our great mistake could be taken out of your timeline.* But they *told* Yul and Sabrina to board that flight—they were not originally supposed to be on Flight 305. They weren't on that flight in this timeline. Only Harper, Grayson, and me . . .

For Oliver the objective was Grayson. A second chance to do something about his one true regret. Which meant for Nicholas . . .

Harper.

It has to be. The love of his life. And she stopped him, knew it was him somehow. That's why he pumped me for information, for an account of every second I spent with her.

She must have known something I don't. She gave her life to stop Nicholas, to keep him away from the device. She took away the one thing he would stop at nothing to possess: her life. And if she was willing to do that, then something is very, very wrong.

"Stop!" I yell, sitting up.

Grayson turns back to me, but Oliver keeps his arm around his son, corralling him, whispering to him.

"He came here for her, didn't he?"

Oliver turns, an amused smile on his face.

"Grayson, get the tablet! Stop the countdown!"

The floor booms below us. All the glass figurines and trinkets rattle and shake, falling, shattering. It's a sickening sound, accompanied by a shower of sharp pieces, debris and dust from the ceiling mixing with it, burying me behind the counter.

I feel Mike's arms around me, pulling me up, around the counter. We stumble over a sharp blanket of broken glass, toward the door and stairway, where Oliver is practically dragging Grayson.

"Help us, Grayson!" I yell.

Oliver turns, fires a shot that catches me in the shoulder, blowing me back into the store. I slide over the bed of glass. The shards cut into my back, a million agonizing slices, jabbing deep, cutting me to shreds.

Mike stands and fires, but Oliver catches him with a shot to the head. He's dead before he lands at my feet.

Grayson grabs his father's arm, forcing the rifle out of it. Our eyes meet, and I see the pain in his, the sadness, the struggle. His moment of hesitation allows his father to trap his arms at his sides. Oliver leans in, speaking, but Grayson frees his right hand and jerks the tablet out of his father's sleeve, tossing it clanging on the marble floor. It settles halfway between us, and Grayson lunges for it, but his father restrains him, pulling him back.

With far too much force.

I watch in horror as they both crash through the glass rail. A second later, I hear the sickening sound of the fountain's granite breaking, more pieces of the Titan statue crumbling away, splashing in the water.

The tablet's screen is cracked, but still lit, displaying the countdown.

I try to sit up. Every movement pushes the glass deeper into my skin. I crawl, the shards grinding into my knees and elbows through my tattered suit.

Footsteps. Boots on the marble. Titans and colonists descending the winding helix of the grand stairway.

My hand reaches the tablet.

"Stop!"

I minimize the countdown.

"Stop, or I'll shoot."

I work my fingers, pulling up the access program for the array of explosives. There's no pass code, just a fingerprint verification, keyed to only two people in the world: Oliver Norton Shaw and Nicholas Stone.

A shot hits the floor three feet from me. I wince, close my eyes, and press my thumb to the screen.

CHAPTER FORTY-ONE

Nick

WHEN THE COUNTDOWN ON THE TABLET STOPS, I toss it away and roll onto my side, the only part of me that isn't coated in jagged glass. Blood oozes from a thousand places on my body. At any moment I expect my guts to spill out on the white marble floor like the contents of a piñata that's finally popped.

Maybe that's what they're waiting for—the easy way out.

I stare up into the barrels of the rifles pointed at me, into the hatred on the faces of the Titans holding them. They circle me, glancing at each other, no doubt silently debating: shoot all at once, so no one knows who fired the killing shot, or conduct a more orderly execution? Or wait—after all, I'll die soon either way. One way or another, that's what's next. No words I can say will change it.

I wear the face of the Titan civil war. When they look down at me, they see Nicholas Stone, the man who destroyed this world and set the Titans against each other. They see the villain who betrayed humanity time and again, slaughtered his fellow Titans at Heathrow, and planned and executed this final assault.

As I wait for the end, I can't help contemplating what Nicholas became, how all his extraordinary achievements changed him, made him arrogant, yet his guilt at his mistakes ate away at his moral compass, drove him inward, to a selfish and ruthless place where he longed only to taste happiness again.

As much as it disgusts me, I don't blame him. Because I guess I felt some of that desperation, the fear that I would never feel whole and happy again, before Flight 305 took off. He was me. He *is* me. I'm capable of everything he did. I guess we're all capable of evil, under the right circumstances.

Movement. The Titans around me shift, form up, getting ready.

A sound track of death and destruction plays behind them. Blood-reddened water gurgles in the mangled fountain below the statue of Nicholas and Oliver that broke the fall of so many Titans, battering them, each body taking with it a small piece of the sculpture. Behind me, shards of glass fall to the store's floor like wind chimes blowing on a lazy day. I focus on the sound of each little piece falling, wondering if it's a piece of my face or that of another Titan. I imagine them settling on the floor, indistinguishable in the sea of shattered glass.

Footsteps, loud on the grand helix stairway. The Titans part.

Sabrina.

"Hello, Nick."

I've never been so glad to hear her voice—or my own name. Just Nick. I'll never use the name Nicholas.

She bends down toward me, a syringe in her hand.

"Wait."

"Your injuries are urgent," Sabrina says in that mechanical tone, the sweetest sound I can imagine right now. "We must—"

"How'd you know?"

"Harper."

"How'd she know?"

Sabrina arches her eyebrows. "That may remain a mystery."

"She's . . ."

Sabrina nods, genuinely sad. That's new. She starts at me again with the syringe, but I hold my hand up, the movement accompanied by a grunt of pain. "You have a plan? To send a warning to 2015 when we go back?"

"Yes. Memories."

"Memories?"

"A detailed brain scan that maps the position of every electron in every neuron. Yul was working on the science, using the Q-net to transmit the data back, but he didn't complete his work."

So Yul's dead as well.

Her syringe still at the ready, Sabrina goes on. "I believe, however, that the colonists can complete his work. Yul was scanned before he died, so we have his memories to transmit."

"And Harper's?"

"No. I'm sorry, Nick."

"Scan her."

"We can't—"

"I saw her fall. Is her body intact?"

"We don't know. It's in the water."

"Get her out. You have one airship left. Go get her and scan her right now."

"Nick, we can't be sure—"

"Do it, Sabrina. You owe us. Please."

I DON'T KNOW HOW LONG I've been in this lab with Harper's corpse. I can't seem to leave. There's so much left unsaid between us. How do you get over someone passing too soon? Someone with so much life left to live. I thought seeing her might . . . help. But it hasn't. Maybe I'll come back tomorrow. Or maybe that will only make things worse.

I run my hand through her blond hair, kiss her cold forehead—our first and only kiss—and walk out of the lab.

FOR THE PAST HOUR SABRINA has lectured me on the likelihood that Harper's memories won't make it to 2015, that none of ours will. That Harper was dead for almost half an hour before her brain was scanned complicates matters, apparently. The key to the whole thing is having the same neurons present in both timelines. Sabrina thinks it would be better not to attempt to send her memories back. Sabrina was scanned during the assault on Titan City, Yul right before.

I'm due to be scanned in an hour. She says I won't remember anything that happens here after that; the memories transmitted back—if it works—will stop after I slide into the machine.

She's run off a list of possible physical calamities, everything from brain damage to stroke to schizophrenia. It's like the warnings during a pharma commercial, except Sabrina talks slower, and this one lasts for sixty minutes (I've been told to hold my questions until the end).

As she plods on, I try to sort through what to do. I think about what I want: the Harper I've come to know. But that's the selfish choice, the choice Nicholas made. And then I think about what Harper would choose, if she were sitting here. That's the key: ignoring my desires, focusing on what she would want. Who am I kidding? That's really impossible. Facts. What do I know? Harper risked her life time and again here in 2147 to save others. At the end, when she knew she was the only person who could stop Nicholas, she gave her life to do that. The journal she found in her flat, what she read, it changed her. She didn't like the choices the version of herself in this world made. I know she would want to do things differently. But she may never have that chance if any of Sabrina's dire warnings come to pass. It comes down to this: leave her the way she was in 2015 and guarantee she lives, or send her memories along with ours, and roll the dice with her life.

"Questions?" Sabrina finally asks.

"How sure are the colonists that they can make Yul's science work?"

"Not sure at all. Yul's mind was far ahead of his time. But time is one thing we have."

"What does that mean?"

"Whether the colonists solve the quantum aspects of the memory transmission tomorrow or a thousand years from now, it makes no difference to us. If the memories do make it back to 2015, we'll remember nothing after the scan. The passage of time in this timeline will have no bearing."

I rub my eyes. Still so hard to wrap my head around all this.

Sabrina's tone softens. "I have a suggestion, Nick."

"Yeah?"

"Decide Harper's fate—whether you want to attempt transmitting her memories or not—after your scan."

I nod. "So I won't remember my choice. No guilt."

"Correct."

She's right. Guilt can be a dangerous thing. Nicholas proved that to me.

And I have time to decide. Maybe years or decades, if the science here takes that long.

"All right."

"Are you ready?"

"Yeah."

SABRINA AND I WALK TO the lab that contains the massive machine in silence.

Inside the lab, she runs through the details of how it works, how groggy I will feel after the procedure, but I barely hear a word, my mind still consumed with the decision I have to make.

Finally I hop onto the frigid white table and wait as the machine spins up, the hum growing louder each second.

To my surprise, Sabrina takes my hand in hers and looks down at me on the table.

"See you in 2015, Nick."

PART THREE

STRANGERS

CHAPTER FORTY-TWO

Harper

IT'S OVER. THE GREATEST SEVEN HOURS AND EIGHT minutes of travel in my thirty-two years on Planet Earth.

Over.

Jillian's voice comes on the speaker, announcing the conclusion of this glorious flight (tear). Her tone's brisk, slightly cheery, completely professional. She welcomes each and every passenger (especially Reward Miles members) to London Heathrow Airport, and says she hopes we had a pleasant flight (understatement) and that she will see us again soon, wherever our travel plans may take us (I would go anywhere in this chair).

I'll never understand the race to get off the plane. It's like a flash strain of flesh-eating bacteria just broke out in the tail section, and it's a live-or-die mad dash to make it to the exits. Can this many people have tight connecting flights?

People swarm the aisles, jerking their carry-ons out of the overheads, hastily shoving tablets, e-readers, and snacks they squirreled away during the flight into their bags, barely bothering to zip them.

There's a cacophony of voices. *Excuse me— Sorry— Is that your bag? Do you mind?*

I'll be the last off. I dread going home. That's where I'll have to make the Decision.

God, just thinking about it puts me in a bad mood.

"You all right?"

The guy from 2A. Short dark hair, chiseled face, American accent. *Like.*

"Yeah," I manage, barely audible over the game of Twister playing out in the aisles.

"Need some help?"

That's an understatement.

He squints. "With your bag?"

"I—"

"Hey, some people have places to be, Casanova." Grayson Shaw. Drunk. Very drunk.

Two A doesn't budge. "Exactly. Why don't you stand aside?"

Grayson mutters a cornucopia of curse words as he turns back, disembarking via the business section exit.

Two A pops the overhead open and fishes out my bag, its heft seeming inconsequential in his hands.

I cringe as he lowers my battered black bag to the aisle. It tilts slightly when he releases it—it's missing one of its four wheels. I received the bag for Christmas one year at uni, and as I travel so seldom, I've never seen the need to fork out the cash to replace it. It teeters there like Her Majesty's government's Exhibit 1 of my impostorhood, my complete unworthiness to be here in the first-class section of Flight 305. The barrister would no doubt direct the jury's attention to the fuzzy white remnants of a sticker that I unsuccessfully tried to peel off, the glue seeming to have melded with the bag's canvas at the molecular level. The sticker was placed there by a drunken friend of mine almost a decade ago, in Spain. It read either "I heart guacamole" or "Viva la revolución"—I can't recall which.

"Thanks," I squeak.

HEATHROW EXPRESS TO PADDINGTON STATION, then the tube, all the while staring at my phone, still off, dreading what awaits.

At home, I finally hold the power button down.

Two voice mails. One from my agent, the other from Mum.

My agent's voice barks in my ear. *"Hi, Harp, hope you had a good flight. Ring me when you're home. They're pressing me to get your decision. If you're out, they're moving to their second choice. They don't want to do that. I don't want them to do that. Huge opportunity, Harp. Let's sort it out, yeah?"*

Mum, just making sure her only child hasn't crashed into the Atlantic or the English countryside somewhere. It's late, but I know she's up, worrying, waiting for me to call, so I do.

The conversation is decidedly one-sided: hers. I sit on my sunken sofa with its cream slipcover, listening to updates about relatives young and old. I know what she's working up to, and I mentally prepare myself. Ethan, my cousin, is headed off to Harrow, but how will my aunt and uncle ever afford it, and speaking of uncles, Clive has bought a horse, which Mum figures is his midlife crisis, which is better than an affair, she supposes, and . . . speaking of dating—

I ring off after that, pace the flat for a while, ruminating on the Decision. I get the Alice Carter notebook out from under my mattress and lay it on the coffee table, eyeing it sympathetically, as you might a child before you break her heart. *Summer vacation will have to wait another year, honey. Mummy has to work.* And that's what I think it will come down to. But then I'll be free to finish Alice, give her the time she deserves.

That sounds like a rational, responsible, adult decision.

Who am I kidding? I'm still teetering, like my shabby three-wheeled bag. Maybe I'll use some of the money to replace it.

Only one thing to do, one thing that can help me decide.

I put my coat back on and ponder on my way down the stairs: vodka or wine?

Since I'm now making only practical, rational, adult decisions, I'll choose vodka. More bang for the buck. More pure revelation-inducing, decision-solidifying power per penny. And less calories. Less calories is good. As Mum just reminded me, I don't want to wind up a spinster with a beer gut, like Cousin Dolly.

CHAPTER FORTY-THREE

Nick

"I KNEW YOUR FATHER, NICK."

I hate when meetings start this way. I'm never sure what to say. Some folks get sappy (my father passed away two years ago); some recall episodes I was too young to remember (which, to be fair, I often enjoy hearing about a great deal); and some, like the man before me, Alastair Hughes, just let the statement hang in the air, awaiting my response.

I stare at the London skyline behind him for a moment, what I can see through the dreary fog. The day is as gray as I feel. Maybe I should move to London. There's a change. Probably a good investment, too. But I hear they're considering taxing homes owned by foreigners. Surprised they haven't yet.

"Were you a diplomat as well?" I finally ask.

He was, as it turns out. He runs through a few of his postings, offers a story about my father, one that took place in 1985, in Nicaragua, one I hadn't heard. It's a good story, well told. I like Alastair

Hughes. And I think that may have been the point of the story. I bet he was a pretty good diplomat.

When the last laughs settle into chuckles, then reflective silence, he gets to the matter at hand.

When he's finished, I simply say, "You want to build a dam across the Strait of Gibraltar?"

Alastair leans forward slightly. "We *will* build a dam across the Strait of Gibraltar."

I glance at the three men, wondering what in the world this has to do with me. Before the meeting, I told them that I typically fund Internet-related companies, mostly at seed stage. The initial investments are low, relatively speaking; assuming things work out, I usually participate in subsequent funding rounds, doubling down on winners. I'm rarely more than twenty million into any one company by the time it either folds or reaches liquidity (IPO or acquisition). They're talking billions to build something like this. And even if they had the money in hand, I doubt they'd get the political buy-in.

"This project will take decades, Nick. It will be the largest construction project in history, a multinational collaboration that will change the face of the earth. The marvels of the ancient world—the Great Pyramid of Giza, the Temple of Artemis at Ephesus, the statue of Zeus at Olympia—most were monuments, ceremonial shrines. This dam will *do* something. It will carve a new destiny for humanity, a future about global cooperation, dreaming big. It will show the world that we can solve big problems. It won't be built with dollars, pounds, or euros, or even man-hours. It will be built with consensus."

He slides a series of artists' renderings over to me. In the center of the dam, a waterfall spills into a blue basin set in a rocky brown valley that turns to green farther out. A few simple low-rise buildings stand at the top.

"Building something this large requires a strong foundation. We're not talking about a foundation of concrete or steel or money. People. Every successful venture starts with the right people. I'm sure that's how it is in start-ups, right? Two companies developing the same technology; the best group of people wins the day."

I nod.

"You chose start-ups because you like to be on the ground floor of something big, something that could have a huge impact."

"I suppose."

"Doesn't get bigger than this, Nick. And this is the ground floor."

"Yeah, but the thing is, I don't see how I fit in. Don't get me wrong: it's impressive, the vision, the potential impact. But . . ."

"You're uniquely qualified, Nick. The people you grew up with, went to school with around the world—over the next few decades, they will become the senators, prime ministers, and CEOs who will decide whether this dam gets built. They're the levers of the future."

"Perhaps, but look—I mean, I was rarely picked last at gym time, but my childhood friends don't like me enough to let me drain their coastlines."

"These people will listen to you, Nick. That's all we need. You didn't become a diplomat like your father. You wanted to do something different. No comparisons. Your own path."

He's done his homework. "Something like that."

"But you're looking for a change, something big. That's why you flew to London, even knowing this wasn't about an IT start-up. We're just asking you to think it over. That's all. We're offering you the opportunity to be the point person on an international initiative that would change the course of history. Your father relished that role. It was the only time he was ever really happy. It's inside you, too."

We spend the last minutes of the meeting talking about small details, ancillary benefits from the project. There's talk of refreezing polar ice using solar shades, technology that's still conceptual. Issues related to sea currents and salinity. The fate of the Black Sea. It's an attempt to convince me that this isn't the half-baked dream of a few aging diplomats. They're trying to close me, convince me that I won't spend the next three decades flying around Europe having the same meeting about a dam that will never get built.

That was my first instinct early in the meeting, but as I look at the artists' renderings a feeling settles over me, a sensation I haven't had in a long time: excitement. It's faint, the desperate flare of a match flickering in the wind, but to me, at this point, it's like a campfire on a cold November night.

I'm confident that this dam will be built.

I keep the drawings and promise them they'll have my answer shortly.

The gray-haired man clears his throat and peers up at me through thick curved glasses that make his eyes appear unnaturally large, nearly cartoonish. "RailCell is faster, safer travel, a network that will link the world. Faster than a train. Safer than a plane. RailCell. Get there quicker, safer, cheaper."

The lines come off well enough, though I can tell he's pretty nervous. Poor guy.

I like scientists. They're my favorite. By far.

Like anybody, they're uncomfortable outside their element. Most don't like selling things. And he's no different.

The scientist sits next to a guy I knew in college but have seen only a few times since. I took the meeting at his request, not knowing what it was about. I was in town and my flight wasn't for a few hours, so I figured what the heck.

My acquaintance is a marketing guy. He should be giving the pitch. He's clearly coached the scientist. That's trouble: the marketing team giving the lines to the scientist, who is inevitably the person investors want to hear from.

I can imagine the primer the scientist was given. "Sell benefits. Don't describe features. *Sell the benefits.*"

There was no doubt an analogy made. "You're not selling breath mints, or fresh breath; you're selling sex appeal, attractiveness—what you become after you take the breath mint. It's not about the shampoo, it's about shiny, sexy, vibrant hair that catches the eye of the cute guy who lives across the hall, causing him to turn, pause, then ask you out. It's not about the shampoo, it's about the big house and beautiful children you'll have with that cute guy who finally notices you. And to seal the deal, said shampoo is infused with countless vitamins and minerals, all clinically proven to strengthen dry or damaged hair. Scientific proof breeds confidence. Hit 'em with the science if you have to, but hook 'em with the benefits first, let them know they want what you're selling."

People in my particular line of work, however, can sort out the benefits themselves. We want to know if it works—whether it's the real deal. Great marketing can sell an inferior product for a short time. Only a strong product can sell itself over the long term.

"*How* does RailCell link the world?"

After some hemming and hawing and verification that I have signed the NDA (so much for my old friend's trust), they come clean: they've bought the patents of a Brazilian mining company for a song. Pretty revolutionary stuff. There's a complicated business model: they'll sell the minerals they get from the underground tunnels, everything from iron ore to gold, silver, and copper, splitting the proceeds with national and local governments in return for a monopoly on the lines. The operation of the passageways will be opened to local operators, ensuring that most of the money paid for tickets goes back into the local economy. It's smart. Maybe a few problems with it, but it could be a global gold mine, both literally and figuratively.

It's also well outside my wheelhouse. I'm usually sitting in meetings about an app that could be worth nothing or billions in two years, depending on whether it catches on with a certain niche audience before going mainstream. So this isn't that.

They want to start in England, which—given the population density and housing issues, especially in London—they feel will be more receptive.

It's very interesting—and I tell them that. But I also let them know it's outside my area of expertise—"Not the sort of thing I typically invest in" are my exact words. Yet I'm intrigued, so I add that I'll help in any way I can.

"What we're looking for at the moment, Nick, is introductions." A pause, and my acquaintance from college quickly adds, "And of course any advice you might have."

Mentally, I start rifling through my Rolodex. "I'll think about who I know, who might be interested."

"We'd cut you in for a finder's fee, of course, on any investment dollars you bring in."

"That's okay. I only do intros for free."

"Best counteroffer I've ever heard!" My old friend slaps the table and cuts his eyes over toward the scientist, a look that says, *See, I told you about this guy. This is why you need me.*

And there it is: the probable history of RailCell to date. The scientist worked for the undercapitalized Brazilian company. When they folded, he got on the phone, desperate to continue his work, to find anyone who could help him buy the patents. He's probably got his house mortgaged and his retirement savings—and maybe some family members' savings, too—in this. My acquaintance likely has very little skin in the game. He just wants to see if some heavy hitters will throw in and make it a reality. Pretty common.

"One thought."

Both men wait, eyebrows raised.

"You can't call it RailCell."

Crickets.

"To me, rail implies slow, old. A train."

"It will replace the trains," my college friend says.

Yep, the name was definitely his idea. The scientist's eyes shift back and forth slowly, giant fish in a bowl behind those glasses.

"True. It will replace trains, but it's a faster, newer technology. And I wouldn't use the word *cell* either. Feels confined. I hear 'cell,' I think prison, cramped, inescapable. Last thing you want for a transportation brand."

"What would you name it, then?" There's an edge to his voice now.

"I don't know. I would come up with two dozen names and test them with diverse groups. It's cheap to do these days with social media. If this thing's going to be as big as you think, a global brand that could reach everyone on earth, the name is crucial. Maybe Pod something. The cars in the tunnels are like pods, right? Pods feel safe. Impregnable. Comfortable. And it sounds like new technology—nobody is going anywhere in a pod right now."

"PodJet? JetPod? Jets are fast." He nods at the scientist, who doesn't react.

"Jets crash," I say.

"Not anymore. I mean, they crash so rarely."

"People think rarely could happen to them. Subways don't crash."

"PodTube?"

"Sounds like TV."

"TubePod."

I shake my head. "Sounds like part of a plant."

"Podway?"

"That could work. Keep playing with that."

THE WORST PLACE TO BE sick is on an airplane. Well, maybe not the worst place, but it's bad, and I'm bad sick, in and out of the first-class lavatory, puking, leaning against the wall, waiting for the pain and nausea to pass or to puke some more. I never know which is next.

I slump back in my seat, pale and drained.

"Get some bad food, partner?" the guy across the aisle asks.

"Must have," I mumble.

It's not bad food. I've never had a migraine in my life. Never felt this sick. Something is wrong with me. Something bad. Heathrow to SFO. Halfway over the Atlantic. Eight hours to go.

I wonder if I'll make it.

CHAPTER FORTY-FOUR

Harper

VODKA BOTTLES DRUNK LAST NIGHT: .25

Hugely important decisions made: 0

Episodes of *Sherlock* watched: 2

I awake to my phone ringing, my agent's number staring me in the face.

It was late enough last night not to return his call—my agent and I aren't that close, after all. Not ringing him up this morning looks like I'm dodging him, though. I start compiling cover stories, mentally rehearsing them to see what might float.

Got a nasty bug, Ron. Bloody planes—you know—laid up all day . . . Mum's been ill . . .

Oh, Ron, my phone, dropped it in the gap where the plane meets the ramp, cracked into a billion pieces when it hit the tarmac. Then a luggage truck ran over it, then a fuel truck, which God bless the driver tried to swerve to miss my poor phone but hit another truck. The explosion was enormous, blew the plane over, right onto my phone. It's still down there somewhere.

May have gone a bit far with that last one. Nothing says you're lying like overselling it.

But none of them will really work anyway. That's the downfall of the digital age: no one can ever really get away. Even if I'd lost my cell, or come down with something, or had to pop out to help my mum, I'd still have e-mail access at home and hers to fire off a quick "Yes." It's rude not to ring him back, after all the work he's put in. He deserves an answer, and so do the publisher and Mr. Shaw.

Tapping at my phone, I fire off an e-mail, thanking my agent for all his efforts to get me this opportunity, but . . . I haven't made a decision yet.

A response pops up almost immediately.

Thanks, Harp. Take the time you need, but I want you to know they're in a hurry to get the ball rolling. I have a call with the editor in an hour, sounds urgent. Will keep you posted.

Vodka didn't shake the decision loose. Time for new tactics.

MILES RUN: 3

Correction, in the interest of complete honesty—

Miles run: 1.5

Miles walked while pondering life and pivotal decisions: 1.5

Decisions made: 0

There are two voice mails waiting when I get back. Both Ron. I tap the first one and listen.

"Just got off with the publisher, Harp. Shaw loved you—of course. The editor wants to be able to ring him in New York this morning and say we're a go. Aaaaand—they've doubled the advance—without me even asking. I might get a touch more. Something's up, will find out. Need your answer soon, Harp. Great opportunity here."

And the next message, not fifteen minutes later.

"Think I know what's brewing, Harp. Heard through the grapevine that Shaw's son, Grayson, is shopping a tell-all. New York publishers won't touch it, but he's got an agent here, and they're making the rounds. Bidding's going to be intense. Rumors are he has juicy secrets. Maybe even criminal accusations. Lives of the rich and famous revealed. Going to be nasty. Oliver Norton Shaw needs someone to

tell his story, the true story, *when this load of bollocks hits the shelves. No matter who writes it, the books will feed off each other. Great opportunity here, Harp. Ring me when you get this."*

Ahhhh. I will make a decision today. And I've decided how.

AFTER A TRIP TO W. H. Smith, I am eight pounds fifty poorer and the proud owner of a myriad of notebooks, writing utensils, and poster boards, which lie sprawled out on my living room floor. I've moved the couch around, pushed the tables and chairs to the walls. It's a big studio now, a temple devoted to Alice Carter.

I'm going to give her the day, pour my heart into her story. If it comes, if it demands to be written, I'll give Alice the attention she needs. If it's a chore—as it has been for years now—I'll put her on the back burner and make the logical choice.

That's what a rational adult would do—after drinking vodka, of course. But I've done that, so I'm going to try this.

I'm feeling better already.

CHAPTER FORTY-FIVE

Nick

I'VE FELT FINE SINCE THE PLANE LANDED IN San Francisco. Well, physically okay. But I have this overwhelming feeling that I've forgotten something. That I'm not doing something important that I need to do. It's like a nervous, nagging type of guilt.

But it's a feeling, at least. That's new.

I call the one person I think might be able to help me. Luckily, he has an opening.

"HOW WAS YOUR WEEK?"

"About the same."

"Explain." Dr. Gomez crosses his legs and gives me the Psychologist Look. It seems like all psychologists are either born with it or taught it in school.

"I feel like I'm just watching my life happen."

"How so?"

"I don't get excited when I should. Barely even get angry. Most of the time, I couldn't care less what happens. I just feel empty. But . . . the past two days, I've felt like there's something urgent I've forgotten. Something drastic."

"Do you feel you're in danger?"

"What?"

"In danger. A danger to yourself or others?"

"No. You're not listening to me. I don't feel enough to hurt myself. I'm not depressed. I'm not manic. I'm *nothing*. It's like the wires in my brain are disconnected. Look, I'm not at risk of offing myself or anyone else. But I'm scared to death I'm going to just watch the best years of my life go by, like I'm staring at a fish tank."

IN MANY WAYS, EARLY-STAGE VENTURE capital is a soap opera.

Most of the sets are the same. The same characters appear and reappear; they have dramatic reversals and successes, fade out for a while, then return with what they swear is the next big thing.

Secrets are kept. Rumors spread at the speed of light.

Companies get hot, and the hotter they are, the more excited— and nervous—investors become. And for the last few days I've gotten e-mail after e-mail insisting I meet with a young man who is white-hot around here, the talk of the town. Or the whisper, actually; they'll talk once their money is in. But everyone I've spoken with has one very big problem with him.

His name is Yul Tan, and we sit alone in the conference room at my office, his laptop on the table beside a stack of folders. He isn't nervous or overconfident, not a talkative type. He's focused, all about his work. And it might be the most interesting work I've heard about in a while.

"I'm calling it Q-net," Yul says, laying a piece of paper in front of me. "Stands for quantum network. The modems will work in existing computers. No wires. It uses quantum entanglement to move massive amounts of data at the speed of light."

He gets into the details, a little too far into the weeds, but I don't stop him. It's incredible. A no-cost, high-speed Internet, no infrastructure required. This will turn the world on its head. The potential is virtually limitless.

"I filed the patents two weeks ago."

I nod. "Smart. Especially before making the rounds. Where do you see this company in five years, Yul? What do you want to happen here?"

The answer that follows is the problem, the issue my compatriots have and perhaps part of their motive for me to meet with him.

Yul Tan isn't terribly interested in commercializing the technology or in money at all, for that matter. He wants to open the patents up to manufacturers for free. He just wants to work on the software, making it more efficient, ensuring that his new network stays secure from hackers and anyone who might use it for ill purposes. In short, he's the real deal—an honest-to-God good human being, out to make this world a better place.

But he's dangerous to investors. They don't mind if the company loses money early, or even if there's no clear plan to make a profit at the outset—but the folks running the thing have to at least want to make money eventually.

I'm not sure Yul does. But I am sure that I'll do anything I can to help him. The world needs what he's created, and it needs more people like Yul Tan and more people who would help someone like him. I want to be one of those people. Maybe that's what I'm investing in. Either way, I feel that flame again, the match that flares and then gutters quickly, but still . . .

At the threshold of my office, Yul pauses. "I have to ask. I have this feeling . . . Have we met before?"

"I don't think so." I would have remembered Yul Tan.

We go through the possibilities: conferences we've both attended, talks I've given, potential mutual acquaintances. Yul's not trying to make a social connection or to become more familiar; he works at the problem, his head down, focused, like he's solving for x in a complex equation.

But we don't find the missing variable.

When he's gone, I sit in my office, pondering. There *is* something familiar about Tan.

My admin, Julia, floats in and lays a sheet of paper on my desk. "Tickets. I know you hate the mobile app."

"Tickets to what?"

"New York."

"What?"

"The Shaw meeting. Did you forget?"

I rub my temples. I definitely forgot. Why would I schedule this the day after I got back from London? But that's not the real issue, I realize suddenly.

For the first time in my life, I'm terrified of flying.

"Want me to cancel it?" Julia asks, arching her eyebrows.

"No. I'll go."

It would be rude to cancel. But . . . I wonder what my chances of landing alive are.

CHAPTER FORTY-SIX

Harper

EXPECTED OUTCOME:

Zero to little progress on Alice Carter.

Decision made. I'll write the bloody Shaw biography.

Agent informed.

Best night of sleep of my life.

Actual outcome:

Alice Carter story explosion.

No decision made. More torn than ever.

Agent annoyed.

Didn't sleep a wink.

It poured out of me. Ideas. Characters. Storylines. Outline after outline. I wrote until my hand hurt. It was effortless, like I was possessed, as if I was writing books I'd written, or at least mapped out, before.

I'm up the creek now.

I sit on the floor of my flat, staring at my poster boards and notes.

Alice Carter and the Eternal Secrets
Alice Carter and the Dragons of Tomorrow
Alice Carter and the Fleet of Destiny
Alice Carter and the Endless Winter
Alice Carter and the Ruins of Yesteryear
Alice Carter and the Tombs of Forever
Alice Carter and the River of Time
What am I going to do?

On the kitchen counter, my phone rings.

I walk over and eye it from a distance like a dead but venomous snake I need to toss in the rubbish heap.

When it stops ringing and the voice-mail tune chimes, I step closer, tap the play button, and close my eyes.

"Harper, if you're out, they're moving to their second choice. They don't want to do that. I don't want them to do that. Call me."

I put the phone back on the counter, drift back to the living room, and collapse into my nest of scribblings.

I lie there thinking about another story, unrelated to Alice Carter. It would be a stand-alone. A thriller. Or is it sci-fi?

I wonder if this is my brain's desperate, last-ditch effort at keeping the kid in me alive, my subconscious's last stand. Is this my last chance to pursue my dream of writing fiction? I turn over and scribble some notes, then draw on the poster board: a gaping dark circle, half a plane, torn open roughly, sinking in a lake under a crescent moon.

It's not the type of story I would normally read—or write—but I like it. It's different. It feels like a potboiler, a simple thriller, a race against time, but it's really about the characters, and how their lives change. About decisions and how they are the keys to the future. Again, the ideas pour out of me. I don't even recall falling asleep, sprawled out on the living room floor, the pen still in my hand.

CHAPTER FORTY-SEVEN

Nick

MILD MIGRAINE AND NAUSEA ON THE FLIGHT TO New York, about a fourth of the agony I experienced during the last flight. Only vomited twice. Maybe it was the shorter flight. For the first time in my life, I'm scared that I could be really sick. I barely slept last night, my mind racing, weird thoughts running through my head.

I contemplate what might be wrong with me while an acquaintance, another investor, devours his overpriced poached eggs.

After the niceties, he gets down to the matter at hand, a promising company that will preside over a new world (his words).

"Orbital colonies?"

"Not just that. We're talking asteroid mining, vacation spots—the most expensive real estate in human history." He leans in. "And we can create as much of it as we want."

He rattles off another half-dozen potential business models, a buffet of enticements for capitalists, then waits, seeing which bait I go for.

The migraine returns, a low pulsing that ratchets up each second, like a building symphony inside my head, playing chords of pain.

I close my eyes and mumble, "It's sort of outside my wheelhouse."

"Word is, you're looking to branch out." He leans in. "This is pretty far out there."

I flag the waiter and ask for a cup of coffee. Maybe that will help.

"It's intriguing," I say, trying to hide the pain as I speak. "But I'm looking for . . . a change in the impact my companies have. I'm looking to do something, I don't know, with more social impact."

"Oh, for God's sake, not you, too, Nick. The whole world's going crazy."

According to my breakfast companion, the dispersal of the world's great fortunes and the epidemic of undeserved wealth syndrome will be the ruin of the Western world.

"You want social impact, Nick? Think about this: there have been five mass extinction events on this planet. It's a matter not of *if* but *when* the lights go out for good." He tosses another piece of egg into his mouth. "We've got to get off this rock."

"How's the survival of the human race for the greater good?"

IN THE CAB RIDE TO Oliver Norton Shaw's home, my phone rings. Yul Tan. It's 9:43 A.M. here, 6:43 A.M. in San Francisco.

Calls this early are rare in my world. Founders stay up late and sleep late. Investors spend the morning reading articles and sending e-mails, or having breakfast with acquaintances with warped worldviews.

I hit the answer button. "Nick Stone."

"Mr. Stone . . ." I told Yul several times in the meeting to call me Nick, but I sense that there are bigger problems at the moment. His voice is nervous, agitated, a stark departure from his composure at our meeting. "I, uh, I thought I'd get your voice mail."

"I can hang up and let you call back, if you prefer."

He doesn't laugh. An awkward silence stretches out, and I wish I hadn't made the joke.

"I've been thinking about you. Where we might have met. I can't stop thinking about it." He coughs. "Can't sleep."

Silence. This is typically the point at which I would politely get off the phone and promptly start calling people about things like restraining orders and making sure that home alarm really does work.

Instead I shift in the backseat of the cab, turning my head away from the driver. "Yes . . . I've been thinking about it, too. Do you have any idea—"

"No."

I wait, but he doesn't say another word, only coughs. I think he called me out of desperation.

Finally I say, "I've had these migraines—"

"Feels like my head is going to explode. Like I'm sick."

"When did it start, Yul?"

"Right after I met you."

SITTING IN OLIVER NORTON SHAW'S study, waiting for him to arrive, I run through what I know: I got sick on the flight from London to San Francisco. I got better after I landed. Yul Tan got sick, seemingly with the same neurological disorder, shortly after he met me. That tells me it's communicable. It's a pathogen I acquired either in London or on the plane. I'll make some calls after this meeting. I'm almost scared to fly home. Nothing I can do about it now, though. I just have to get through this meeting. I try to focus on my surroundings, anything but the nagging thought that I'm really sick.

Shaw's study is decorated in the classical master-of-the-universe motif: mahogany panels, Persian rugs, two stories of bookshelves filled with ancient tomes he's probably never read, floor-to-ceiling windows that look out on Central Park, the type of view only acquired through inheritance or quick action, an all-cash bid the same day such a property hits the market.

Despite the lavish office, the sixtysomething-year-old man who shuffles in is warm and unassuming, almost grandfatherly. That surprises me. His reputation is just the opposite: a driven, borderline ruthless, uncompromising captain of industry who never relents once he sets a goal.

He extends his hand, but I beg off, saying I'm fighting a cold. That seems less jarring than "a mysterious illness of unknown origin."

We recount the few times we've met: a few years ago in Sun Valley, an IPO party here in New York, possibly at the funeral of a friend of my father's. Then he gets to it.

"I appreciate you coming, Nick. I requested this meeting because I'm interested in investing heavily in a few early-stage ventures. High risk. High impact."

"That's great. Unfortunately, our current fund is closed. We'll probably raise again in two years." Staying on good terms with folks like Oliver Norton Shaw is part and parcel of my business. Wealthy individuals form the bulk of our investors, and they're usually the easiest to manage. But my words come out without conviction, and I realize that I'm not sure I'll raise another fund in two years. This could be it for me—and I have no idea what's next.

"I'm not looking for that kind of investment."

Shaw talks at length about the type of investments he *is* looking for: global endeavors with the potential to impact every person on the planet, which may or may not make money. "I'm not interested in charity either, Nick."

"What are you interested in?"

"I want to find the lever that moves the world. I'm looking for that nascent invention that will be the portal to humanity's future—not something like the airplane, but something like the *wheel*. Hell—like *fire*. Paradigm shifts that I can help usher to the rest of the world. I don't want to measure my return in dollars and cents, or positive press, or pats on the back at parties. All my friends are giving away their fortunes. I applaud them. Projects in the third world, inner-city initiatives, libraries, free Internet access, disease eradication. It's all important. But it's not who I am. I'm a builder. And I want to build something that will last an eternity, that will be the beacon that guides the human race into the long tomorrow, making us better, year after year. That's why you're here. I have a vision of what I want to build, but I need the pieces. I need the right people. I need access to those inventions and companies that could change history. There's a hole in the world, Nick. That hole lies at the intersection of capitalism and government. There are countless inventions and organizations wait-ing down there in the dark. Their potential to benefit humanity is

limitless, but they'll never see the light of day. They're too unwieldy
for governments: they're global, risky. Capitalism ignores them: it's
not their kind of return on investment. Some won't make money at
all. Some will take decades, maybe centuries, to build. Generations.
Money isn't as patient as it once was. I want to plug that hole. I want
to build an organization, a foundation that can reach down, long and
deep, across the ages, bringing these innovations to the surface."

"Fascinating."

"You know the kinds of ventures I'm talking about?"

I don't know if it's all coincidence or fate or whatever, but I'm
starting to believe that I was meant to be right here, right now for a
very good reason.

"I know of a few."

I tell him about Yul Tan, about Q-net, and about the scientist who
bought the mining patents and his ideas for RailCell, or possibly
Podway—how the two technologies could link the world, one virtually, one physically.

We talk at length about how both companies could be ruined by the
wrong investors, never reaching their true potential. How the world
would benefit from both. He asks me about others, and I can't resist telling him about the Gibraltar Project. Shaw comes alive, looking younger
than his years, the ideas flowing out of him, how his connections and
existing companies might move the project along. We talk about my
meeting this morning, the orbital colonies. Shaw sees the true potential
of the project, which isn't about real estate or asteroid mining or anything else on the investment buffet I was shown: it's about inspiring
the human race, about making us dream again, about creating a cause
that's bigger than nations or races, a grand goal that unifies humanity.
And I realize that's what I saw, too, and why I was so turned off by the
pitch this morning, focused as it was on profit and not people. It was the
right product—as my acquaintance said, far out there, not my typical
investment. A project with huge potential impact. The approach was my
problem. I see the world as Shaw does. He's speaking as if he's reading
my mind. With every word I come alive a little more, ideas occurring to
me, us feeding off each other. Gradually phrases like "You could" and "I
would" transition to "*We should*," and then, ultimately, "*We will*."

I don't know exactly what we're building, but it's taking shape right here in this room. It's like a new venture capital fund, his resources and mine (which pale in comparison), and our complementary know-how: start-ups for me, large-scale organizations for him. "We're bookends" are his words.

As the clock's hands near twelve, I realize I don't want the meeting to end. I'm unsure where things go from here, even whose court the ball is in or who's in charge.

"How long are you in town for, Nick?"

"Not sure," I say, in lieu of *I'm a little nervous about flying right now—I seem to have a mysterious disease that's activated by air travel.*

"Good—we have a lot more to talk about."

I couldn't agree more. I nod.

"We're going to need a lot of help to build what we're planning, Nick. Visionaries, scientists. And money. Fortunes. Billions, possibly trillions, of dollars. You know about raising money. You brought me a gift today, and it was more than I could have asked for—and more than I expected to accomplish today, if I'm being honest. Yet, I had a feeling about you, and I know you have a talent for getting people to reach deep and see an idea the way you do. That's why I thought you would be perfect for this, and I don't think I'm wrong. We just have to think about how we package what we're selling."

"I agree."

"To me, we're selling the only thing money can't buy."

My mind flashes to the word *love.*

"Status," says Shaw. "The issue is how to value status. There are two components—extrinsic and intrinsic value. How much do others value status, the people the beholder respects? That's the extrinsic value. And how much benefit does the status hold for you personally, excluding all external factors and influence? That's the intrinsic value. In my mind, I've been calling this . . . *venture* the Titan Foundation. Its members will be Titans. It will be the most exclusive club in the world. But the people we'll recruit are used to status and exclusive clubs. We need something else. I have someone coming in at three. She's been working on a key to convincing these people to join us. Something irresistible. Her name is Sabrina Schröder, and I can't wait for you to meet her."

CHAPTER FORTY-EIGHT

Nick

WHEN I RETURN TO OLIVER'S HOME IN THE afternoon, his assistant doesn't lead me to the master-of-the-universe study where we met before. Rather, she leaves me in a much smaller space, an office with a simple, worn desk, two chairs, and a couch. The shelves are filled not with collector's editions of books, but with personal photographs and popular nonfiction books, mostly history and science—books the masses read.

This is Shaw's personal study, and its simplicity and humility reflect the man I met earlier today, the person the public has never seen. He sits on the couch, a keyboard and trackpad on the coffee table in front of him. "Hi," he says, pushing up from the couch to greet me.

"Hi." I hold a hand up, urging him to keep his seat. It's strange. I only met him this morning, but I feel like I've known Oliver Norton Shaw for a hundred years or more.

He focuses on the screen on the wall opposite, a high-resolution panel that must have cost a small fortune.

To my surprise, he pulls up Facebook: the profile of a girl in her late twenties or early thirties. Blond hair. A twinkle in her eyes and a slightly mischievous smile on her lips, as if the picture was taken just before she laughed out loud at a prank pulled on a friend.

He studies the screen intently, reading the latest posts.

"Didn't figure you for a Facebook user." I pause, then shrug. "No offense."

"None taken. I'm not. My assistant's idea. Apparently it's become somewhat acceptable to stalk people on the Internet."

I take a seat on the couch beside him. "Just some harmless stalking, huh? Glad it's not anything weird."

He chuckles as he works the keyboard.

"She's a biographer, a really talented young lady. I met with her recently. I want her to write my story, but I haven't been able to get an answer from her. My assistant suggested looking her up to see if she'd posted any clues as to what she might do. This new generation . . . they revel in putting it all out there, dirty laundry and all." He gives me a sly sidelong glance. "No offense."

"None taken," I say, smiling. I scan the profile. Harper Lane. *Harper Lane.* I don't know the name, but . . . I know the face. For a moment, my mind flickers between memories, places I think I've seen her. On a plane. Her captivating eyes looking up at mine. The plane shaking. No. That's not right. A guy behind me, long blond hair. Jerk. Me turning to him. Then . . . I get her bag out of the overhead and set it in the aisle for her, pausing a second to hold the handle, afraid it will topple over.

Oliver pauses, registering the look on my face. "You know her?"

"I . . . think I was on a flight with her to London."

"She lives there. She was probably headed home after our meeting. She's a big part of this, Nick. We won't have a lot to show for years, maybe decades. We'll be selling the sizzle for a long time, the promise of what's to come. There's only so much you can accomplish sitting in a room, telling these people firsthand. This biography will lay out my vision, where I'm coming from. I want it to inspire and explain. I want it to be a call to arms—written by an outsider. She's the one. I hope she takes the job."

"How's it looking?"

"Doubtful."

He scrolls down, revealing Harper Lane's latest post.

Harper: Can't bloody sleep for two days. Losing it. The Decision.
The Decision is crushing me :(Remedies anyone?

The comments section is a mix of wisecracks from guys and action-able advice from women, everything from Ambien to chamomile tea, with several recommendations to hide all snacks if she opts for the Ambien route.

So she's undecided. But that isn't what really interests me.

I can't tear my eyes away from her. There's something about her, maybe—

"Sir, your three o'clock is here."

Oliver's assistant retreats, returning quickly with a woman about my age, perhaps slightly older, late thirties or early forties. She's fit, and her eyes are intense, unblinking. Her hair is black, about shoulder length. She strides in mechanically.

"Nick Stone, this is Dr. Sabrina Schröder."

She extends her hand and I take it without thinking, an automatic reaction.

When her skin touches mine, the study disappears, and I'm no longer standing. I'm lying on my back on a cold metal surface, blinding lights shining down on me. I can barely see her standing above me, holding my hand in a different way, squeezing as the table I'm on slides away.

Her hand slips from mine as the lights fade, and I'm once again standing in Oliver's study, her hand still in mine, as if we had never left this place.

I open my mouth to speak but stop, not sure what to say. What's happening to me?

For a brief moment, I think Sabrina might have seen it, too. She blinks, searches my face, then turns toward Harper Lane's Facebook profile on the screen, looking confused.

"Do you two . . . know each other?" Oliver asks, glancing between us.

A pause.

If she says yes—

"No," Sabrina answers curtly, releasing my hand.

And then the woman who walked in is back, the unblinking eyes and expressionless mask. She takes the seat opposite Oliver and me on the couch and begins without any prompting.

I rub my temples and close my eyes, wondering what exactly is happening to me.

"You all right, Nick?"

That's a very good question.

"Yeah, sorry—lots of travel in the past few days. Dr. Schröder?"

"Yes. Mr. Shaw asked me here to describe my research, which relates to progeria syndrome . . ."

INCREDIBLE. AFTER SABRINA LEAVES, OLIVER and I sit in his private study, reflecting on the day's conversations, him sipping tea, me drinking water, pacing occasionally.

The scale and genius of his plan is finally gripping me. Immortality is the key, the linchpin that will ensure that what we build is never destroyed. I've bought in. Completely. I know it now. This is *the* change. What I must do. What's been missing. Excitement. Energy. I feel inspired again, curious about what tomorrow holds. There's so much to do.

I imagine our cabal, a hundred people marching across time together, the world's best and brightest, carrying the torch for a better tomorrow. I'm humbled to be involved, and yet I know I am meant to be a part of this. To help *lead* this.

The Titan Foundation isn't about a handful of innovations—Q-net, Podway, Orbital Dynamics, or the Gibraltar Dam. It's about an endless flow of projects on the same scale, generation after generation. An endless human renaissance.

We're not talking about feeding a single starving village for a year, providing clean water for a war-torn region in ruins, or curing a plague in the third world. We're talking about an end to all humanity's problems, any that come, in any age. A group to guide us, watch over the world. Continuity. I feel as though I'm standing at a turning point in human history.

Oliver's phone rings. He apologizes for taking the call, which he says is urgent. I insist he take it and get up to leave, but he gestures for me to stay.

He picks up and listens attentively, shaking his head every few seconds. Whatever the caller says disturbs him deeply. He seems to deflate with every word, slumping back into the brown leather chair behind the desk. Finally he starts asking questions quickly. He's out of his element, that's clear. The talk is of the British court process, gag orders, whether he can sue for conspiracy to libel before anything has been published.

After he hangs up, he stares at the bookshelf beside his desk for a long moment.

"We're all going to have to make sacrifices for this foundation, Nick."

I nod, sensing that he wants to say more.

"My son's very upset about my decision. He's throwing a selfish, irrational fit, the type a child might throw when you take his toys away, which is essentially what's happening. And it's my fault. His mother died twenty years ago, of cancer, far too young. Broke my heart. She's the only thing I ever loved, besides my company. That company was all I had left, and it never would have grown into what it is if she hadn't passed away.

"I was a sorry father. I doted on Grayson. Coddled him. Never said no. The worst thing you can do for a child is give him everything he wants. Humans should grow up a little hungry, struggle a little, be made to strive for something. That's what builds character. Struggle reveals who we really are. That journey shows us what we want from this world. Now Grayson wants what he's always taken for granted: my money."

"What do you want to do?"

"He says if I give him a little money now, that'll be the end of it. If not, he promises he'll extract his inheritance by other means, and it will cost me a lot more. He thinks he knows me, thinks I'll figure up the dollar amounts and pay out the lesser: cash to keep him quiet, hush money that will keep my reputation intact. That reputation is essential to building this foundation."

I don't envy Oliver's situation. He walks over and stares at a picture on the wall: a young man in his twenties with long, flowing blond hair, the smile on his face just a little too self-confident. I've seen that face, slightly older, but wearing the same smirk. On a plane. Then outside it. Him shoving me. My fist connecting with that face.

No. That's wrong. We were on the plane, shoving. He walked away muttering obscenities.

It's like there are two memories.

I reach up, touching my temple. The migraine is back. It's nearly blinding. I close my eyes, hoping it will pass.

I can barely hear Oliver's words.

"If there's one thing I've learned in business, it's that giving a tyrant what he wants doesn't solve your problem. It only makes it worse. My son has to grow up sometime. This is as good a time as any."

I say nothing to this. But I want to. The kid in the picture is acting like a brat, but the truth is that he just wants his father's attention. That's all. I have my own feelings about my father. I've come to terms with them, and I was lucky enough to find my own way. There's so many things I want to say, but flashes are going off in my head, washing over me, plunging me into darkness, and then blinding light.

I stumble, groping my way to a chair. I sense Shaw near me, yelling something—I think getting his assistant—but I wave him off. I just need to sit . . .

CHAPTER FORTY-NINE

Nick

I WAS ONLY PASSED OUT FOR A FEW minutes, Shaw told me. I apologized profusely—the idea that my . . . episode might have jeopardized what we were talking about today almost brings on a new wave of nausea—but he assured me he was only concerned for my welfare. The concern in his eyes, the way his hand rested on my shoulder—it was genuine. *Is* genuine. He ordered a car for me, waited for me to get in, and told me to get some rest.

"Seriously—get some sleep. You're health's important, Nick." He smiles. "Soon, we're going to have all the time in the world."

THE MIGRAINE FADED DURING THE ride from Oliver's home to the hotel, but I can still feel it idling at the back of my head, waiting to attack, almost taunting me, the dread as oppressive as the pain. I've been lucky. For my entire life, I've been pretty healthy. Now I'm beginning to understand what it's like for a few of my friends with chronic medical conditions. The uncertainty. The lurking fear. Knowing when you go to bed that tomorrow your health could be markedly worse. Knowing that right when you have to be someplace important, when people are counting on you to be at your best, you might not be able to, and there's nothing you can do about it. Committing anyway—that takes guts. I know, because I'm scared now. I'm scared this won't just be an episode, a bump in the road I get past. I'm scared this will persist. I'm scared it will limit what I can do, keep me from this incredible opportunity with Oliver. That's new. Yesterday I didn't have that kind of hope, or fear for that matter. Feeling. That's something.

I need help. I'm desperate enough to risk another flight back to San Francisco. Seeing a doctor there, at home, where I know people, feels a lot less scary. I'm sure I'll need to find a specialist.

In my room I instinctively turn on the TV to the six o'clock news—my postwork ritual—and get my laptop out, ready to search for flights.

The travel site flashes my most recent trips, and my eyes lock on one.

Flight 305: New York (JFK) → London (Heathrow)

A bolt of pain shoots from the back of my head to the front, bulging there. The pressure pushes at my eye sockets like water from a fire hose. The surge passes, the pain tapering to a drip.

My eyes still tightly closed, I stand and stagger to the sink. I feel around, find a glass, fill it with tap water, and gulp it down. What could help? Advil. Anything. I don't have any. Maybe the front desk does.

I'm reaching for the phone when the newsreader catches my attention.

"*. . . lost contact with the plane around four fourteen p.m. Eastern time. At this time, authorities don't believe the flight was hijacked. However, they have activated search-and-rescue teams to begin . . .*"

Every word is a sledgehammer to my head. I stumble toward the table, grabbing for the remote, almost blind from the pain.

The report about the missing plane goes off before I can reach it, and the pain fades.

Sight returns. I glance at the papers strewn across the table.

The sketches of the Gibraltar Dam. They're wrong. I pick one up.

The buildings—they're too short. They look like nubs. Nubs of what? Fingers. Fingers that have been cut off. Why would buildings be fingers? Makes no sense. But they were. That's what I remember. Not imagine—*remember.* I rifle through the rest of the papers, everything from the last two days of meetings. This is the only sketch of the dam. It's wrong. It should be a giant hand, reaching out of the dam . . . a symbol.

A wave of pressure. I squeeze my eyes shut. A single tear rolls down my face.

This is it. The origin point. I think.

It all started after the Gibraltar Dam meeting. Or did it? Was it after the Podway meeting? Or the flight?

I glance at the stack of papers. The letterhead reads RAILCELL. It's wrong, too. It will never be called RailCell. Why am I so certain? The cars are off, too. They're too big. They'll be smaller.

Another pulse through my brain, like a balloon being inflated, pushing out in every direction.

I lay my head on the table.

The first attack was on the plane back from London to San Francisco. I must have contracted this before then.

When?

What do I know?

What was the next event?

Yul Tan. Q-net. That meeting. The entire time I felt a nagging sensation. His voice echoes in my head.

It works with quantum entanglement. Particles encounter each other and become linked. After that, their states become dependent upon each other. I use that quantum phenomenon to transmit data across space and time.

His research is the key.

Key to what?

Q-net.

No. That's not right. It's not about Q-net.

What's happening to me? I rub my eyes.

Yul's voice is in my head again. *I've had some interference the past few days, like static on the network. I was worried, but it just stopped.*

It just stopped.

But something started for Yul after we met. He was sick, too. Just like me. He felt something, as if we had met before. Memories he couldn't reach.

The next attack: the flight to New York. But it wasn't as bad. Wasn't the same.

Breakfast. The orbital colonies. The pitch that was wrong.

Shaw knew it was wrong. The way it was presented was wrong. But the idea was right.

The whole time with Shaw, everything was right.

Sabrina.

When I touched her hand, I was gone, on a hard, cold table, staring up. The lights. She was there.

She knew. I saw it in her eyes.

The touch was the key.

The woman on Facebook. The biographer. The sensation when I saw her. Sabrina looked at her, too. Knew her.

I focus on my laptop. My eyes catch on the open window, on Flight 305, and a strike splits my head, sending me reeling back.

That's a flash point. Flight 305. What does it mean? Is it because the flight from London was total agony?

My eyes closed, I find the Windows key, hold it down, and press M, minimizing all the windows. I open a new browser and navigate to Harper Lane's Facebook profile.

The instant I see her face, chills run through me, growing stronger, numbing my body.

I replay the moment we met. On the plane. In the aisle. It was dark, and half the plane was gone.

No. Wrong.

Our plane was whole, sitting on the tarmac at Heathrow.

The tarmac at Heathrow. A sea of grass.

I shake my head. That's impossible.

Planes overturned, crumbling.

Not right.

Our plane was whole, sitting at the jet bridge. She was there, in a first-class seat, waiting to get off. I stood up, helped her with her bag. She peered up at me, her beautiful eyes wide.

I blink and she's trapped in the seat, her leg caught.

Water all around her.

She's scared, can't get free.

No. Impossible. A flooded plane at the jet bridge?

Focus.

I scan the screen.

There's a new post on her profile.

Harper: Indecision 2015 Update. Finally slept for a few hours and dreamed I was on sinking plane after it crashed. I was pulled underwater and couldn't get out :(

She saw it, too. How is that possible?

Sweat springs up on my forehead. I feel the memories slipping away, the two versions of reality separating again, a kite I can see clearly at first, carried away by the wind, drifting up until it's just a tiny speck and then invisible, as if it were never there.

I reach for the remote, intending to turn the TV off, but the words from a new report stop me cold. *"Authorities say if the plane did crash into the water, that makes it much harder to find and decreases the chances that there will be any survivors—"*

A new wave of numbing spasms battles with the surging pain in my head.

I close my eyes.

The plane did hit the water. But they lived. Some of them.

I tried to save them.

How could a plane hit the water without disintegrating? It would be like hitting concrete at six hundred miles per hour.

The answers are in my head—how, I don't know.

Facts emerge, as if answering my unspoken question.

The plane slowed down after the turbulence. The pilots deployed the landing gear to further slow it down. It broke apart and the tail section spun and dragged against the trees, which also decreased its speed. It hit the lake backward, tail first. Something—trees under the water, maybe—kept it from sinking right after impact. I can almost see it sticking out of the water.

I feel dizzy. I'm going to throw up. I grip the table, then push myself up. I stagger to the sink, push the handle back quickly, and watch the water pour out, gushing down the drain, which has a single bar across a round circle. The water flows in, like water into a sinking plane, a plane torn in half.

For a second I don't see the sink drain. I see a plane in cross-section, a jagged dark circle.

Then it's gone.

I splash more water on my face. It's so cold, but . . . it helps. I remember the feeling. Cold water on my face, numbing it as I swim. I turn the faucet all the way to cold, cup my hands until my fingers tingle, start to burn, then go numb. With each second it hurts more, but I can feel less. As the burning, numbing sensation creeps up my hand, my mind becomes clearer. I splash the water on my face and inhale, shivering.

I'm running through the woods. A dozen points of light bounce in the dark forest before me. My breath flows out, white steam against the beads of light.

Then I'm back in my hotel room, the water flowing from the sink, the TV silent in the background.

I'm giving a speech. On the lake bank in the dark. *No one will save those people if we don't. Their lives are in our hands. . . .*

I look at the laptop screen. At her eyes. I hear the running water. Like a waterfall.

My head explodes. Waves coalesce into a bolt of pain. A hammer strike. Pain so bad I lose feeling in my extremities, and for a brief moment I think I'm paralyzed, but I can see my hand moving in the mirror.

I bring another handful of water to my face, pressing it into my eyes, and when I take my hands away, I'm standing on a muddy bank before a torn plane sticking up out of the lake. Every exhalation sends white steam into the night, and there's no sound, no other sensation. The world, save for my breathing, seems frozen.

Slowly, with great effort, I turn to my right, where a woman stands still, her face unreadable. "How about you?" I ask.

"Yeah . . . I'm good. I'm a good swimmer."

I turn back to the plane in the lake, but it's gone. I'm in my hotel room. The newscast is ending. The glowing computer screen stares at me. The face. The woman on Facebook. It was her.

CHAPTER FIFTY

Nick

I'M LOSING IT.

My hands are slick with sweat. The voice over the loudspeaker booms, "*All passengers, this is a final boarding call for Flight 314 to London Heathrow. All passengers...*"

But I'm the only passenger left in the waiting area for this flight. I sit, staring at the woman working the counter. She's holding the radio with its curling cord, the button depressed as she speaks, staring directly at me.

She knows there's only one booked seat unfilled, one person left to board the flight who has cleared security and is somewhere in the concourse. She figures it's me.

This is crazy. I should turn around and go home, get my head checked.

Instead I stand and walk over, hand her my boarding pass. She glances at my sweat-drenched hair and pale, clammy skin. "Are you all right, sir?"

"Fine . . . It's just . . . I've had some bad transatlantic flights recently."

I DON'T KNOW HARPER LANE'S number. I searched for it. No landline. No way to find her cell. Don't know her e-mail. I thought about a Facebook friend request, but . . . how creepy is that? What would I say? "Remember me? I got your carry-on down after a flight we shared. Hey, do you happen to remember that flight crashing in the English countryside? 'Cause I do, and things got really crazy after that . . ."

What I do know—about all I know—is where she lives.

Because I've been there. In 2147.

And now I'm walking there. In 2015. The thing I need to figure out at this point is what I will tell the police when I'm arrested.

An elderly man wearing an argyle sweater and a flat cap holds the door to her building open for me as I approach.

I skip to catch it, thanking him.

Up the first flight of stairs.

Second.

Third.

On the fourth, I see her door.

Crazy.

I knock, every tap sending a sensation like an electric shock from my fingers to the pit of my stomach. I fight the urge to turn on my heel and run.

On the other side of the door, I hear the sound of socked feet on the wooden floor. I wipe the sweat from my forehead.

The tiny point of light in the peephole goes dark.

A thud on the other side of the door. The peephole is light again. She's likely going for her phone, calling the police.

A clicking sound.

The door swings in slowly, and she steps into the narrow opening.

My voice comes out a whisper. "Hi."

Her jaw falls as she turns white as a sheet. Her eyes go wide, making them seem even bigger, more endless, more captivating, than they already are.

"Hi," she breathes, barely audible.

She lets her hands fall to her sides, and the heavy wooden door creaks open, revealing the room. It's a wreck. Wadded-up pieces of notebook paper lie in drifts at the edges of the room. Layers of construction paper cover the floor like unraked autumn leaves. Markers are scattered everywhere. It looks like a day-care center. Maybe her children? Nieces and nephews?

On the couch and two chairs, seven big sheets of poster board are propped up, facing out, like artworks on easels at an exhibition. Actually, they're more like scientific papers at a conference: titles scrawled at the top, rough drawings and timelines below. Dragons. Ships. Pyramids. And endless notes, scribblings. Arrows and strikethroughs. And a name.

Alice Carter.

They're all about Alice Carter.

Who the hell is Alice Carter? Another passenger? Possibly. I only got a few names.

As the door swings completely open, I see an eighth sheet of poster board. A final exhibit. FLIGHT 305 is scrawled across the top in big block letters. Below it: "Stand-alone novel? Sci-fi? Thriller? Time travel?"

She thinks it's all in her head. Another story she made up.

Below the subtitle, there's a sketch: the round, torn end of a plane jutting above a placid lake, a crescent moon in the sky.

Names fill the space below.

Nick Stone. Sabrina Schröder. Yul Tan.

Not fiction?

Hope fills me, gives me the courage to step into the room. She keeps her feet planted, her body still. Only her eyes follow me.

Time to take a chance. "How much do you remember?"

She swallows, blinks, but her voice comes out clear, confident. "Everything."

I exhale. For the first time the pounding in my head subsides, every passing second washing it away.

She steps closer and scrutinizes my face, especially my forehead, where the gashes were after the Titans invaded the camp, the wound she cared for in the abandoned stone farmhouse. She reaches up, touches that place where my hairline meets my forehead, just as she did in the Podway, in the only moment we had alone in all the time we spent in 2147. I wrap my fingers firmly around her wrist and let my thumb slide into her palm, just as before.

"What do you want to do now?" I ask.

"I want to finish what we started on the way to London."

CHAPTER FIFTY-ONE

Harper

WE LIE IN THE BED WHERE I FOUND the notebooks, where I read them, a few days ago—or 132 years from now, depending on how you choose to see it. Either way, this is the exact place where I saw what my life had become. I was horrified then, and I'm terrified now. But more than that, I'm excited.

Then, when I found the journals, Nick walked in, sat on the end of this very bed, beside me, and told me that the journal wasn't my future, that it didn't have to be. That I could make a different choice.

It seemed like an empty promise at the time, kind words said to ease my pain and quiet my mind.

But it came true. Here I am. Back in my time. With the knowledge of everything that happened.

The terrible future I almost repeated will never be.

And Nick Stone is here in this bed with me. With all his memories. And none of his clothes.

Perfect.

WHEN THE SUNLIGHT THROUGH THE wide window in my bedroom becomes too bright to ignore, Nick sits up and pulls his boxers on, then his trousers.

I panic a little.

How clean is the shower?

Not as clean as I would like it to be.

And breakfast. I bet a starving vagabond wouldn't eat what's left in my fridge.

He pulls his shirt on and glances back at me. "Gonna get some breakfast. What would you like?"

I want to go with him, but I'm a fright. I didn't get a great deal of sleep last night—not that I'm complaining about that. But I could use every precious second he's gone to address the previously mentioned domestic concerns. I request a muffin and coffee and suggest a reliable spot around the corner, and then he's gone.

I turn over in bed and put my face in my hands. Why am I so bloody scared?

It's not about the memories anymore, or the decision that has haunted me. It comes down to this: I like Nick Stone very much, and I've no idea what he thinks. In fact, I don't know him at all.

That's not true. Not one bit. I know him very well indeed. I feel like I know every inch of his soul, what kind of person he is. I knew it the first few moments I met him, when he came to the defense of Jillian before the plane crashed, when he stopped the stampede in the nose section and saved a lady who would have been trampled, and those cold, electric moments on the bank of the lake when he rallied the hesitant survivors to swim out to the plane. When he saved my life, at great risk to his own.

That's the man I'm in love with.

But I have no idea how he feels about me. That's what's nerve-racking. I don't know what this means to him: one sleepless night together.

It's not something I've ever done without knowing someone for a long time. It's a big deal to me, and I wonder if it is to him.

I hope it is.

But what if it's not? What if it's something he does all the time? What if this doesn't mean anything to him at all?

The door pops open, and I spring up. God. I haven't done a thing to the flat. It's still a mess, and I've lain here naked in bed like a lazy tart the entire time he was gone.

He holds a brown bag up, and I motion to the kitchen area. I pull a tank top and some pajama pants on and stroll out, trying to look only 10 percent as crazy as the thoughts in my head.

"Breakfast is over. Apparently it's eleven thirty."

He spreads out some sandwiches on the table, four in fact—he wasn't sure what I would want. We sit, nibbling them, talking about matters infinitely less important than the real question at hand.

We work up to more serious matters. The memories, for one. Nick figures dumping them at once in our minds must have presented a problem. Maybe the human psyche has limitations in how it deals with conflicting memories, or maybe the neurons in the brain needed time to integrate the new memories. He thinks the pieces were triggered by the four of us—Yul, Sabrina, him, and me. I was the last piece for him. I smiled when he said that, and he paused and smiled, too.

He's not sure if Sabrina and Yul have recovered all their memories yet, but he's in contact with both of them.

"But there's another call I need to make first." He punches at his cell phone. "What time is it in New York? Almost seven. Close enough."

He drifts over to the window, stands by the chair that holds the poster board with FLIGHT 305 written across the top, and dials a number. He waits as it rings, staring out the window at the people milling about on the street, heading off to lunch.

"Oliver, it's Nick Stone. I hope I didn't wake you."

A short pause.

"No, everything's all right." He looks over at me. "Better than all right, in fact. I've been thinking about Grayson. I think we should include him in the Titan Foundation. I think if we give him the opportunity, the chance to make a change, to be involved at the ground level in how the Shaw fortune is spent . . . I believe he might jump at it."

Nick waits again, his eyes still, then darting back and forth. I like that—it's almost like I can see the wheels inside his brain turning.

"I agree. I think it has to be framed correctly to him. But I have this feeling that if it's presented the right way, if we just give him a chance and a say, he might surprise us. Let's give him the opportunity to do the right thing. You want him to do something with his life, something he has to earn. So *do* that. Let's start by trusting him and involving him and letting him make the decision."

Another pause, and Nick's voice changes, softens.

"No, it's nothing like that. It might sound crazy, but I have this feeling that if you don't give him one last chance, you're going to regret it for the rest of your life."

He rings off after that, and we sit, finishing our coffee at the small, square wooden table in my kitchen, its white paint chipped, a little too authentic to be shabby chic.

When he's finished, and our conversation dies down, he pushes up and goes for his coat, which is buried in a pile of clothes that came off rather quickly last night.

"Don't know what your schedule is, but I have a few errands to run. Should only take a few hours."

"Right. Well, I'll just be here. No plans." Try not to sound crazy. "Nick," I begin, my voice changed, the use of his name already weird, drawing his eyes. God. I'm that crazy chick the morning after, pressing the Talk. This can only end in disaster, yet I know I'm not crazy: this is definitely more than a fling. We've been exposed to each other, and not just in the bedroom, and I can't let him leave—even just for a few hours—without knowing. I force myself to sound casual. "We writers, we don't get out that much." I shrug, trying not to look nervous. "Don't date that much either. Well, I haven't . . . recently."

He scans my face, his expression serious. "Me either, Harper. Look, my work has pretty much been my life since college. Hasn't been much time for anything else. Or anyone." His eyes cut to the bedroom, the sheets still in disarray. "It's a big deal for me, too. I'll show you how big tonight."

CHAPTER FIFTY-TWO

Harper

PANIC LEVEL: ONE MILLION (ON A SCALE OF one to ten).

After those words—*It's a big deal for me, too. I'll show you how big tonight*—Nick kissed me on the forehead and was out the door before I could say a word. It took several minutes to collect my jaw from the floor.

I'm terrified. Even more terrified than this morning, when I thought he was going to roll over in bed, pinch me on the cheek, and say, "Fun times, Harp. Thanks for the memories." Wink. "Catch ya later."

I can't decide if this is better or worse.

I don't want Nick out of my life, but I'm not bloody ready to make a major commitment.

And the reason has nothing to do with him. It's me. I need to get my own life in order, figure out what I want to be when I grow up before I'll be ready for anything like this. But it's here, now, standing—just seconds ago, literally—in my flat. Will I regret it for the rest of my life if things fizzle out between us? I've regretted not being able to be with him before—for a whole lifetime.

Ahhhh!

Got to settle down. Focus. Think.

A solution. When he comes through that door, I will convey to him that I have things in my life I need to put straight, to get on track before I'm ready for anything that serious. It's the truth. I feel like, for the first time, I have it together—I know exactly what I need to be doing in life.

I wouldn't have that without the time I spent in 2147. I also wouldn't have met Nick. I wouldn't trade either for the world.

I know what I need to be doing with my professional life.

Alice Carter.

Because when you're young, life is about pursuing dreams. I have the rest of my life to take the safe road. If I don't write Oliver Norton Shaw's biography, someone will. They might even be better than me. Or maybe a little worse. But it will get done.

No one else will write Alice Carter's story. No one but me. She's depending on me.

That's what life is about: finding something you can do that no one else can, and working your hardest at it. It's about finding someone you love like no one else, someone who loves you like no one else does. That person might be Nick Stone. But I don't know him as well as I know Alice Carter. Not yet.

Now it's about making a plan to ensure I get to know them both. It's going to be risky.

MY AGENT SITS QUIETLY, LISTENING, nodding.

When I finish, he glances around his office, as if looking for the words.

I cringe, mentally bracing for the barrage that will cut me to the bone. *Throwing your career away. Wasting this opportunity I worked so hard to get you. Irresponsible decision.*

Those words never come. Instead I hear, "I respect your decision, Harper. I believe you owe it to yourself to follow your dream. I'll do my best to help you." The words are like a parachute I sway beneath, holding me up, saving my life as my feet land firmly on the ground.

One down.

MY FATHER PASSED AWAY EIGHT years ago from a heart attack. I miss him very much, and so does my mum. He was a schoolteacher in my small hometown, and the years after he passed have been tough, emotionally and financially, for my mum, who is a photographer. He left her two assets of value: our family home and a flat in London that he inherited from his parents, who had been quite well off at one time.

She rents that flat, and for the past few years, she's rented it to me. It's a good trade: I insist on paying her slightly more than the unit would fetch on the market, and on occasion, when I'm between projects and a bit late with the rent—well, she's the best landlord a girl could have.

If I'm vacating, if I'm about to make the change I'm contemplating, something will have to happen with the flat. I want to present her with some options, a clear plan. I want to save her the trouble of coming to London and going through it all. She deserves that. Plus, she's even worse at decisions than I am.

With that in mind, I sit in the estate agent's messy office, listening to him rattle off figures and facts, some more comprehensible than others. The London market is up this percent over last year. The average price has risen to . . . Interest rates are hovering at . . . but they're expected to rise this much more, especially if the BOE tightens next quarter, though the labor market has thrown that into question. Your particular neighborhood has this many properties currently offered, with the average days on the market being . . .

Finally I hold my hand up and try to get down to it. I'm not sure when Nick will be back, and he doesn't have a key. "That's all well and interesting, thank you, really—but what do you reckon my particular flat might fetch?"

He raises his eyebrows and leans back in the seat, as if I've really put him to the test on that one. "Tough to say. But I'll tell you"—he leans in a bit, speaking a little more quietly, as if to shield this now-confidential conversation from passersby in the hall—"if we were to get it on the market directly, we stand a good chance of commanding top dollar." He rattles off some numbers, which, to be fair, do sound quite good. More than I expected.

"If we wait—say, go further into winter—the market's going to get soft. Might already be getting soft. There's talk of a bubble in the paper all the time, and that's got some buyers spooked." He quickly adds, "But probably not for a property your size. There's strong demand for those . . . *at this very moment, at least.*"

I nod. "And if I let it? What might I expect?"

He doesn't like that idea. He would have to hand it off to the letting agent in his office, and when it comes off lease, he assures me it will fetch a great deal less at sale. He details various ways it could go wrong, from bad renters to the distaste in potential buyers' minds. He reminds me that the property has been in my family for generations. That it's remained a single-owner property will add a premium at sale—"For the right buyer," he adds.

I remind him that my income will likely be nonexistent for years to come, that letting it is the only way to hang on to it, which would have been important to my father. I tell him I suppose he would have approved of letting it over selling it, even if it needs a paint job when the lease is up.

Still, the estate agent is sour on the idea, for obvious reasons.

I leave with one more decision to make.

But the bottom line is, I can either advise Mum to sell it or to let it to someone else. Either way, I'm moving back in with her until I can sell the first Alice Carter novel.

NICK ISN'T WAITING BY THE door when I get home, and I'm relieved. I do, however, see my neighbor in the hall, and she's as happy as the day is long, bouncing around like she's won the lottery.

And she sort of has. Apparently you don't even need to list your flat to sell it in London.

She cups her hand over her mouth, "Unsolicited offer, Harp. Foreign buyer. All cash."

Though she won't tell me the price, she does say she didn't even have to think about it.

No doubt the estate agent will call tomorrow with this bit of news, pointing out that it just increases the value of my place and that the new neighbors might be dreadful. "Sell now," he'll say, "or risk losing even more."

Inside my flat, I tidy up some, but I can't help checking the window every few minutes, hoping to catch a glimpse of Nick on his way up.

CHAPTER FIFTY-THREE

Harper

I'M LYING ON THE FLOOR, WRITING IN THE Alice Carter notebook, when the door swings open and Nick strides in, carrying brown bags that waft delicious smells into the flat: chicken and mashed potatoes.

How does he do that? Always get past the front door?

He smiles. "That's the cutest thing I've ever seen."

I look back and watch him pass the fire and the large windows that look out on the street, where the last rays of sunset paint the shops and bustling pedestrians in an orange glow. He sets the bags on the shabby table in the kitchen, and my nerves rise as one last mental rehearsal of my speech plays in my mind.

"Got dinner," he calls.

"Great, I'm famished."

I push up and join him in the small kitchen.

He reaches into his pocket, and my heart stops.

His fingers fumble for something. He looks up, grinning. His hand comes out . . . with his cell phone.

"Listen to this." He places the phone on the table and clicks play on a voice mail.

"Nick, it's Oliver. I just got through with Grayson. It was incredible. He's excited, Nick. It was the best two hours we've ever spent together. We talked about the foundation some—he's got so many ideas, so much energy for it. And we talked about everything else, his mother, things we should have talked about a long, long time ago. I can't tell you how glad I am that you called me this morning. I'm not a religious person. Never have been. But I believe things happen for a reason, and I think people come into our lives at the right time for the right reasons. I think that's why we met, Nick. Anyway, I'm feeling sentimental, and I've been drinking." Shaw laughs quietly. *"So you might want to delete this. Give me a call right after you do."*

Nick glances up, his eyebrows raised.

"Amazing," I say. This is the perfect segue. "It's great news. And hopefully it'll soften the blow when he hears I've said no to the biography."

Nick begins unpacking the takeout. "So you've decided."

"I have. Alice Carter. I'm going to pursue her. My dream."

I pace behind the table, my hands shaking. I stuff them into my pajama pant pockets to hide them—or am I subliminally trying to remove any targets for expensive metallic devices that hold precious gemstones? I imagine I look like a mental patient with my arms strapped to my waist. Despite that, I try to make my voice normal. "I've been doing some figuring all day. Meetings and such. Trying to get my affairs in order."

He looks up from the bags. "Really? Me, too."

Oh no.

"Also," he says, unwrapping a side of mashed potatoes that I can't smell, I'm so nervous, "I talked to Yul. He's remembered a little more. I told him I wanted to get the four of us together. I'll see him when I go back to San Francisco to pack my things for the movers."

Pack my things for the movers.

"I'm moving, too," I blurt out, an act of desperation. "My mum owns the flat. She'll have to let it to someone else—someone who can actually pay the rent." I manage a weak smile. "I'll be pretty strapped while I finish the first Alice novel. Will take some time. I'm in such a transition period. Lot of moving pieces. Will be hectic for a bit. So many decisions. Can't imagine making one more, not a single one. My mind's about to explode as it is."

I wait.

Seconds tick by. All the food's out now. Mashed potatoes, carrots, and chicken.

"Do you want to wait?" he asks.

"Waiting is good, I think." The words come out harsh, defensive. I try to soften my tone, appear casual. "For some things. Gotta wait until the time is right. Doesn't mean you're saying no."

"I wouldn't think so."

"I'm not." I say firmly.

"Right." He glances around. "Well, I could put it in the oven."

Is he crazy? "Why would you do that?"

"To keep it warm."

I stare at him.

He shrugs. "I just can't eat cold chicken."

"Oh." Dinner. He's talking about waiting on dinner. I take my hands out of my pants, freeing myself, trying to look less like the mental patient I seem to be at the moment. "Well . . . we can eat now. Certainly no problem with that."

We sit, and he digs in. He must not have eaten all day. I pick at the chicken and roll a few carrots around my plate, unable to eat.

He motions to the living room. "Seems like you've got a good start on Alice. How long do you think for the first novel?"

"Hard to say. Inspiration keeps its own schedule. Maybe a year. Maybe more."

"Your mom owns the flat?"

"Yep. I saw an estate agent today, wanted to get her some options. He says the flat will fetch a good sum. That will last her a while, maybe to her retirement. Letting it is also a good option, but she'll have to pay a management fee, and there's a bit of uncertainty there. The London market's a madhouse. Flat next door just sold—unsolicited, in fact. Bloody foreigners. They're buying up every square inch of London. Heard Norway bought a big chunk of Mayfair the other day,

Savile Row included. Pretty soon there won't be any Londoners left in London."

"Everybody's looking for alternative investments. That's been the topic of my day, in fact. I've been thinking about what to do. About the Titan Foundation. In particular, I've asked myself what I can learn from what I saw in 2147."

That sounds like it could be working up to—

"Human nature."

I put my fork down. "Human nature?"

"That's what they missed, the Titans. Nicholas said it to me a few times. It might have been the most honest thing he said to me. All the Titan Marvels, all their technology, they just sped up the world. But they didn't solve our real problem: human nature. They didn't make humanity kinder or more understanding. They didn't make us more accepting. Didn't inherently change what's inside us. That's the great challenge. That's what they should have been working on. Not technology, or innovation, or construction projects. I think the great work left to do is about changing how we treat each other. That's what's been missing in my life, that kind of challenge. That's why I was so unhappy." He looks right in my eyes. "Well, half of it. That's what I realized in 2147. Anyway, changing human nature—not building dams or new technology—that's what I want to work on."

"How?"

"I haven't quite figured that out yet. Been thinking about it all day."

My nerves have settled a bit, and I can't resist having a bit of fun with him.

"I actually know of a technology that addresses human nature, nurtures understanding, enhances compassion—some of those very issues you cited, Mr. Stone."

"Yeah?"

"It's an ancient technology."

"Ancient?"

"And incredibly powerful. It has the ability to instantly transport people—en masse, by the millions and billions at a time—to other worlds, where they learn from people strangely like them. They make revelations they carry back to their own lives. Learn skills. Gain inspiration to make change on a global scale."

"Cost?" he asks, the start of a smile forming on his lips.

"Minimal. No infrastructure needed."

"Sounds too good to be true."

"Wrong. It's already here." I walk to my bookshelf, pull a paperback off. "Books."

"Books?"

"That's right."

"I could get behind that," he says, leaning back in the chair. "It's an interesting idea: writing a book about what happened to us in 2147 and releasing it to give people something to think about. That's a venture I wouldn't mind investing in."

"That . . . would be interesting."

"And," he says, "it could give you working capital—without selling or letting this cozy little flat."

I raise my eyebrows. "Are you negotiating with me?"

He laughs out loud. "I am. This could be the best investment I've made in some time. But you know, we'd have to work closely on this. It would be half my story, half yours. You'd have to help me with my part."

"I might be willing to do that."

"Since we'd be working together so much, I would need to be close by. Say, next door."

My jaw drops. "You didn't."

" 'Bloody foreign investors,' " he says, mimicking me.

I shake my head, embarrassed.

"I meant what I said this morning, Harper. I'm serious about seeing where things go with us. If you're not ready, I'll stay in San Francisco. But if you are, I'll be next door. That wall doesn't have to come down any time soon. Or ever, if you don't want it to."

I nod. I do want that wall to come down. At some point. I'm certain about that now. I know it came down in the other world, so it's possible here.

I like possibilities. Used to hate them. Possibilities meant choices—decisions. But I've gotten a lot better at making decisions lately.

We talk about that, the book we'll write together, and the future for a few hours, the fire crackling in the living room that's littered with construction paper, drawings, and worn notebooks.

Through the tall windows, the first snow of winter is beginning to fall, and bundled-up people are hurrying home under the yellow glow of streetlamps.

When the dinner is half gone, we wrap up the leftovers, place them in the fridge for tomorrow, stoke the fire for the night, and head to the bedroom.

For the first time since I can remember, I'm not the least bit worried about the future.

The story continues!

Read the epilogue to *Departure* and browse extras at my web site:

agriddle.com/post-departure

On the web site, enter your boarding pass number below for full access:

X47NHSY4

The post-departure lounge includes:

| The *Departure* Easter Egg | The *Departure* Epilogue | Harper's Alice Carter Board | Titan Foundation Documents | Sabrina's Mortality Talk |

and much more!

Author's Note

Thank you for reading. I really hope you've enjoyed *Departure*.

This novel was challenging to write at times, perhaps because the story draws on some of my personal experiences (not the part in 2147, though). While *The Atlantis Gene* was about the origins of the human race, *Departure* is sort of about the origins of my writing career, or at least, why I chose to leave Internet start-ups and do something I felt passionate about.

It seems like the world around us gets faster every year. We're knee-deep in new technologies, but I'm still scratching my head, wondering if we're making the world better or just speeding it up. I guess time will tell. Maybe we'll all be Titans someday. Or maybe we're smart enough to avoid that fate altogether.

That's what *Departure* is about to me: an exploration of where technology might take us, and the possible consequences. It's the sort of cerebral, "what if?" story I enjoy reading and (most of the time) enjoy writing.

To me, the best stories are the ones that leave the reader better than they were. And the best of those nurture both our minds and our souls. I don't know if my craft is quite there yet, but I'm working on it, and I truly appreciate you coming along for the journey.

Take care,
Gerry

Acknowledgments

I'm beginning to think it takes a village, not an author, to write a novel. This year, I've been very lucky to see my little village grow by leaps and bounds.

My wife, Anna, makes sure the trains run on time here at the Riddle household (and that we never miss our plane when we're on the road). Without her, I would likely still be in a train station somewhere in Europe and you wouldn't be reading this novel. And past that, my life wouldn't be the same.

Professionally, I'm blessed to have some incredibly talented people working to get my books into readers' hands. Gray Tan of Grayhawk Agency took a chance on me when I was a promising start-up author. A million copies later, he's still selling my rights throughout Asia and doing an incredible job.

Danny Baror and Heather Baror-Shapiro represent me in Europe and the rest of the world with every bit as much passion and skill.

Between the two agencies, they've sold the Origin Mystery series in twenty territories and counting. I've been amazed, and I'm humbled to have Gray, Danny, and Heather representing me.

Departure's journey into your hands is almost as incredible as Harper and Nick's adventure, and in a way some time travel was involved. I originally self-published the novel in December of 2014. Miranda Ottewell was my outside editor and did a fantastic job (she's edited novels by some of the world's most beloved authors, including Mitch Albom, Elizabeth Gilbert, Daniel Silva, and Barbara Kingsolver; I was very happy she lowered her standards long enough to work with me). To my delight, *Departure* became a smash hit, selling over a quarter of a million copies in its first several months. 20th Century Fox secured the movie rights, and HarperVoyager, the science fiction imprint of HarperCollins, made a compelling offer to buy the publishing rights. It was a tough decision; I had never traditionally published and was very nervous—*Departure* was and is an incredibly personal and special novel to me. Giving up control of the things we love is hard. But I took the plunge, and the people at HarperVoyager have verified my decision at every turn. David Pomerico's edits and suggestions helped take the story to the next level (which I didn't think was possible). David's work, together with Greg Villepique's copy edits, made *Departure* my most polished novel to date and it's the one I'm most proud of. I'm incredibly grateful to Rebecca Lucash, Shawn Nicholls, and Pam Jaffee for their outstanding work making the *Departure* release happen in a major way—everything from PR, to advertising, to in-store placement. The entire HarperVoyager team is a well-oiled machine, and I was glad to be a small cog in that machine this year. Lastly, I need to say a special thanks to Liate Stehlik, the lady at the top of the Voyager food chain, for all her support and for making Departure's re-release happen. Almost a year after I self-published the novel, it hit bookstores with new content, new edits, and better than ever. It was quite a journey.

And before I go, I need to thank some folks at the beginning of that journey: my alpha readers. In 2014, they once again saved the day with some invaluable catches and suggestions. I learn so much with every novel I write, and I truly appreciate all the time they put in. They are: Fran Mason, Carole Duebbert, Lisa Weinberg, and Michael Hattig.

My beta readers provided a source of encouragement and timely feedback right before the launch. They are: Lee Ames, Sue Arnett,

Ivan Arrington, Laura Avramidis, Jeff Baker, Joshua Baker, Paula Barrett, Eris Barzman, Jen Bengtson, Tracy Big Pond, Ben Bird, Casey Boatman, Steve Boesen, Paul Bowen, Jacob Bulicek, Michael Camenisch, Stephanie Campbell, Emily Chin, Lianne Christian, Markel Coleman, Robin Collins, Heather Comerford, Jacky Cook, Frank Cowan, Ken Cuddeback, Terry Daigle, Sue Davis, Sylvie Delézay, Joe Devous, Kathy Dickinson, Adam Dorrell, Debbie Dowdy, Michelle Duff, Matt Egan, Christopher Eix, Maisha Elonai, Amanda Flies, Skip Folden, Kay Forbes, Ben Forrest, Holly Fournier, N. J. Fritz, Ben Fury, Matthew Fyfe, Brenda Gehrmann, Zachary Gershman, Kathy Gianneschi, Vicky Gibbins, Christine Girtain, Julie Godnik, Carl Gray, Julia Greenawalt, Mike Gullion, Chet Hale, Miora Hanson, Dustin Hermon, Aimee Hess, Matthias Hüls, Ted Hust, Mary Jakobowski, Paul Jamieson, Sam Jarvie, Christopher Kazu Williams, Shawn Kerker, Jeannine Klos, Linda Koch, Karin Kostyzak, Matt Lacey, Kendall Lane, Daniel Lewis, Cameron Lewis, Marina Lobato, Dee Lopez, Peter Lynch, Kelly Mahoney, Jane Marconi, Angela Marx, Virginia McClain, Leanne McGiveron, Steven McKenney, James McMullen, Jake Meals, Saquib Mian, Kristen Miller, Brian Miller, Thomas Mitchum, Tera Montgomery, Kim Myers, Steven Nease, Kevin Nguyen, Jordan Nguyen, Amber O'Connor, Anne Palmer, Sara Patterson, Mike Pease, Cindy Prendergast, Nikita Puhalsky, Brandon Pulliam, Brian Puzzo, Rachael Qualls, Deborah and Cary Radunz, Akash Rajpal, Katie Regan, Terri Reilly, Dave Renison, Teodora Retegan, Lionel Riem, Timothy Rogers, Andy Royl, Mike Russell, Dennis Sable, John Scafidi, Stefano Scaglione, Scott Scheffler, Andreas Schild, John Schmiedt, Chere Schoning, Cameron Schutza, Shane Schweitzer, Debbie Sembera, Anjulie Semenchuk, Keith Shurmer, Russell Simkins, Andrea Sinclair, Rhonda Sloan, Christine Smith, Duane Spellecacy, Linda Spotz, George Stalling, Elizabeth Steininger Wolf, Alex Stevens, Kady Stewart, Tiffany Tanner, Paula Thomas, Macy Tindel, Kevin Veneskey, Andrew Villamagna, Tom Vogel, Jimmy Von Riesen, Liz W., Lauren Wall, Louise Ward, Ron Watts, Chris Watts, Sylvia Webb, Scott Weiner, Dana Westphal, Charlie White, Linda Winton, Robert Wiseman, Samantha Woracek, John Woughter, Lew Wuest, Athena, and TeResa.

I also have to thank a group of people whose inquisitive minds encourage my playful side. They are: Jason Barroca, Bader Bouarki, Steve Brenckle, Lee Davis, Michael De Feo, Christopher Dunham, David Galli Carrera, eRin Hanson, Rob Hanus, Matt Isaacs, Josh Jacobs, Samuel Lynch, Kostas Mavraganis, Desiree Melkovitz, Jonathan Moore, Bryan Nelson, Jonathan Palmer, Sam Penry, Darin Powell, Zach Renshaw, and Evan Roy.

And finally, to you, wherever you are, whatever time it is: thanks for reading.

See you next time.

About the Author

A.G. RIDDLE spent ten years starting Internet companies before retiring to pursue his true passion: writing fiction.

His debut novel, *The Atlantis Gene*, is the first book in a trilogy (The Origin Mystery) that has sold a million copies in the United States, is being translated into eighteen languages, and is in development to be a major motion picture.

He grew up in a small town in North Carolina and currently lives in Lake Lure with his wife, who endures his various idiosyncrasies in return for being the first to read his new novels.

No matter where he is, or what's going on, he tries his best to set aside time every day to answer e-mails and messages from readers.

You can find him at these fine Internet locations:

Web site: agriddle.com

E-mail: ag@agriddle.com

For a sneak peek of new novels, free stories, and more, join the e-mail list at agriddle.com/email.

If you don't want to miss any Riddle news, you can:

Like the A.G. Riddle Facebook page: facebook.com/agriddle

Follow A.G. Riddle on Twitter: twitter.com/riddlist